THE CROGAN ADVENTURES
"LAST OF THE LEGION"

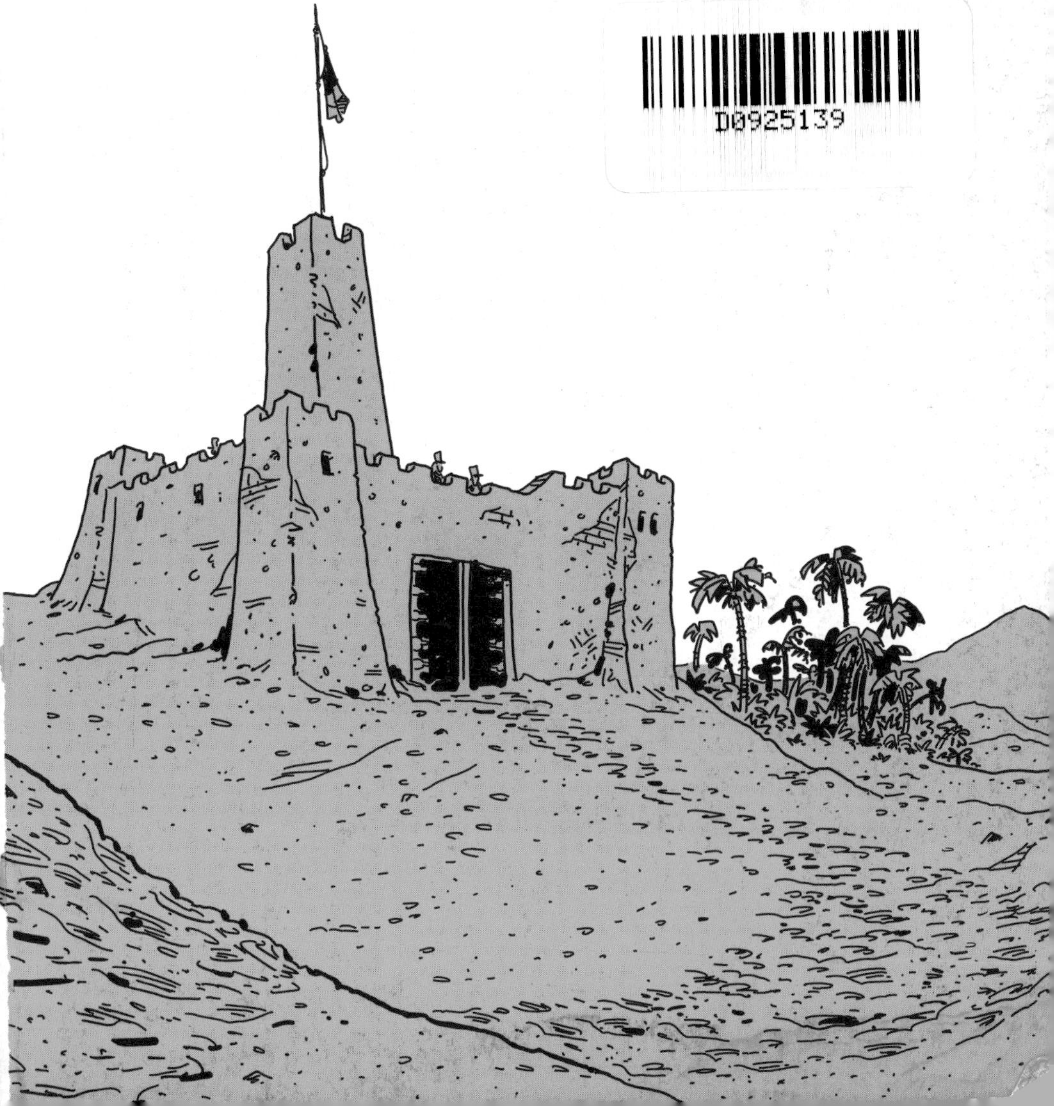

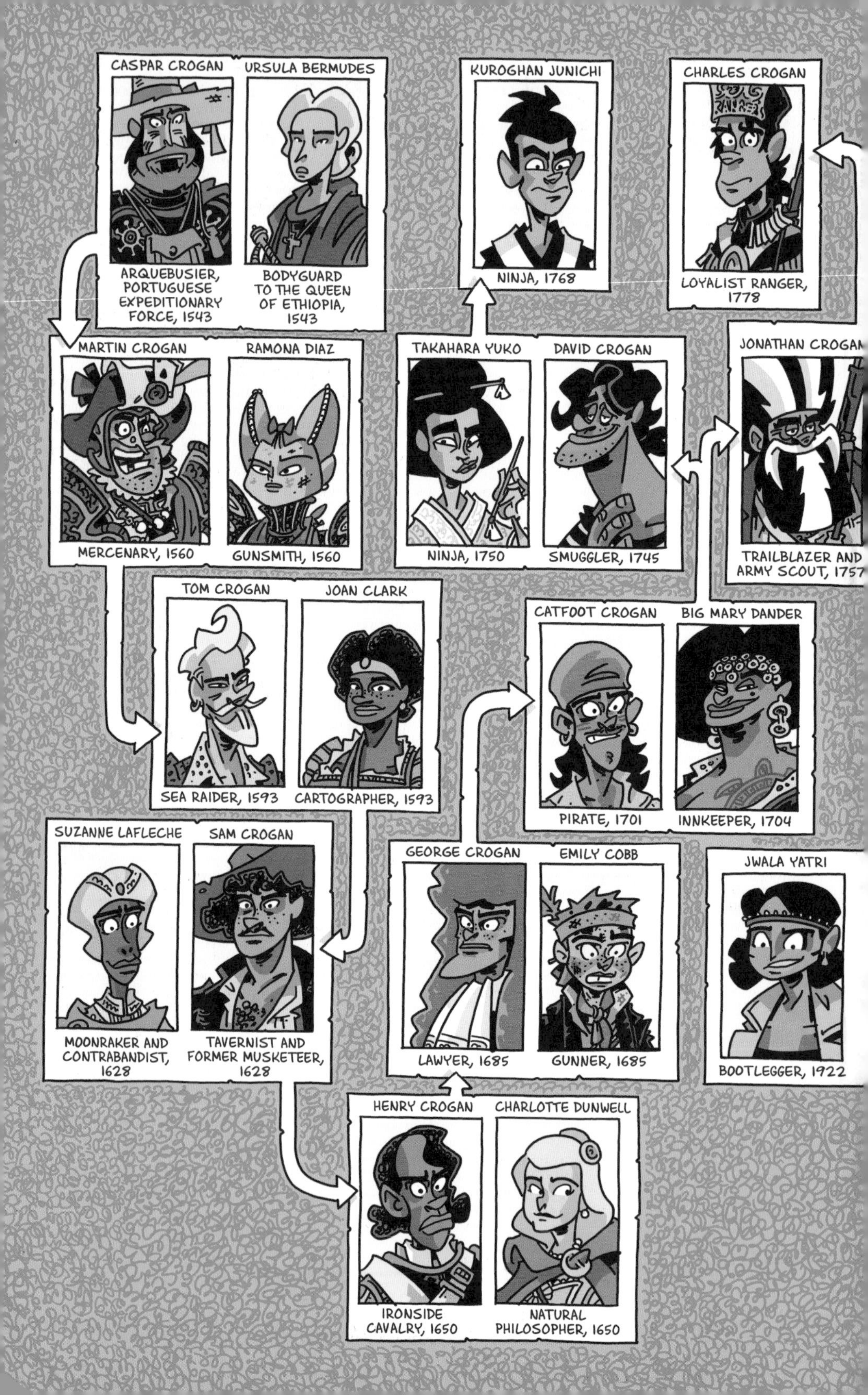
CASPAR CROGAN
ARQUEBUSIER, PORTUGUESE EXPEDITIONARY FORCE, 1543
URSULA BERMUDES
BODYGUARD TO THE QUEEN OF ETHIOPIA, 1543
KUROGHAN JUNICHI
NINJA, 1768
CHARLES CROGAN
LOYALIST RANGER, 1778
MARTIN CROGAN
MERCENARY, 1560
RAMONA DIAZ
GUNSMITH, 1560
TAKAHARA YUKO
NINJA, 1750
DAVID CROGAN
SMUGGLER, 1745
JONATHAN CROGAN
TRAILBLAZER AND ARMY SCOUT, 1757
TOM CROGAN
SEA RAIDER, 1593
JOAN CLARK
CARTOGRAPHER, 1593
CATFOOT CROGAN
PIRATE, 1701
BIG MARY DANDER
INNKEEPER, 1704
SUZANNE LAFLECHE
MOONRAKER AND CONTRABANDIST, 1628
SAM CROGAN
TAVERNIST AND FORMER MUSKETEER, 1628
GEORGE CROGAN
LAWYER, 1685
EMILY COBB
GUNNER, 1685
JWALA YATRI
BOOTLEGGER, 1922
HENRY CROGAN
IRONSIDE CAVALRY, 1650
CHARLOTTE DUNWELL
NATURAL PHILOSOPHER, 1650

WILL CROGAN
COLONIAL SCOUT, 1778

BESS DOCKREY
FARMER, 1778

GEOFFREY CROGAN
MARINE, 1805

HODA BINT BASHAW
CORSAIR, 1805

NANCY REDLEGS BUTLER MESHAWAY
SHAWNEE WARRIOR CHIEF, 1760

MABEL COTTONSHOT
TRICK-SHOOTER, 1870

BEN CROGAN
GUNFIGHTER, 1870

MATTHEW CROGAN
PUNJAB FRONTIER CAVALRY, 1857

SADA SINGH
HORSE TRADER AND STRATEGIST, 1857

AGNES MORLEY
MINE OWNER, 1879

JOSEPH CROGAN
DIAMOND MINER, 1878

MARJA TOLLIVER
COMMANDO, 1900

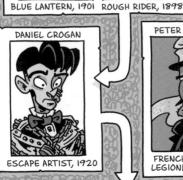

LEI YANG
BLUE LANTERN, 1901

ROBERT CROGAN
ROUGH RIDER, 1898

PETER CROGAN
FRENCH FOREIGN LEGIONNAIRE, 1912

RUTH GILLETTE
FILMMAKER, 1925

JOHN TOLLIVER CROGAN
PILOT, 1917

DANIEL CROGAN
ESCAPE ARTIST, 1920

"CALLOWAY" CROGAN
PRIVATE EYE, 1947

ALEX CROGAN
SECRET AGENT, 1962

SEAN CROGAN
HOMICIDE DETECTIVE, 1971

THE CROGAN ADVENTURES
"LAST OF THE LEGION"

BY
CHRIS SCHWEIZER

COLORED BY
JOEY WEISER & MICHELE CHIDESTER

BOOK DESIGN BY
CHRIS SCHWEIZER & KEITH WOOD

EDITED BY
JAMES LUCAS JONES
WITH JILL BEATON

ONI PRESS

AN ONI PRESS PUBLICATION

FOR LIZ, WHO LETS ME DO WHAT
I LOVE, AND GIVES ME A REASON
FOR DOING IT.

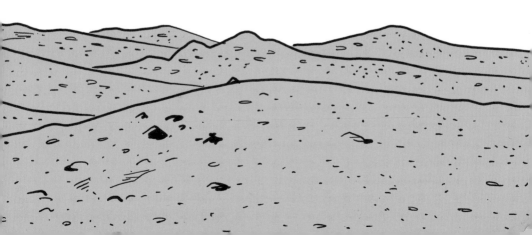

Published by Oni Press, Inc.

Joe Nozemack, publisher · James Lucas Jones, editor in chief

Cheyenne Allott, director of sales · Fred Reckling, director of publicity

Troy Look, production manager · Charlie Chu, senior editor · Robin Herrera, editor

Ari Yarwood, associate editor · Hilary Thompson, graphic designer

Jared Jones, production assistant · Brad Rooks, inventory coordinator

Jung Lee, office assistant

Oni Press, Inc.
1305 SE Martin Luther King Jr. Blvd.
Suite A
Portland, OR 97214
USA

facebook.com/onipress · twitter.com/onipress · onipress.tumblr.com
onipress.com

croganadventures.blogspot.com · @schweizercomics
tragic-planet.com · @joeyweiser
michelechidester.com · @drogochideseter

First edition: December 2015

ISBN 978-1-62010-243-5
eISBN 978-1-62010-176-6

Library of Congress Control Number: 2015938925

1 3 5 7 9 10 8 6 4 2

PRINTED IN CHINA.

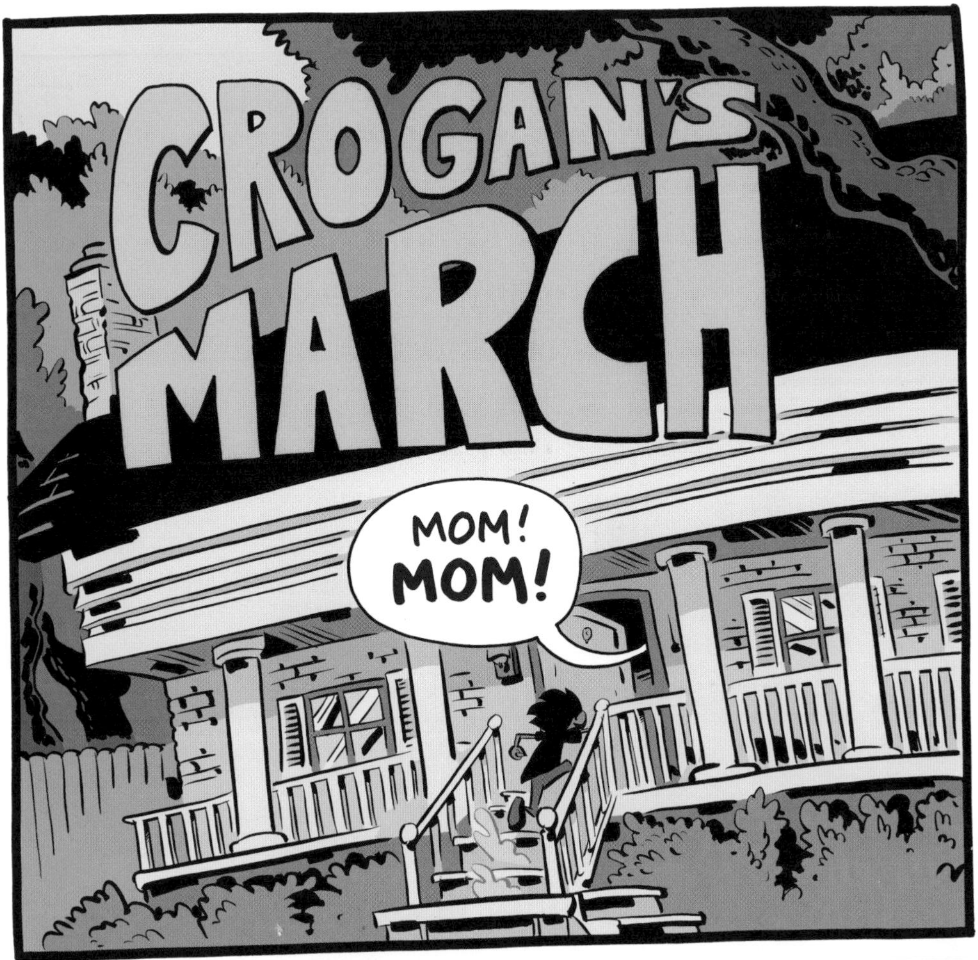
CROGAN'S MARCH
MOM! MOM!

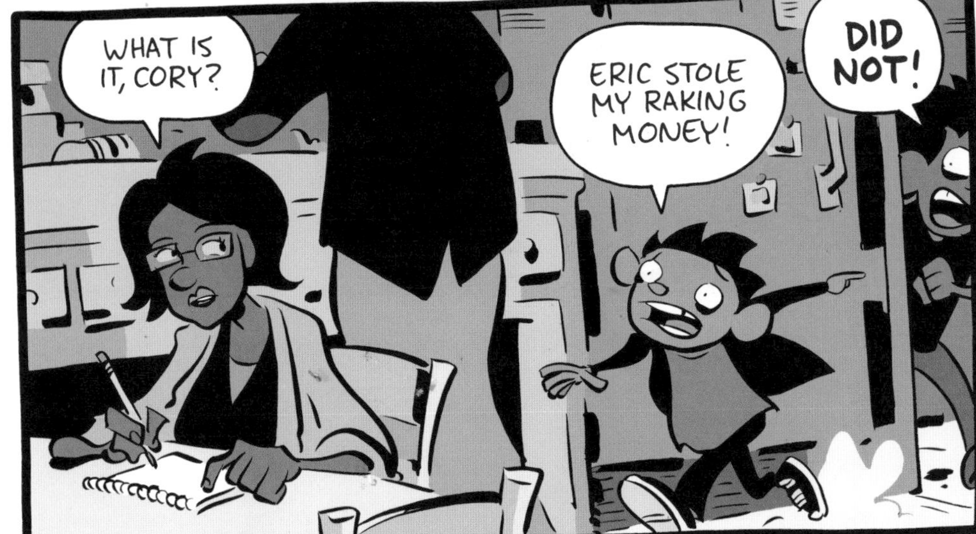
WHAT IS IT, CORY?
ERIC STOLE MY RAKING MONEY!
DID NOT!

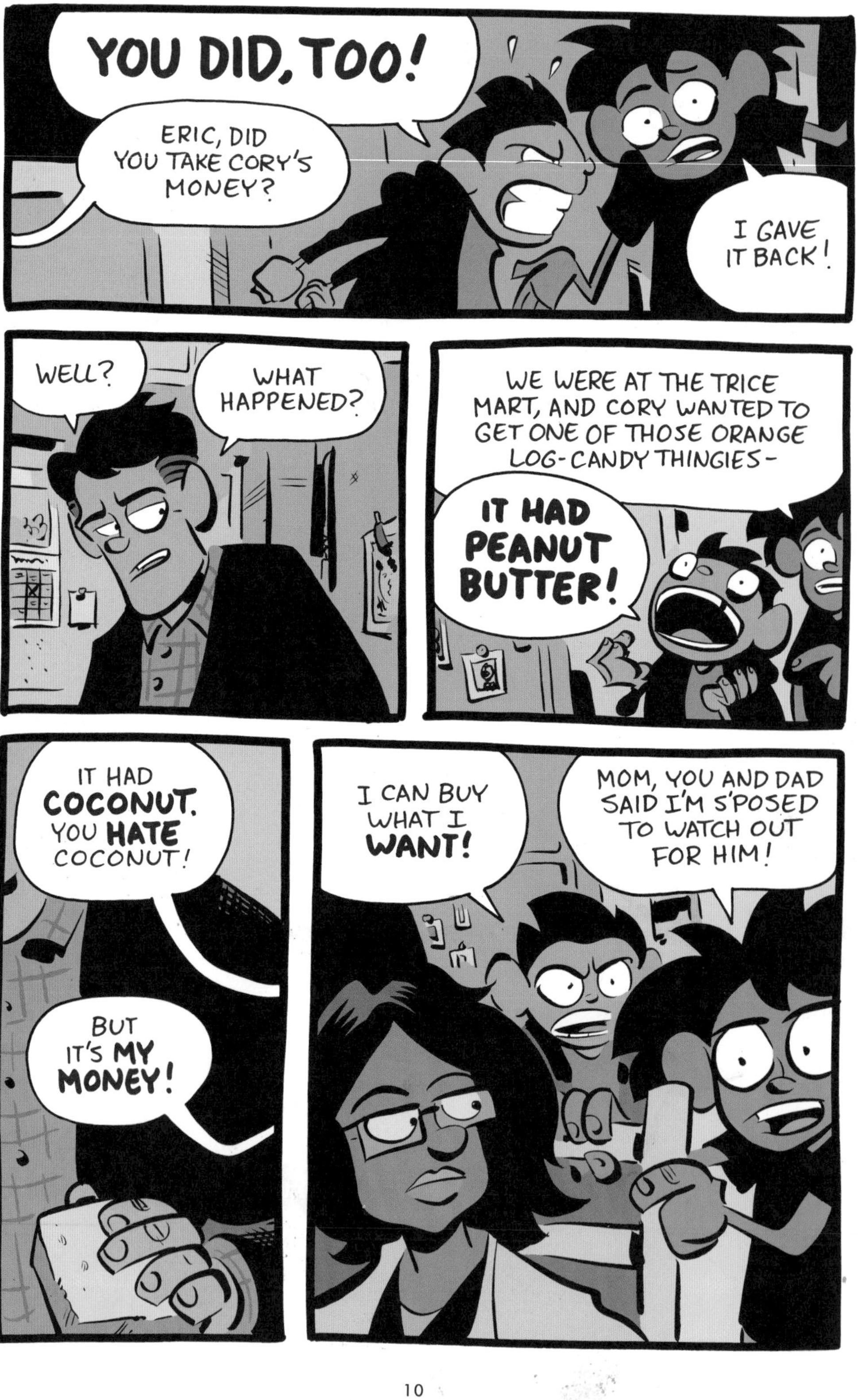
YOU DID, TOO!
ERIC, DID YOU TAKE CORY'S MONEY?
I GAVE IT BACK!
WELL?
WHAT HAPPENED?
WE WERE AT THE TRICE MART, AND CORY WANTED TO GET ONE OF THOSE ORANGE LOG-CANDY THINGIES-
IT HAD PEANUT BUTTER!
IT HAD COCONUT. YOU HATE COCONUT!
BUT IT'S MY MONEY!
I CAN BUY WHAT I WANT!
MOM, YOU AND DAD SAID I'M S'POSED TO WATCH OUT FOR HIM!

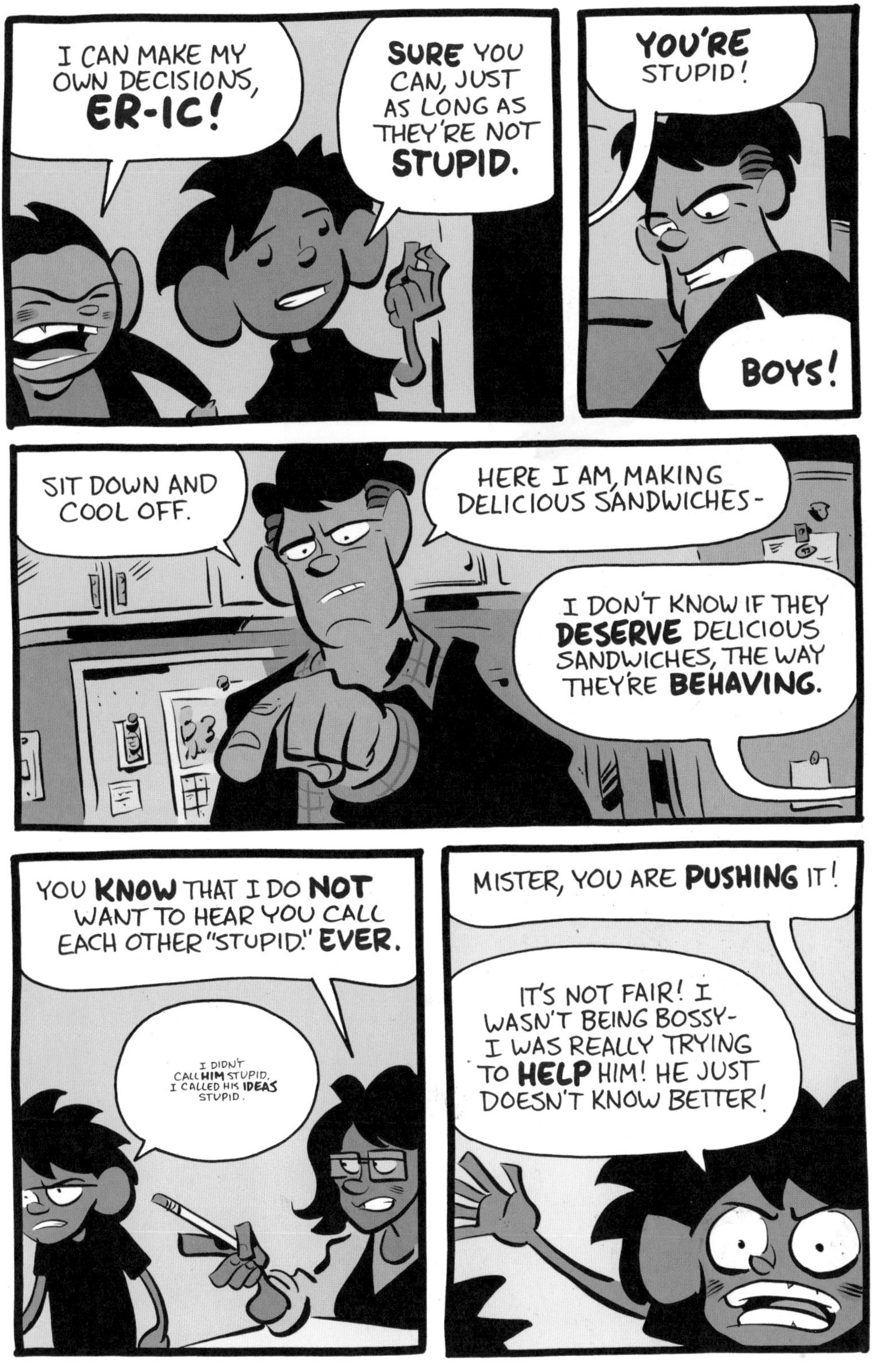
I CAN MAKE MY OWN DECISIONS, ER-IC!
SURE YOU CAN, JUST AS LONG AS THEY'RE NOT STUPID.
YOU'RE STUPID!
BOYS!
SIT DOWN AND COOL OFF.
HERE I AM, MAKING DELICIOUS SANDWICHES-
I DON'T KNOW IF THEY DESERVE DELICIOUS SANDWICHES, THE WAY THEY'RE BEHAVING.
YOU KNOW THAT I DO NOT WANT TO HEAR YOU CALL EACH OTHER "STUPID." EVER.
I DIDN'T CALL HIM STUPID, I CALLED HIS IDEAS STUPID.
MISTER, YOU ARE PUSHING IT!
IT'S NOT FAIR! I WASN'T BEING BOSSY- I WAS REALLY TRYING TO HELP HIM! HE JUST DOESN'T KNOW BETTER!

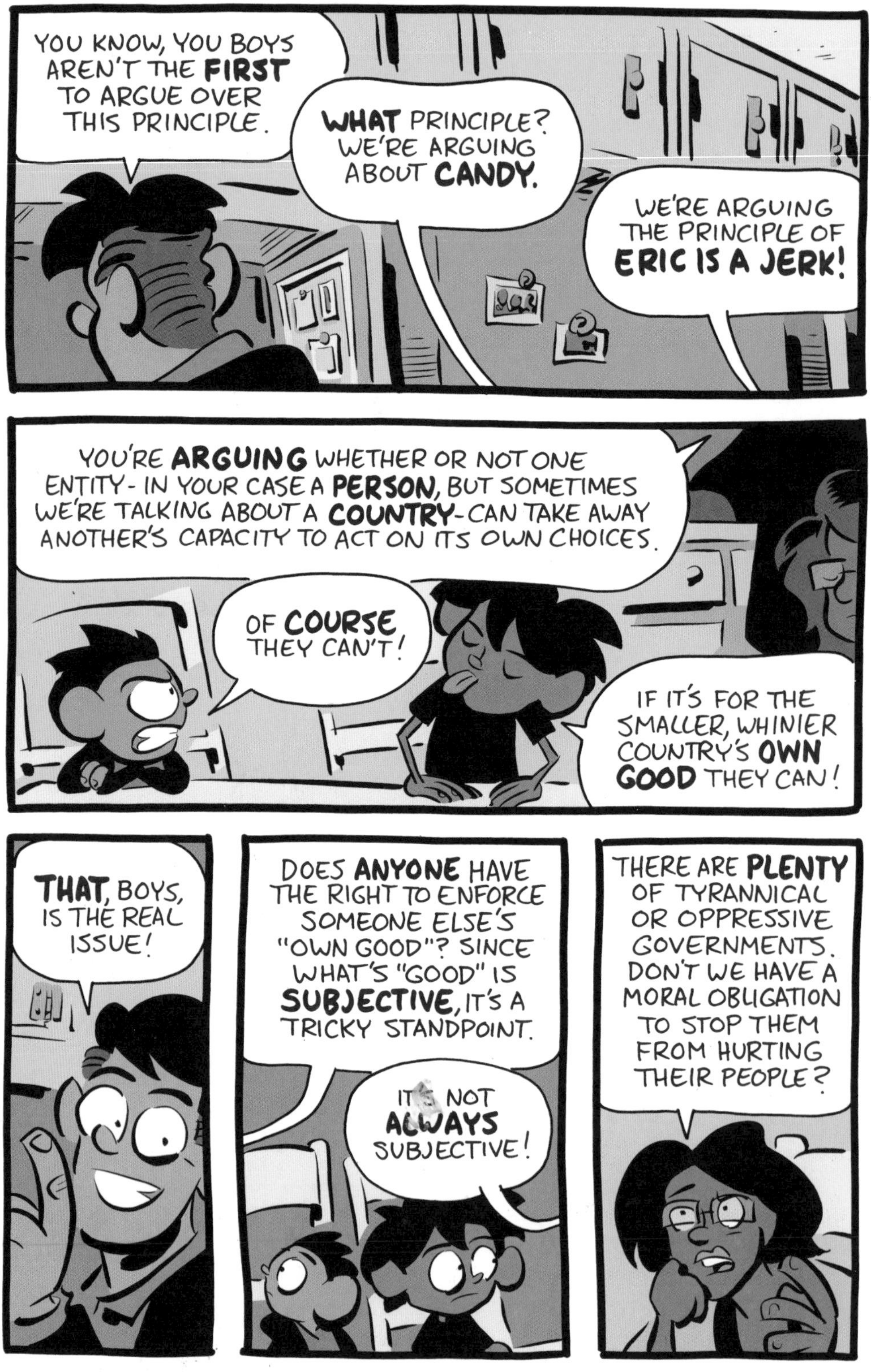
YOU KNOW, YOU BOYS AREN'T THE **FIRST** TO ARGUE OVER THIS PRINCIPLE.
WHAT PRINCIPLE? WE'RE ARGUING ABOUT **CANDY.**
WE'RE ARGUING THE PRINCIPLE OF **ERIC IS A JERK!**
YOU'RE **ARGUING** WHETHER OR NOT ONE ENTITY- IN YOUR CASE A **PERSON,** BUT SOMETIMES WE'RE TALKING ABOUT A **COUNTRY**-CAN TAKE AWAY ANOTHER'S CAPACITY TO ACT ON ITS OWN CHOICES.
OF **COURSE**, THEY CAN'T!
IF IT'S FOR THE SMALLER, WHINIER COUNTRY'S **OWN GOOD** THEY CAN!
THAT, BOYS, IS THE REAL ISSUE!
DOES **ANYONE** HAVE THE RIGHT TO ENFORCE SOMEONE ELSE'S "OWN GOOD"? SINCE WHAT'S "GOOD" IS **SUBJECTIVE,** IT'S A TRICKY STANDPOINT.
IT'S NOT **ALWAYS** SUBJECTIVE!
THERE ARE **PLENTY** OF TYRANNICAL OR OPPRESSIVE GOVERNMENTS. DON'T WE HAVE A MORAL OBLIGATION TO STOP THEM FROM HURTING THEIR PEOPLE?

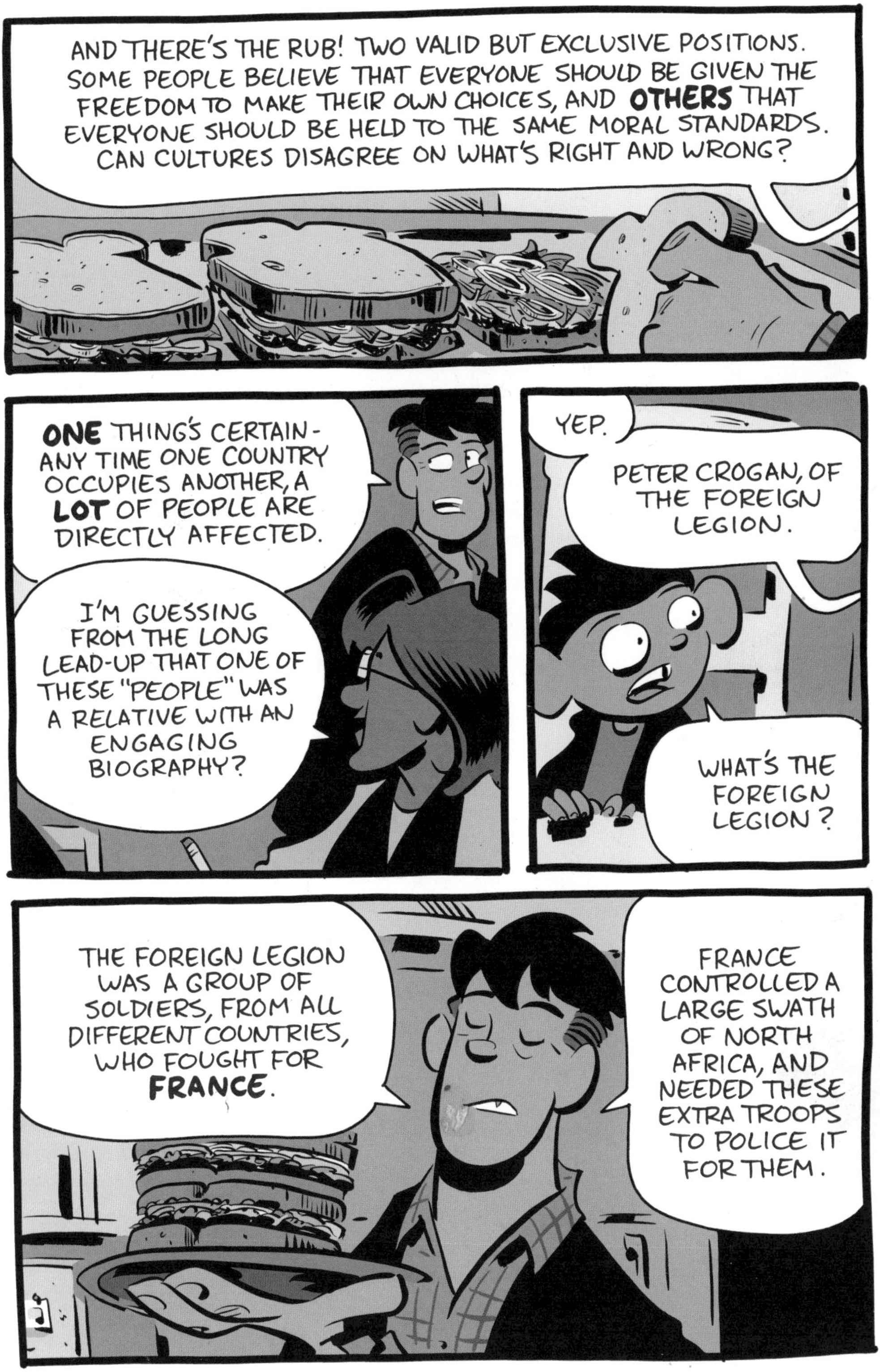
AND THERE'S THE RUB! TWO VALID BUT EXCLUSIVE POSITIONS. SOME PEOPLE BELIEVE THAT EVERYONE SHOULD BE GIVEN THE FREEDOM TO MAKE THEIR OWN CHOICES, AND **OTHERS** THAT EVERYONE SHOULD BE HELD TO THE SAME MORAL STANDARDS. CAN CULTURES DISAGREE ON WHAT'S RIGHT AND WRONG?
ONE THING'S CERTAIN- ANY TIME ONE COUNTRY OCCUPIES ANOTHER, A **LOT** OF PEOPLE ARE DIRECTLY AFFECTED.
I'M GUESSING FROM THE LONG LEAD-UP THAT ONE OF THESE "PEOPLE" WAS A RELATIVE WITH AN ENGAGING BIOGRAPHY?
YEP.
PETER CROGAN, OF THE FOREIGN LEGION.
WHAT'S THE FOREIGN LEGION?
THE FOREIGN LEGION WAS A GROUP OF SOLDIERS, FROM ALL DIFFERENT COUNTRIES, WHO FOUGHT FOR **FRANCE**.
FRANCE CONTROLLED A LARGE SWATH OF NORTH AFRICA, AND NEEDED THESE EXTRA TROOPS TO POLICE IT FOR THEM.

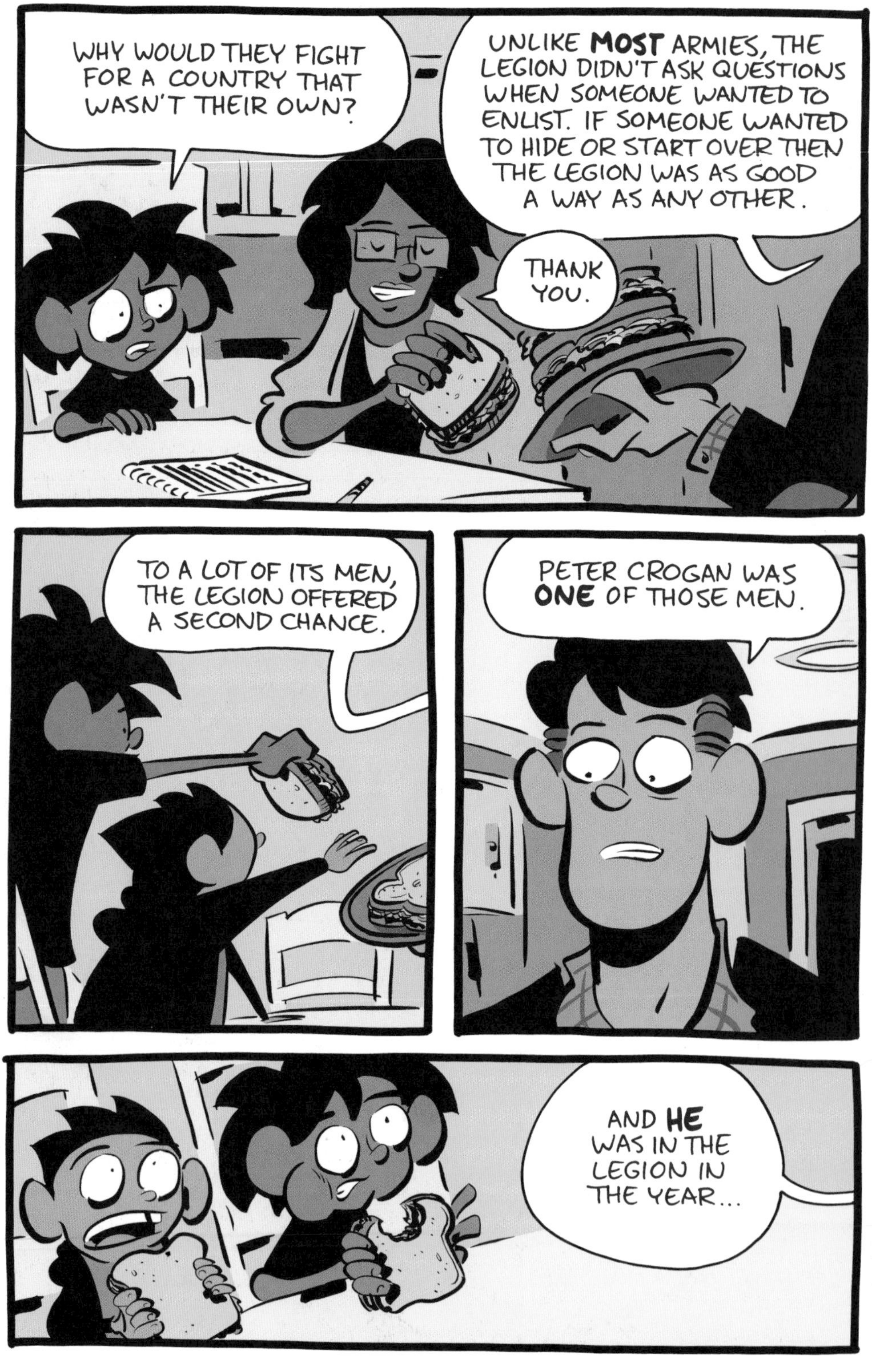
WHY WOULD THEY FIGHT FOR A COUNTRY THAT WASN'T THEIR OWN?
UNLIKE **MOST** ARMIES, THE LEGION DIDN'T ASK QUESTIONS WHEN SOMEONE WANTED TO ENLIST. IF SOMEONE WANTED TO HIDE OR START OVER THEN THE LEGION WAS AS GOOD A WAY AS ANY OTHER.
THANK YOU.
TO A LOT OF ITS MEN, THE LEGION OFFERED A SECOND CHANCE.
PETER CROGAN WAS **ONE** OF THOSE MEN.
AND **HE** WAS IN THE LEGION IN THE YEAR...

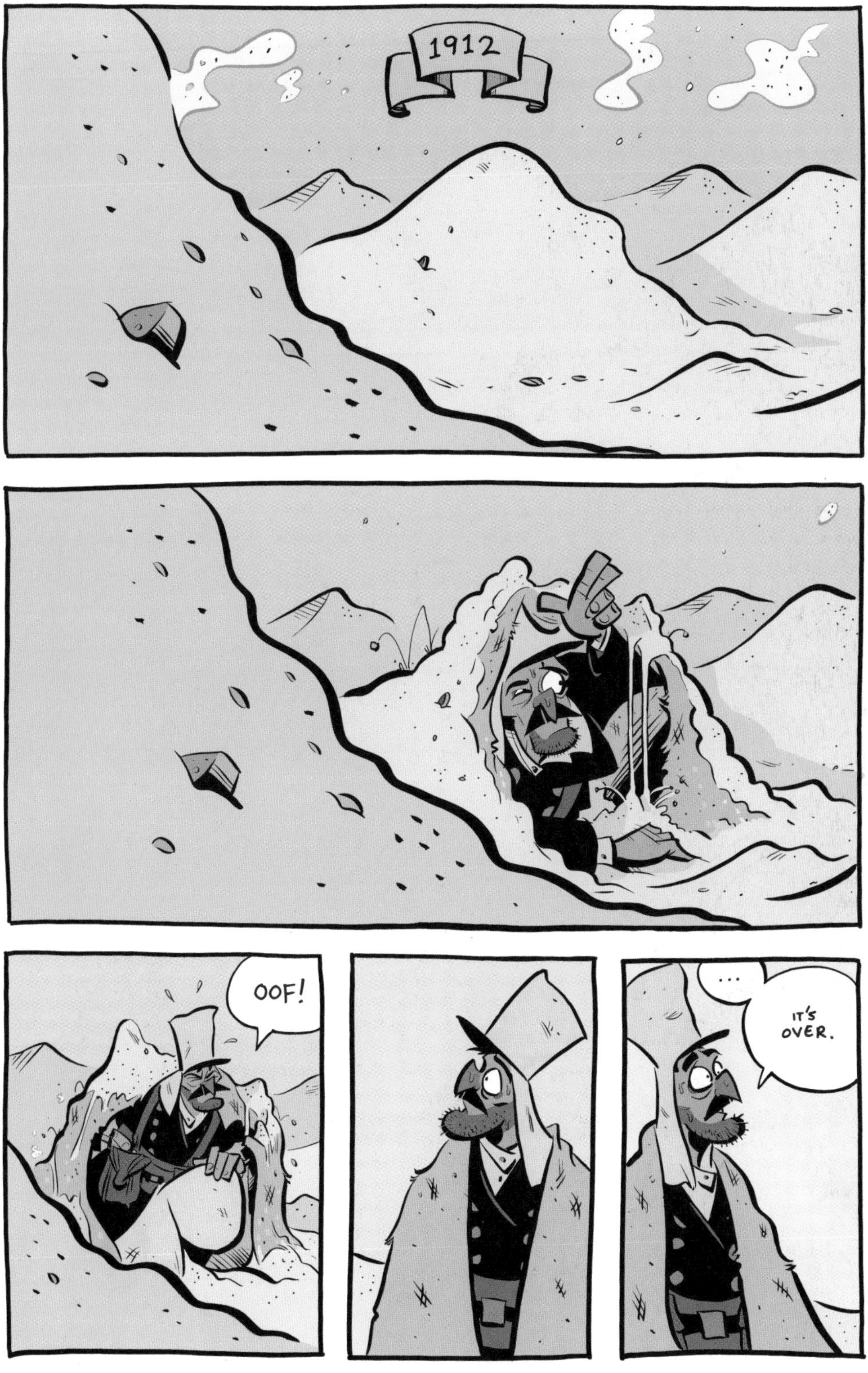
1912
OOF!
...
IT'S OVER.

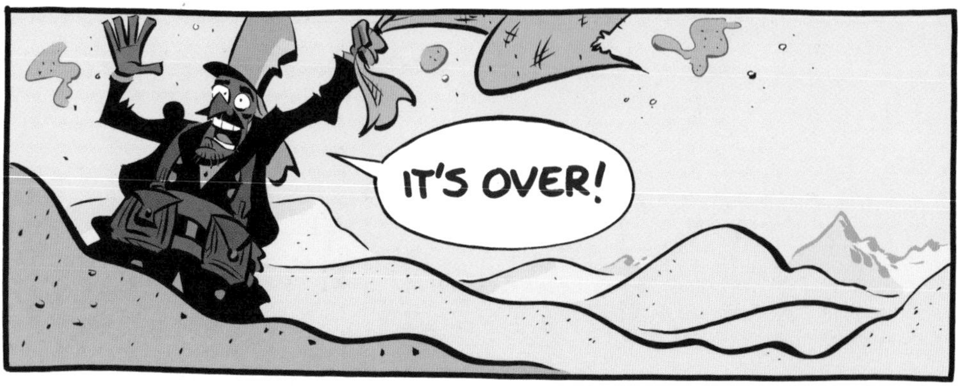
IT'S OVER!

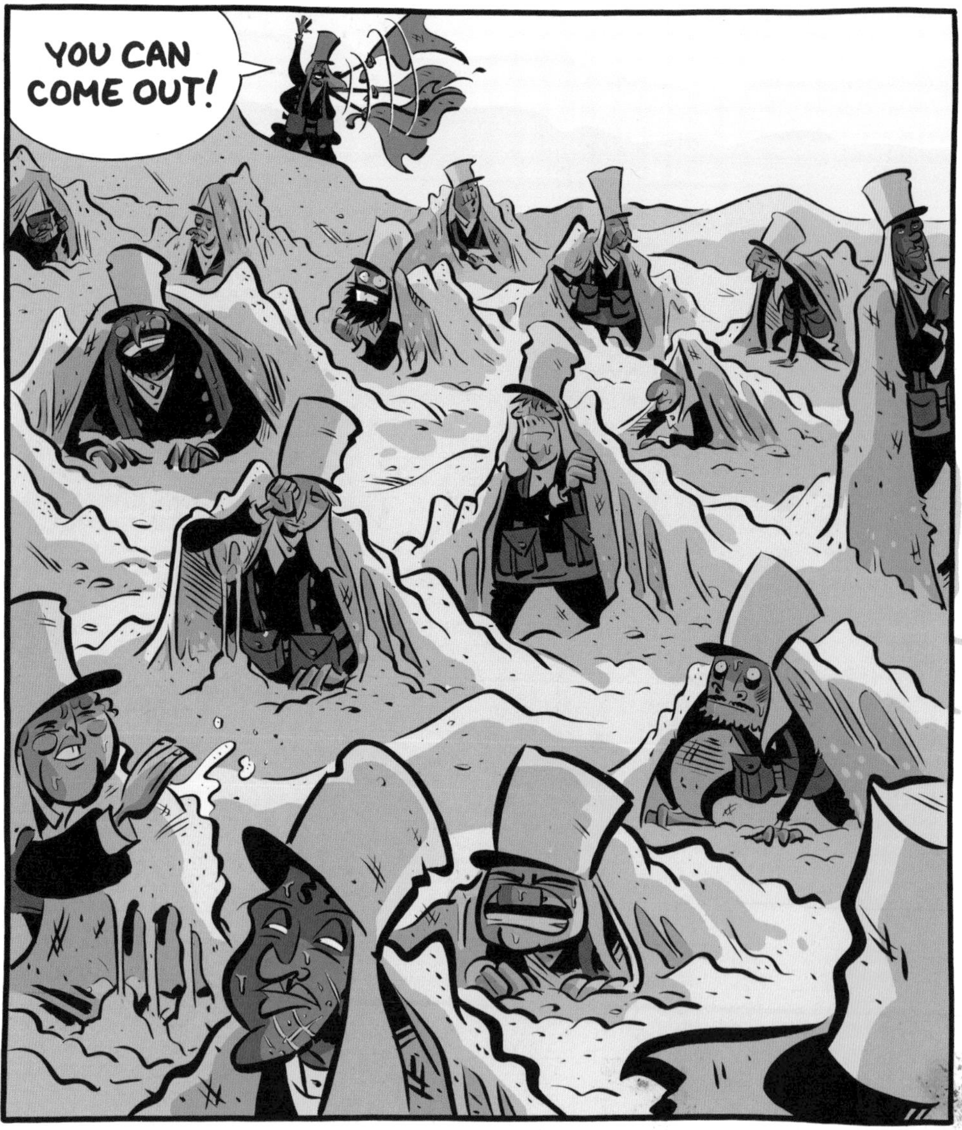
YOU CAN COME OUT!

18

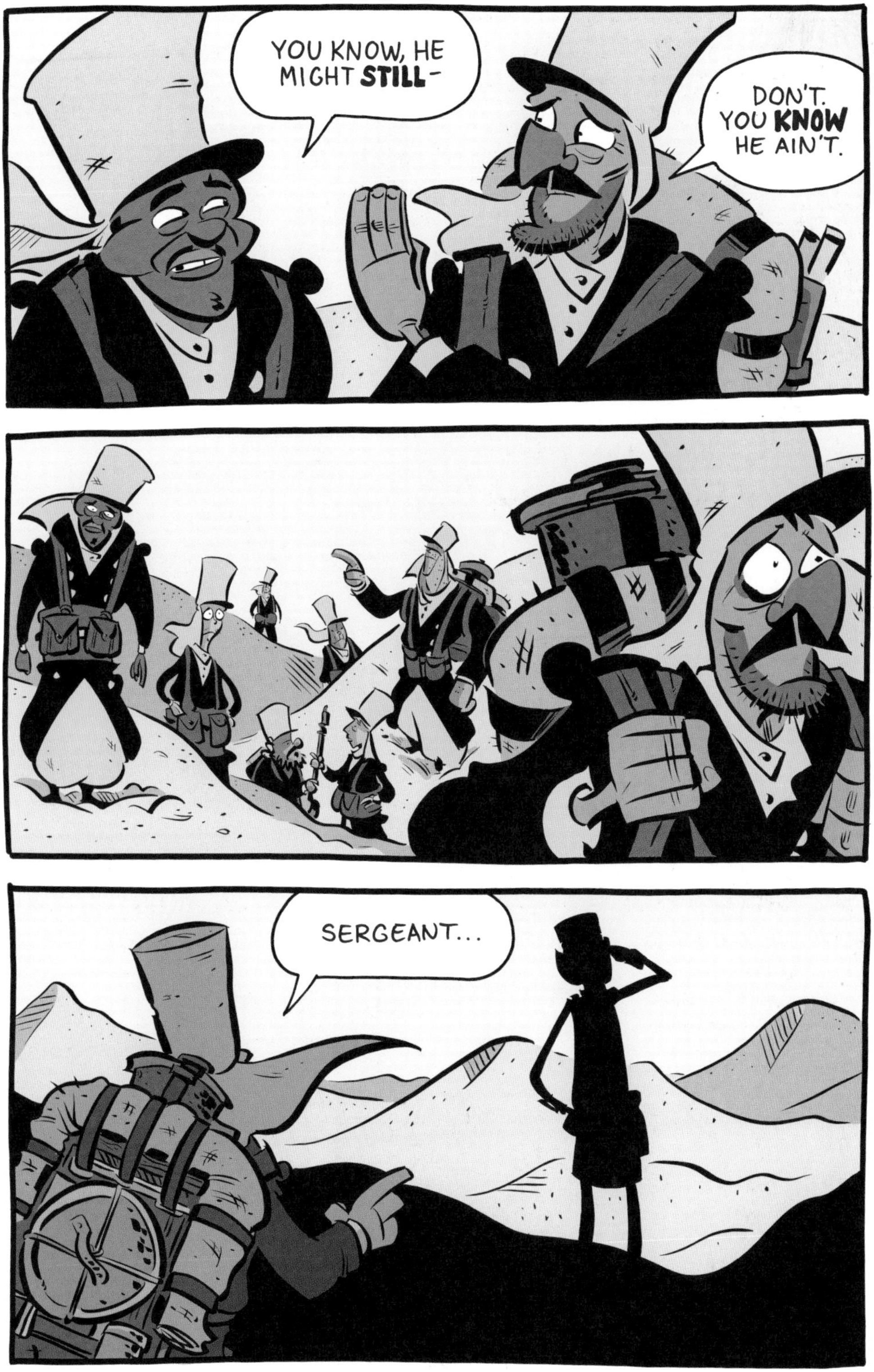
YOU KNOW, HE MIGHT STILL-
DON'T. YOU KNOW HE AIN'T.
SERGEANT...

LEMME GIVE YOU A HAND, KID.

OH. THANKS, PETER.

OOF!

THERE YA' GO.

THANK YOU.

BAILEY! GERALD!

YEAH, PETE!

WHO'S GOT THE RIFLES?

JOMERE. HE'S HANDIN' 'EM OUT.

WELL, WHO'DA THOUGHT IT? THE KID'S STILL IN ONE PIECE!

BE EASY ON HIM, EH? HE AIN'T DONE NUTHIN'.

'COURSE HE HASN'T, **YET**. HE'S ONLY... TWELVE? FIFTEEN?

THAT DON'T MEAN NUTHIN'! I WAS MAKIN' ALL **SORTS** OF TROUBLE AT FIFTEEN.

YEAH, WE JUST WANNA MAKE HIM AS TOUGH AS BAILEY!

HEY, PETER!

21

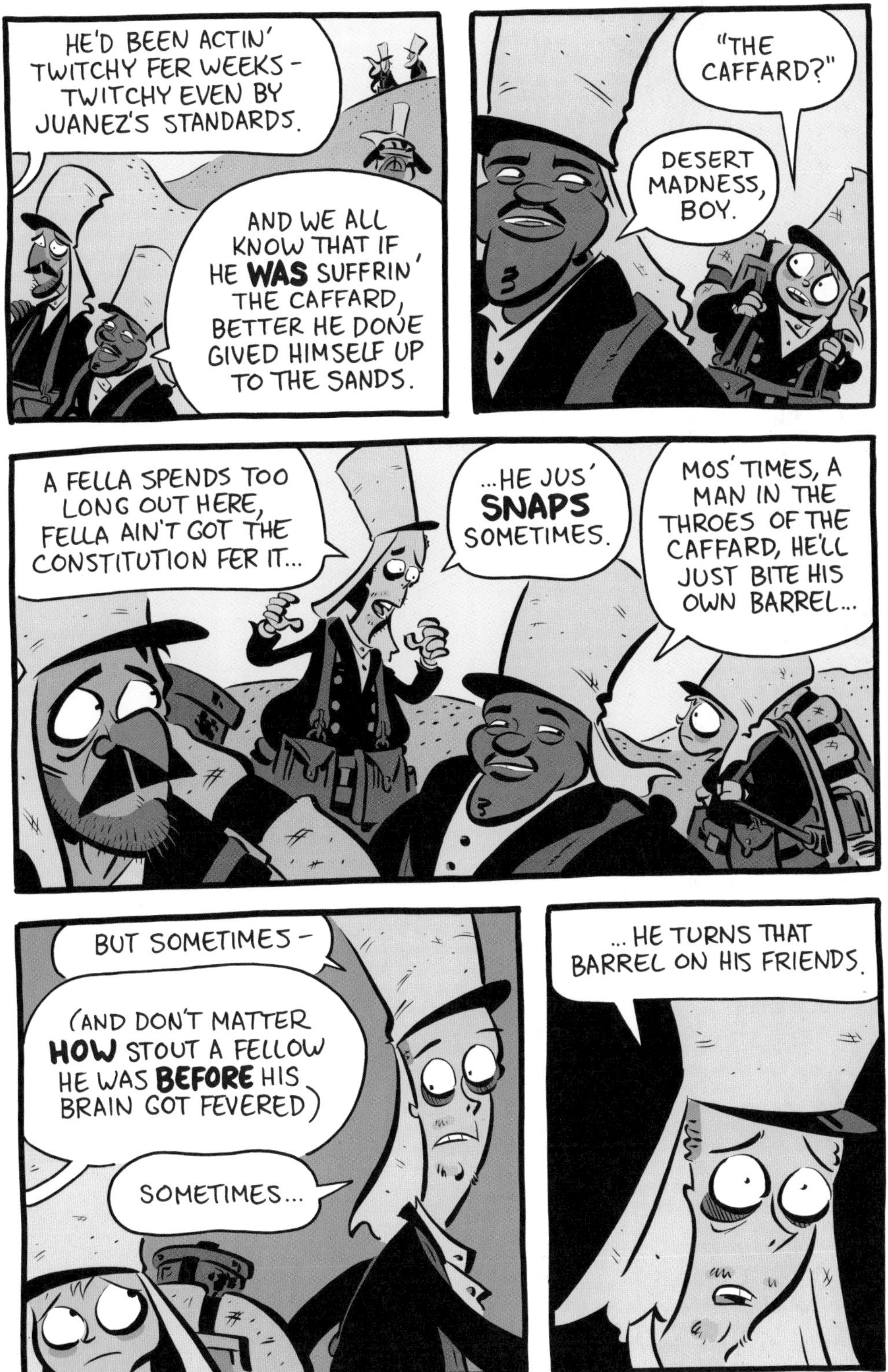
HE'D BEEN ACTIN' TWITCHY FER WEEKS - TWITCHY EVEN BY JUANEZ'S STANDARDS.
AND WE ALL KNOW THAT IF HE **WAS** SUFFRIN' THE CAFFARD, BETTER HE DONE GIVED HIMSELF UP TO THE SANDS.
"THE CAFFARD?"
DESERT MADNESS, BOY.
A FELLA SPENDS TOO LONG OUT HERE, FELLA AIN'T GOT THE CONSTITUTION FER IT...
...HE JUS' **SNAPS** SOMETIMES.
MOS' TIMES, A MAN IN THE THROES OF THE CAFFARD, HE'LL JUST BITE HIS OWN BARREL...
BUT SOMETIMES -
(AND DON'T MATTER **HOW** STOUT A FELLOW HE WAS **BEFORE** HIS BRAIN GOT FEVERED)
SOMETIMES...
... HE TURNS THAT BARREL ON HIS FRIENDS.

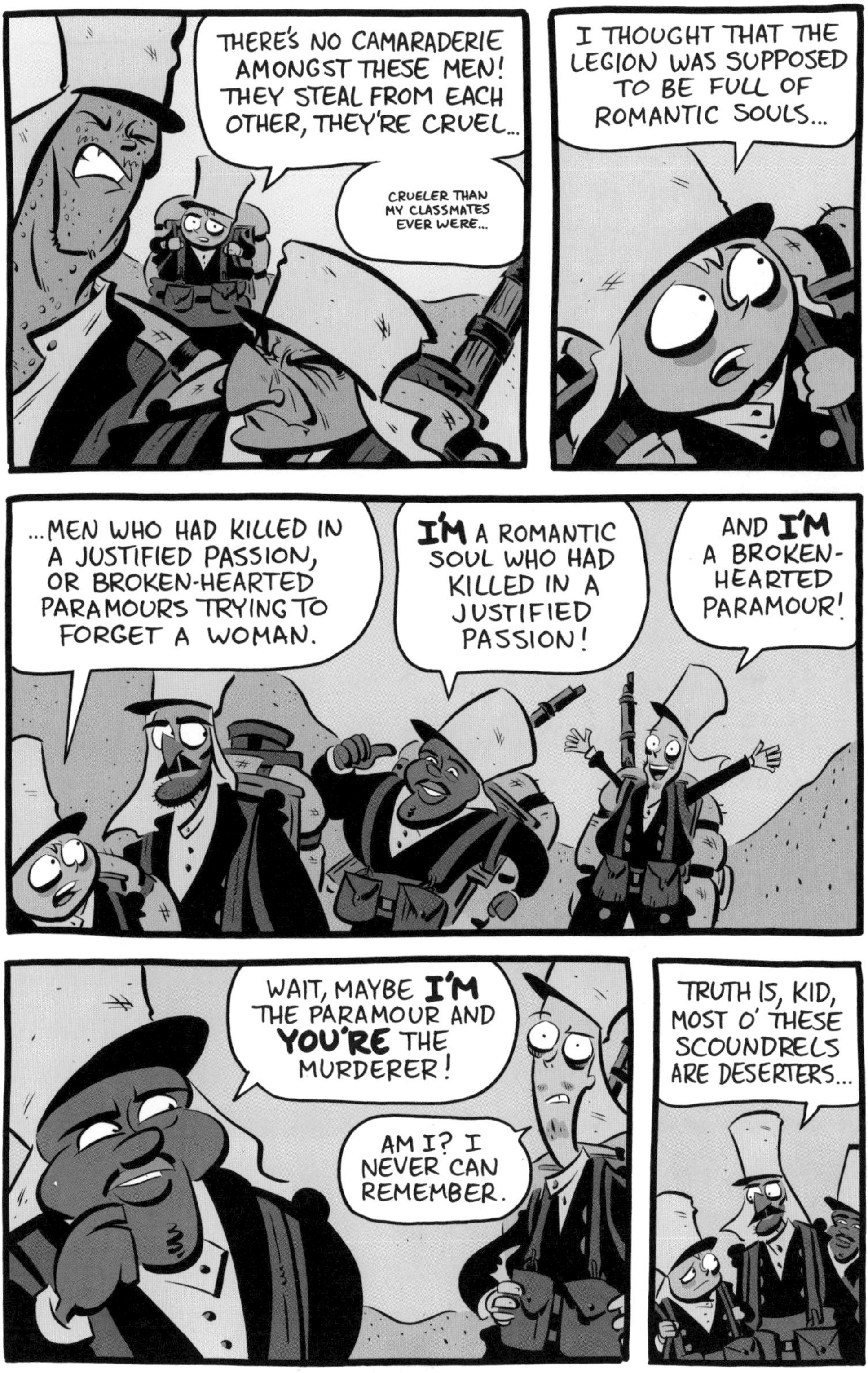
THERE'S NO CAMARADERIE AMONGST THESE MEN! THEY STEAL FROM EACH OTHER, THEY'RE CRUEL...
CRUELER THAN MY CLASSMATES EVER WERE...
I THOUGHT THAT THE LEGION WAS SUPPOSED TO BE FULL OF ROMANTIC SOULS...
...MEN WHO HAD KILLED IN A JUSTIFIED PASSION, OR BROKEN-HEARTED PARAMOURS TRYING TO FORGET A WOMAN.
I'M A ROMANTIC SOUL WHO HAD KILLED IN A JUSTIFIED PASSION!
AND **I'M** A BROKEN-HEARTED PARAMOUR!
WAIT, MAYBE **I'M** THE PARAMOUR AND **YOU'RE** THE MURDERER!
AM I? I NEVER CAN REMEMBER.
TRUTH IS, KID, MOST O' THESE SCOUNDRELS ARE DESERTERS...

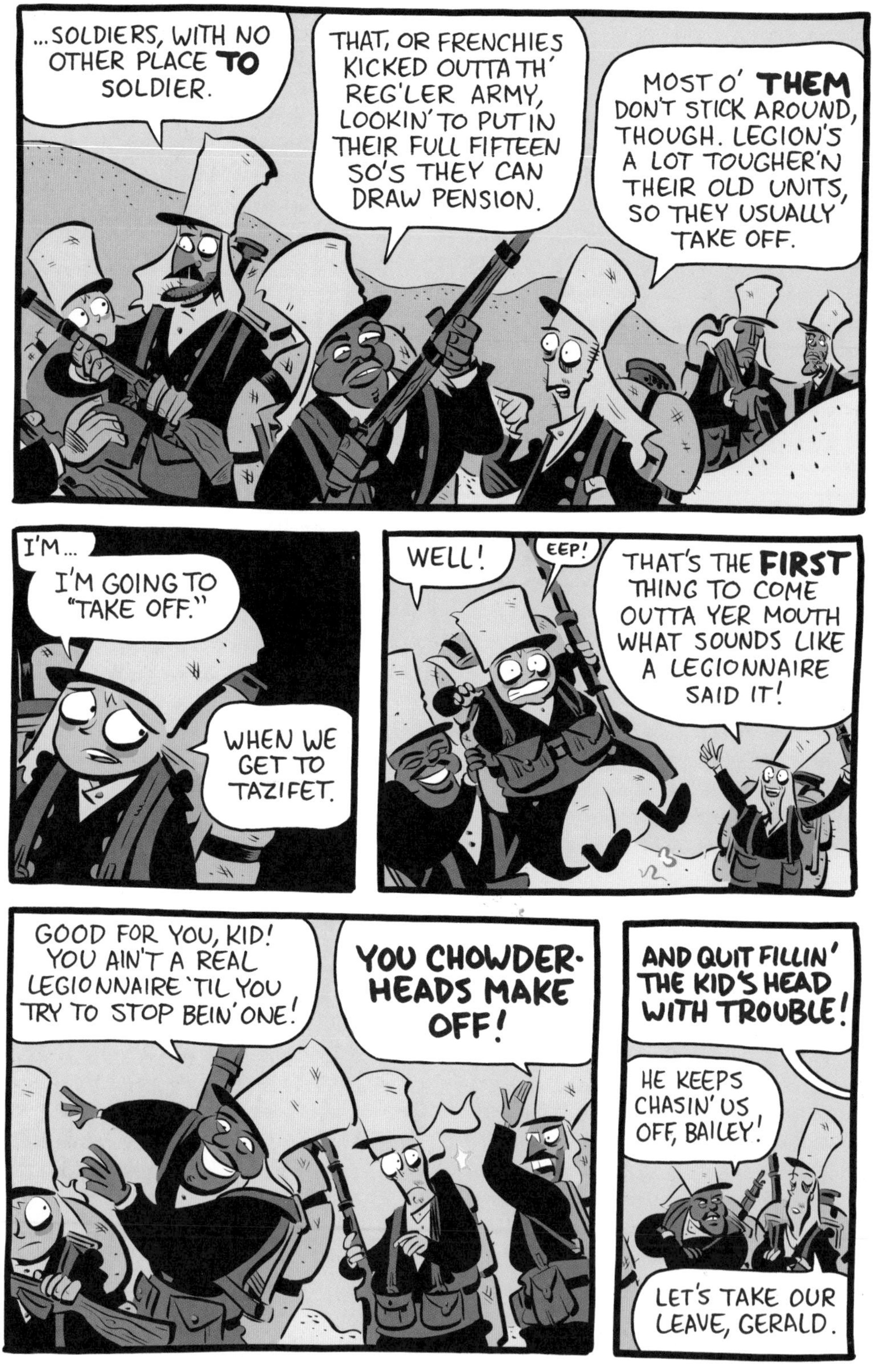
...SOLDIERS, WITH NO OTHER PLACE **TO** SOLDIER.
THAT, OR FRENCHIES KICKED OUTTA TH' REG'LER ARMY, LOOKIN' TO PUT IN THEIR FULL FIFTEEN SO'S THEY CAN DRAW PENSION.
MOST O' **THEM** DON'T STICK AROUND, THOUGH. LEGION'S A LOT TOUGHER'N THEIR OLD UNITS, SO THEY USUALLY TAKE OFF.
I'M...
I'M GOING TO "TAKE OFF."
WHEN WE GET TO TAZIFET.
WELL!
EEP!
THAT'S THE **FIRST** THING TO COME OUTTA YER MOUTH WHAT SOUNDS LIKE A LEGIONNAIRE SAID IT!
GOOD FOR YOU, KID! YOU AIN'T A REAL LEGIONNAIRE 'TIL YOU TRY TO STOP BEIN' ONE!
YOU CHOWDER-HEADS MAKE OFF!
AND QUIT FILLIN' THE KID'S HEAD WITH TROUBLE!
HE KEEPS CHASIN' US OFF, BAILEY!
LET'S TAKE OUR LEAVE, GERALD.

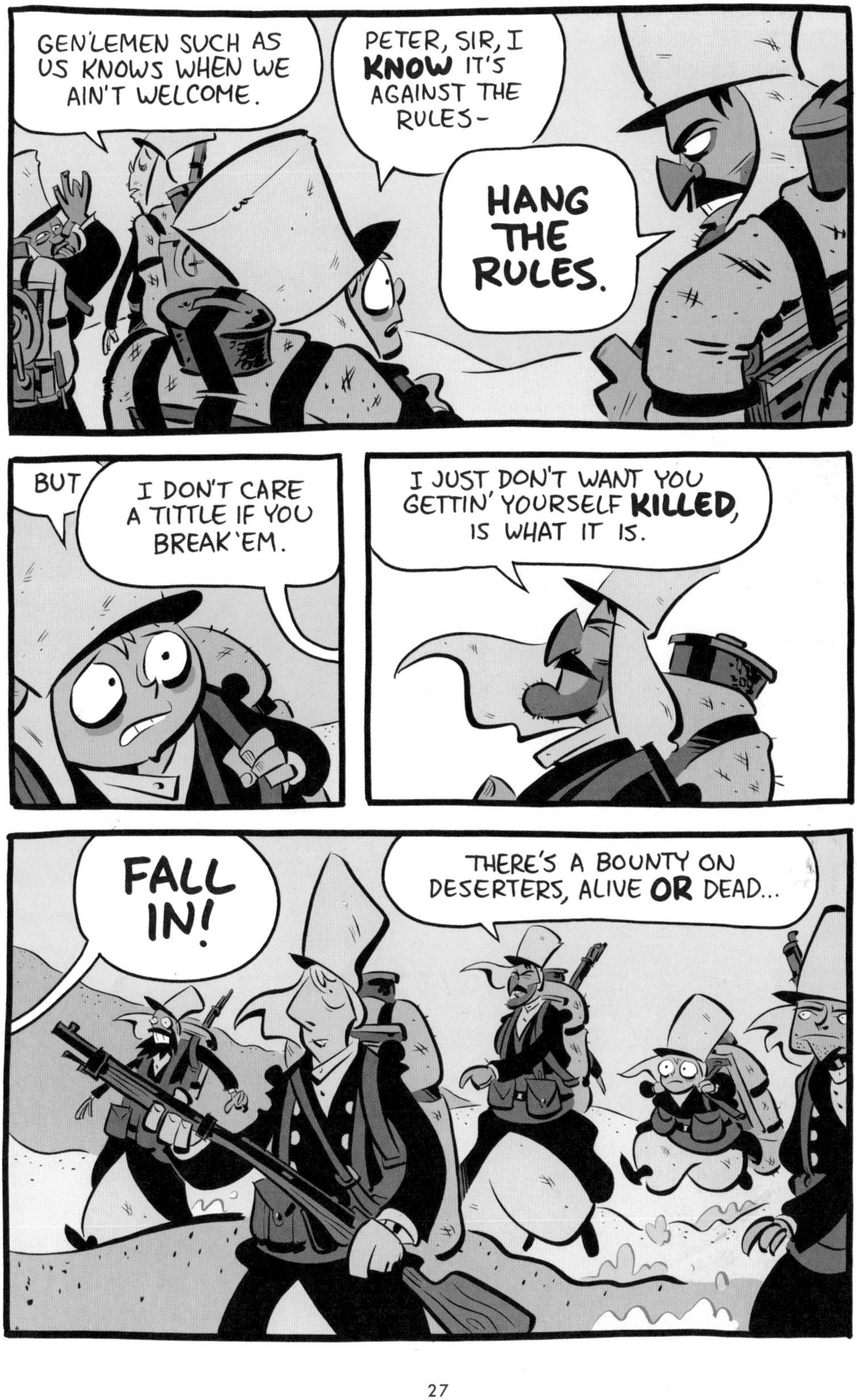
GEN'LEMEN SUCH AS US KNOWS WHEN WE AIN'T WELCOME.
PETER, SIR, I **KNOW** IT'S AGAINST THE RULES-
HANG THE RULES.
BUT
I DON'T CARE A TITTLE IF YOU BREAK 'EM.
I JUST DON'T WANT YOU GETTIN' YOURSELF **KILLED**, IS WHAT IT IS.
FALL IN!
THERE'S A BOUNTY ON DESERTERS, ALIVE **OR** DEAD...

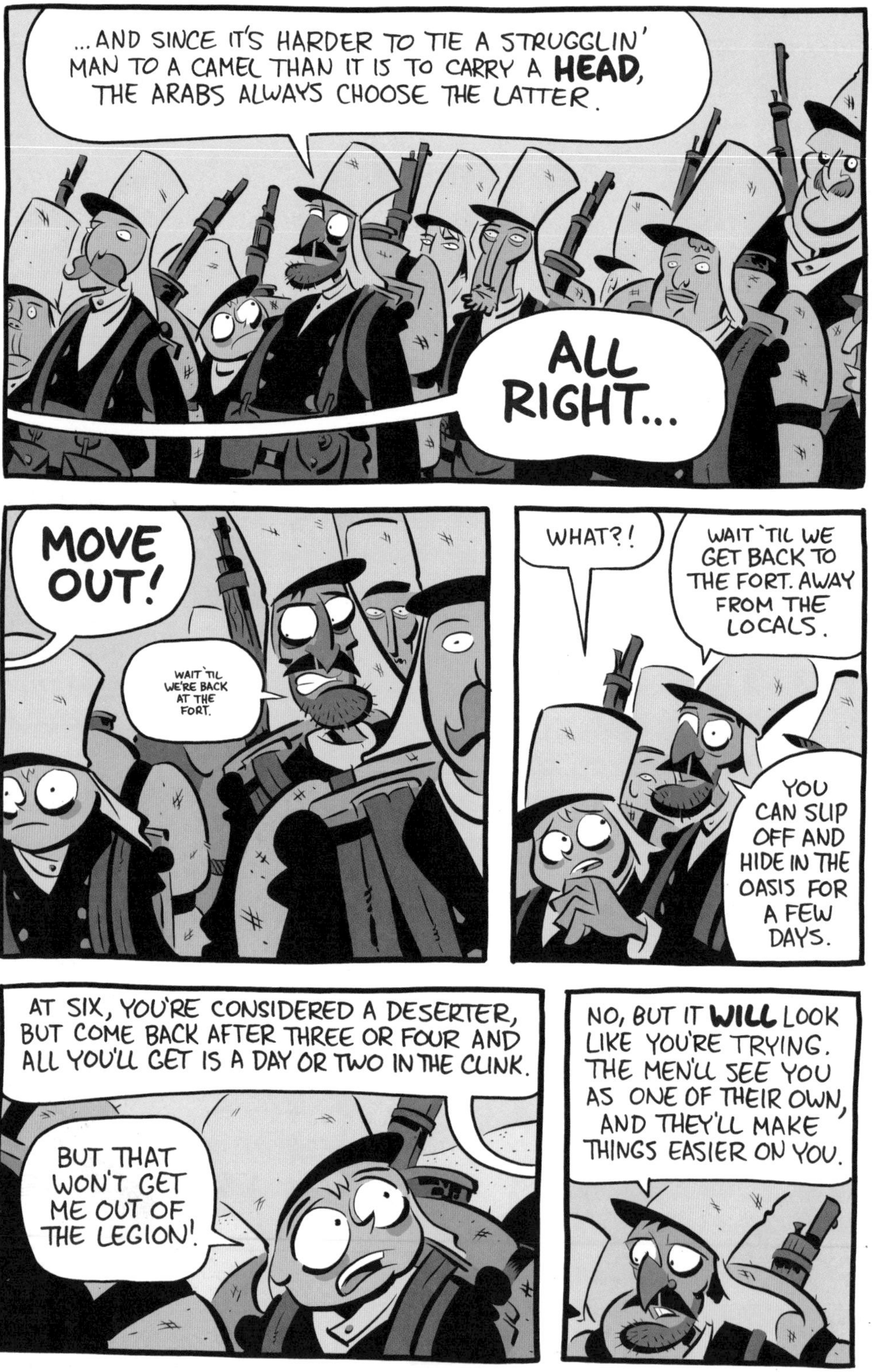
...AND SINCE IT'S HARDER TO TIE A STRUGGLIN' MAN TO A CAMEL THAN IT IS TO CARRY A **HEAD**, THE ARABS ALWAYS CHOOSE THE LATTER.
ALL RIGHT...
MOVE OUT!
WAIT 'TIL WE'RE BACK AT THE FORT.
WHAT?!
WAIT 'TIL WE GET BACK TO THE FORT. AWAY FROM THE LOCALS.
YOU CAN SLIP OFF AND HIDE IN THE OASIS FOR A FEW DAYS.
AT SIX, YOU'RE CONSIDERED A DESERTER, BUT COME BACK AFTER THREE OR FOUR AND ALL YOU'LL GET IS A DAY OR TWO IN THE CLINK.
BUT THAT WON'T GET ME OUT OF THE LEGION!
NO, BUT IT **WILL** LOOK LIKE YOU'RE TRYING. THE MEN'LL SEE YOU AS ONE OF THEIR OWN, AND THEY'LL MAKE THINGS EASIER ON YOU.

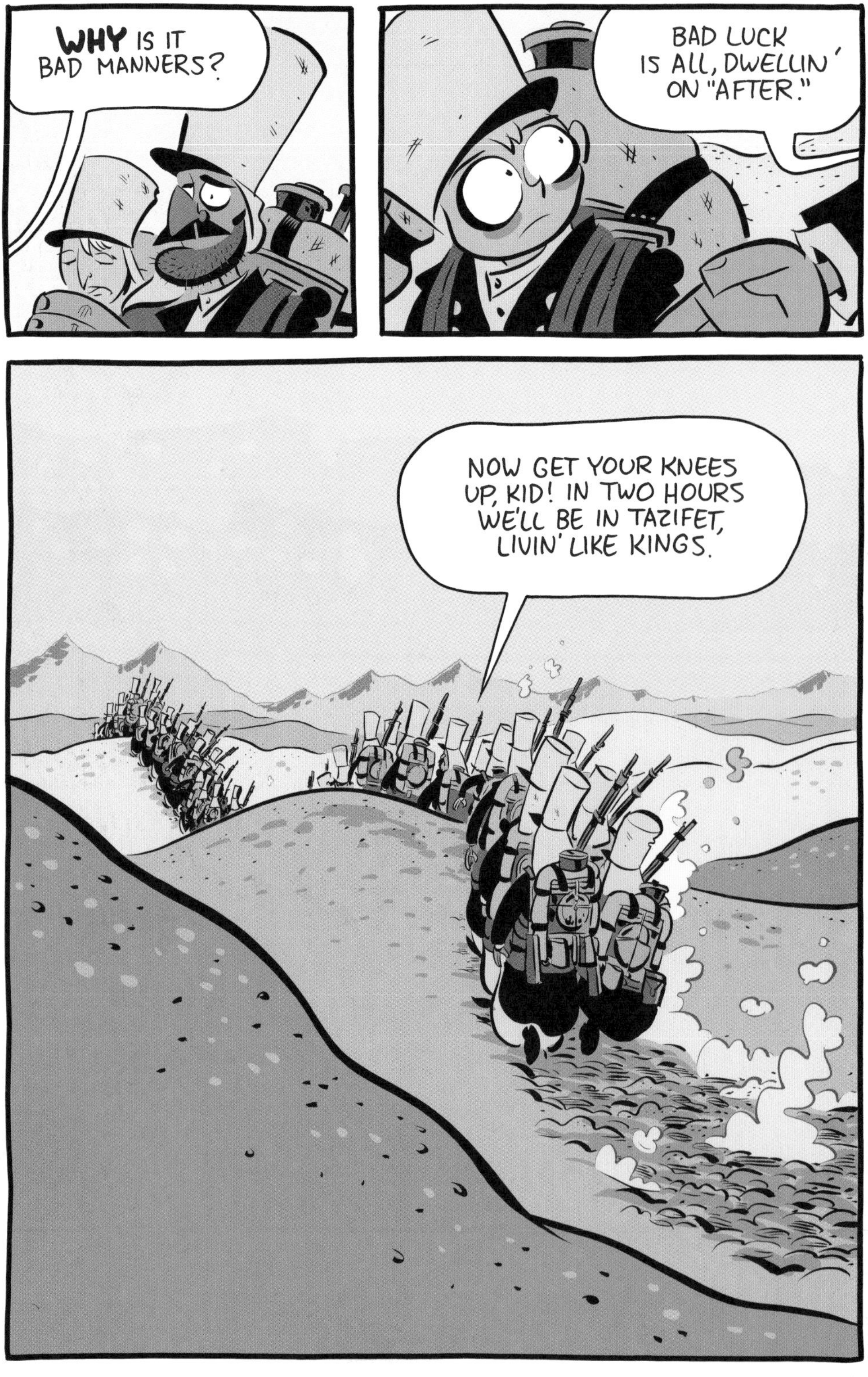
WHY IS IT BAD MANNERS?
BAD LUCK IS ALL, DWELLIN' ON "AFTER."
NOW GET YOUR KNEES UP, KID! IN TWO HOURS WE'LL BE IN TAZIFET, LIVIN' LIKE KINGS.

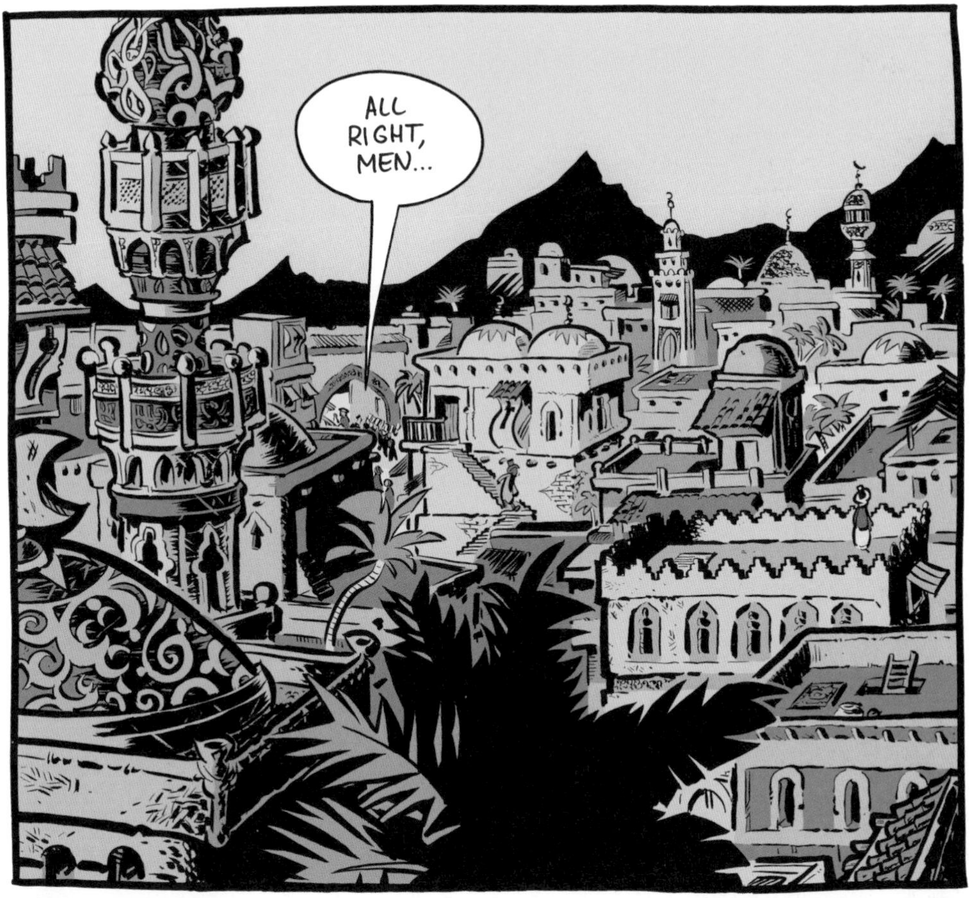
ALL RIGHT, MEN...

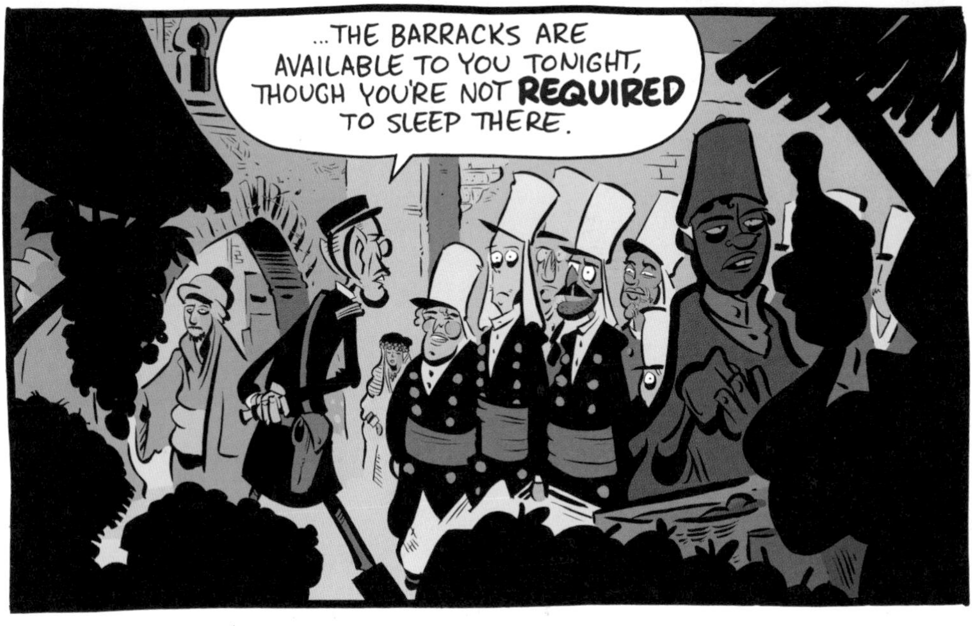
...THE BARRACKS ARE AVAILABLE TO YOU TONIGHT, THOUGH YOU'RE NOT **REQUIRED** TO SLEEP THERE.

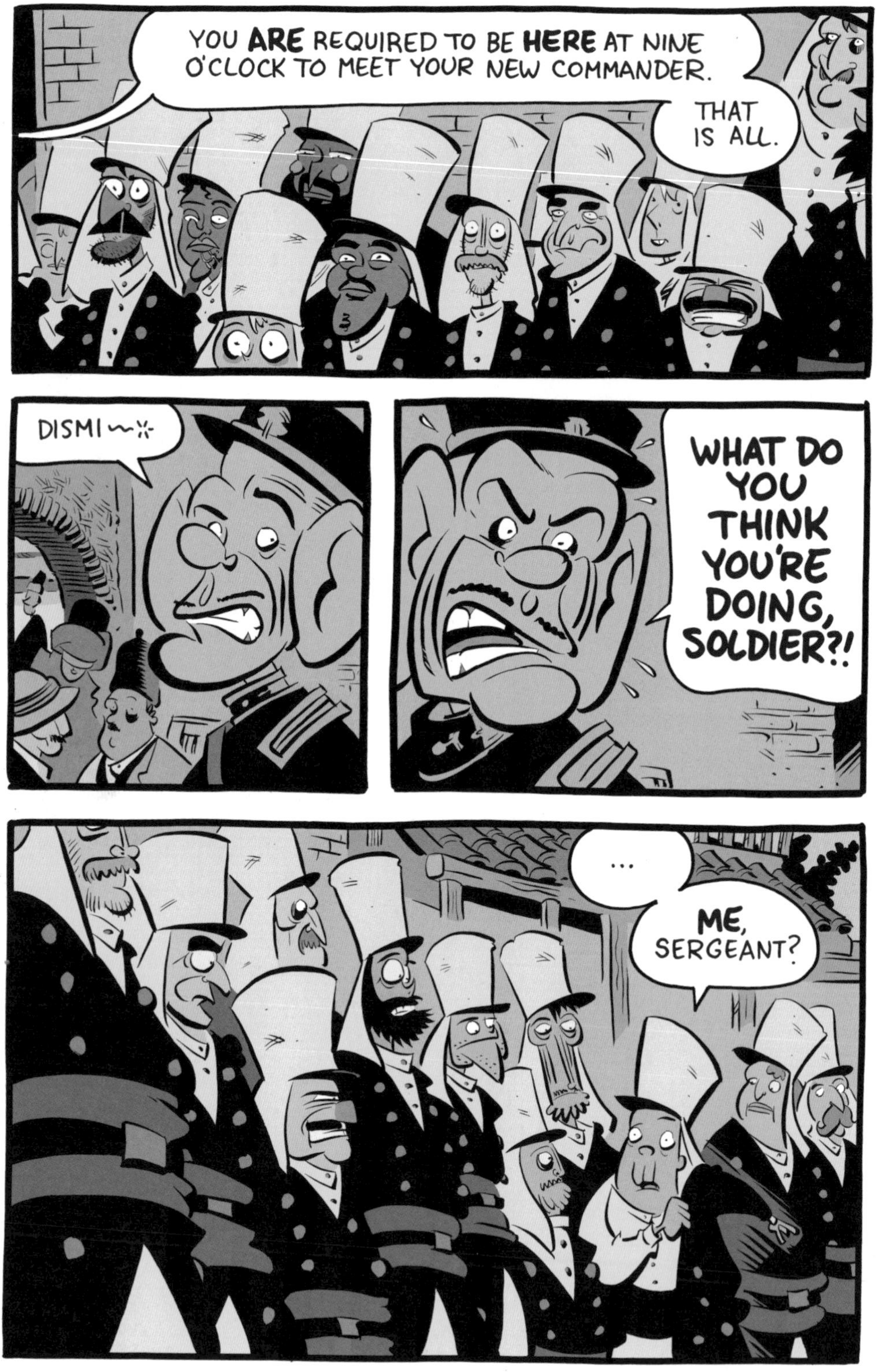
YOU **ARE** REQUIRED TO BE **HERE** AT NINE O'CLOCK TO MEET YOUR NEW COMMANDER.
THAT IS ALL.
DISMI—
WHAT DO YOU THINK YOU'RE DOING, SOLDIER?!
...
ME, SERGEANT?

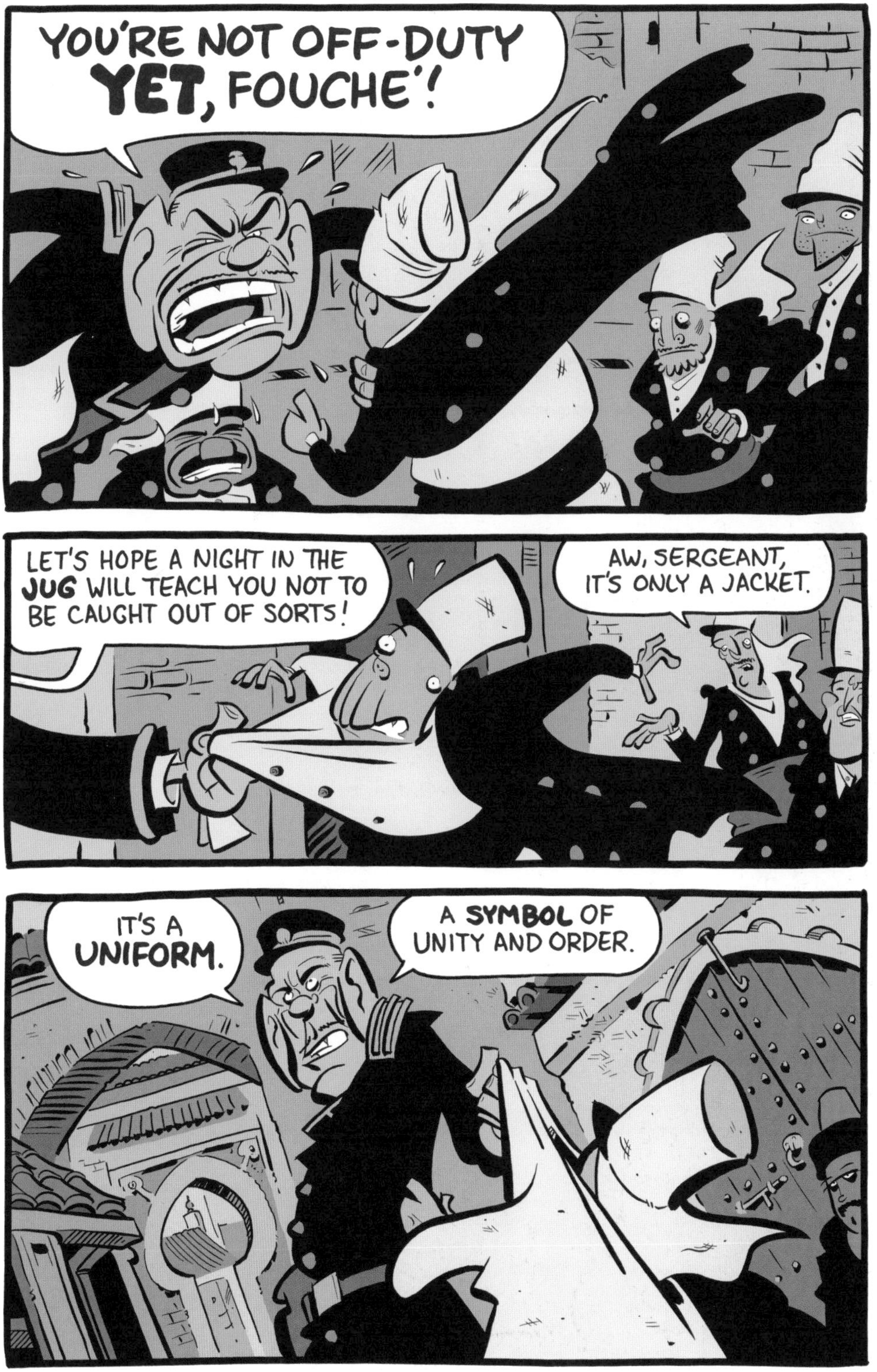
YOU'RE NOT OFF-DUTY YET, FOUCHE'!
LET'S HOPE A NIGHT IN THE JUG WILL TEACH YOU NOT TO BE CAUGHT OUT OF SORTS!
AW, SERGEANT, IT'S ONLY A JACKET.
IT'S A UNIFORM.
A SYMBOL OF UNITY AND ORDER.

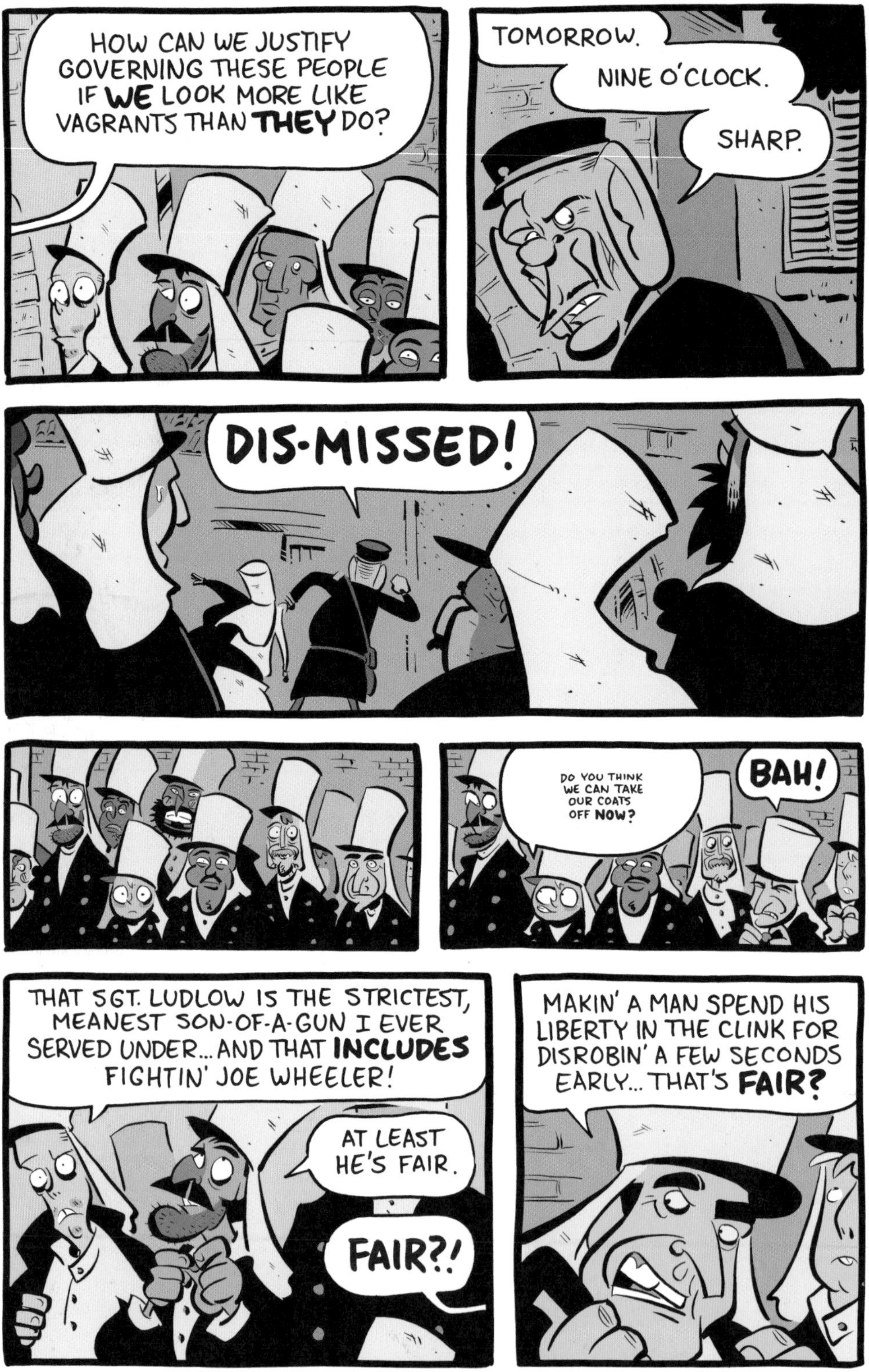
HOW CAN WE JUSTIFY GOVERNING THESE PEOPLE IF WE LOOK MORE LIKE VAGRANTS THAN THEY DO?
TOMORROW.
NINE O'CLOCK.
SHARP.
DIS-MISSED!
DO YOU THINK WE CAN TAKE OUR COATS OFF NOW?
BAH!
THAT SGT. LUDLOW IS THE STRICTEST, MEANEST SON-OF-A-GUN I EVER SERVED UNDER... AND THAT INCLUDES FIGHTIN' JOE WHEELER!
AT LEAST HE'S FAIR.
FAIR?!
MAKIN' A MAN SPEND HIS LIBERTY IN THE CLINK FOR DISROBIN' A FEW SECONDS EARLY... THAT'S FAIR?

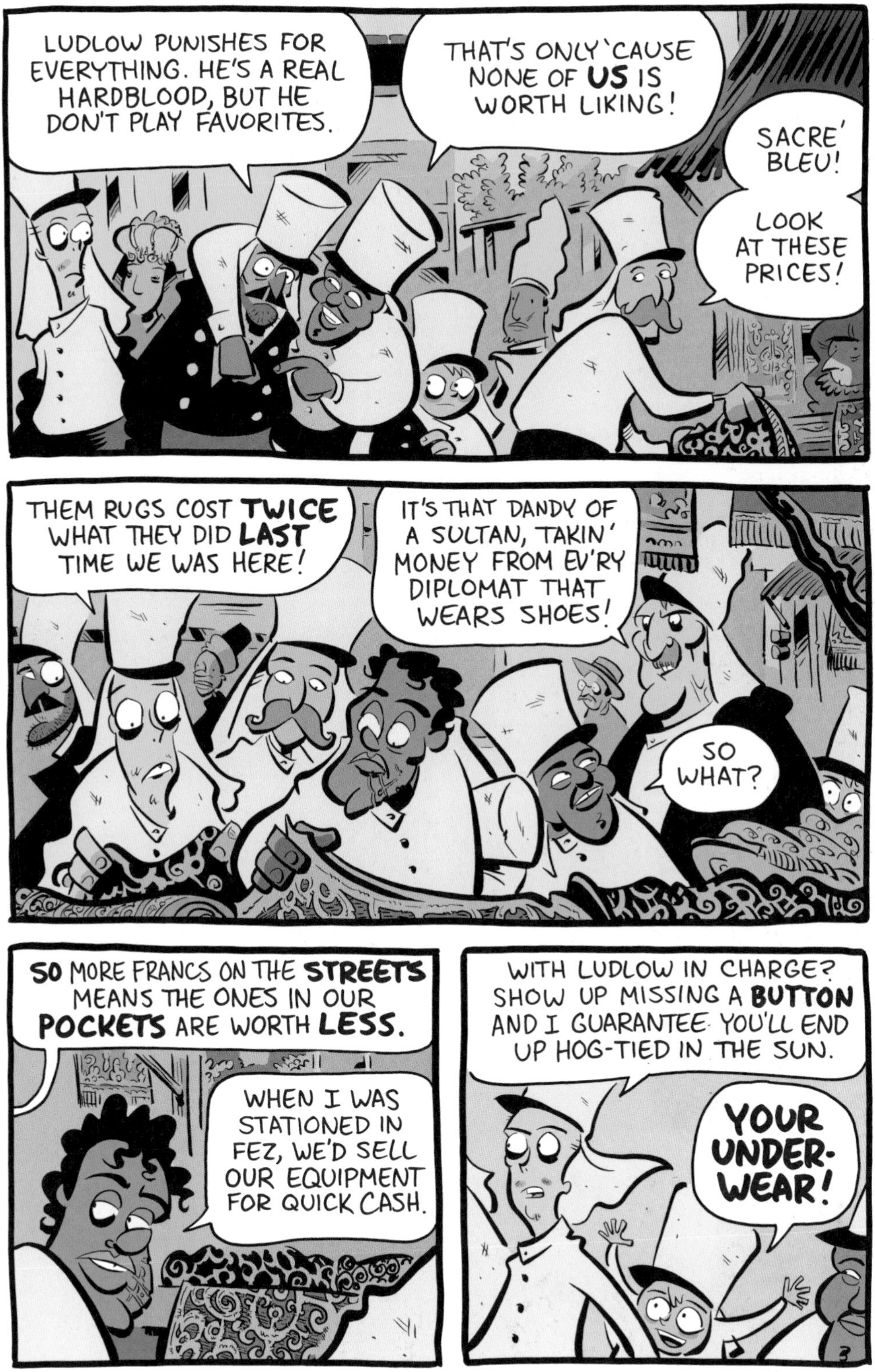
LUDLOW PUNISHES FOR EVERYTHING. HE'S A REAL HARDBLOOD, BUT HE DON'T PLAY FAVORITES.
THAT'S ONLY 'CAUSE NONE OF **US** IS WORTH LIKING!
SACRÉ BLEU!
LOOK AT THESE PRICES!
THEM RUGS COST **TWICE** WHAT THEY DID **LAST** TIME WE WAS HERE!
IT'S THAT DANDY OF A SULTAN, TAKIN' MONEY FROM EV'RY DIPLOMAT THAT WEARS SHOES!
SO WHAT?
SO MORE FRANCS ON THE **STREETS** MEANS THE ONES IN OUR **POCKETS** ARE WORTH **LESS**.
WHEN I WAS STATIONED IN FEZ, WE'D SELL OUR EQUIPMENT FOR QUICK CASH.
WITH LUDLOW IN CHARGE? SHOW UP MISSING A **BUTTON** AND I GUARANTEE YOU'LL END UP HOG-TIED IN THE SUN.
YOUR UNDER-WEAR!

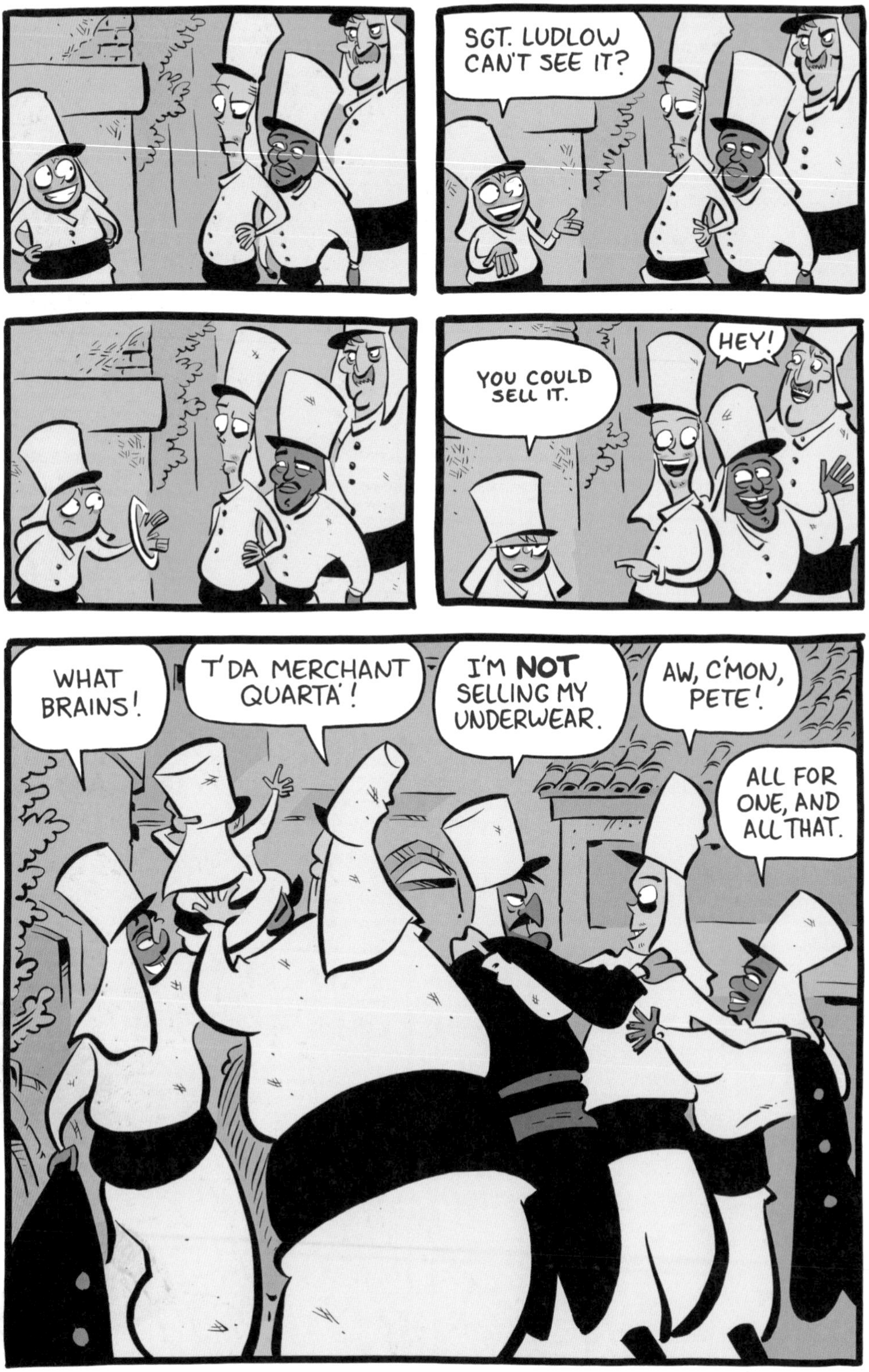
SGT. LUDLOW CAN'T SEE IT?
YOU COULD SELL IT.
HEY!
WHAT BRAINS!
T'DA MERCHANT QUARTA'!
I'M **NOT** SELLING MY UNDERWEAR.
AW, C'MON, PETE!
ALL FOR ONE, AND ALL THAT.

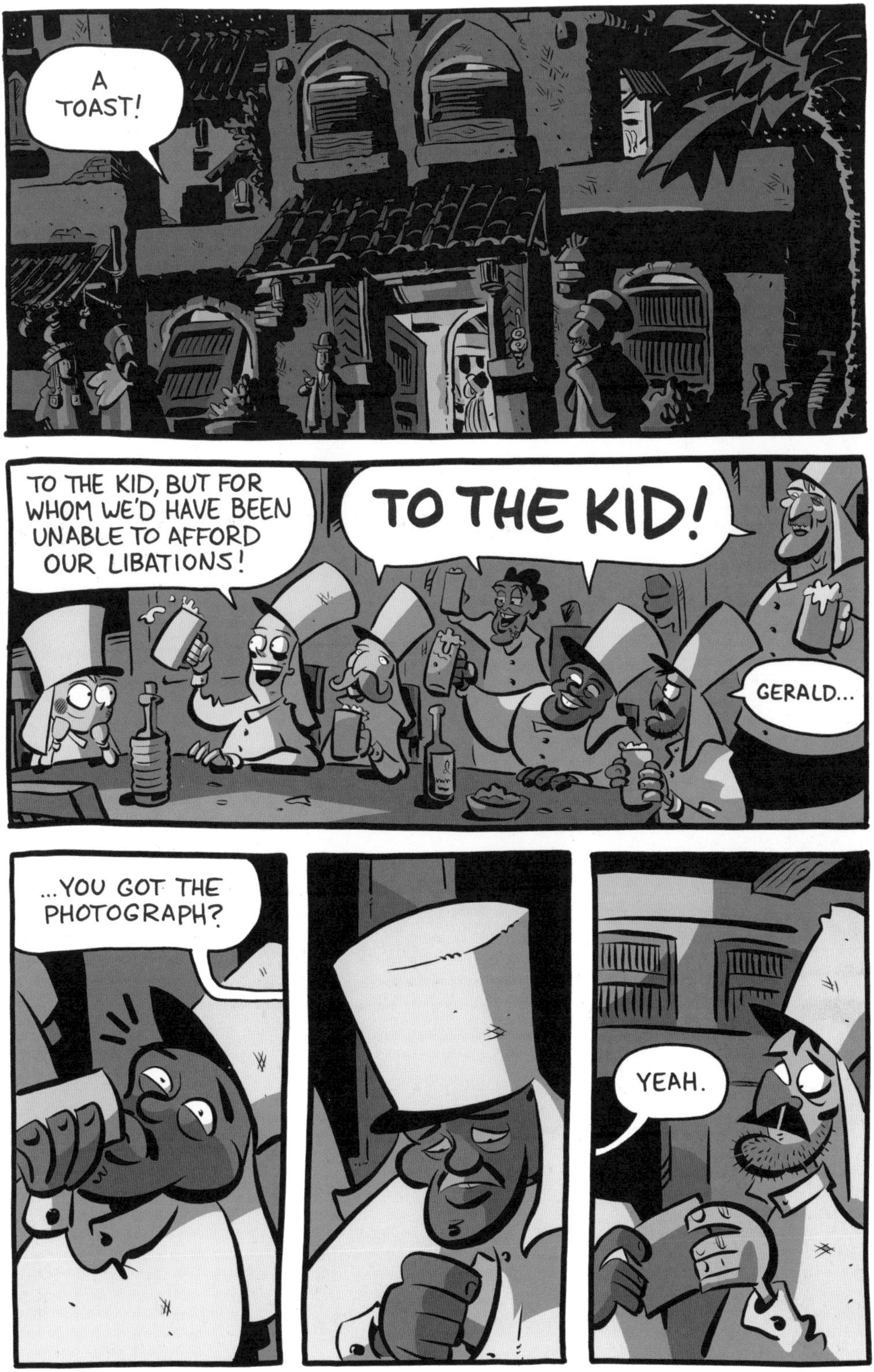
A TOAST!
TO THE KID, BUT FOR WHOM WE'D HAVE BEEN UNABLE TO AFFORD OUR LIBATIONS!
TO THE KID!
GERALD...
...YOU GOT THE PHOTOGRAPH?
YEAH.

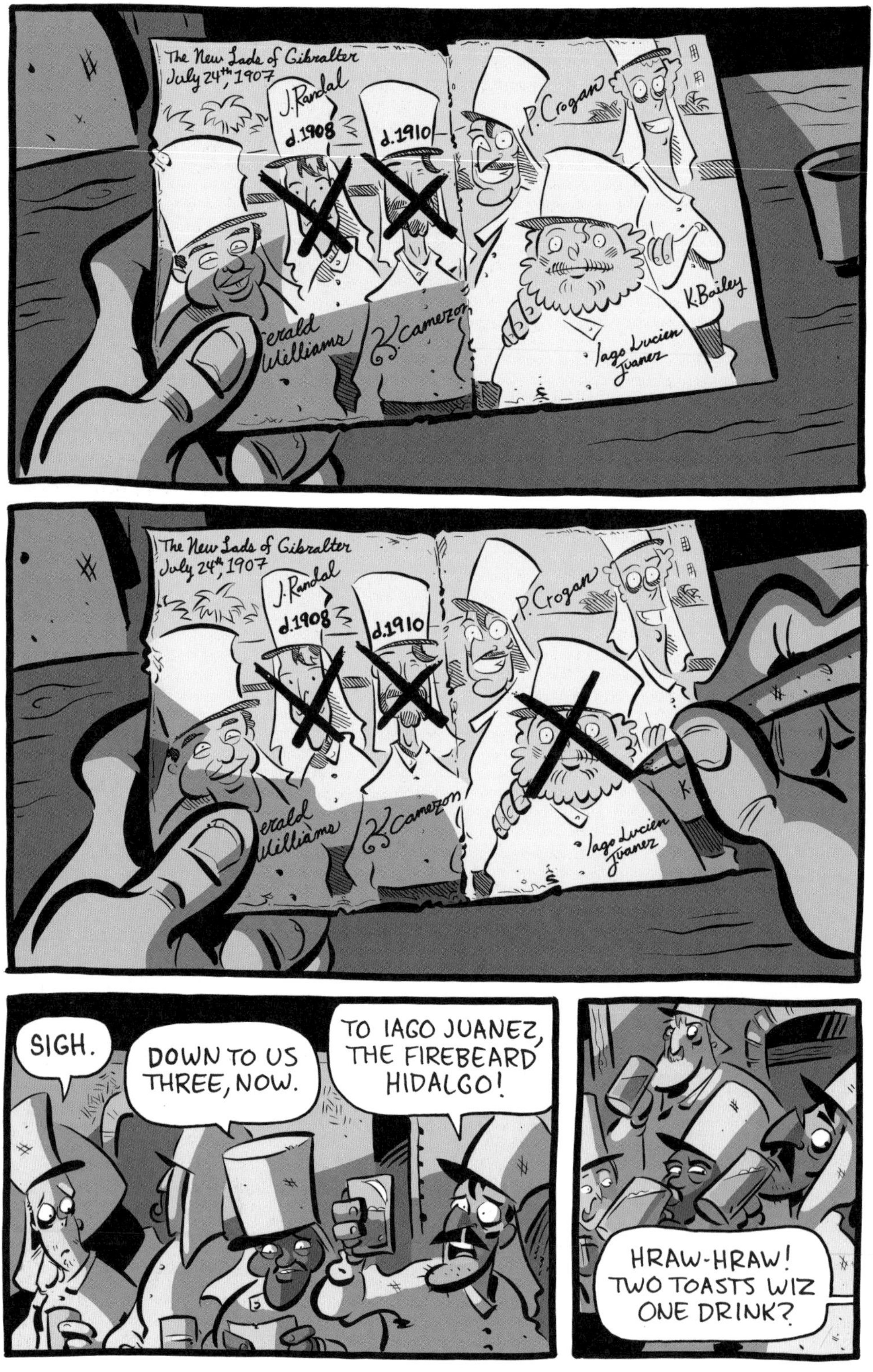
The New Lads of Gibralter
July 24th, 1907
J. Randal
d.1908
d.1910
P. Crogan
K. Bailey
erald Williams
K. Camezon
Iago Lucien Juanez
The New Lads of Gibralter
July 24th, 1907
J. Randal
d.1908
d.1910
P. Crogan
K.
erald Williams
K. Camezon
Iago Lucien Juanez
SIGH.
DOWN TO US THREE, NOW.
TO IAGO JUANEZ, THE FIREBEARD HIDALGO!
HRAW-HRAW! TWO TOASTS WIZ ONE DRINK?

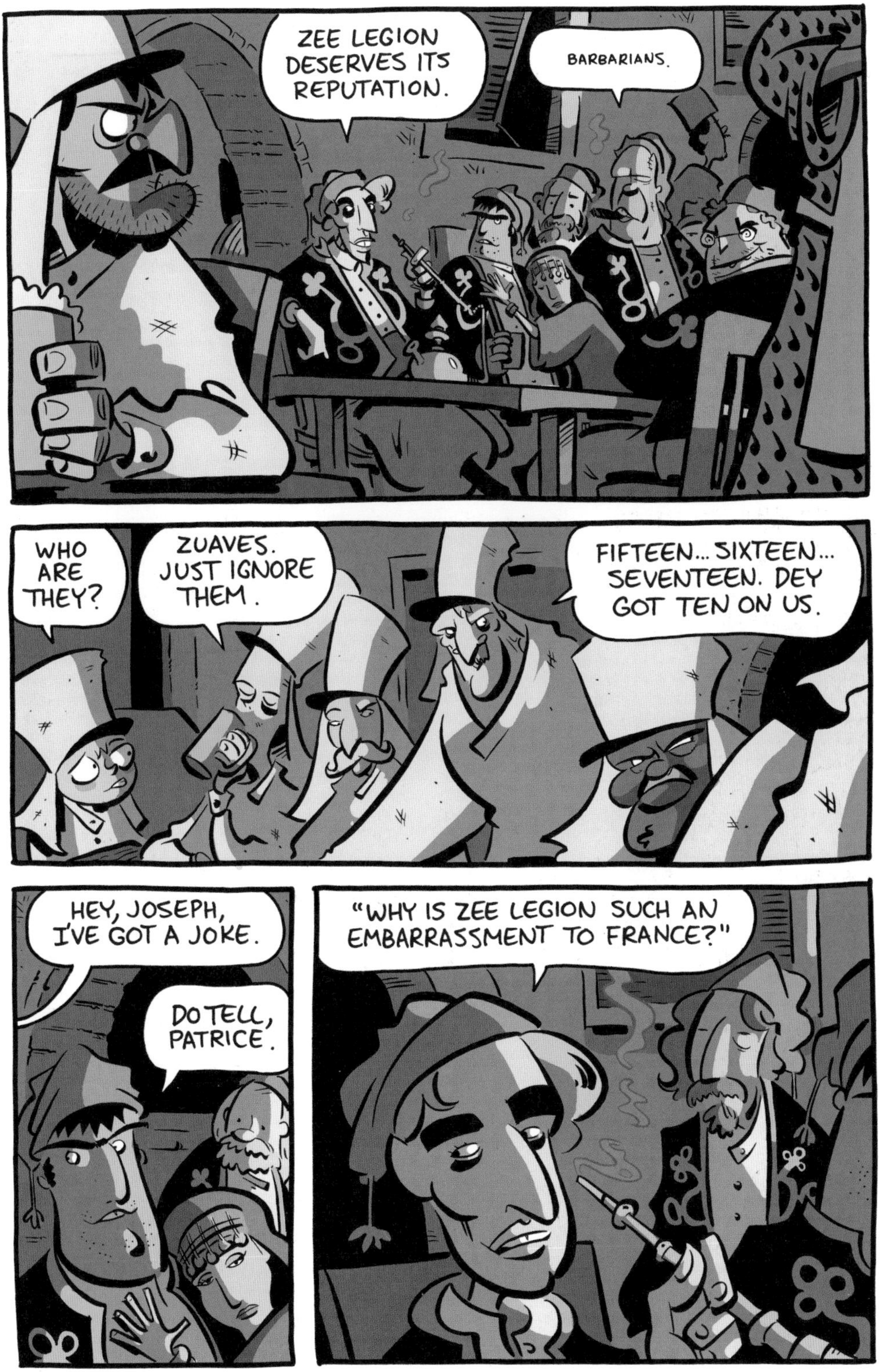
ZEE LEGION DESERVES ITS REPUTATION.
BARBARIANS.
WHO ARE THEY?
ZUAVES. JUST IGNORE THEM.
FIFTEEN... SIXTEEN... SEVENTEEN. DEY GOT TEN ON US.
HEY, JOSEPH, I'VE GOT A JOKE.
DO TELL, PATRICE.
"WHY IS ZEE LEGION SUCH AN EMBARRASSMENT TO FRANCE?"

I DON'T KNOW, PATRICE. **WHY** IS ZEE LEGION SUCH AN EMBARRASSMENT TO FRANCE?

"BECAUSE ZEY'RE ALL A BUNCH OF DESERTERS, DRUNKARDS, AND CRIMINALS!"

HRAW·HRAW·HRAW!

YOU WOULDN'T BE SO FREE WITH YOUR WORDS IF OUR NUMBERS WERE MATCHED!

HRAW!

LITTLE CHANCE WE'LL FIND OUR-SELVES IN **ZAT** CIRCUMSTANCE!

IT'S ZEE UNIFORMS. WHO **WOULDN'T** WANT TO LOOK LIKE ZIS?

WE **ARE** POPULAR.

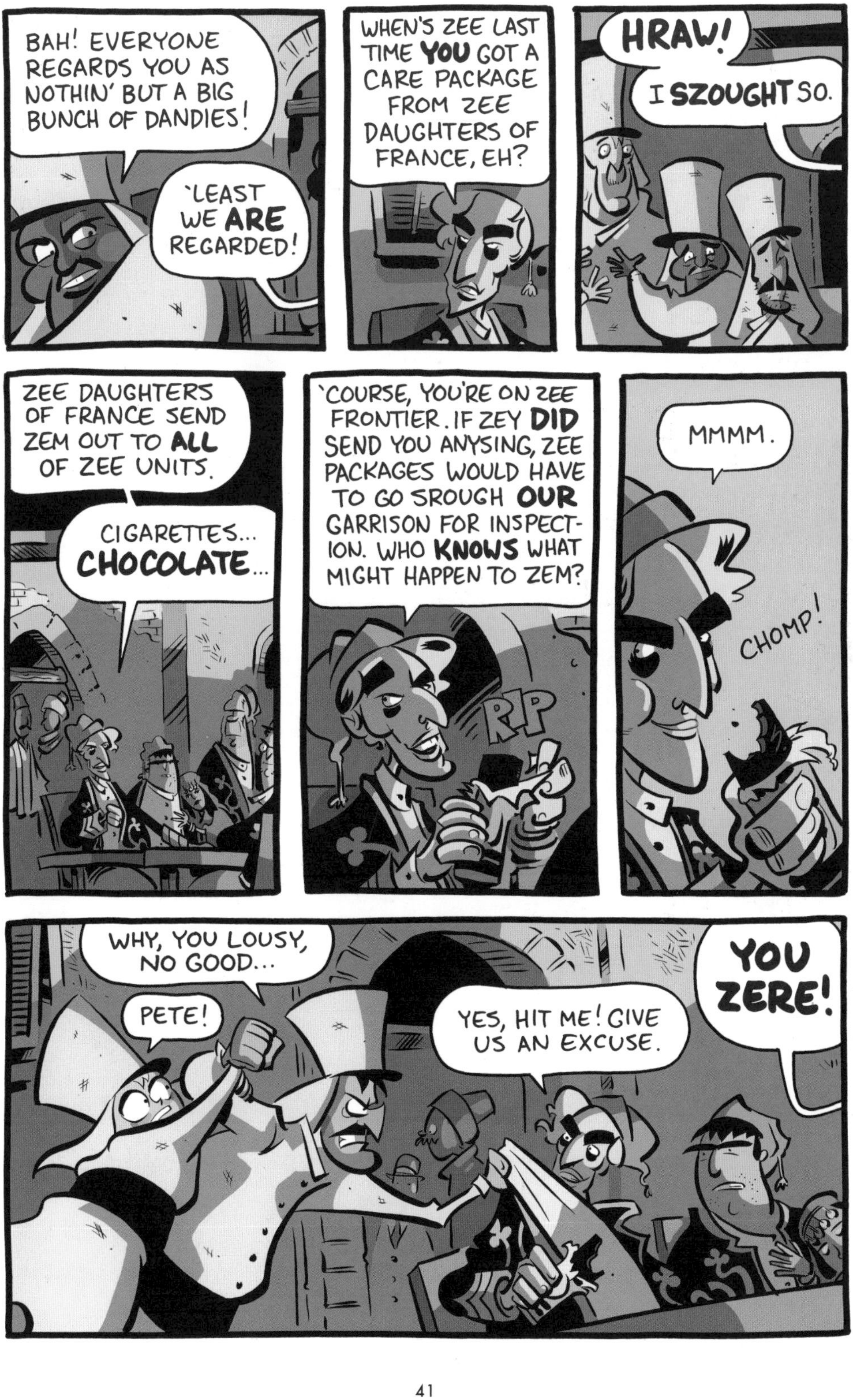
BAH! EVERYONE REGARDS YOU AS NOTHIN' BUT A BIG BUNCH OF DANDIES!
`LEAST WE **ARE** REGARDED!
WHEN'S ZEE LAST TIME **YOU** GOT A CARE PACKAGE FROM ZEE DAUGHTERS OF FRANCE, EH?
HRAW!
I **SZOUGHT** SO.
ZEE DAUGHTERS OF FRANCE SEND ZEM OUT TO **ALL** OF ZEE UNITS.
CIGARETTES... **CHOCOLATE**...
`COURSE, YOU'RE ON ZEE FRONTIER. IF ZEY **DID** SEND YOU ANYSING, ZEE PACKAGES WOULD HAVE TO GO SROUGH **OUR** GARRISON FOR INSPECTION. WHO **KNOWS** WHAT MIGHT HAPPEN TO ZEM?
RIP
MMMM.
CHOMP!
WHY, YOU LOUSY, NO GOOD...
PETE!
YES, HIT ME! GIVE US AN EXCUSE.
YOU ZERE!

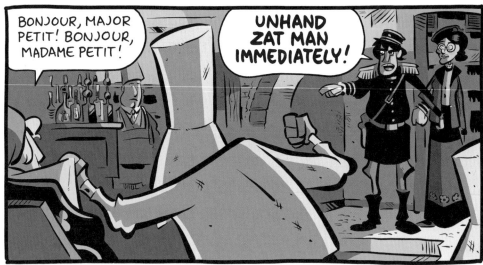

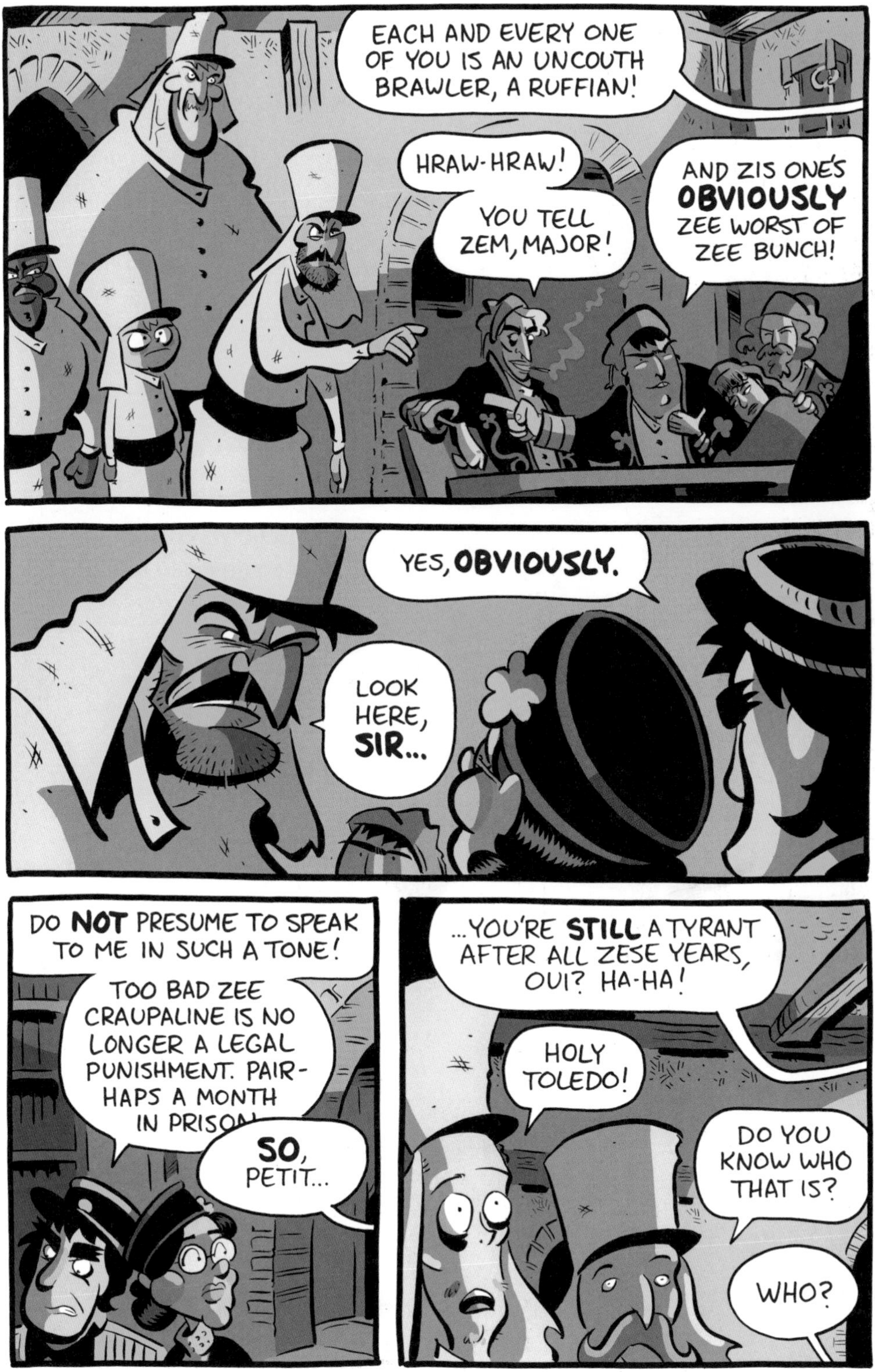
EACH AND EVERY ONE OF YOU IS AN UNCOUTH BRAWLER, A RUFFIAN!
HRAW-HRAW!
YOU TELL ZEM, MAJOR!
AND ZIS ONE'S **OBVIOUSLY** ZEE WORST OF ZEE BUNCH!
YES, **OBVIOUSLY.**
LOOK HERE, **SIR...**
DO **NOT** PRESUME TO SPEAK TO ME IN SUCH A TONE!
TOO BAD ZEE CRAUPALINE IS NO LONGER A LEGAL PUNISHMENT. PAIR-HAPS A MONTH IN PRISON
SO, PETIT...
...YOU'RE **STILL** A TYRANT AFTER ALL ZESE YEARS, OUI? HA-HA!
HOLY TOLEDO!
DO YOU KNOW WHO THAT IS?
WHO?

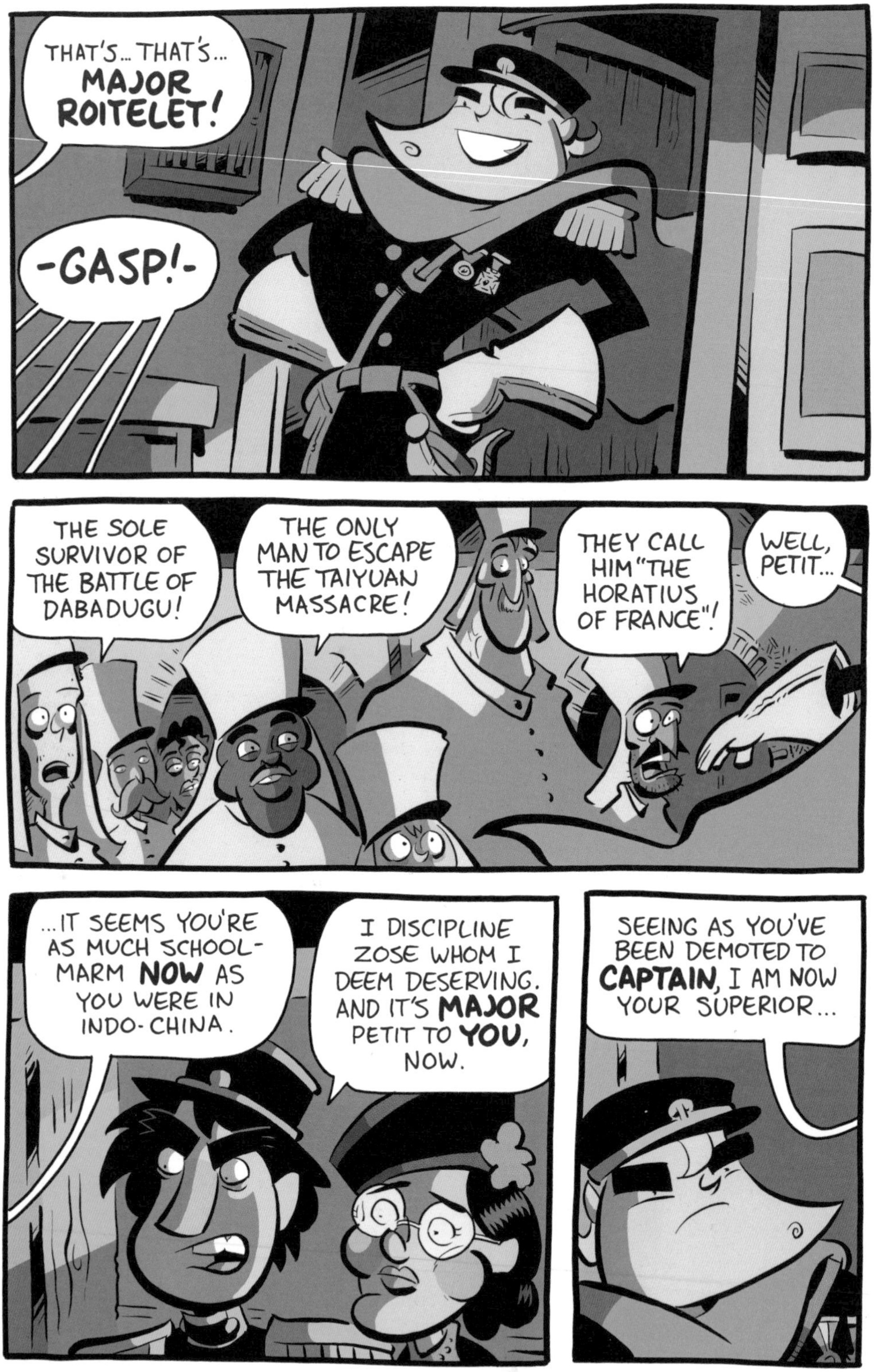
THAT'S... THAT'S... **MAJOR ROITELET!**
-GASP!-
THE SOLE SURVIVOR OF THE BATTLE OF DABADUGU!
THE ONLY MAN TO ESCAPE THE TAIYUAN MASSACRE!
THEY CALL HIM "THE HORATIUS OF FRANCE"!
WELL, PETIT...
...IT SEEMS YOU'RE AS MUCH SCHOOL-MARM **NOW** AS YOU WERE IN INDO-CHINA.
I DISCIPLINE ZOSE WHOM I DEEM DESERVING. AND IT'S **MAJOR** PETIT TO **YOU**, NOW.
SEEING AS YOU'VE BEEN DEMOTED TO **CAPTAIN**, I AM NOW YOUR SUPERIOR...

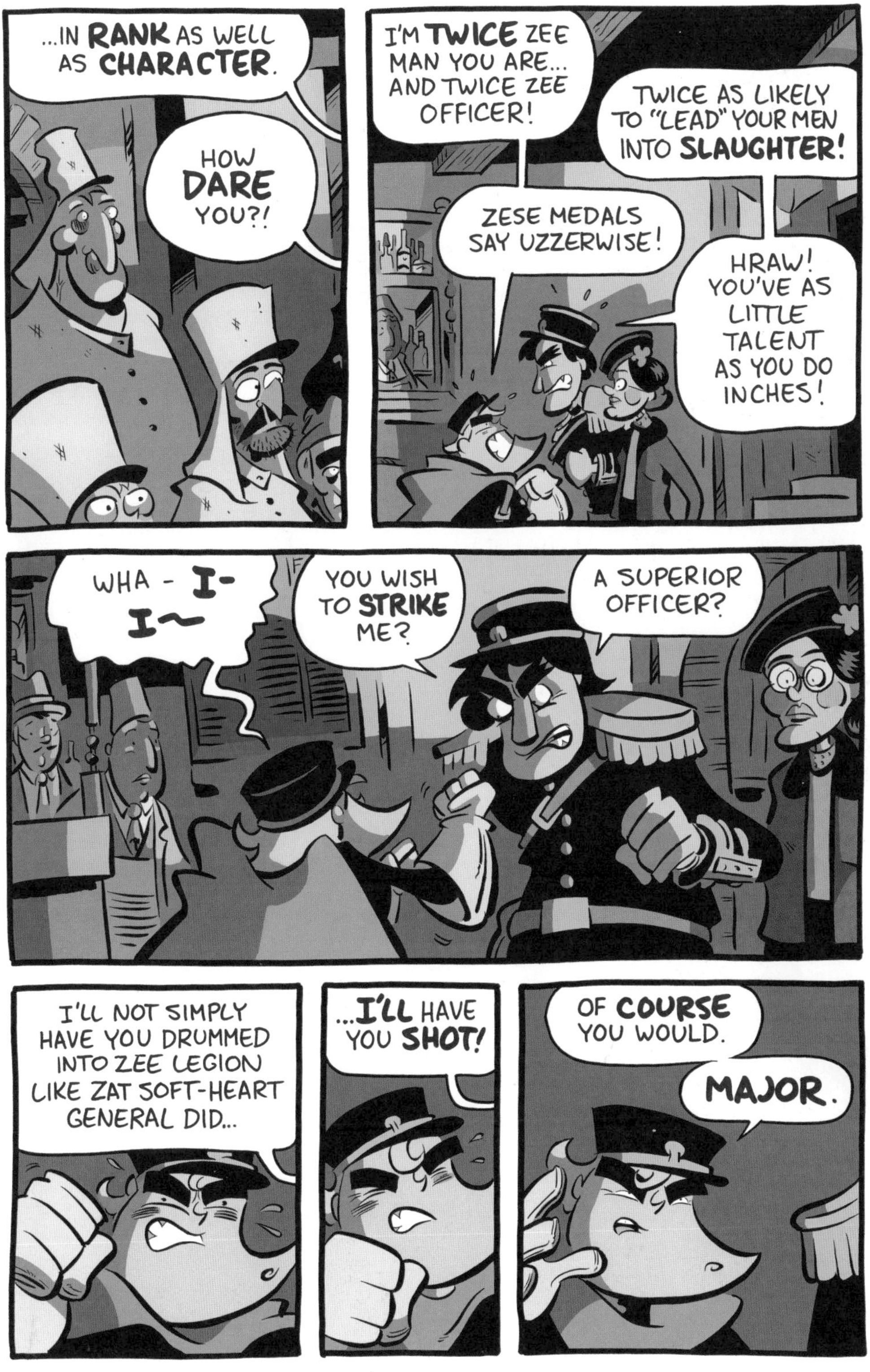
...IN RANK AS WELL AS CHARACTER.
HOW DARE YOU?!
I'M TWICE ZEE MAN YOU ARE... AND TWICE ZEE OFFICER!
TWICE AS LIKELY TO "LEAD" YOUR MEN INTO SLAUGHTER!
ZESE MEDALS SAY UZZERWISE!
HRAW! YOU'VE AS LITTLE TALENT AS YOU DO INCHES!
WHA - I- I~
YOU WISH TO STRIKE ME?
A SUPERIOR OFFICER?
I'LL NOT SIMPLY HAVE YOU DRUMMED INTO ZEE LEGION LIKE ZAT SOFT-HEART GENERAL DID...
...I'LL HAVE YOU SHOT!
OF COURSE YOU WOULD.
MAJOR.

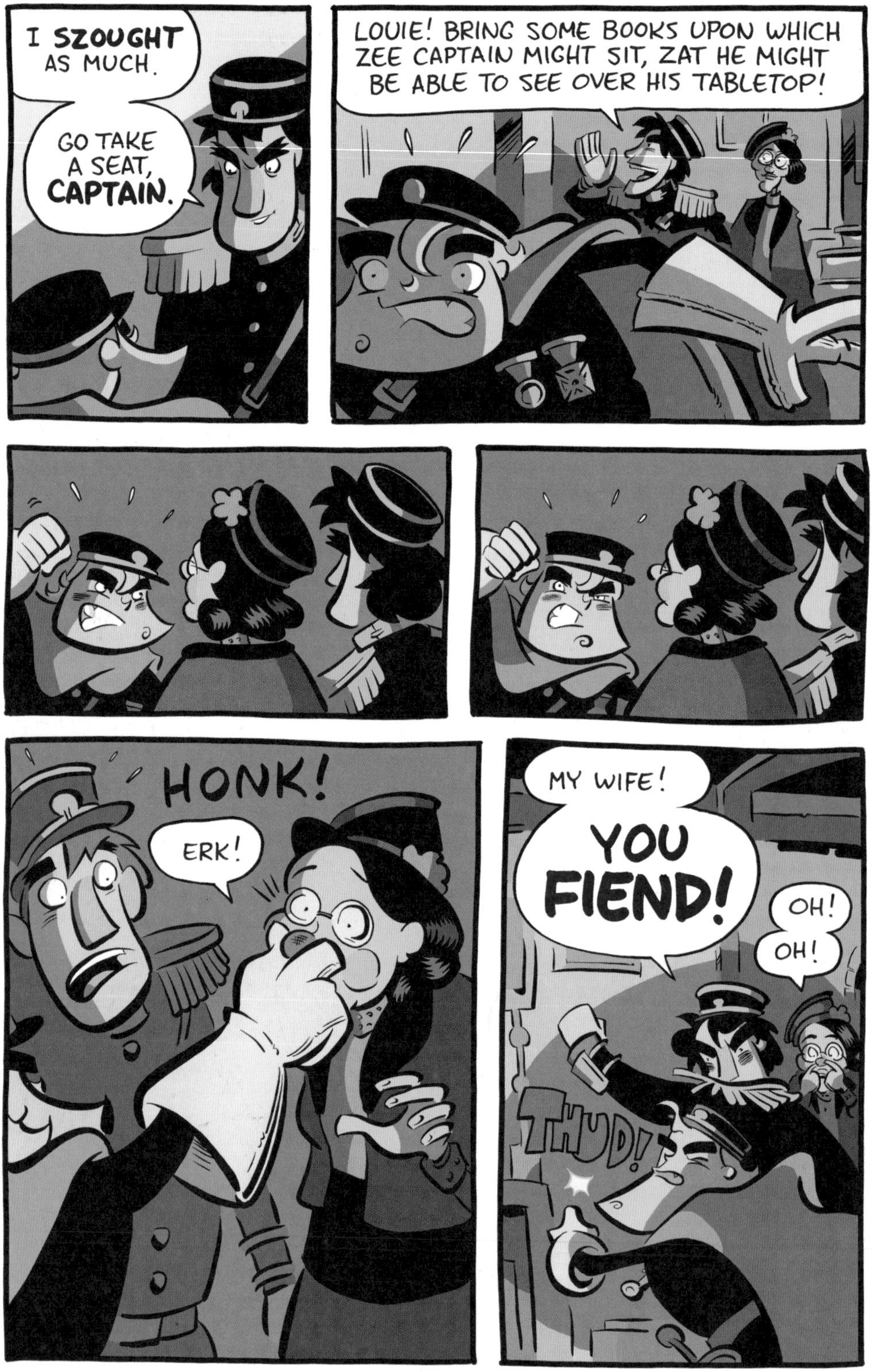
I SZOUGHT AS MUCH.
GO TAKE A SEAT, CAPTAIN.
LOUIE! BRING SOME BOOKS UPON WHICH ZEE CAPTAIN MIGHT SIT, ZAT HE MIGHT BE ABLE TO SEE OVER HIS TABLETOP!
HONK!
ERK!
MY WIFE!
YOU FIEND!
OH!
OH!
THUD!

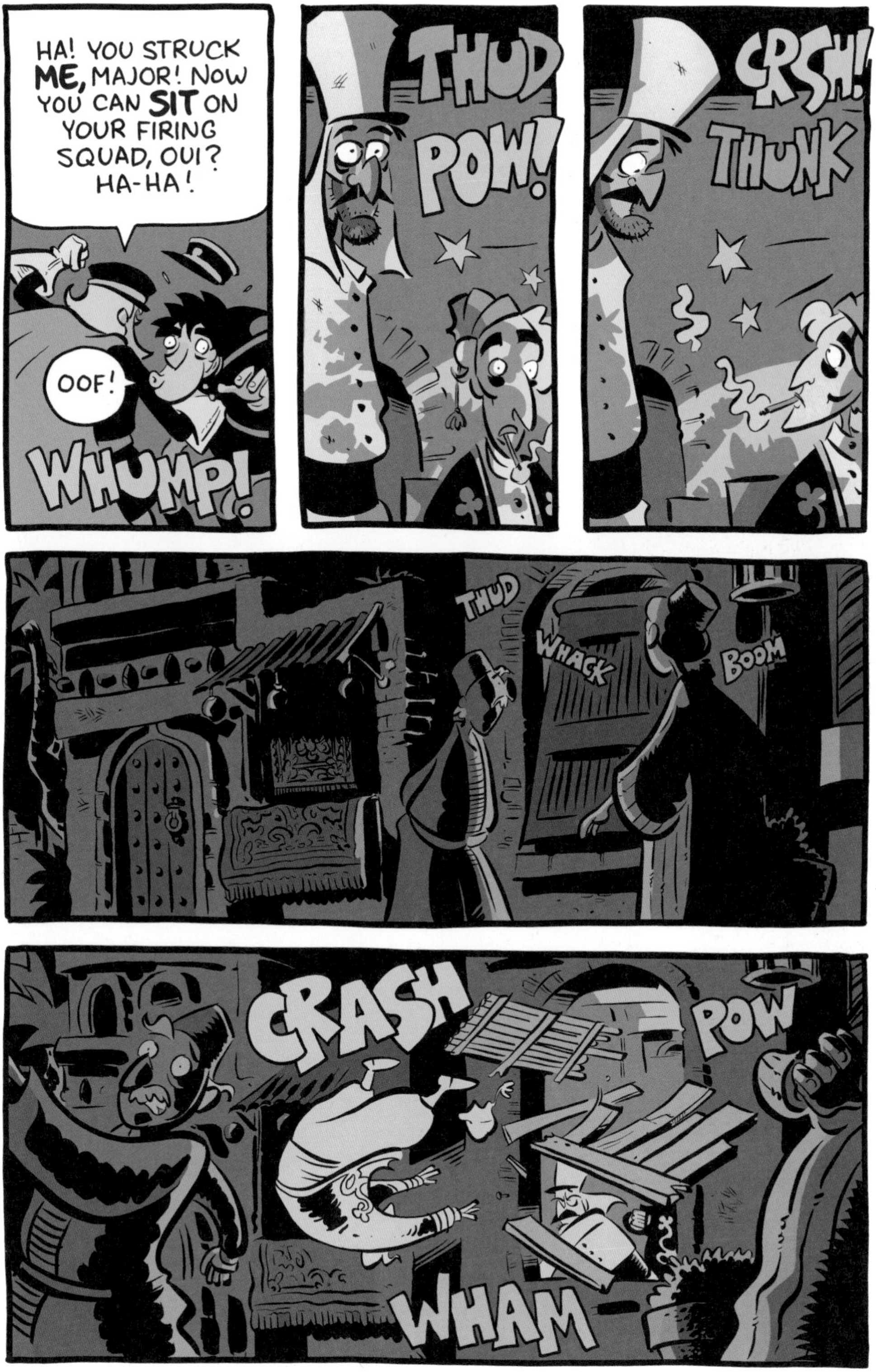
HA! YOU STRUCK **ME,** MAJOR! NOW YOU CAN **SIT** ON YOUR FIRING SQUAD, OUI? HA-HA!
OOF!
WHUMP!
THUD
POW!
CRSH!
THUNK
THUD
WHACK
BOOM
CRASH
POW
WHAM

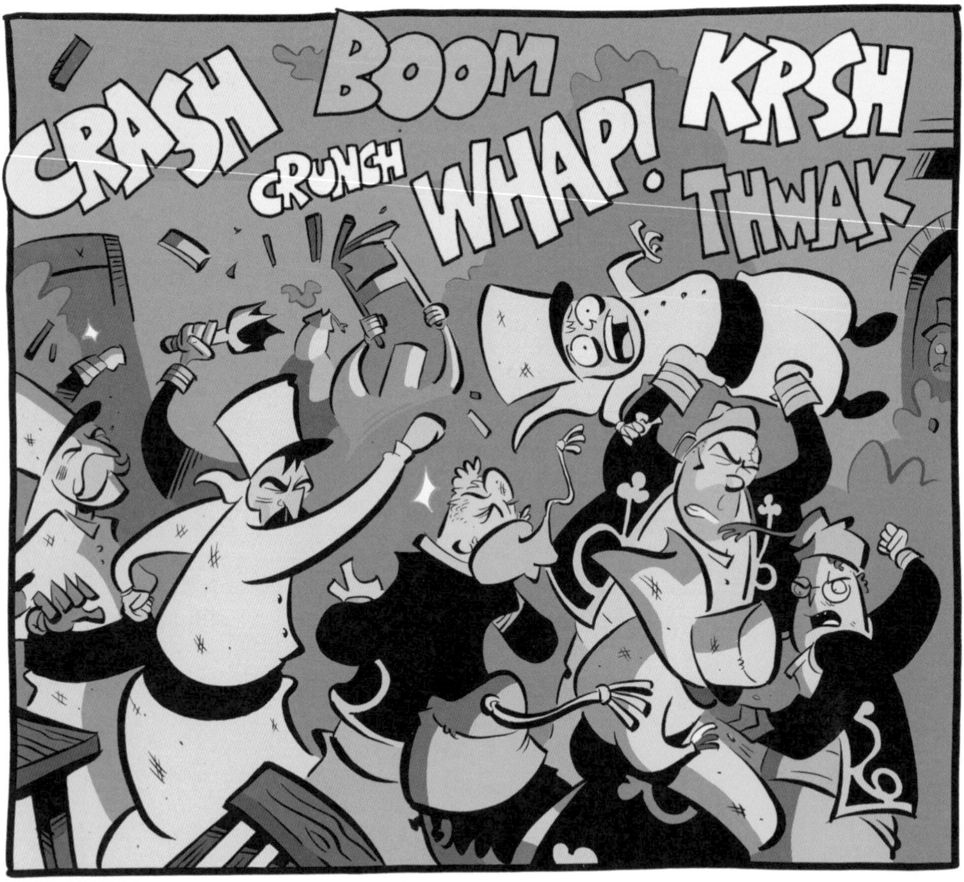
CRASH
BOOM
CRUNCH
WHAP!
KRSH
THWAK

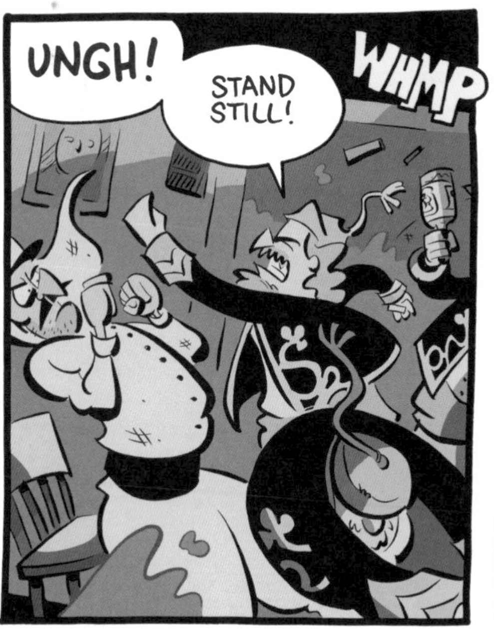
UNGH!
STAND STILL!
WHMP

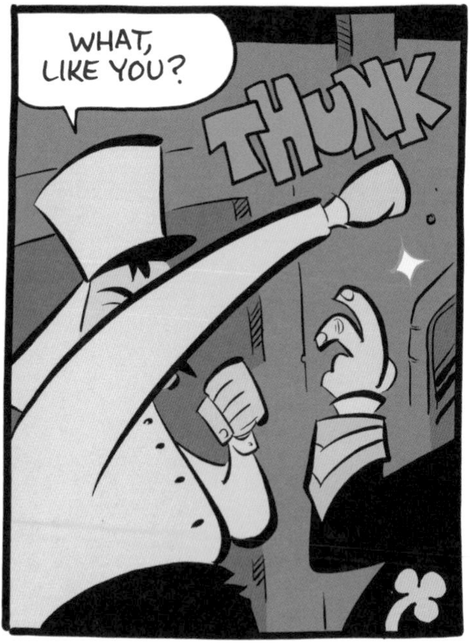
WHAT, LIKE YOU?
THUNK

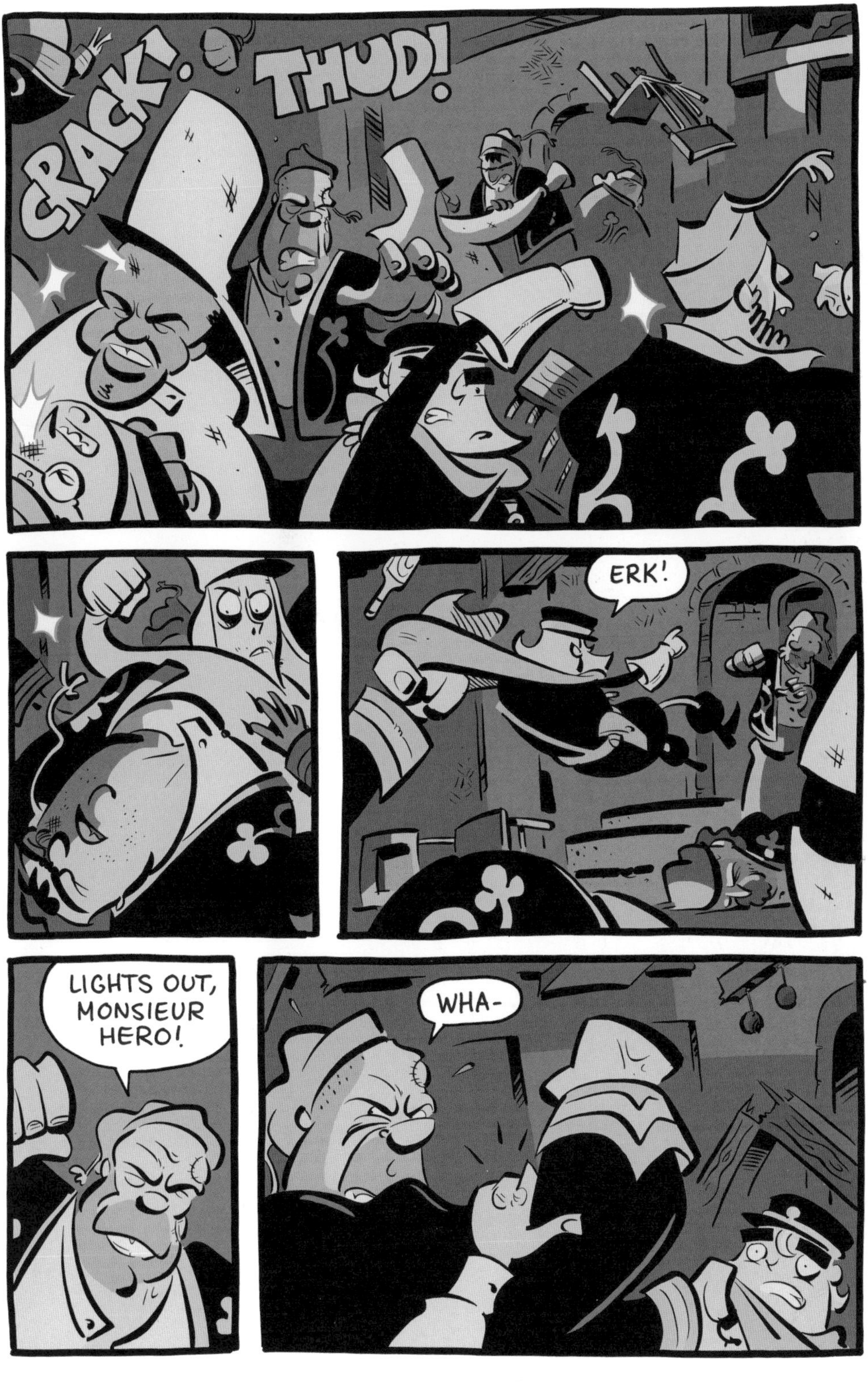
CRACK!
THUD!
ERK!
LIGHTS OUT, MONSIEUR HERO!
WHA-

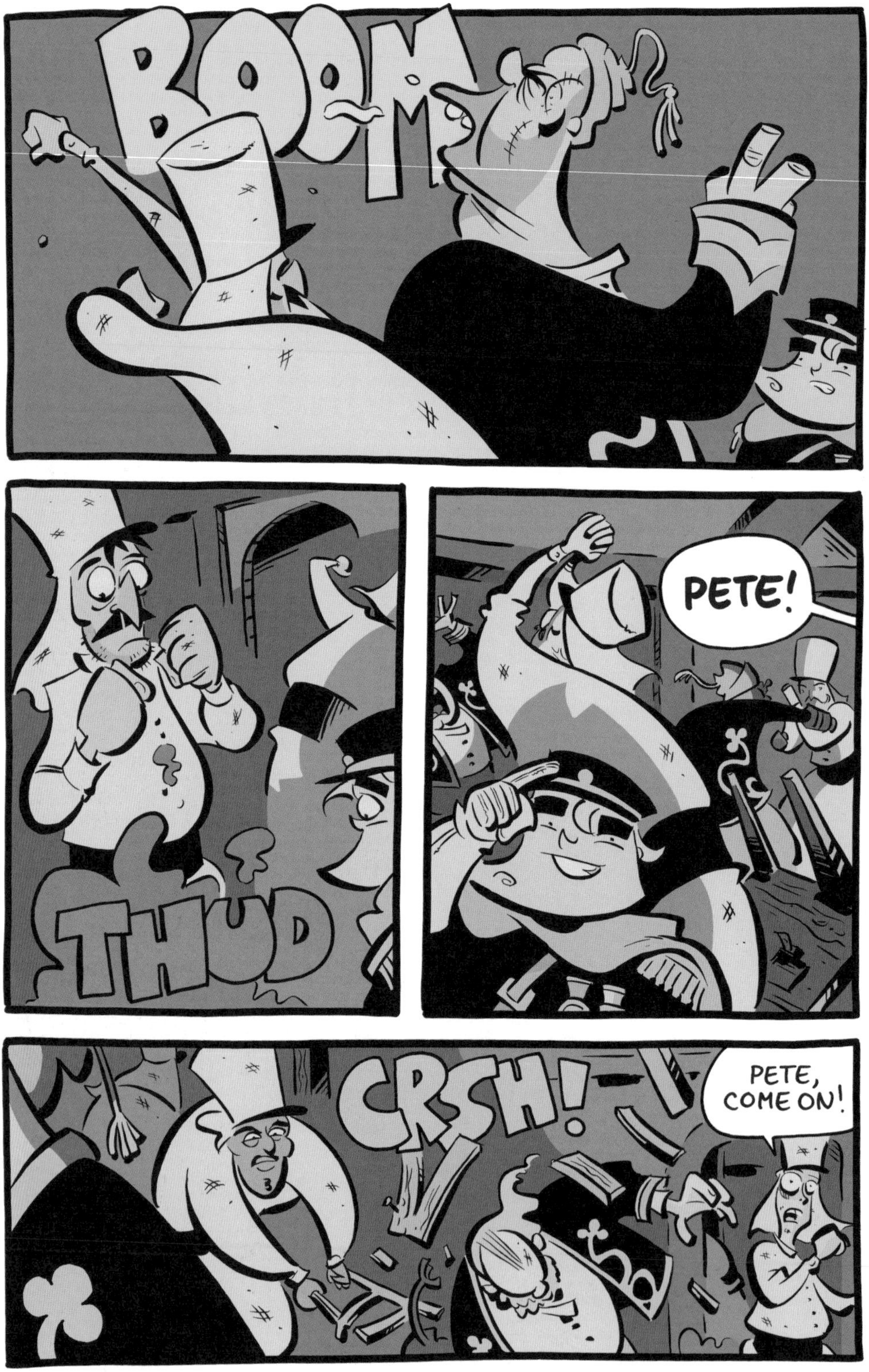
BOOM
THUD
PETE!
CRSH!
PETE, COME ON!

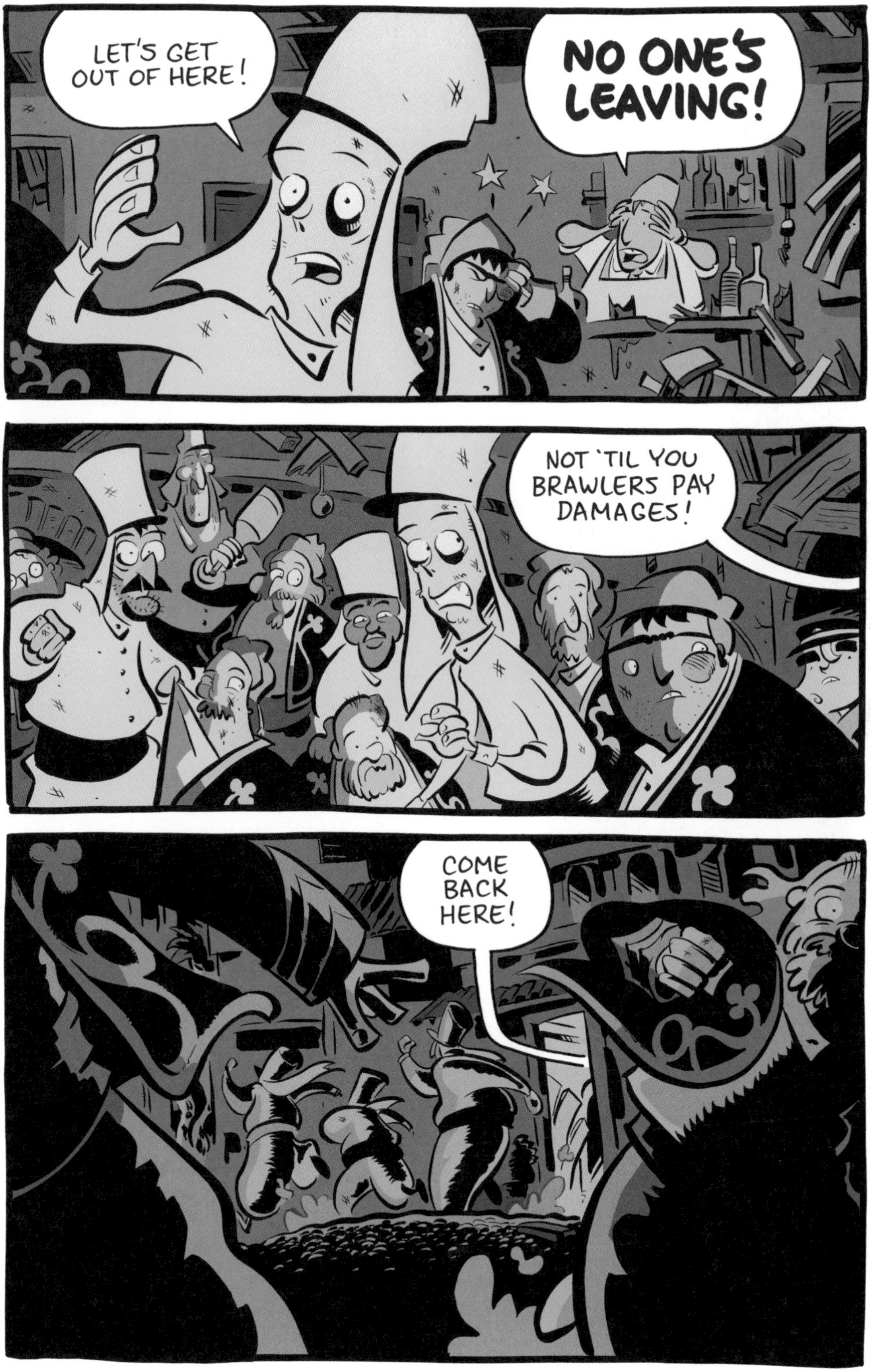
LET'S GET OUT OF HERE!
NO ONE'S LEAVING!
NOT 'TIL YOU BRAWLERS PAY DAMAGES!
COME BACK HERE!

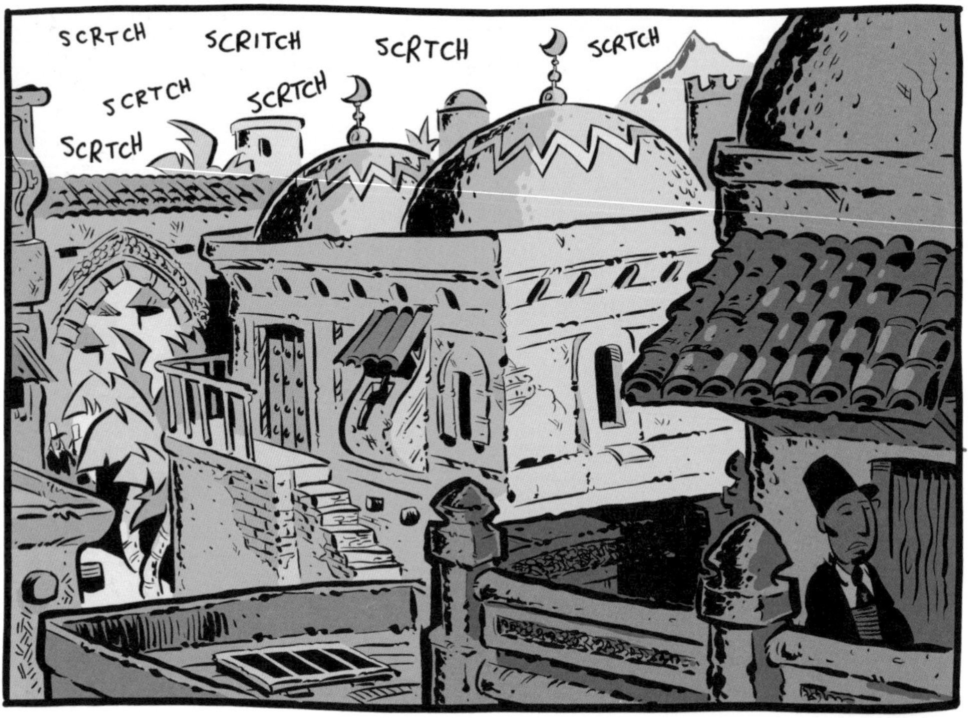
SCRTCH
SCRITCH
SCRTCH
SCRTCH
SCRTCH
SCRTCH
SCRTCH

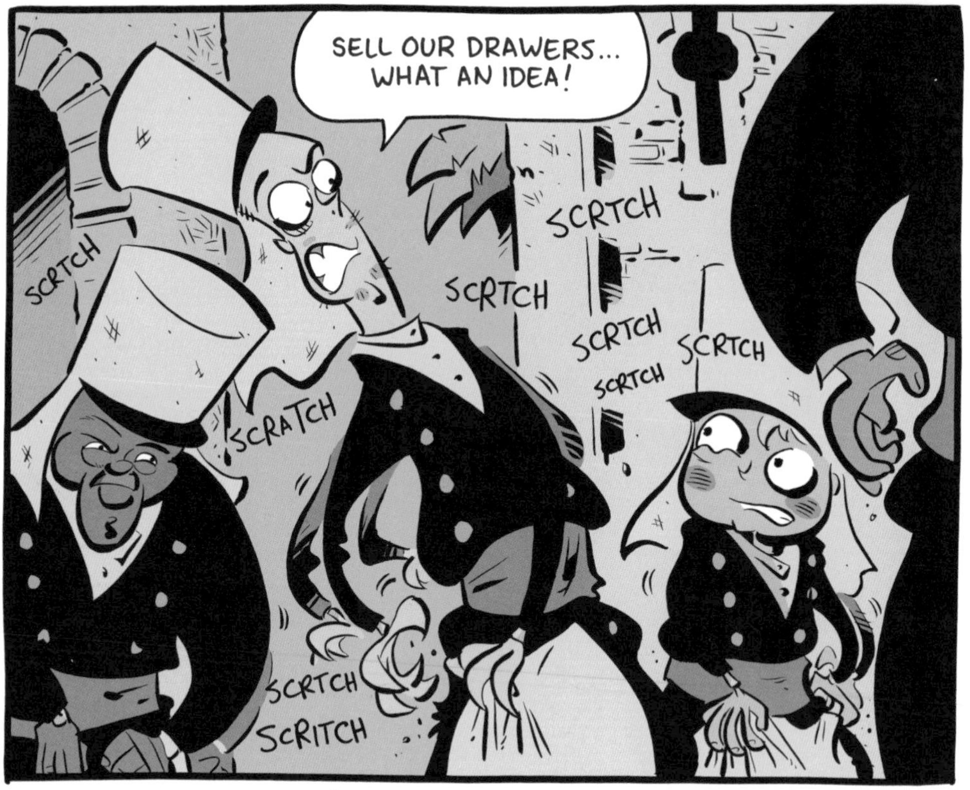
SELL OUR DRAWERS... WHAT AN IDEA!
SCRTCH
SCRTCH
SCRTCH
SCRTCH
SCRTCH
SCRTCH
SCRATCH
SCRTCH
SCRITCH

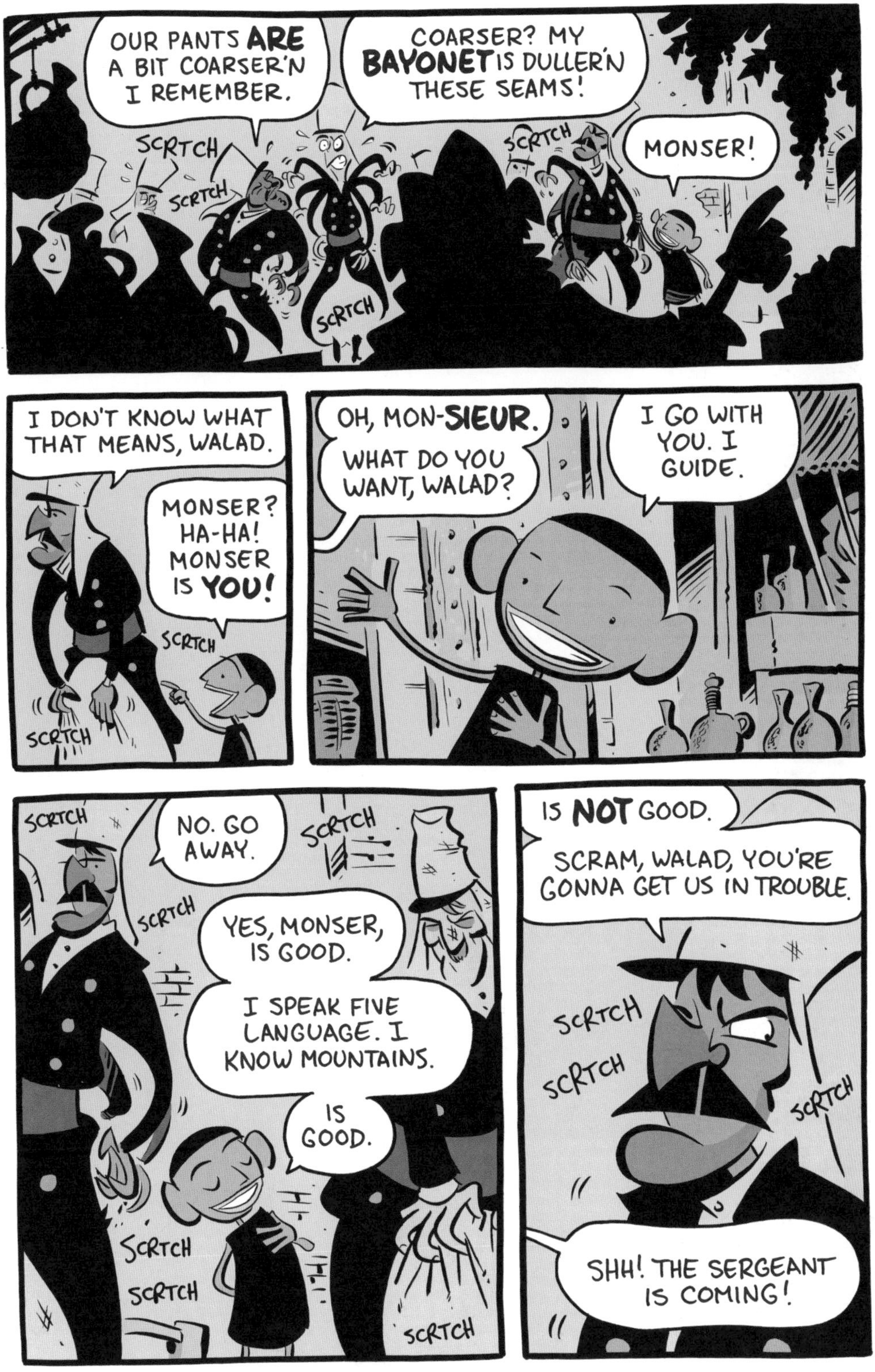
OUR PANTS ARE A BIT COARSER'N I REMEMBER.
COARSER? MY BAYONET IS DULLER'N THESE SEAMS!
SCRTCH
SCRTCH
SCRTCH
SCRTCH
MONSER!
I DON'T KNOW WHAT THAT MEANS, WALAD.
MONSER? HA-HA! MONSER IS YOU!
SCRTCH
SCRTCH
OH, MON-SIEUR.
WHAT DO YOU WANT, WALAD?
I GO WITH YOU. I GUIDE.
SCRTCH
NO. GO AWAY.
SCRTCH
SCRTCH
YES, MONSER, IS GOOD.
I SPEAK FIVE LANGUAGE. I KNOW MOUNTAINS.
IS GOOD.
SCRTCH
SCRTCH
SCRTCH
IS NOT GOOD.
SCRAM, WALAD, YOU'RE GONNA GET US IN TROUBLE.
SCRTCH
SCRTCH
SCRTCH
SHH! THE SERGEANT IS COMING!

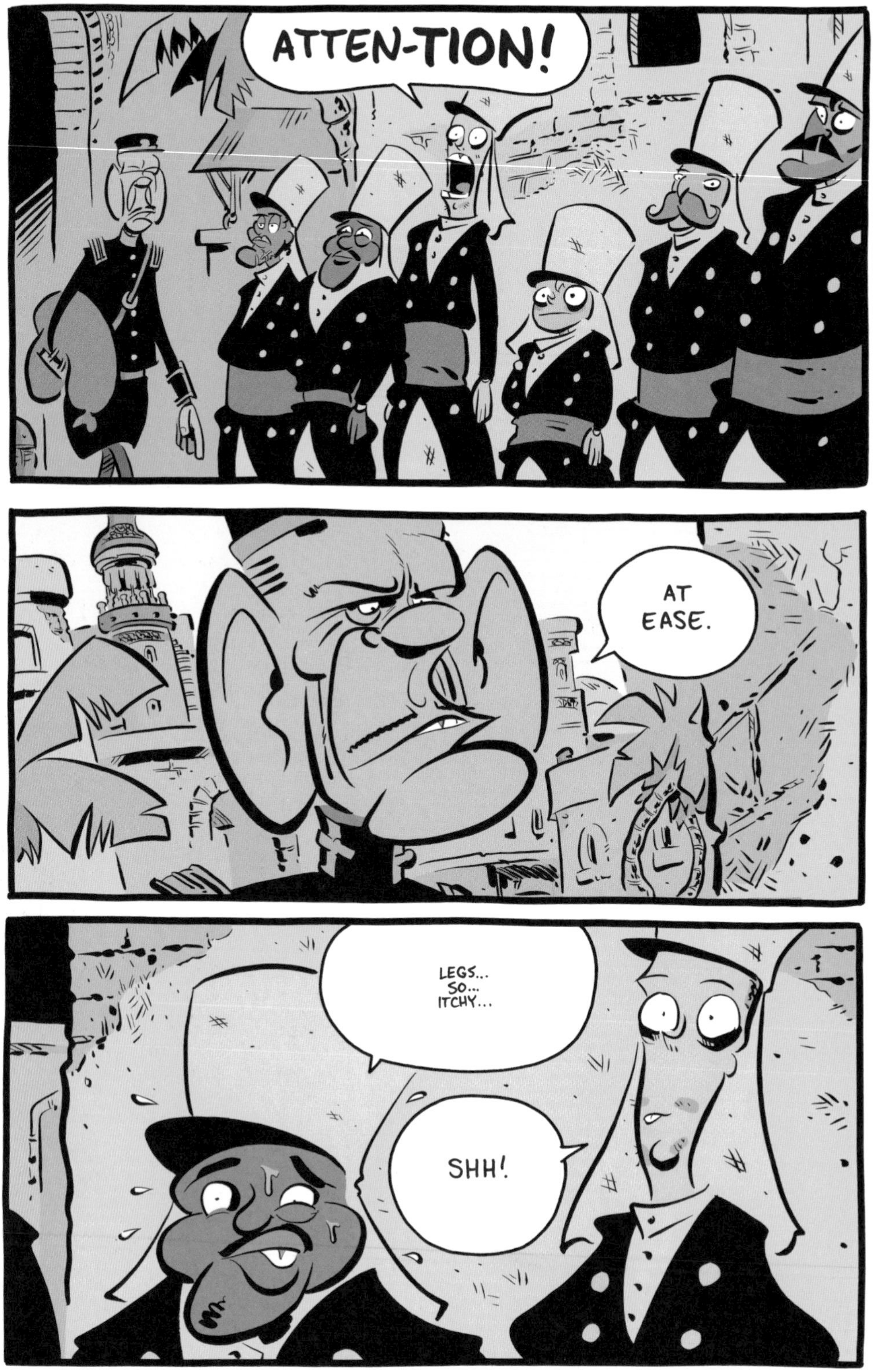
ATTEN-TION!
AT EASE.
LEGS... SO... ITCHY...
SHH!

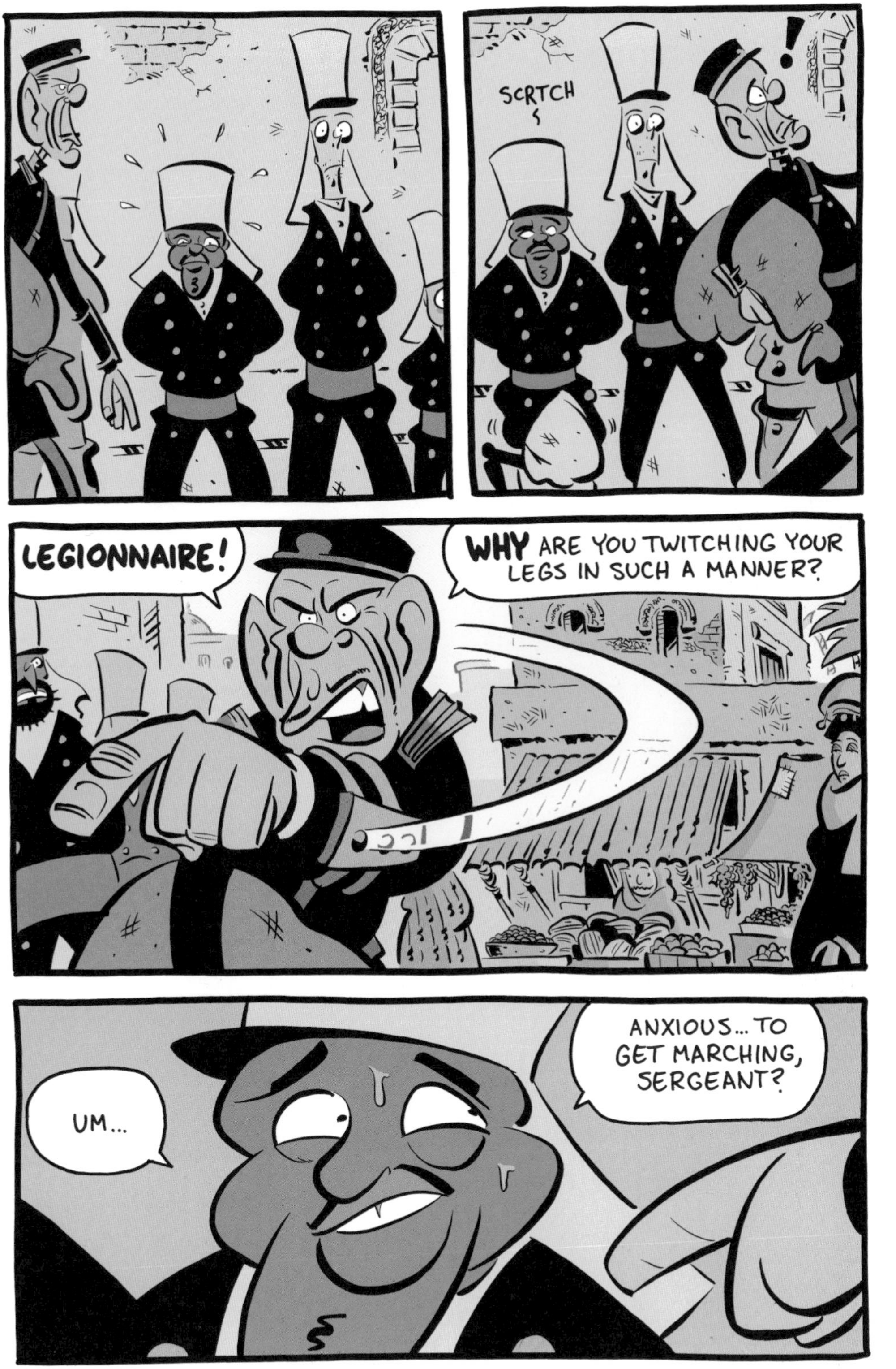
SCRTCH
LEGIONNAIRE!
WHY ARE YOU TWITCHING YOUR LEGS IN SUCH A MANNER?
UM...
ANXIOUS... TO GET MARCHING, SERGEANT?

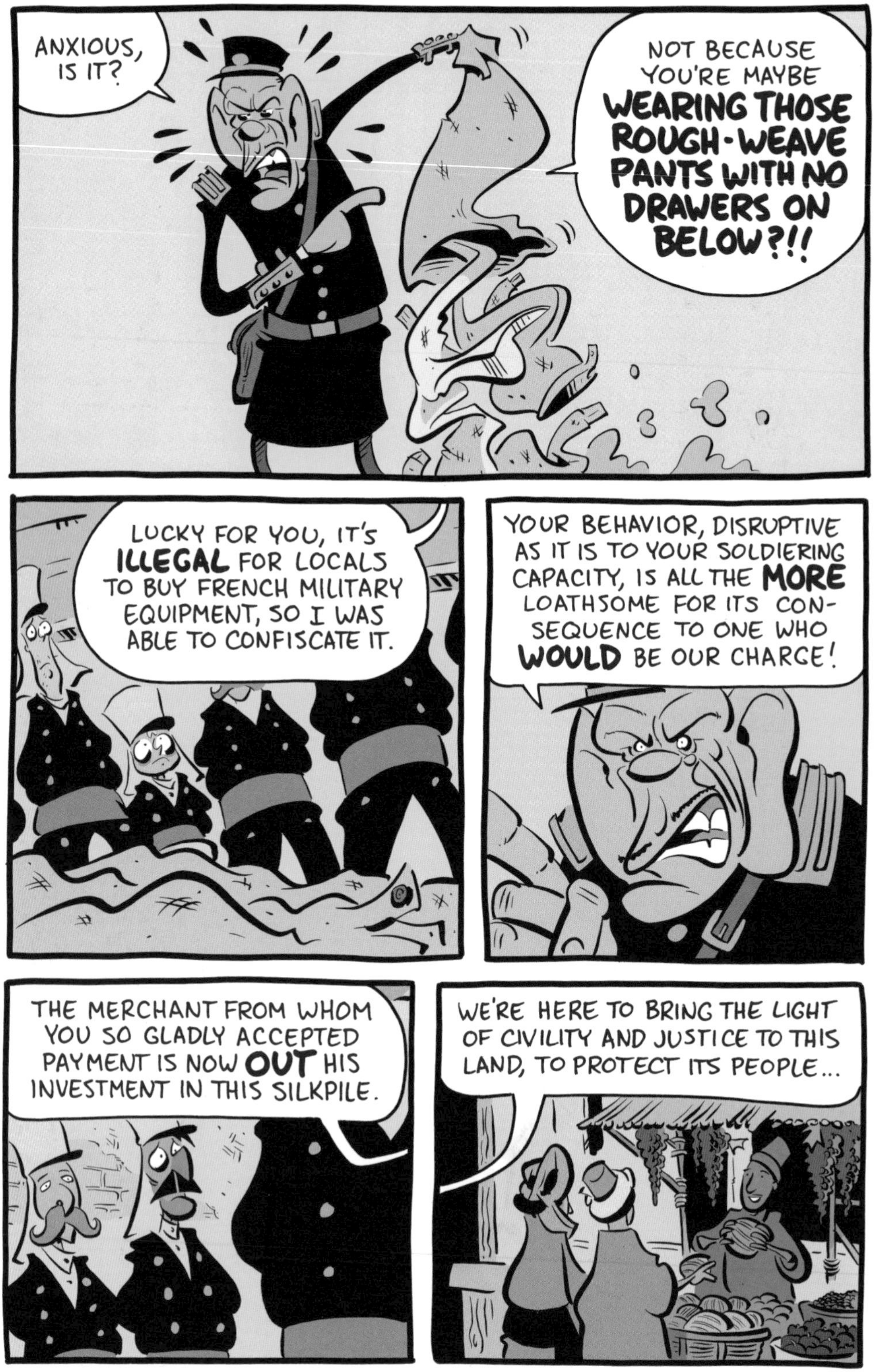
ANXIOUS, IS IT?
NOT BECAUSE YOU'RE MAYBE WEARING THOSE ROUGH-WEAVE PANTS WITH NO DRAWERS ON BELOW?!!
LUCKY FOR YOU, IT'S ILLEGAL FOR LOCALS TO BUY FRENCH MILITARY EQUIPMENT, SO I WAS ABLE TO CONFISCATE IT.
YOUR BEHAVIOR, DISRUPTIVE AS IT IS TO YOUR SOLDIERING CAPACITY, IS ALL THE MORE LOATHSOME FOR ITS CON-SEQUENCE TO ONE WHO WOULD BE OUR CHARGE!
THE MERCHANT FROM WHOM YOU SO GLADLY ACCEPTED PAYMENT IS NOW OUT HIS INVESTMENT IN THIS SILKPILE.
WE'RE HERE TO BRING THE LIGHT OF CIVILITY AND JUSTICE TO THIS LAND, TO PROTECT ITS PEOPLE...

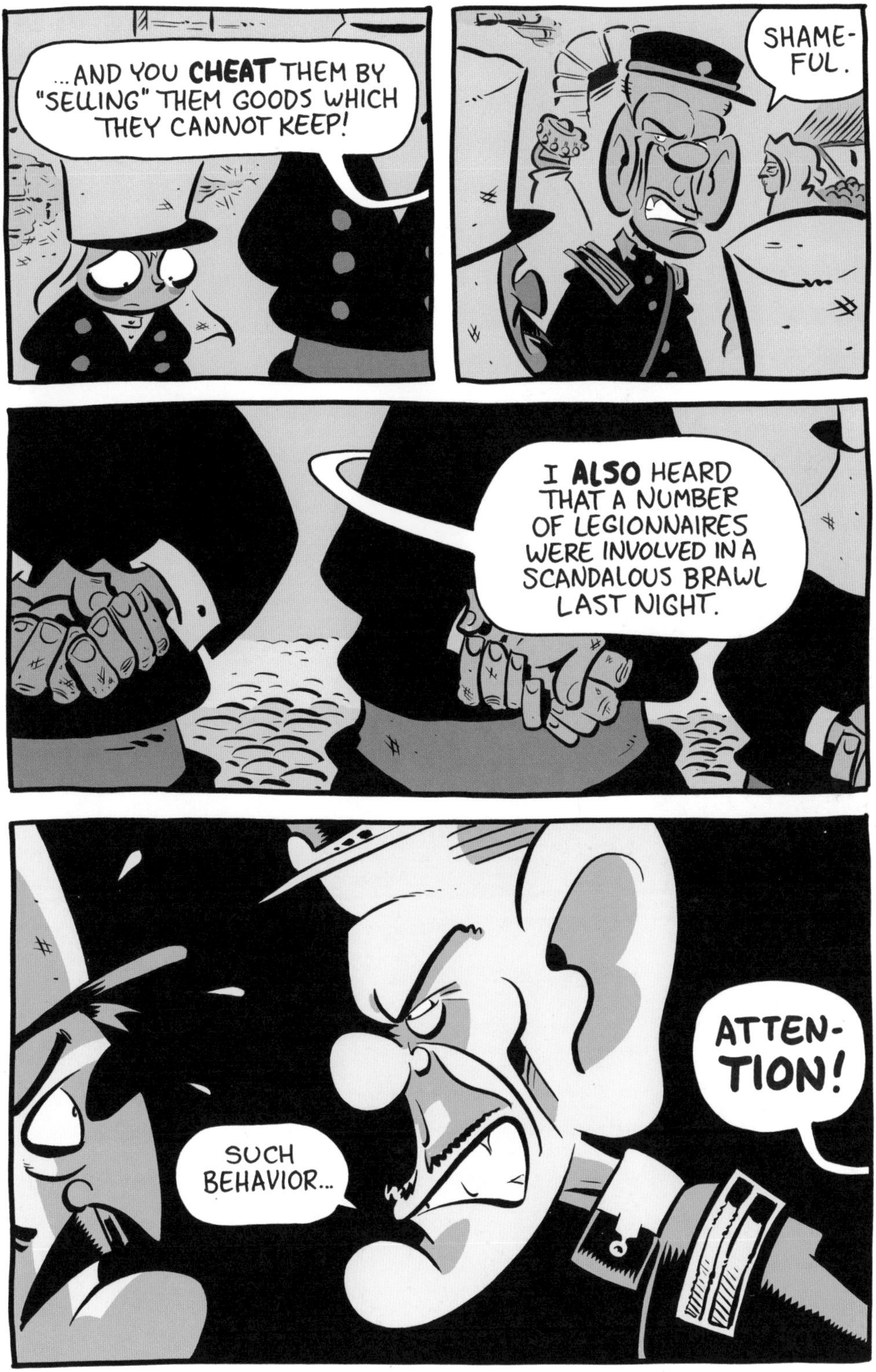
...AND YOU **CHEAT** THEM BY "SELLING" THEM GOODS WHICH THEY CANNOT KEEP!
SHAME-FUL.
I **ALSO** HEARD THAT A NUMBER OF LEGIONNAIRES WERE INVOLVED IN A SCANDALOUS BRAWL LAST NIGHT.
ATTEN-TION!
SUCH BEHAVIOR...

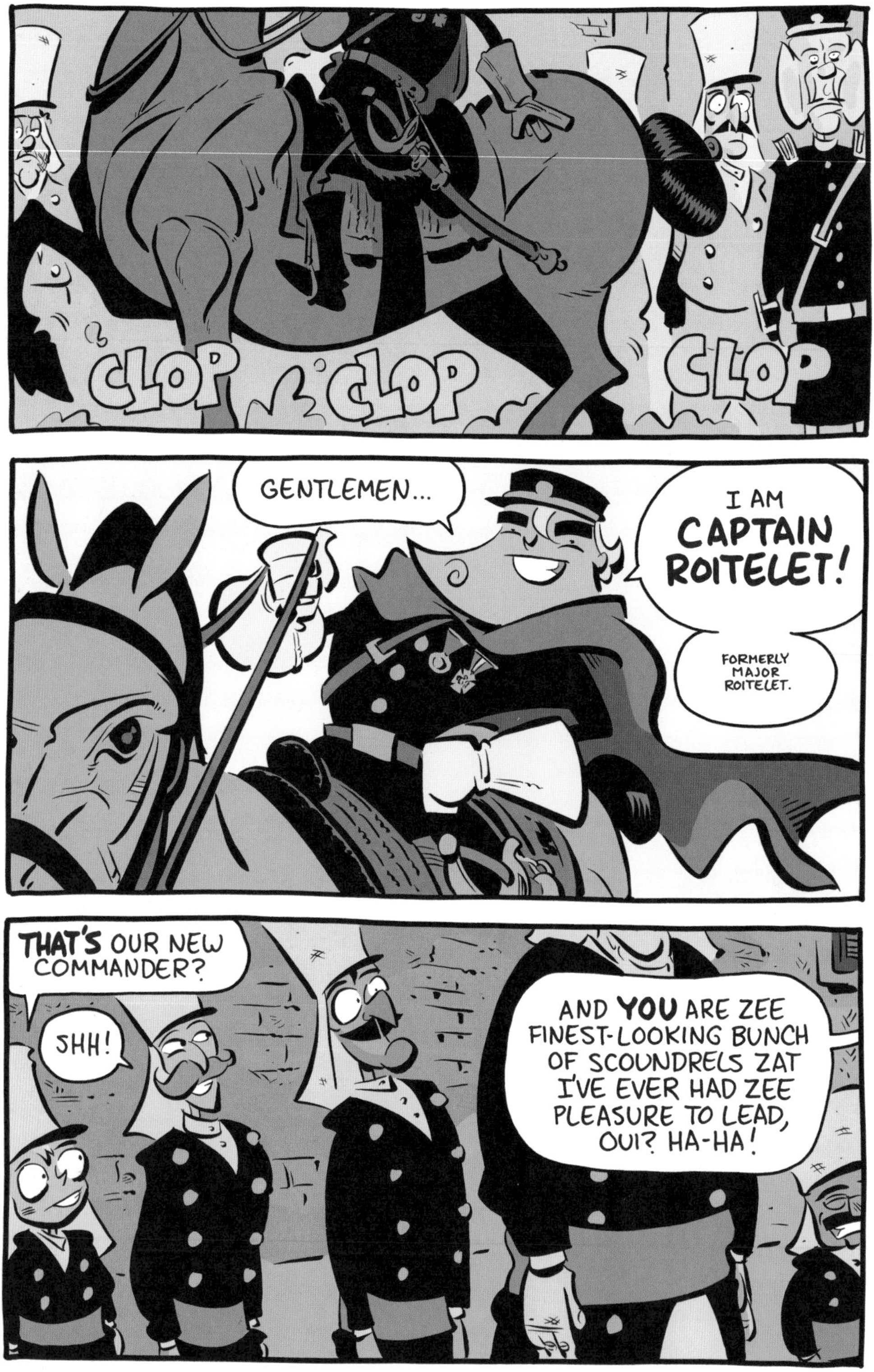
CLOP CLOP CLOP
GENTLEMEN...
I AM CAPTAIN ROITELET!
FORMERLY MAJOR ROITELET.
THAT'S OUR NEW COMMANDER?
SHH!
AND YOU ARE ZEE FINEST-LOOKING BUNCH OF SCOUNDRELS ZAT I'VE EVER HAD ZEE PLEASURE TO LEAD, OUI? HA-HA!

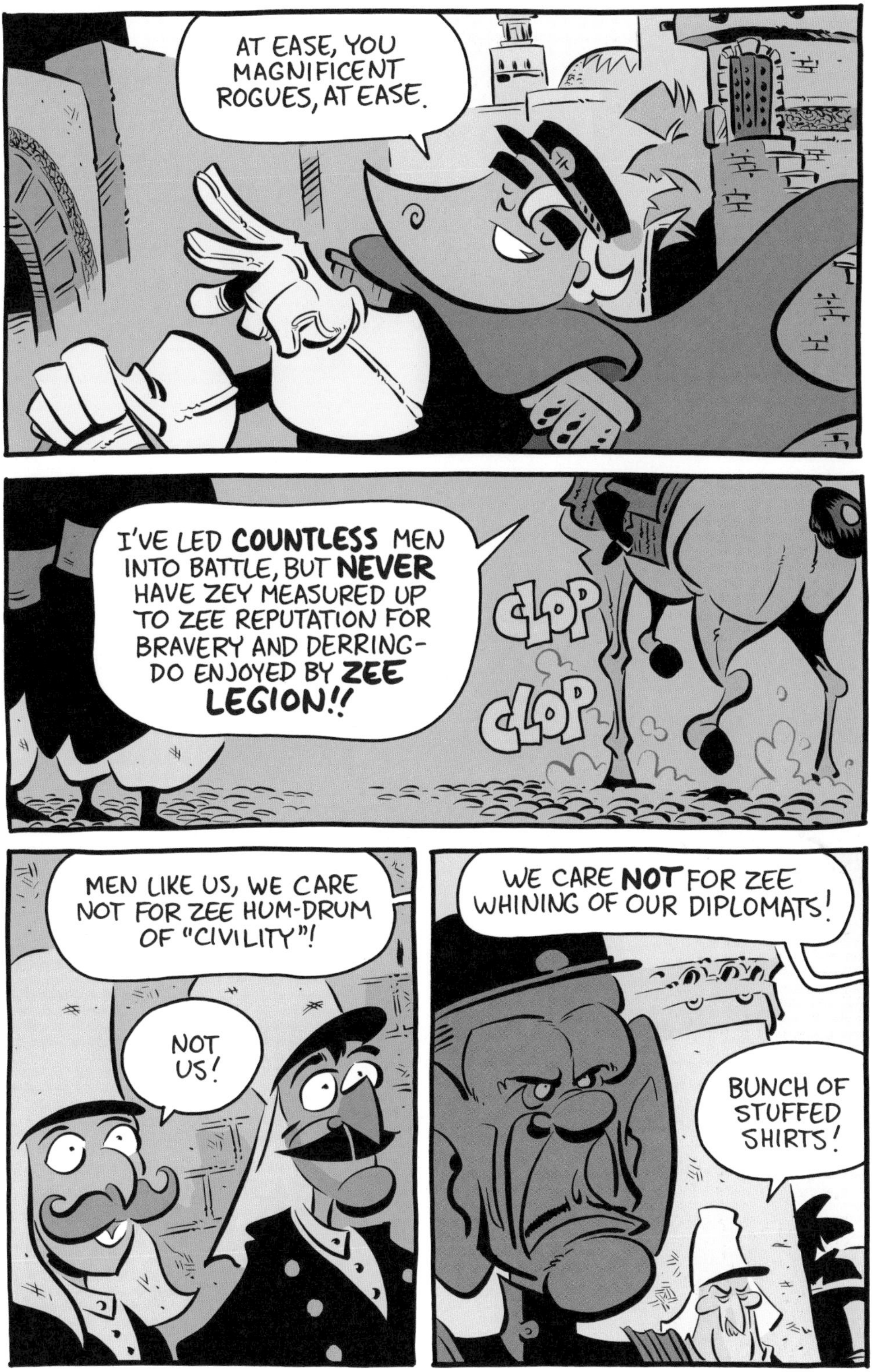
AT EASE, YOU MAGNIFICENT ROGUES, AT EASE.
I'VE LED **COUNTLESS** MEN INTO BATTLE, BUT **NEVER** HAVE ZEY MEASURED UP TO ZEE REPUTATION FOR BRAVERY AND DERRING-DO ENJOYED BY **ZEE LEGION!!**
CLOP
CLOP
MEN LIKE US, WE CARE NOT FOR ZEE HUM-DRUM OF "CIVILITY"!
NOT US!
WE CARE **NOT** FOR ZEE WHINING OF OUR DIPLOMATS!
BUNCH OF STUFFED SHIRTS!

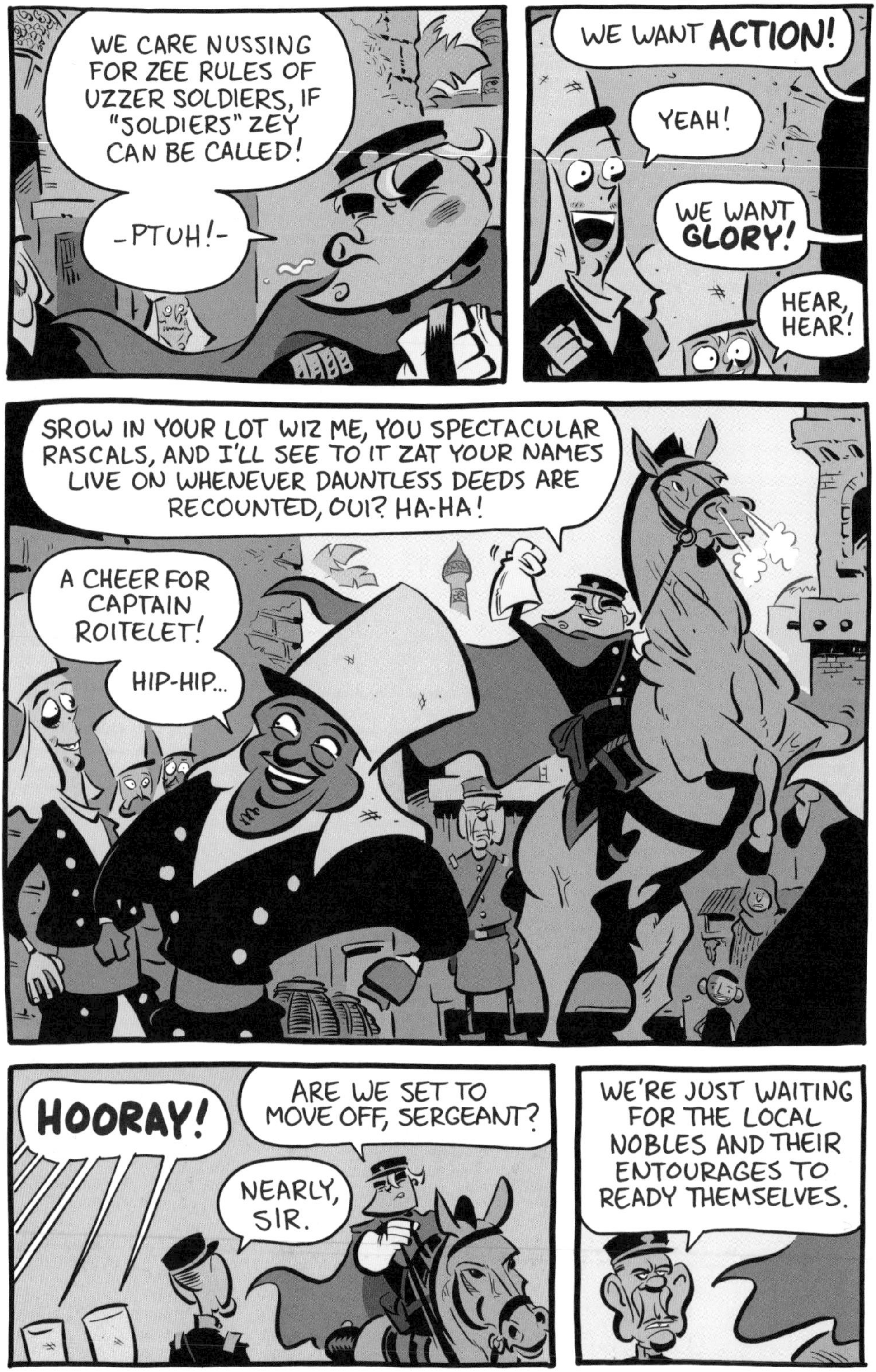
WE CARE NUSSING FOR ZEE RULES OF UZZER SOLDIERS, IF "SOLDIERS" ZEY CAN BE CALLED!
-PTUH!-
WE WANT **ACTION!**
YEAH!
WE WANT **GLORY!**
HEAR, HEAR!
SROW IN YOUR LOT WIZ ME, YOU SPECTACULAR RASCALS, AND I'LL SEE TO IT ZAT YOUR NAMES LIVE ON WHENEVER DAUNTLESS DEEDS ARE RECOUNTED, OUI? HA-HA!
A CHEER FOR CAPTAIN ROITELET!
HIP-HIP...
HOORAY!
ARE WE SET TO MOVE OFF, SERGEANT?
NEARLY, SIR.
WE'RE JUST WAITING FOR THE LOCAL NOBLES AND THEIR ENTOURAGES TO READY THEMSELVES.

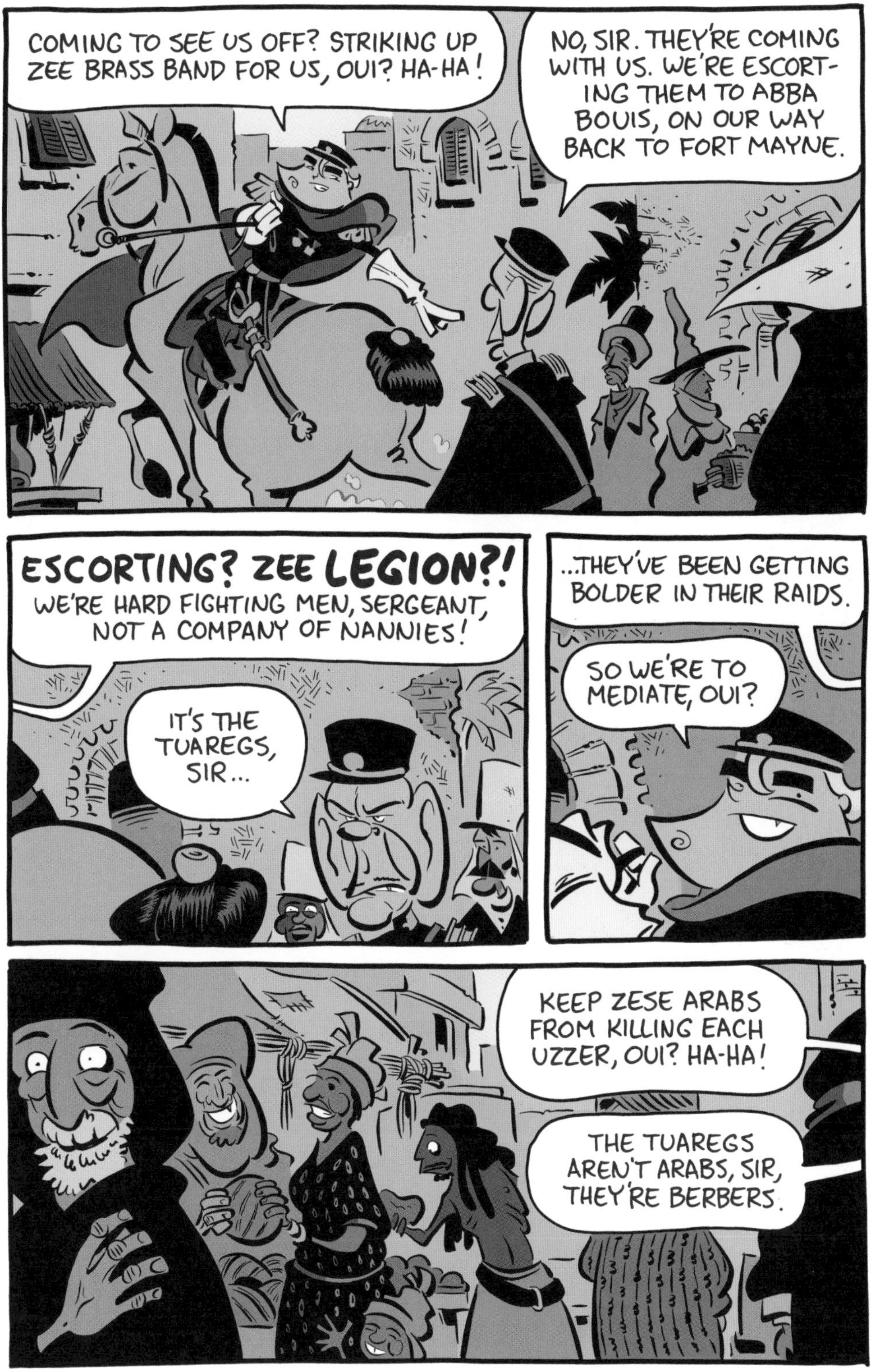
COMING TO SEE US OFF? STRIKING UP ZEE BRASS BAND FOR US, OUI? HA-HA!
NO, SIR. THEY'RE COMING WITH US. WE'RE ESCORTING THEM TO ABBA BOUIS, ON OUR WAY BACK TO FORT MAYNE.
ESCORTING? ZEE LEGION?! WE'RE HARD FIGHTING MEN, SERGEANT, NOT A COMPANY OF NANNIES!
IT'S THE TUAREGS, SIR...
...THEY'VE BEEN GETTING BOLDER IN THEIR RAIDS.
SO WE'RE TO MEDIATE, OUI?
KEEP ZESE ARABS FROM KILLING EACH UZZER, OUI? HA-HA!
THE TUAREGS AREN'T ARABS, SIR, THEY'RE BERBERS.

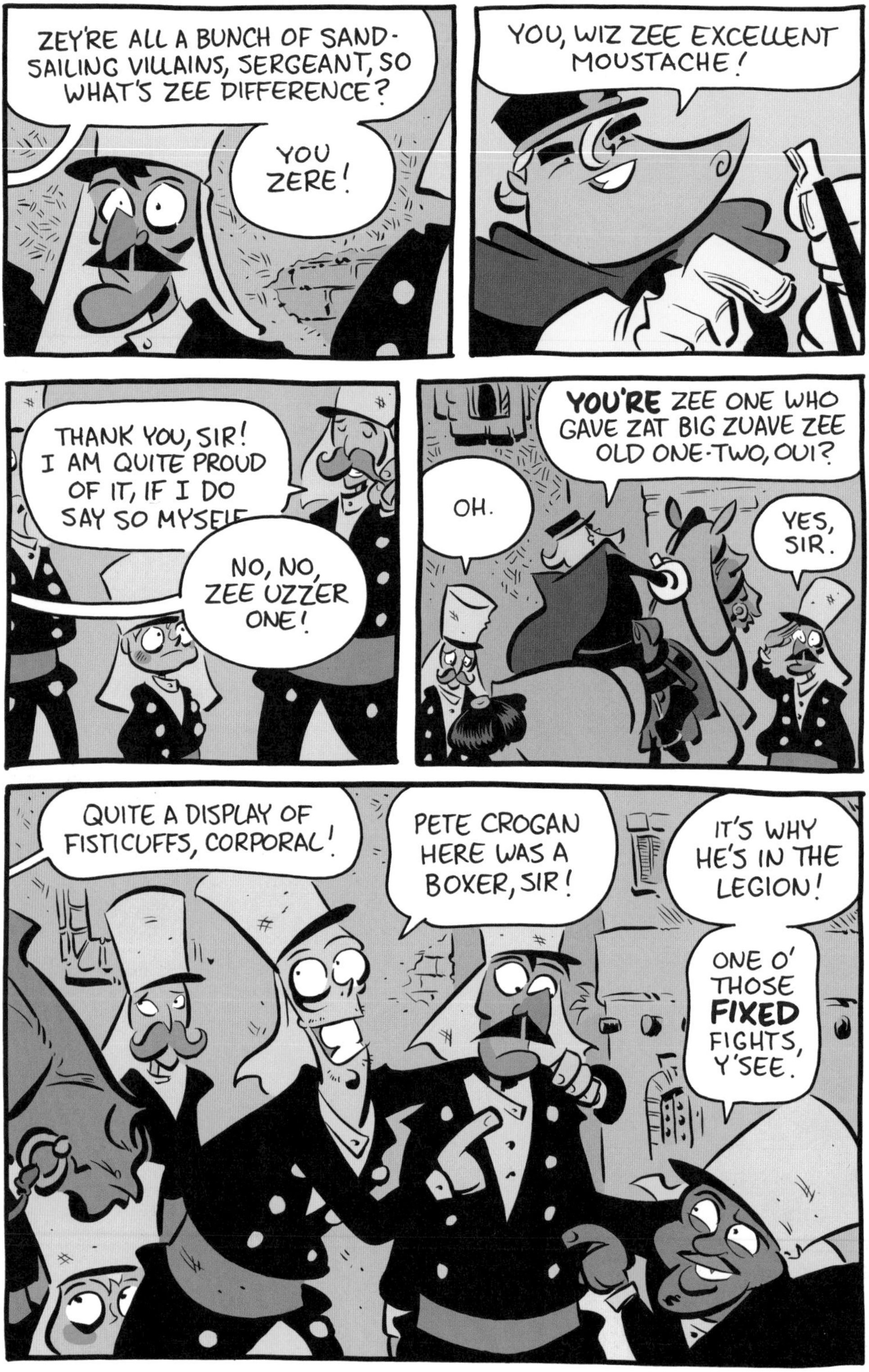
ZEY'RE ALL A BUNCH OF SAND-SAILING VILLAINS, SERGEANT, SO WHAT'S ZEE DIFFERENCE?
YOU ZERE!
YOU, WIZ ZEE EXCELLENT MOUSTACHE!
THANK YOU, SIR! I AM QUITE PROUD OF IT, IF I DO SAY SO MYSELF
NO, NO, ZEE UZZER ONE!
YOU'RE ZEE ONE WHO GAVE ZAT BIG ZUAVE ZEE OLD ONE-TWO, OUI?
OH.
YES, SIR.
QUITE A DISPLAY OF FISTICUFFS, CORPORAL!
PETE CROGAN HERE WAS A BOXER, SIR!
IT'S WHY HE'S IN THE LEGION!
ONE O' THOSE **FIXED** FIGHTS, Y'SEE.

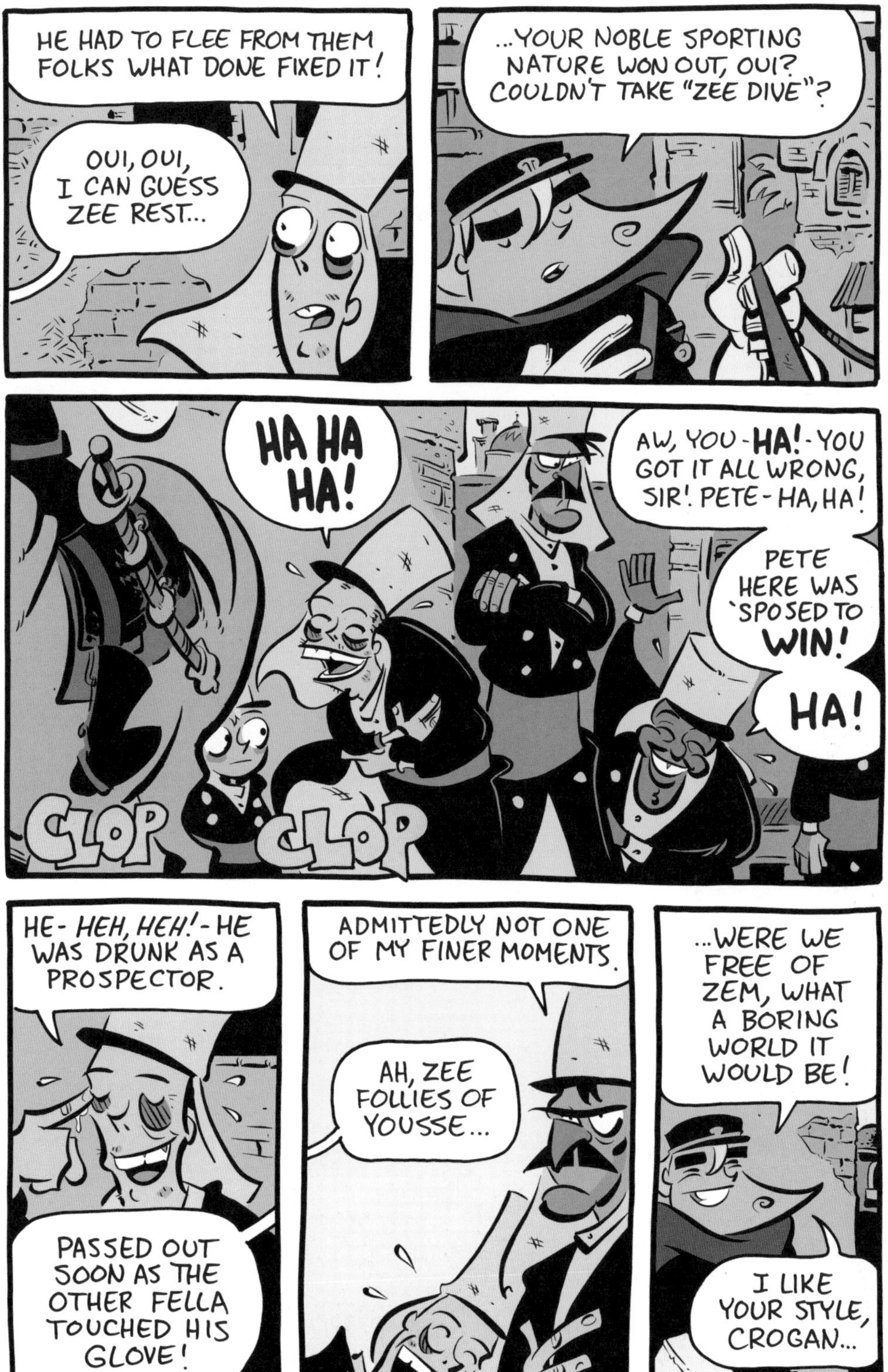
HE HAD TO FLEE FROM THEM FOLKS WHAT DONE FIXED IT!
OUI, OUI, I CAN GUESS ZEE REST...
...YOUR NOBLE SPORTING NATURE WON OUT, OUI? COULDN'T TAKE "ZEE DIVE"?
HA HA HA!
AW, YOU-HA!-YOU GOT IT ALL WRONG, SIR! PETE-HA, HA!
PETE HERE WAS 'SPOSED TO WIN!
HA!
CLOP CLOP
HE- HEH, HEH!- HE WAS DRUNK AS A PROSPECTOR.
PASSED OUT SOON AS THE OTHER FELLA TOUCHED HIS GLOVE!
ADMITTEDLY NOT ONE OF MY FINER MOMENTS.
AH, ZEE FOLLIES OF YOUSSE...
...WERE WE FREE OF ZEM, WHAT A BORING WORLD IT WOULD BE!
I LIKE YOUR STYLE, CROGAN...

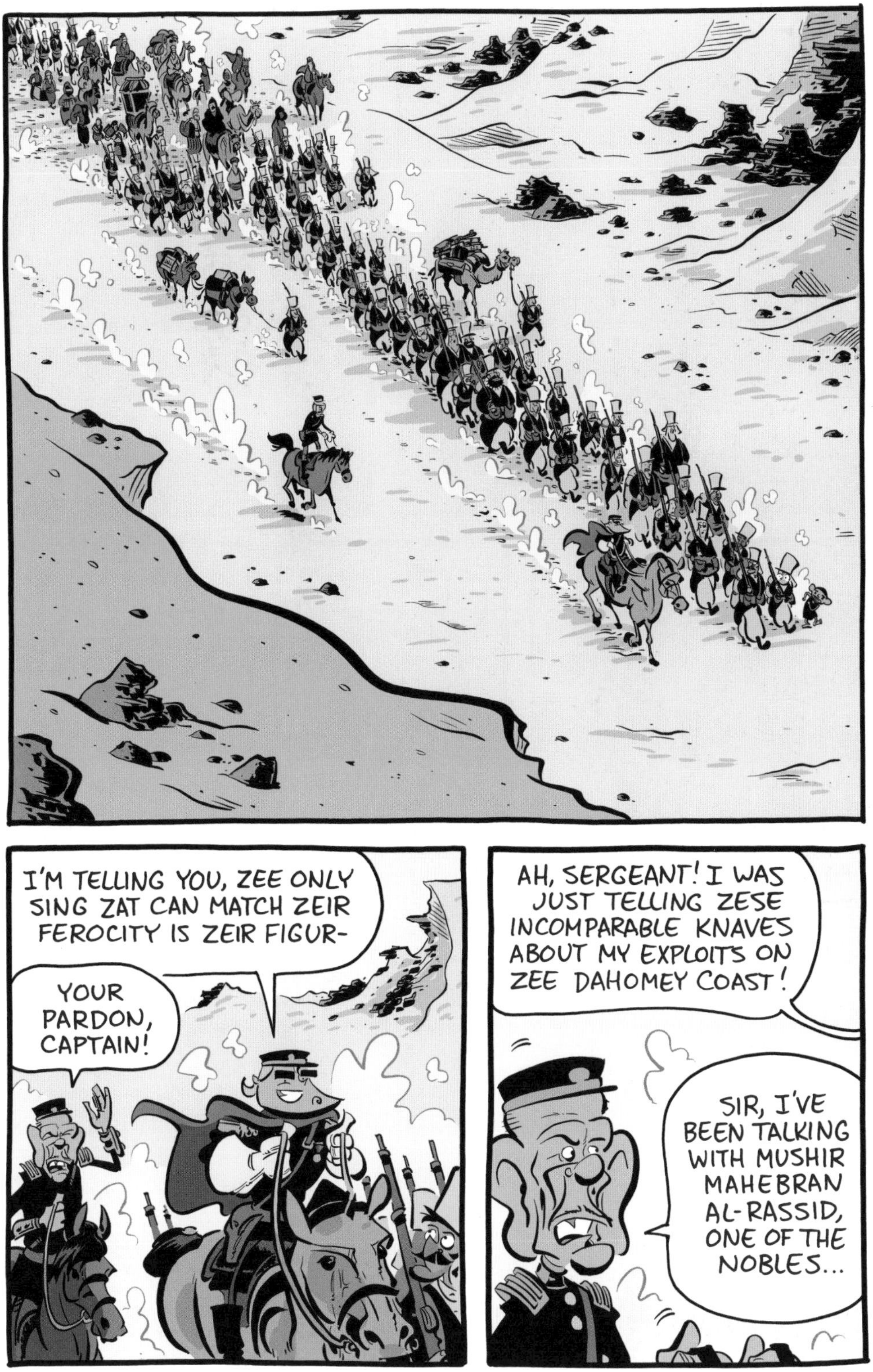
I'M TELLING YOU, ZEE ONLY SING ZAT CAN MATCH ZEIR FEROCITY IS ZEIR FIGUR-
YOUR PARDON, CAPTAIN!
AH, SERGEANT! I WAS JUST TELLING ZESE INCOMPARABLE KNAVES ABOUT MY EXPLOITS ON ZEE DAHOMEY COAST!
SIR, I'VE BEEN TALKING WITH MUSHIR MAHEBRAN AL-RASSID, ONE OF THE NOBLES...

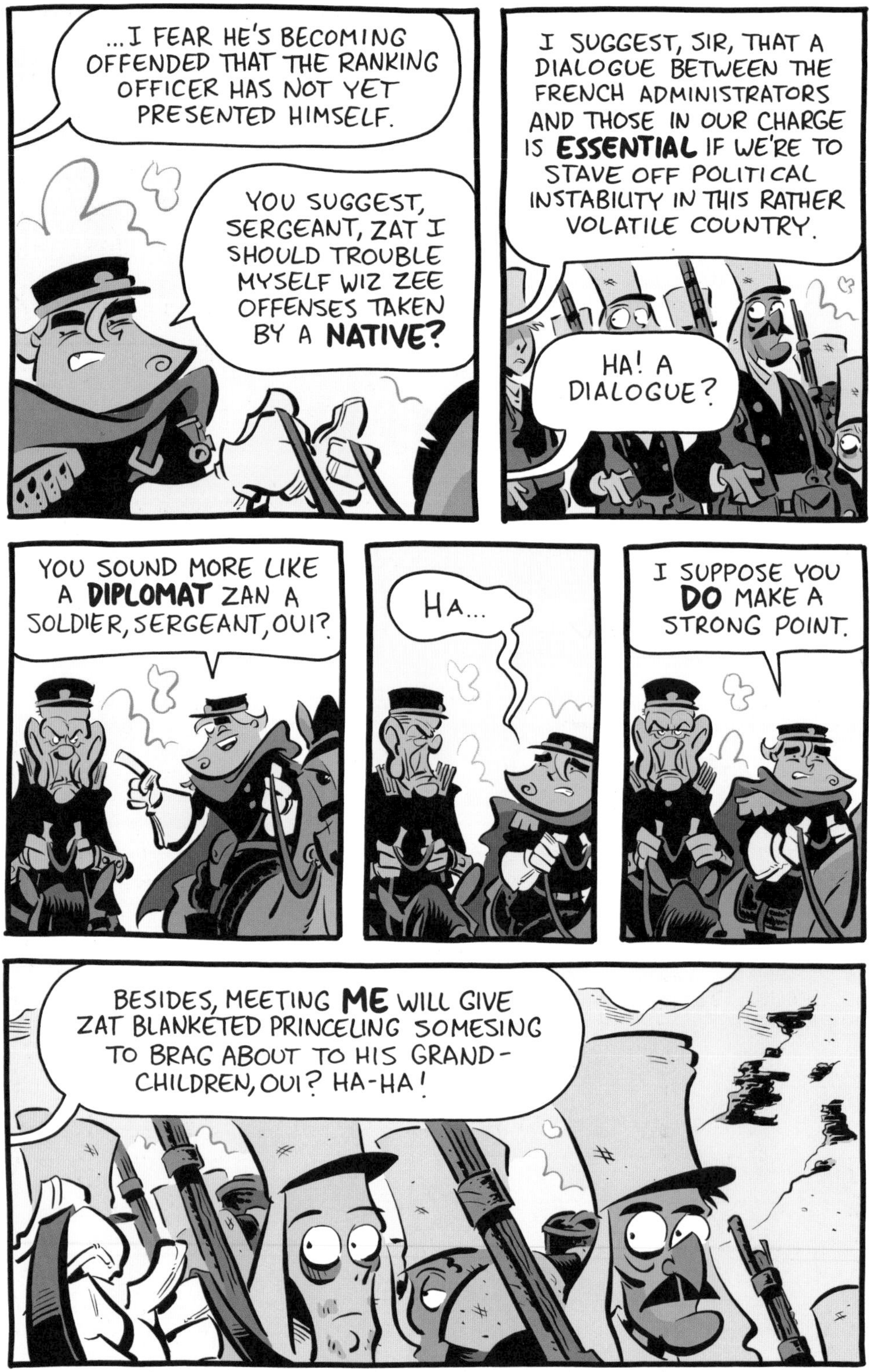
...I FEAR HE'S BECOMING OFFENDED THAT THE RANKING OFFICER HAS NOT YET PRESENTED HIMSELF.
YOU SUGGEST, SERGEANT, ZAT I SHOULD TROUBLE MYSELF WIZ ZEE OFFENSES TAKEN BY A **NATIVE?**
I SUGGEST, SIR, THAT A DIALOGUE BETWEEN THE FRENCH ADMINISTRATORS AND THOSE IN OUR CHARGE IS **ESSENTIAL** IF WE'RE TO STAVE OFF POLITICAL INSTABILITY IN THIS RATHER VOLATILE COUNTRY.
HA! A DIALOGUE?
YOU SOUND MORE LIKE A **DIPLOMAT** ZAN A SOLDIER, SERGEANT, OUI?
HA...
I SUPPOSE YOU **DO** MAKE A STRONG POINT.
BESIDES, MEETING **ME** WILL GIVE ZAT BLANKETED PRINCELING SOMESING TO BRAG ABOUT TO HIS GRAND-CHILDREN, OUI? HA-HA!

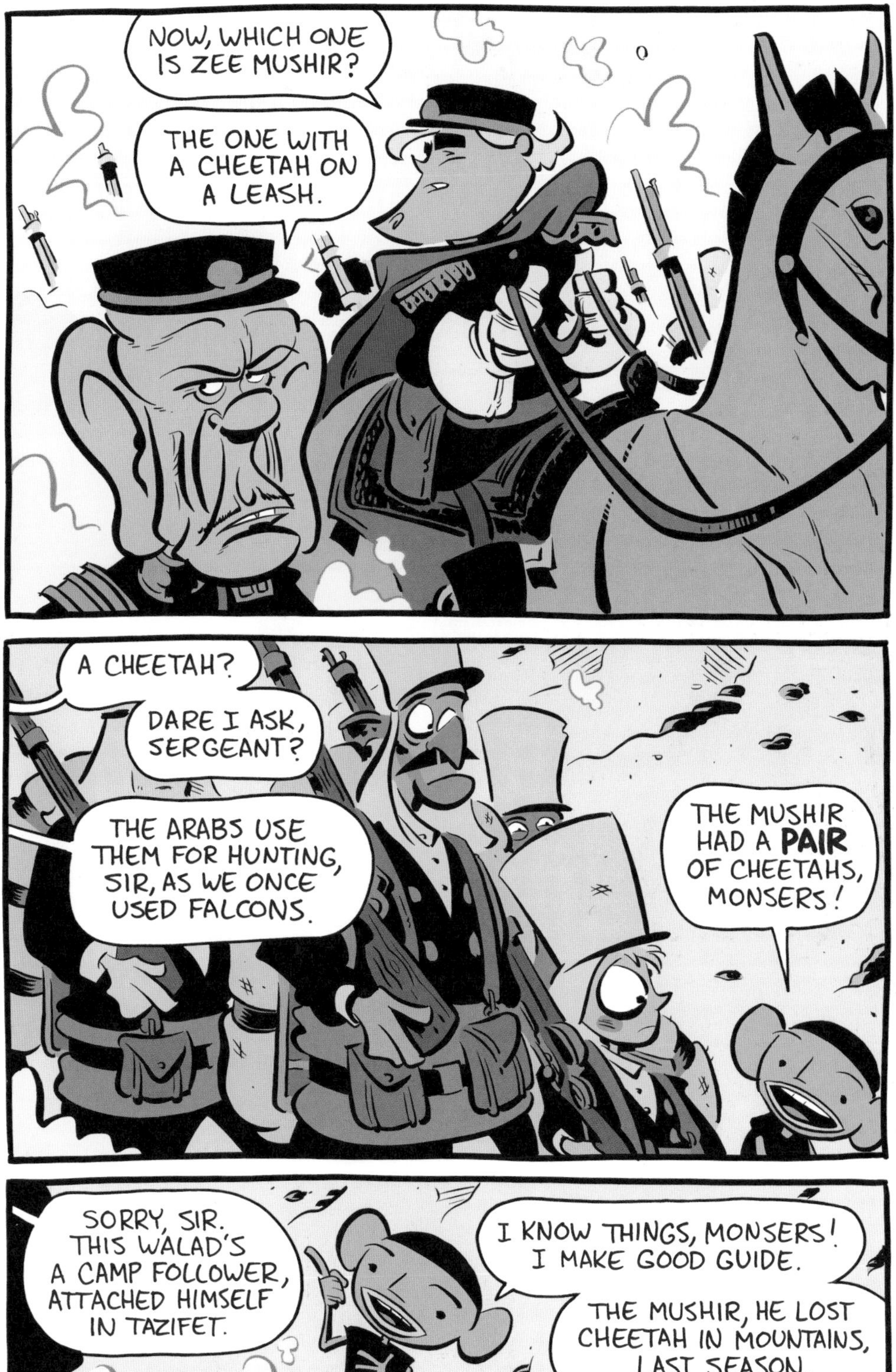
NOW, WHICH ONE IS ZEE MUSHIR?
THE ONE WITH A CHEETAH ON A LEASH.
A CHEETAH?
DARE I ASK, SERGEANT?
THE ARABS USE THEM FOR HUNTING, SIR, AS WE ONCE USED FALCONS.
THE MUSHIR HAD A **PAIR** OF CHEETAHS, MONSERS!
SORRY, SIR. THIS WALAD'S A CAMP FOLLOWER, ATTACHED HIMSELF IN TAZIFET.
I KNOW THINGS, MONSERS! I MAKE GOOD GUIDE.
THE MUSHIR, HE LOST CHEETAH IN MOUNTAINS, LAST SEASON.

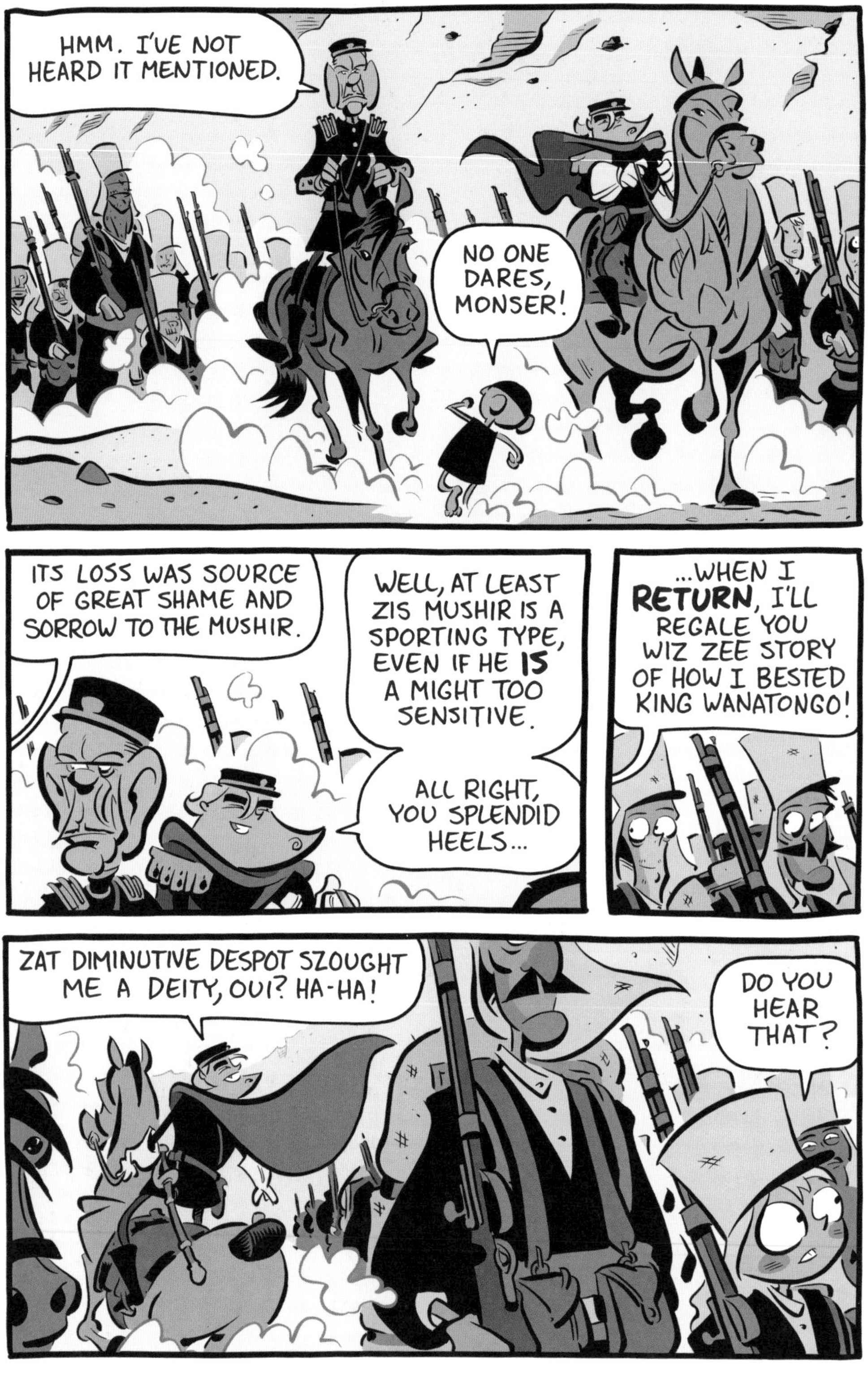
HMM. I'VE NOT HEARD IT MENTIONED.
NO ONE DARES, MONSER!
ITS LOSS WAS SOURCE OF GREAT SHAME AND SORROW TO THE MUSHIR.
WELL, AT LEAST ZIS MUSHIR IS A SPORTING TYPE, EVEN IF HE IS A MIGHT TOO SENSITIVE.
ALL RIGHT, YOU SPLENDID HEELS...
...WHEN I RETURN, I'LL REGALE YOU WIZ ZEE STORY OF HOW I BESTED KING WANATONGO!
ZAT DIMINUTIVE DESPOT SZOUGHT ME A DEITY, OUI? HA-HA!
DO YOU HEAR THAT?

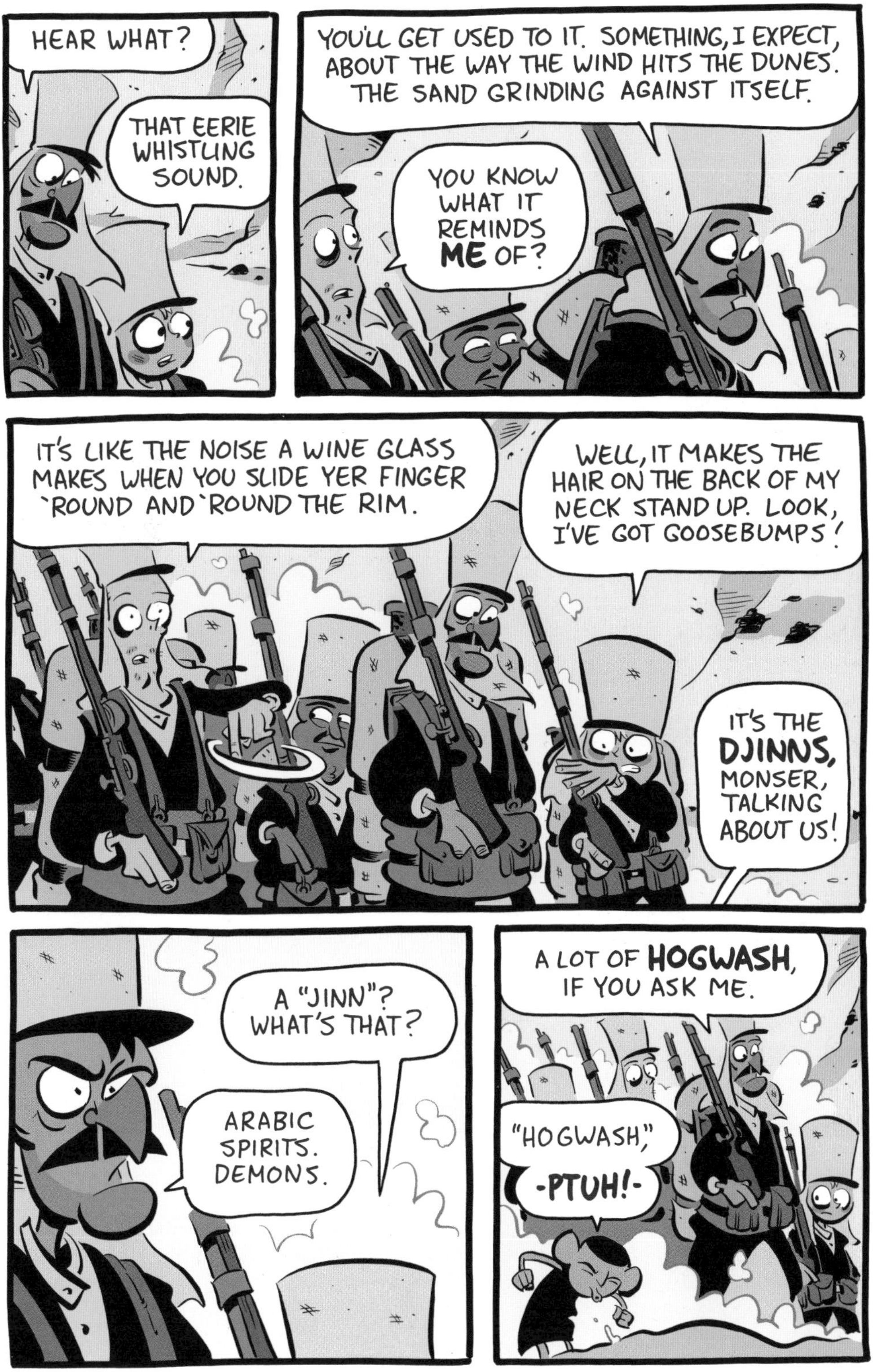
HEAR WHAT?
THAT EERIE WHISTLING SOUND.
YOU'LL GET USED TO IT. SOMETHING, I EXPECT, ABOUT THE WAY THE WIND HITS THE DUNES. THE SAND GRINDING AGAINST ITSELF.
YOU KNOW WHAT IT REMINDS **ME** OF?
IT'S LIKE THE NOISE A WINE GLASS MAKES WHEN YOU SLIDE YER FINGER `ROUND AND `ROUND THE RIM.
WELL, IT MAKES THE HAIR ON THE BACK OF MY NECK STAND UP. LOOK, I'VE GOT GOOSEBUMPS!
IT'S THE **DJINNS,** MONSER, TALKING ABOUT US!
A "JINN"? WHAT'S THAT?
ARABIC SPIRITS. DEMONS.
A LOT OF **HOGWASH**, IF YOU ASK ME.
"HOGWASH,"
-PTUH!-

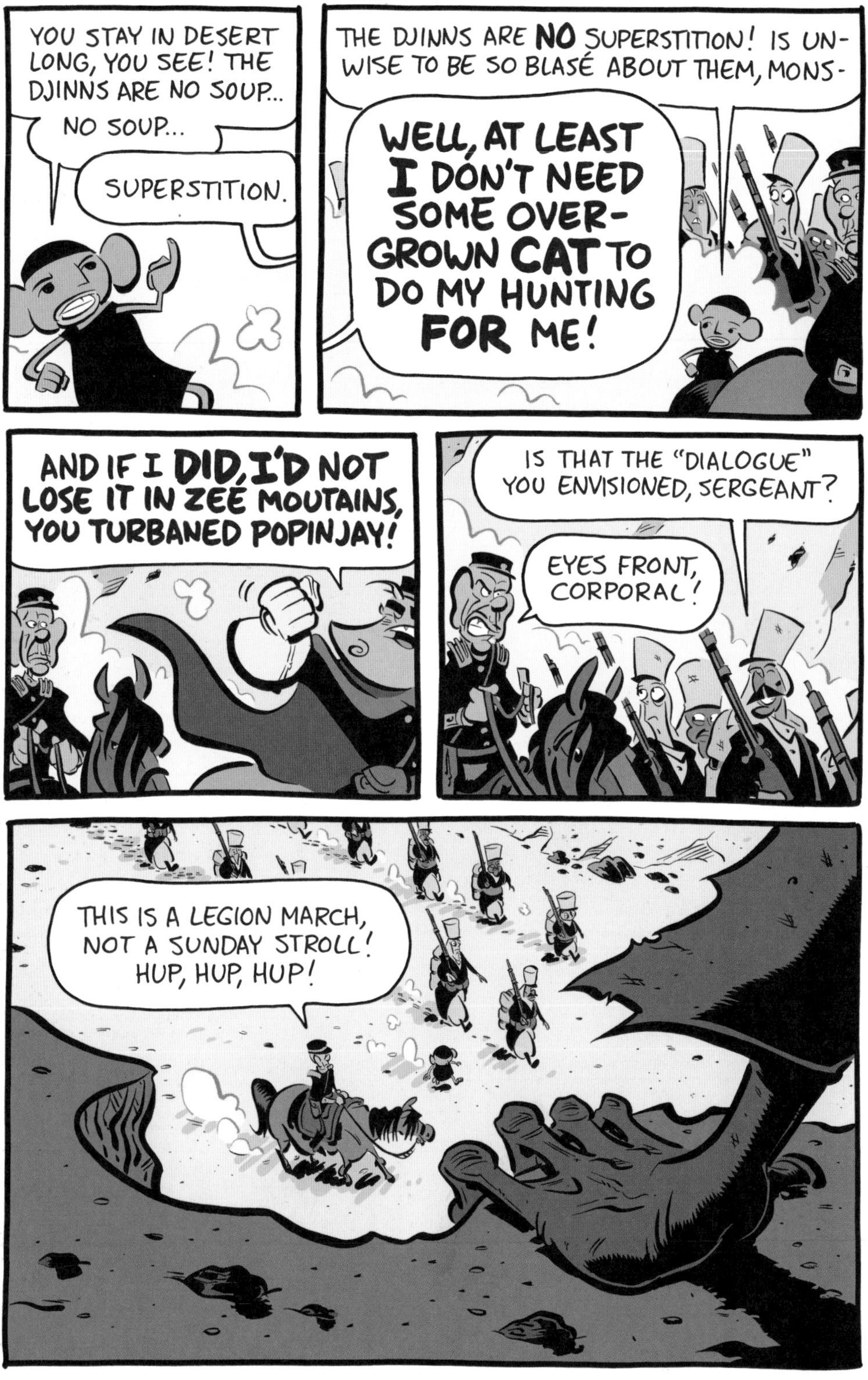
YOU STAY IN DESERT LONG, YOU SEE! THE DJINNS ARE NO SOUP...
NO SOUP...
SUPERSTITION.
THE DJINNS ARE NO SUPERSTITION! IS UN-WISE TO BE SO BLASÉ ABOUT THEM, MONS-
WELL, AT LEAST I DON'T NEED SOME OVER-GROWN CAT TO DO MY HUNTING FOR ME!
AND IF I DID, I'D NOT LOSE IT IN ZEÉ MOUTAINS, YOU TURBANED POPINJAY!
IS THAT THE "DIALOGUE" YOU ENVISIONED, SERGEANT?
EYES FRONT, CORPORAL!
THIS IS A LEGION MARCH, NOT A SUNDAY STROLL! HUP, HUP, HUP!

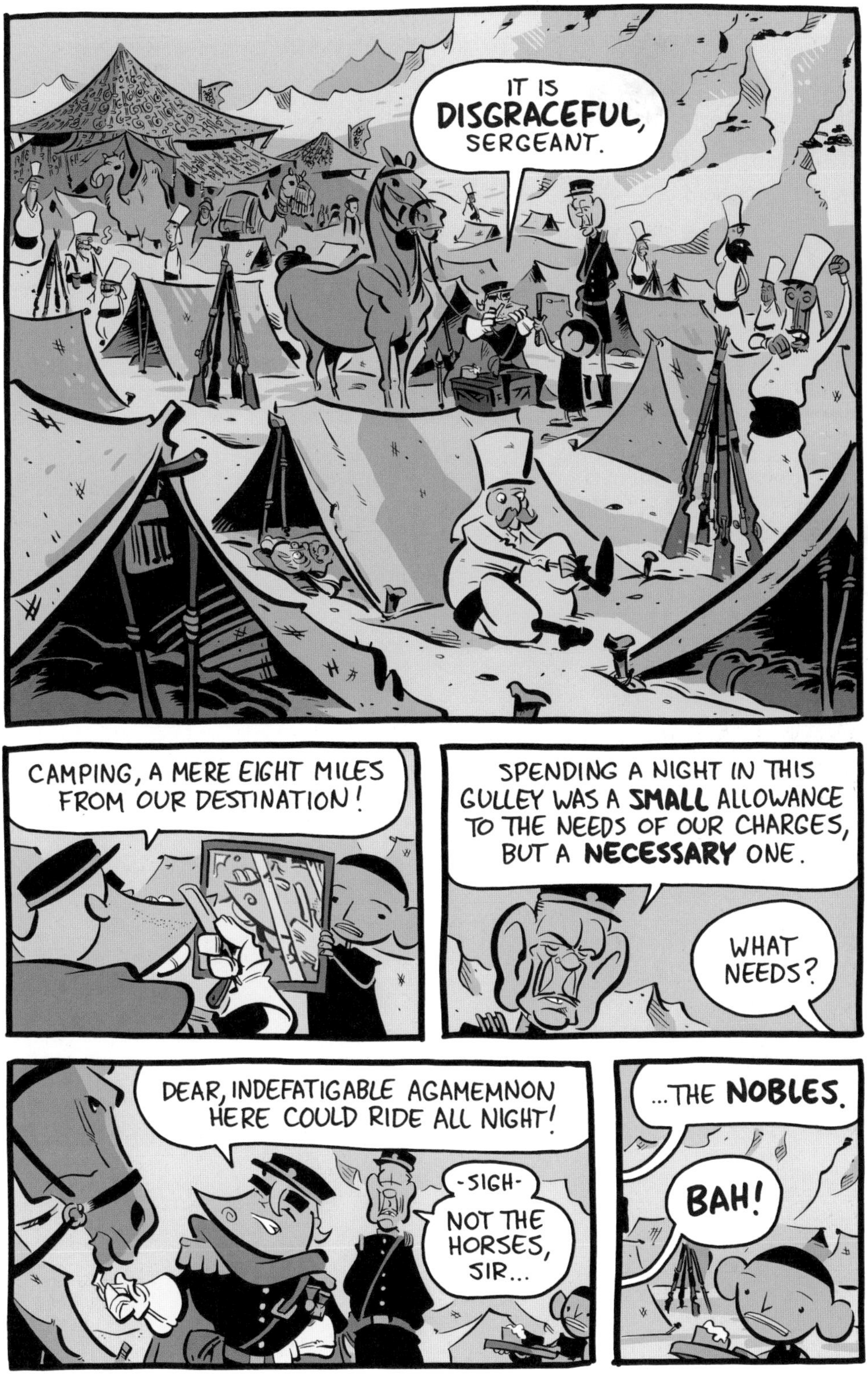
IT IS DISGRACEFUL, SERGEANT.
CAMPING, A MERE EIGHT MILES FROM OUR DESTINATION!
SPENDING A NIGHT IN THIS GULLEY WAS A SMALL ALLOWANCE TO THE NEEDS OF OUR CHARGES, BUT A NECESSARY ONE.
WHAT NEEDS?
DEAR, INDEFATIGABLE AGAMEMNON HERE COULD RIDE ALL NIGHT!
-SIGH-
NOT THE HORSES, SIR...
...THE NOBLES.
BAH!

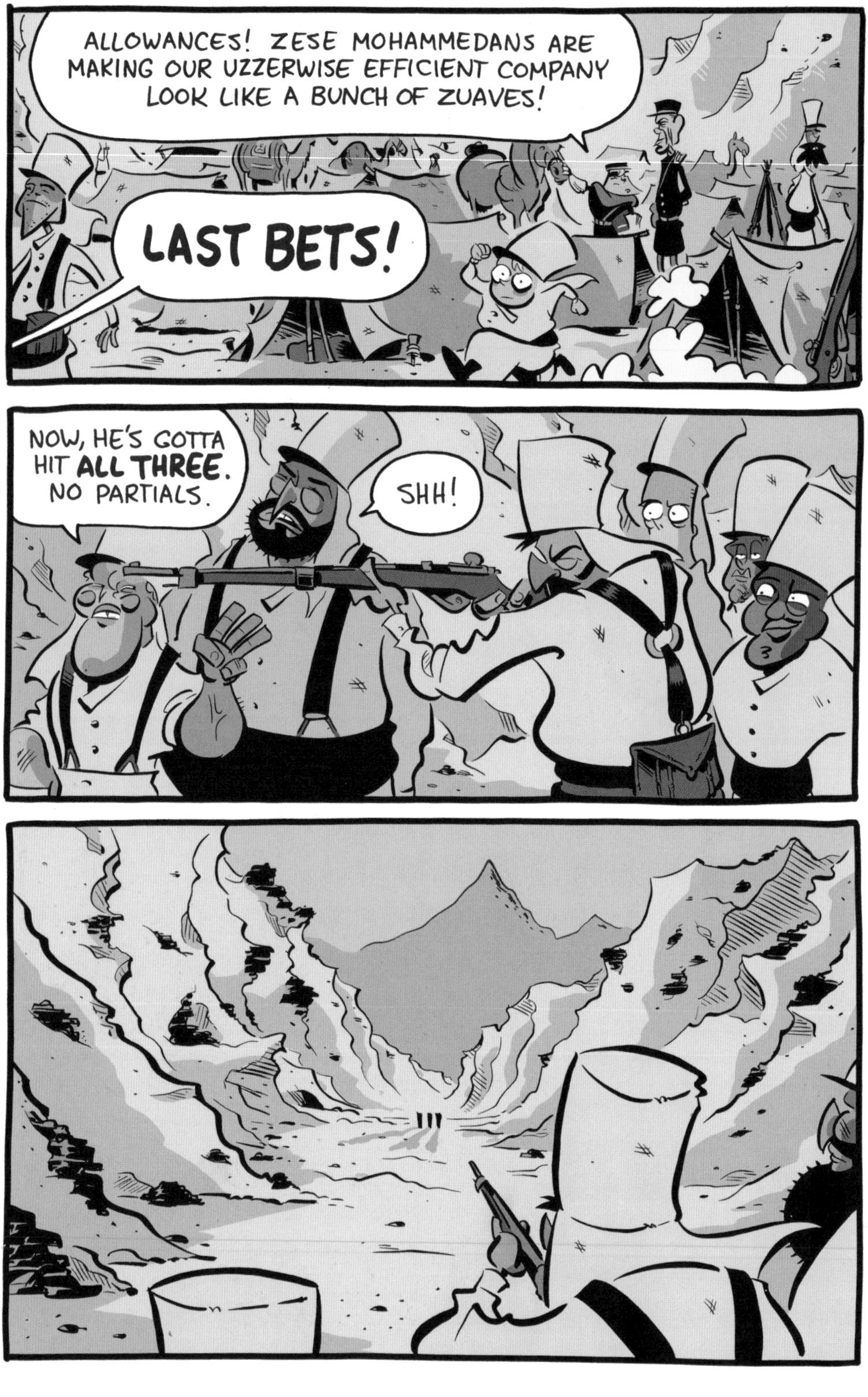
ALLOWANCES! ZESE MOHAMMEDANS ARE MAKING OUR UZZERWISE EFFICIENT COMPANY LOOK LIKE A BUNCH OF ZUAVES!
LAST BETS!
NOW, HE'S GOTTA HIT ALL THREE. NO PARTIALS.
SHH!

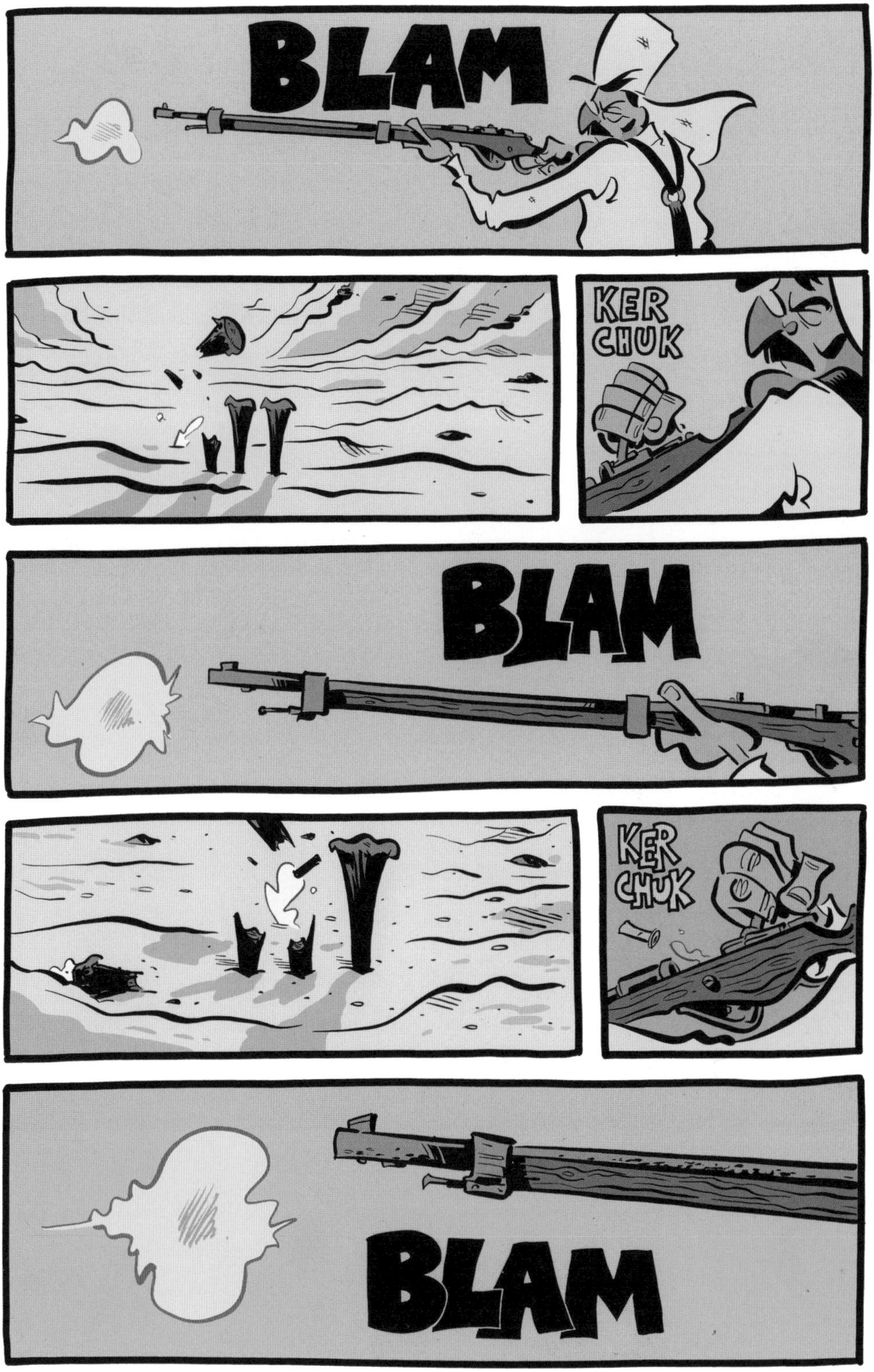
BLAM
KER CHUK
BLAM
KER CHUK
BLAM

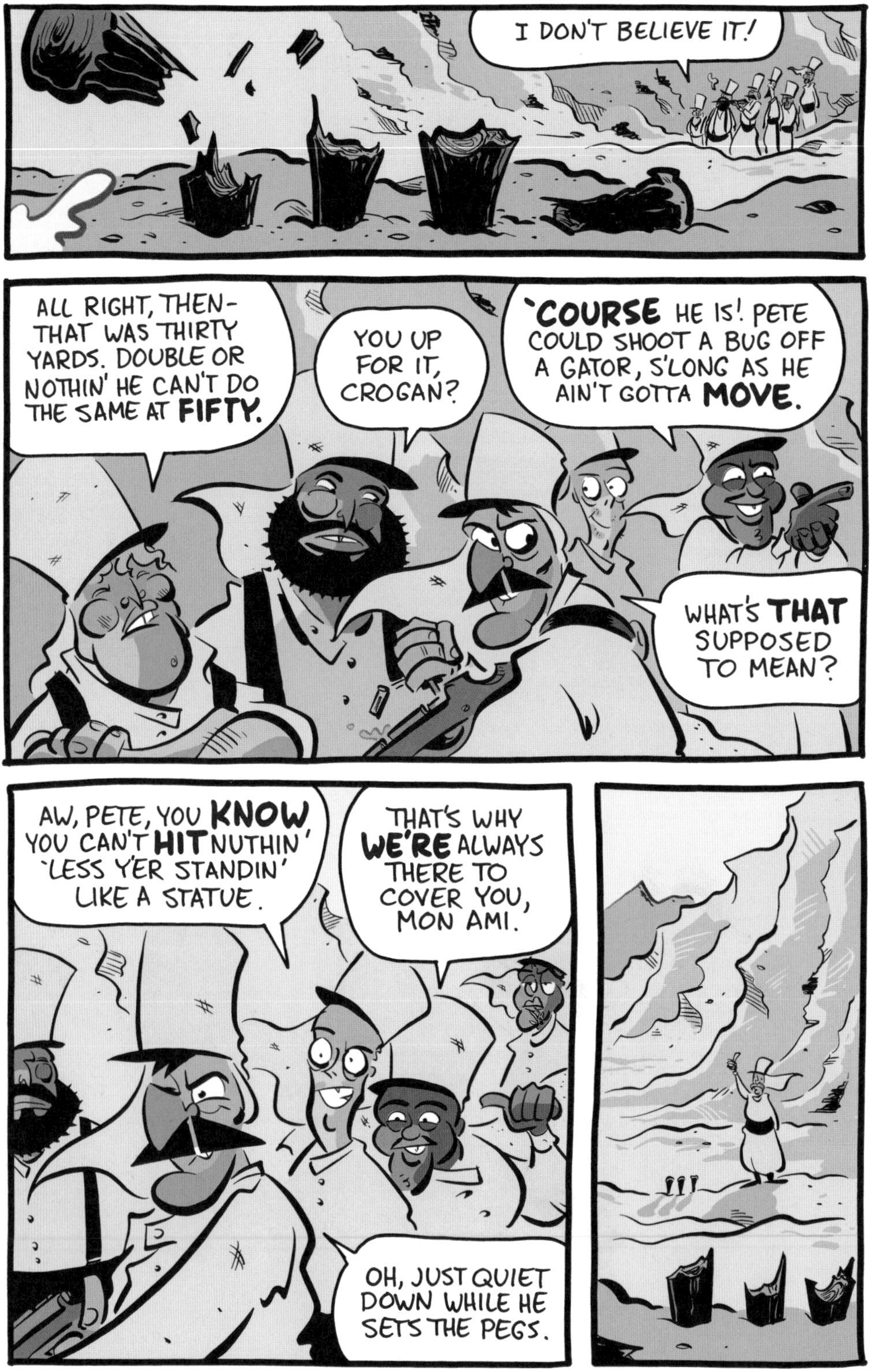
I DON'T BELIEVE IT!
ALL RIGHT, THEN- THAT WAS THIRTY YARDS. DOUBLE OR NOTHIN' HE CAN'T DO THE SAME AT FIFTY.
YOU UP FOR IT, CROGAN?
`COURSE HE IS! PETE COULD SHOOT A BUG OFF A GATOR, S'LONG AS HE AIN'T GOTTA MOVE.
WHAT'S THAT SUPPOSED TO MEAN?
AW, PETE, YOU KNOW YOU CAN'T HIT NUTHIN' `LESS Y'ER STANDIN' LIKE A STATUE.
THAT'S WHY WE'RE ALWAYS THERE TO COVER YOU, MON AMI.
OH, JUST QUIET DOWN WHILE HE SETS THE PEGS.

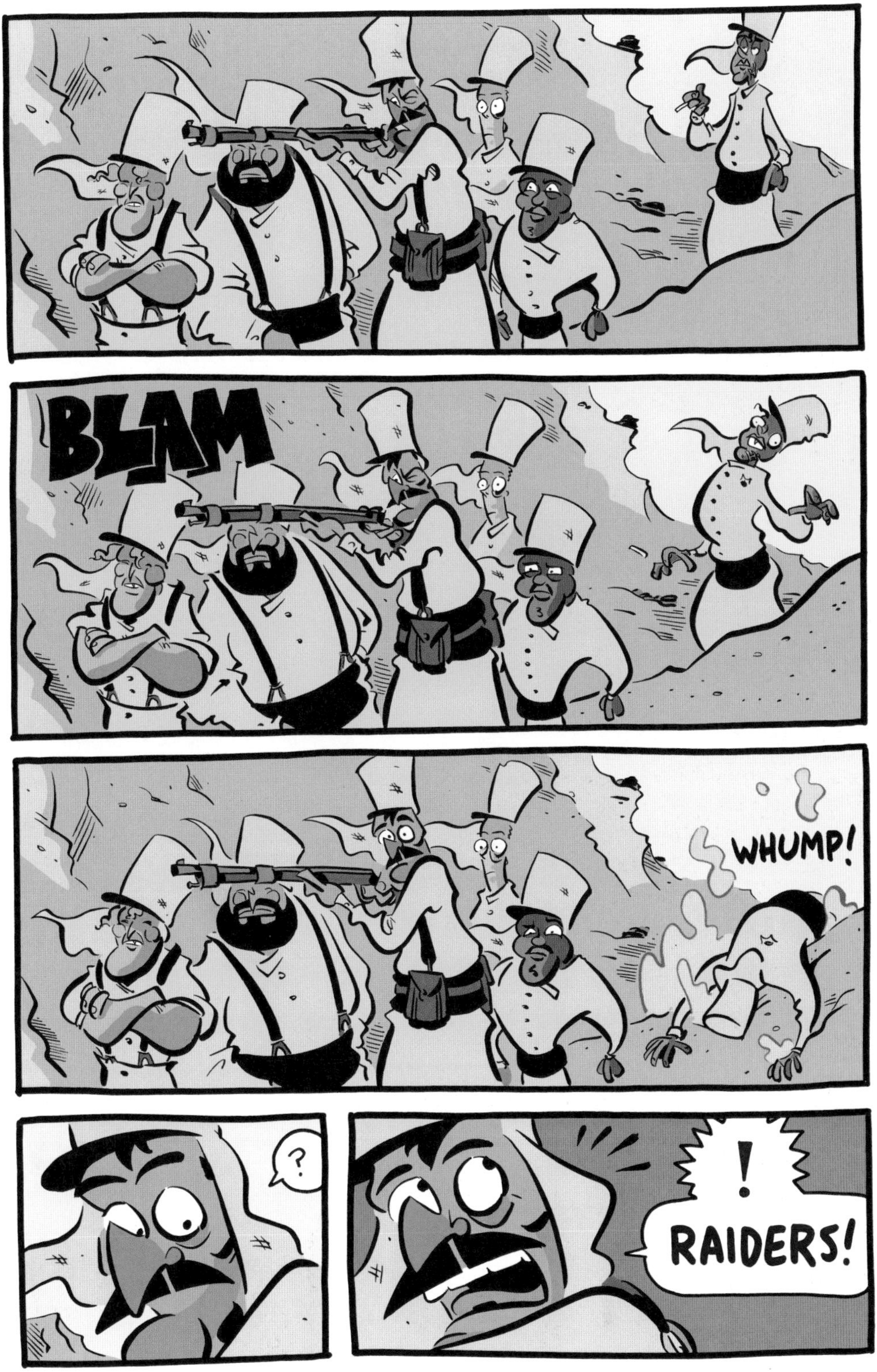
BLAM
WHUMP!
?
!
RAIDERS!

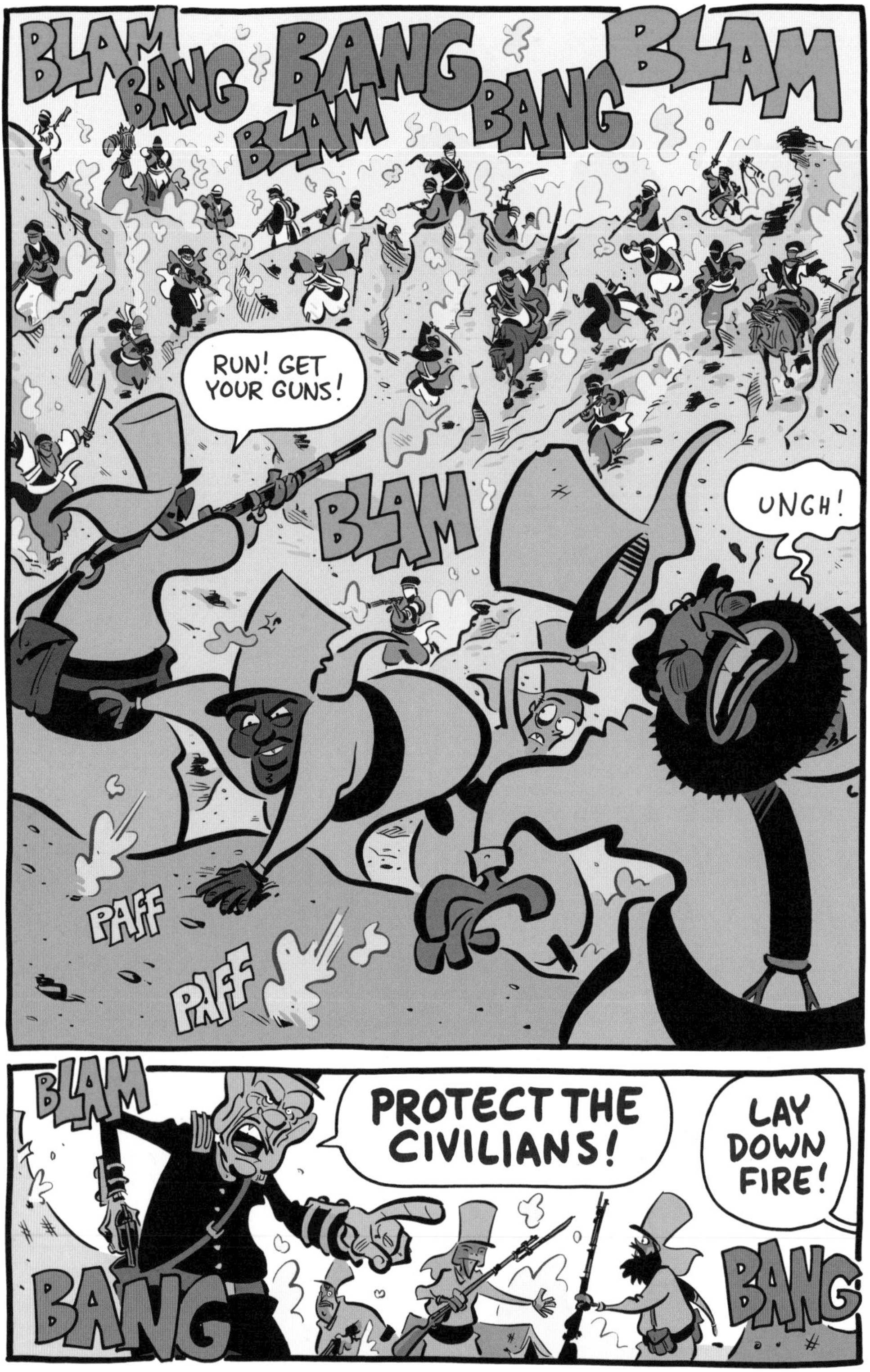
BLAM
BANG
BANG
BLAM
BANG
BLAM
RUN! GET YOUR GUNS!
BLAM
UNGH!
PAFF
PAFF
BLAM
PROTECT THE CIVILIANS!
LAY DOWN FIRE!
BANG
BANG

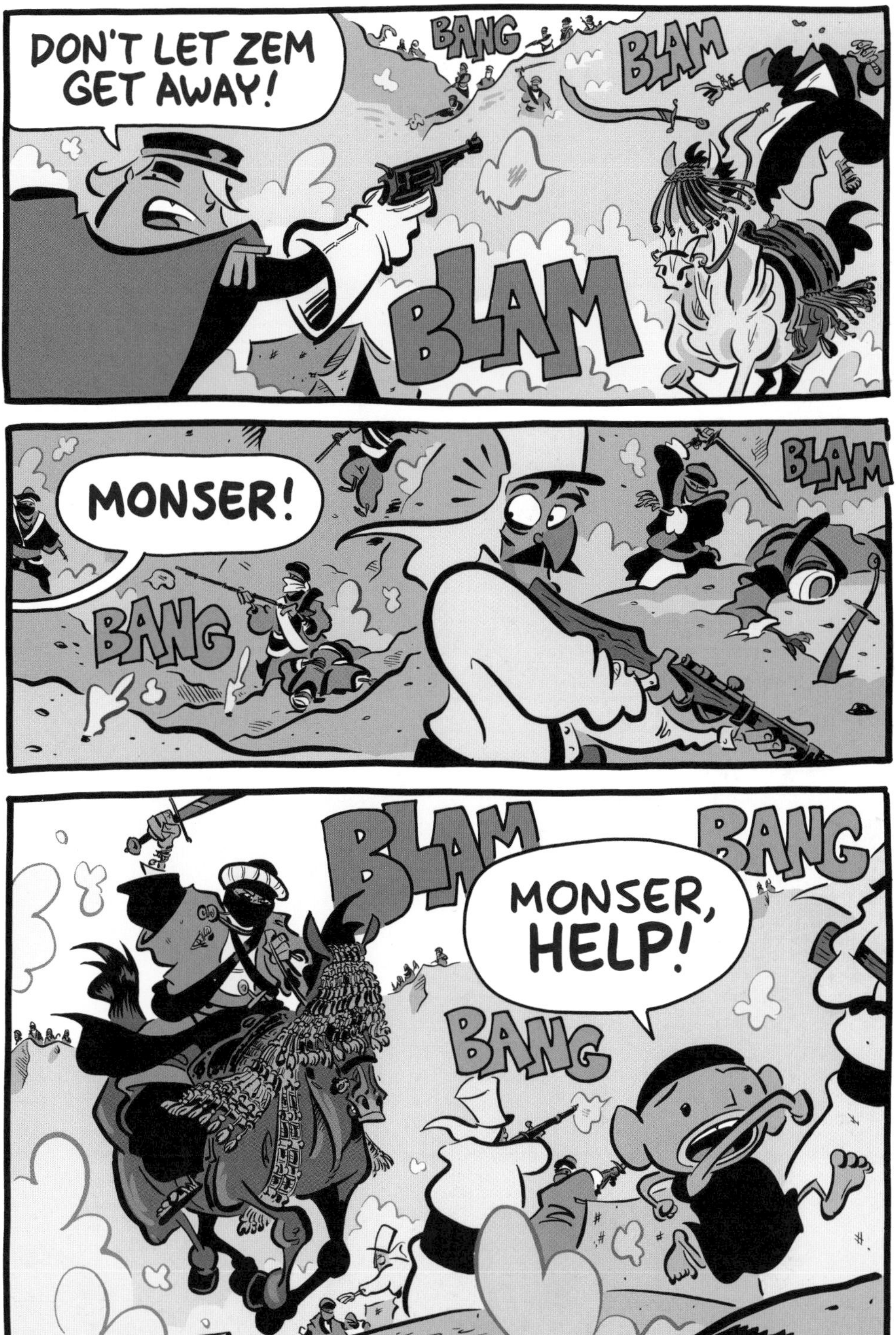
DON'T LET ZEM GET AWAY!
BANG
BLAM
BLAM
MONSER!
BLAM
BANG
BLAM
BANG
MONSER, HELP!
BANG

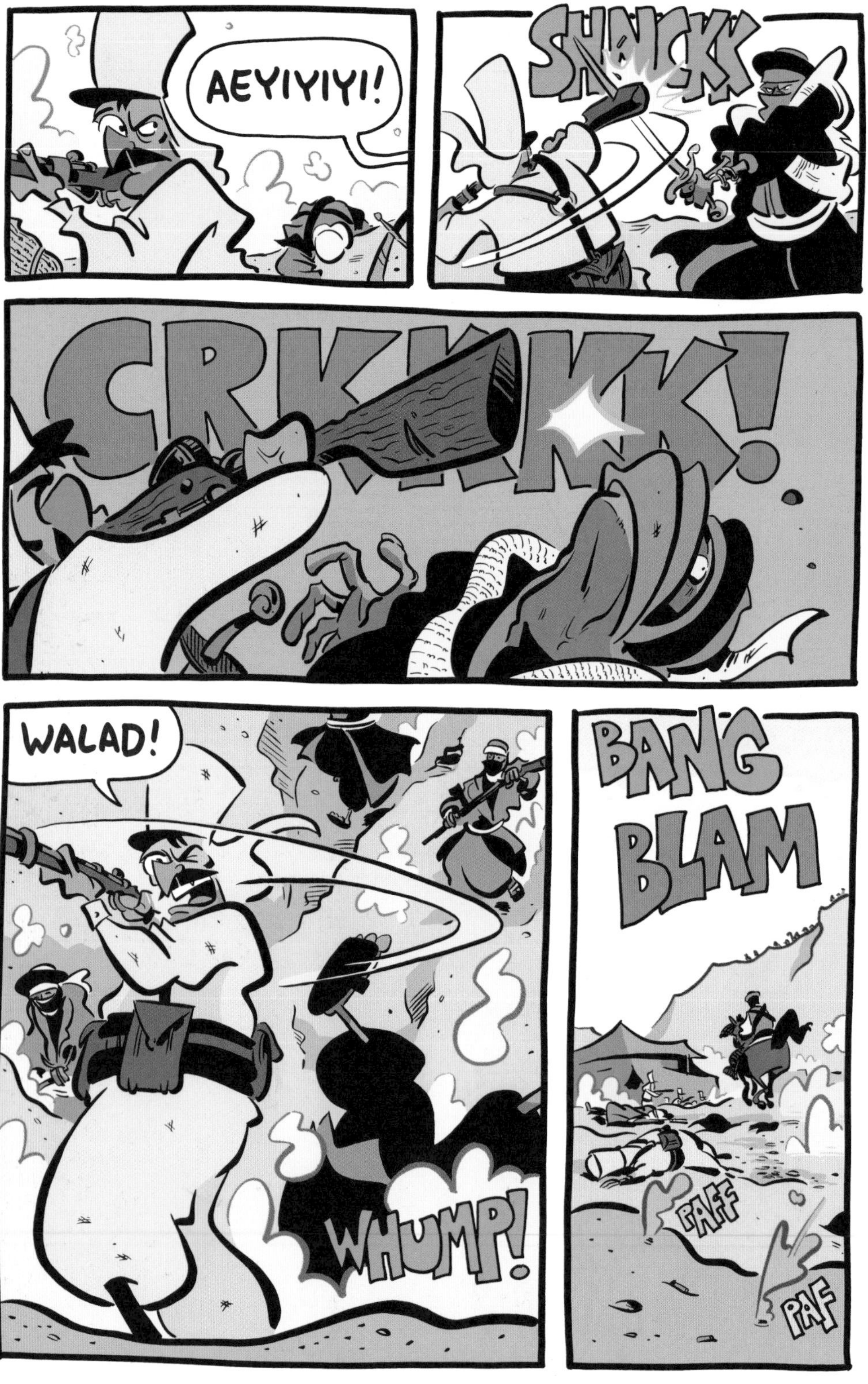
AEYIYIYI!
SHNICKK
CRKKKK!
WALAD!
WHUMP!
BANG
BLAM
PAFF
PAF

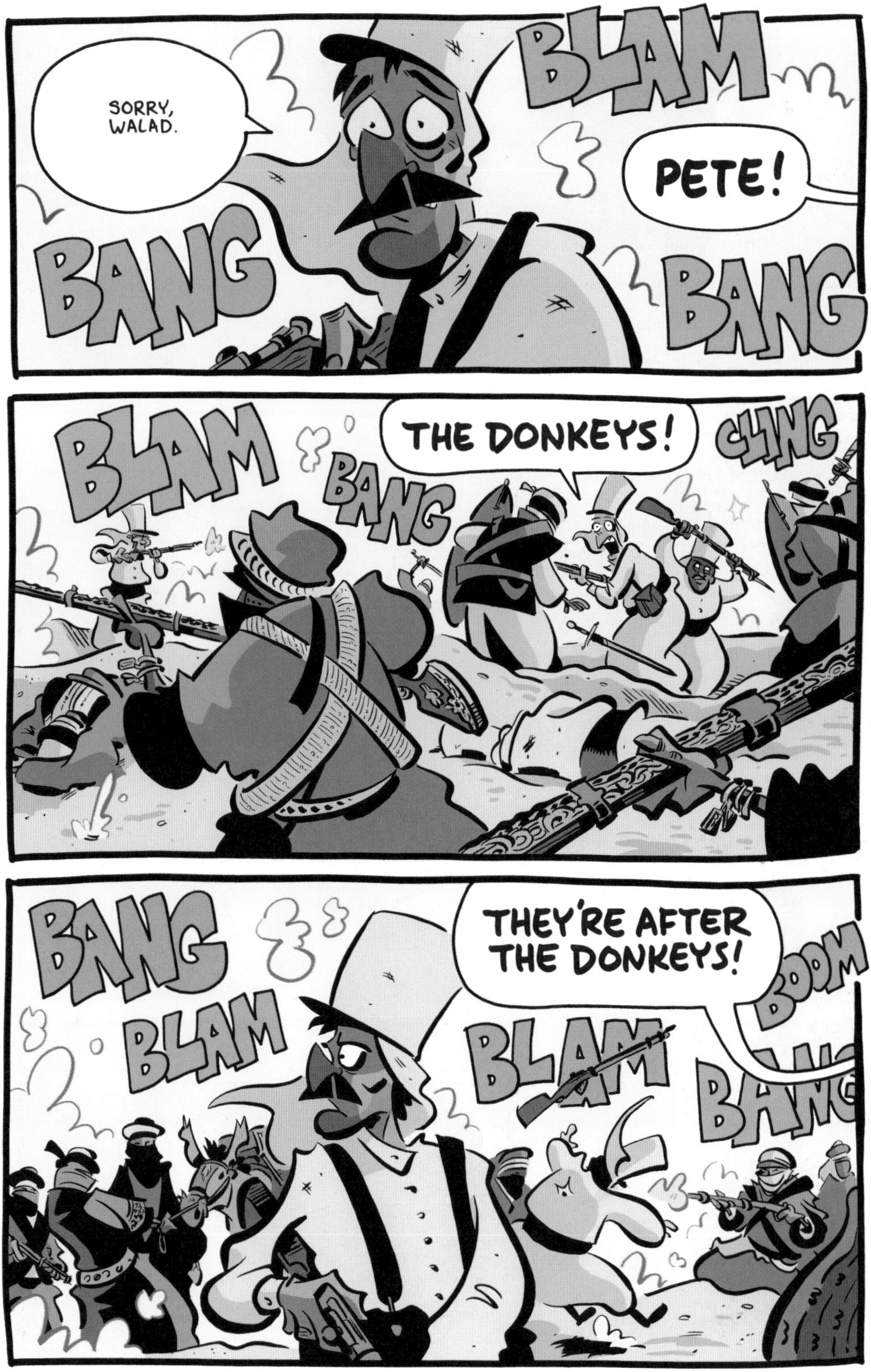
SORRY, WALAD.
BLAM
PETE!
BANG
BANG
BLAM
BANG
THE DONKEYS!
CLING
BANG
BLAM
THEY'RE AFTER THE DONKEYS!
BOOM
BLAM

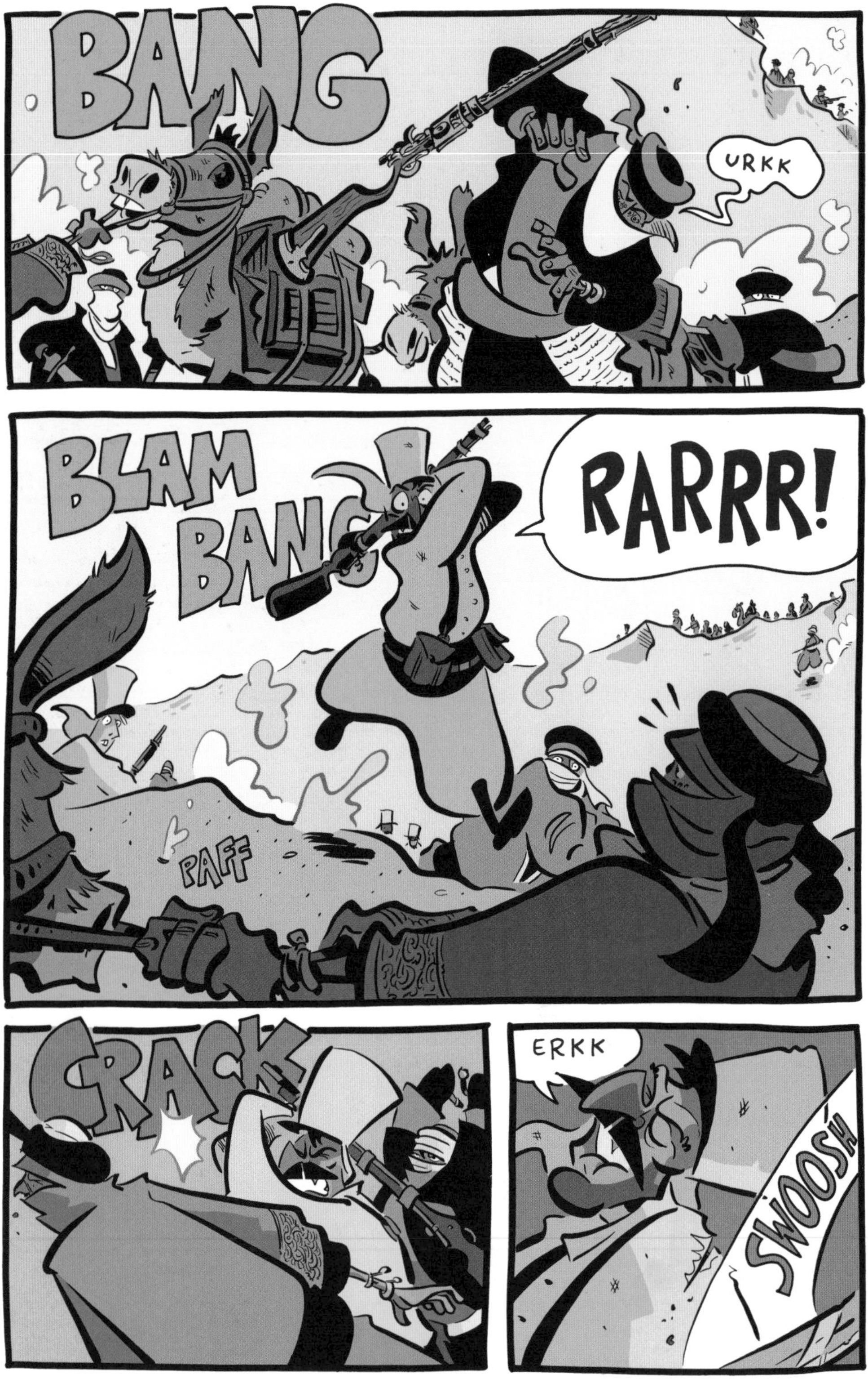
BANG
URKK
BLAM
BANG
RARRR!
PAFF
CRACK
ERKK
SWOOSH

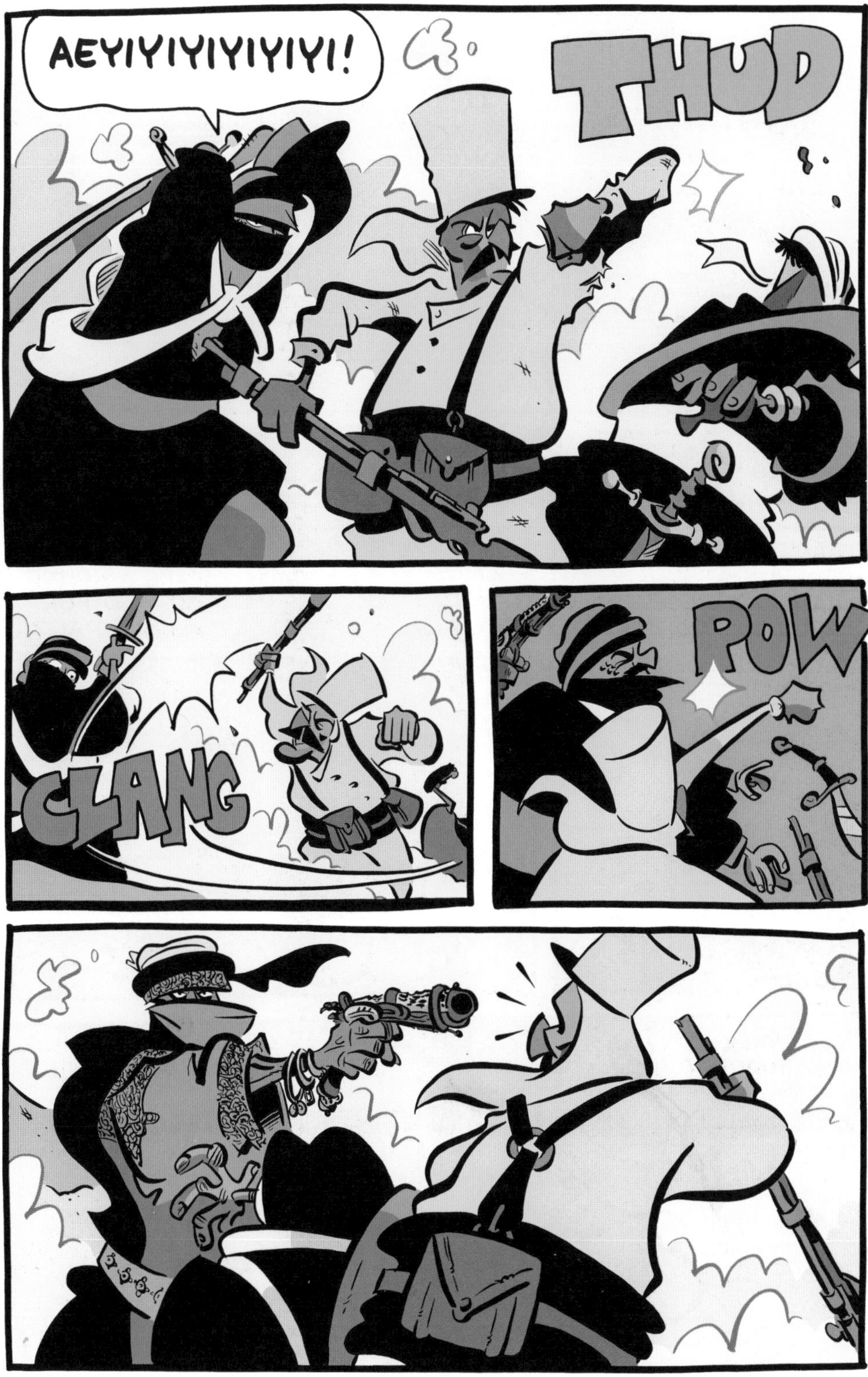
AEYIYIYIYIYIYIYI!
THUD
CLANG
POW

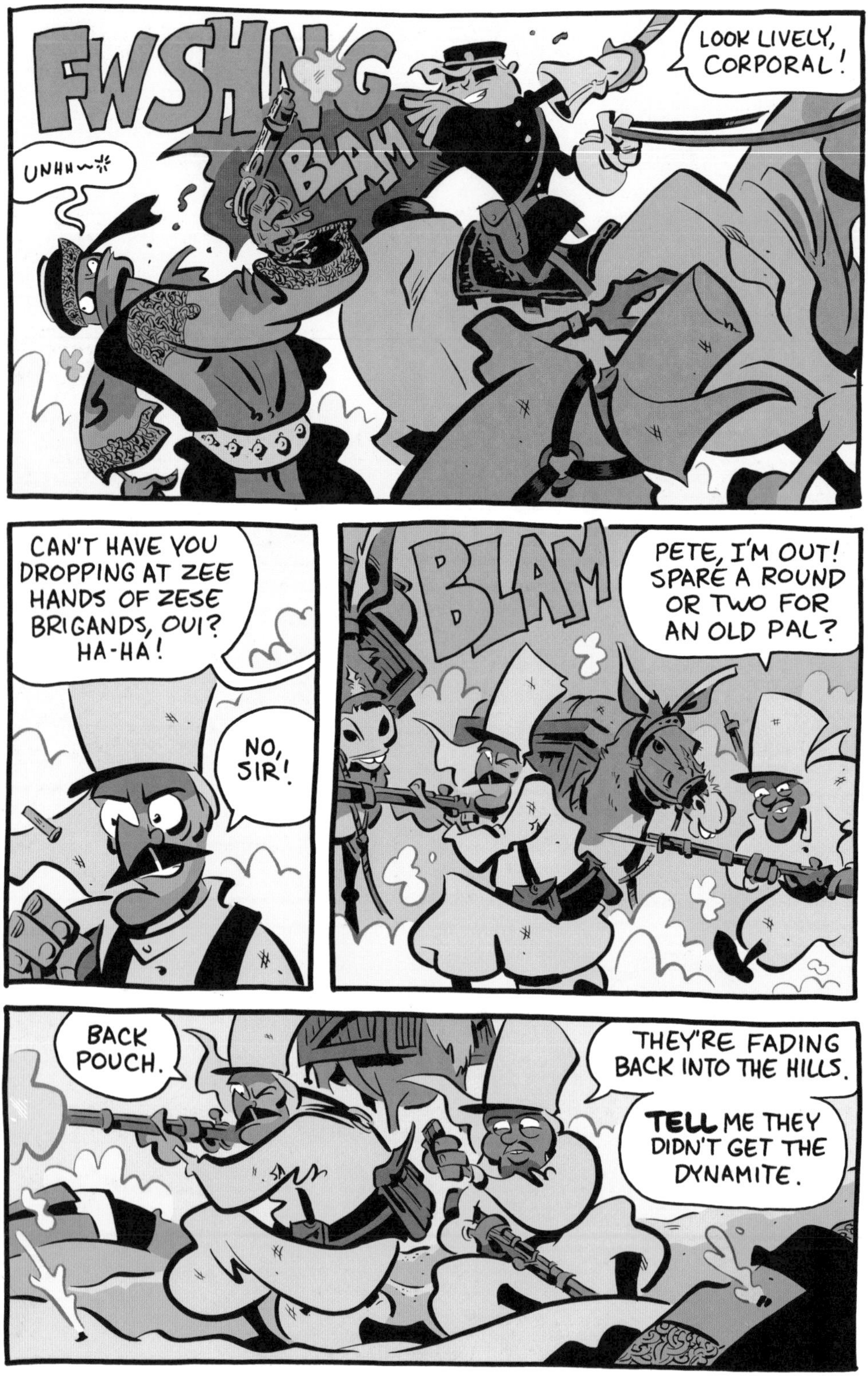
FWSHNG
BLAM
LOOK LIVELY, CORPORAL!
UNHH~
CAN'T HAVE YOU DROPPING AT ZEE HANDS OF ZESE BRIGANDS, OUI? HA-HA!
NO, SIR!
BLAM
PETE, I'M OUT! SPARE A ROUND OR TWO FOR AN OLD PAL?
BACK POUCH.
THEY'RE FADING BACK INTO THE HILLS.
TELL ME THEY DIDN'T GET THE DYNAMITE.

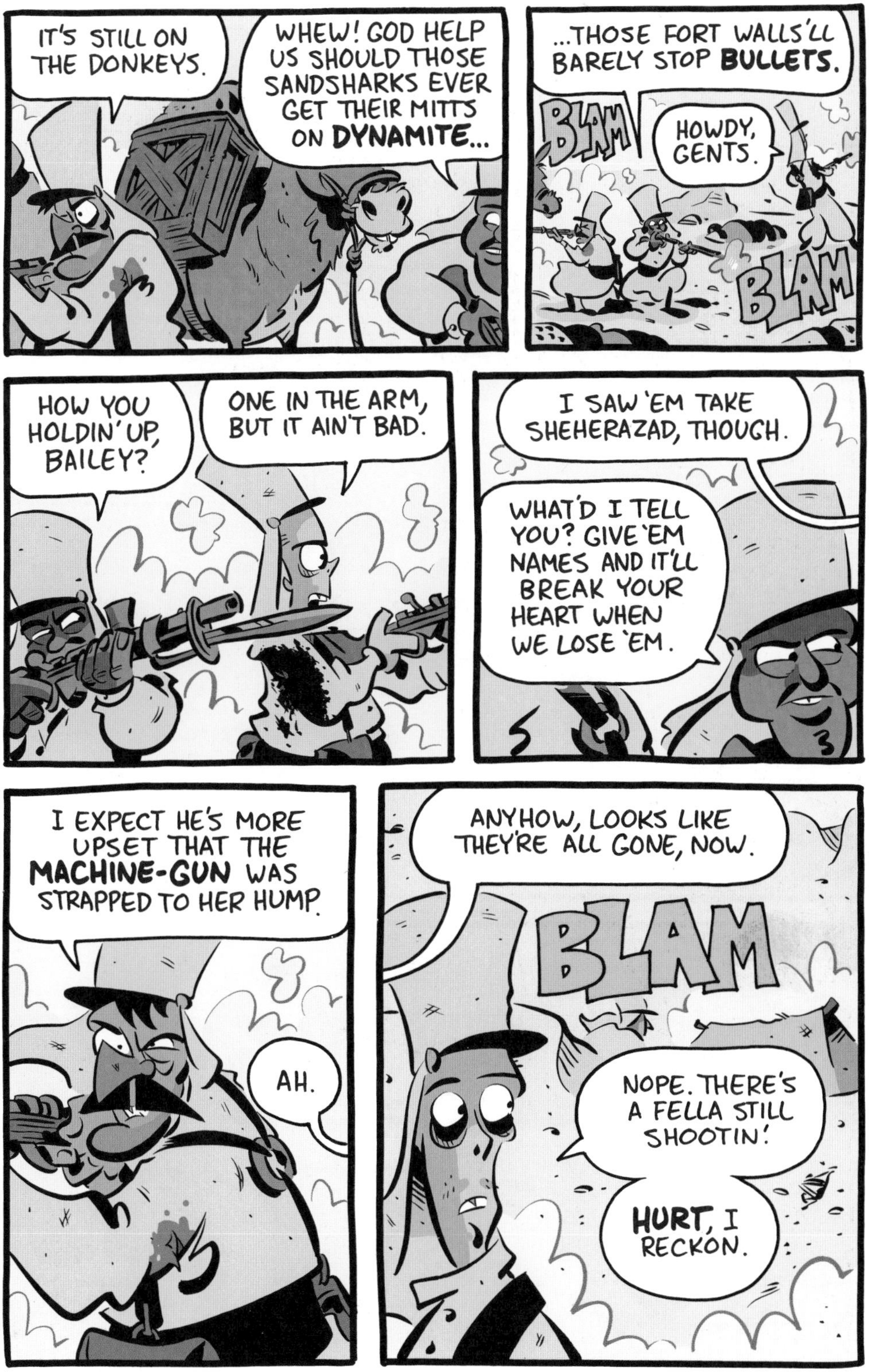

IT'S STILL ON THE DONKEYS.
WHEW! GOD HELP US SHOULD THOSE SANDSHARKS EVER GET THEIR MITTS ON **DYNAMITE**...
...THOSE FORT WALLS'LL BARELY STOP **BULLETS**.
BLAM
HOWDY, GENTS.
BLAM
HOW YOU HOLDIN' UP, BAILEY?
ONE IN THE ARM, BUT IT AIN'T BAD.
I SAW 'EM TAKE SHEHERAZAD, THOUGH.
WHAT'D I TELL YOU? GIVE 'EM NAMES AND IT'LL BREAK YOUR HEART WHEN WE LOSE 'EM.
I EXPECT HE'S MORE UPSET THAT THE **MACHINE-GUN** WAS STRAPPED TO HER HUMP.
AH.
ANYHOW, LOOKS LIKE THEY'RE ALL GONE, NOW.
BLAM
NOPE. THERE'S A FELLA STILL SHOOTIN'.
HURT, I RECKON.

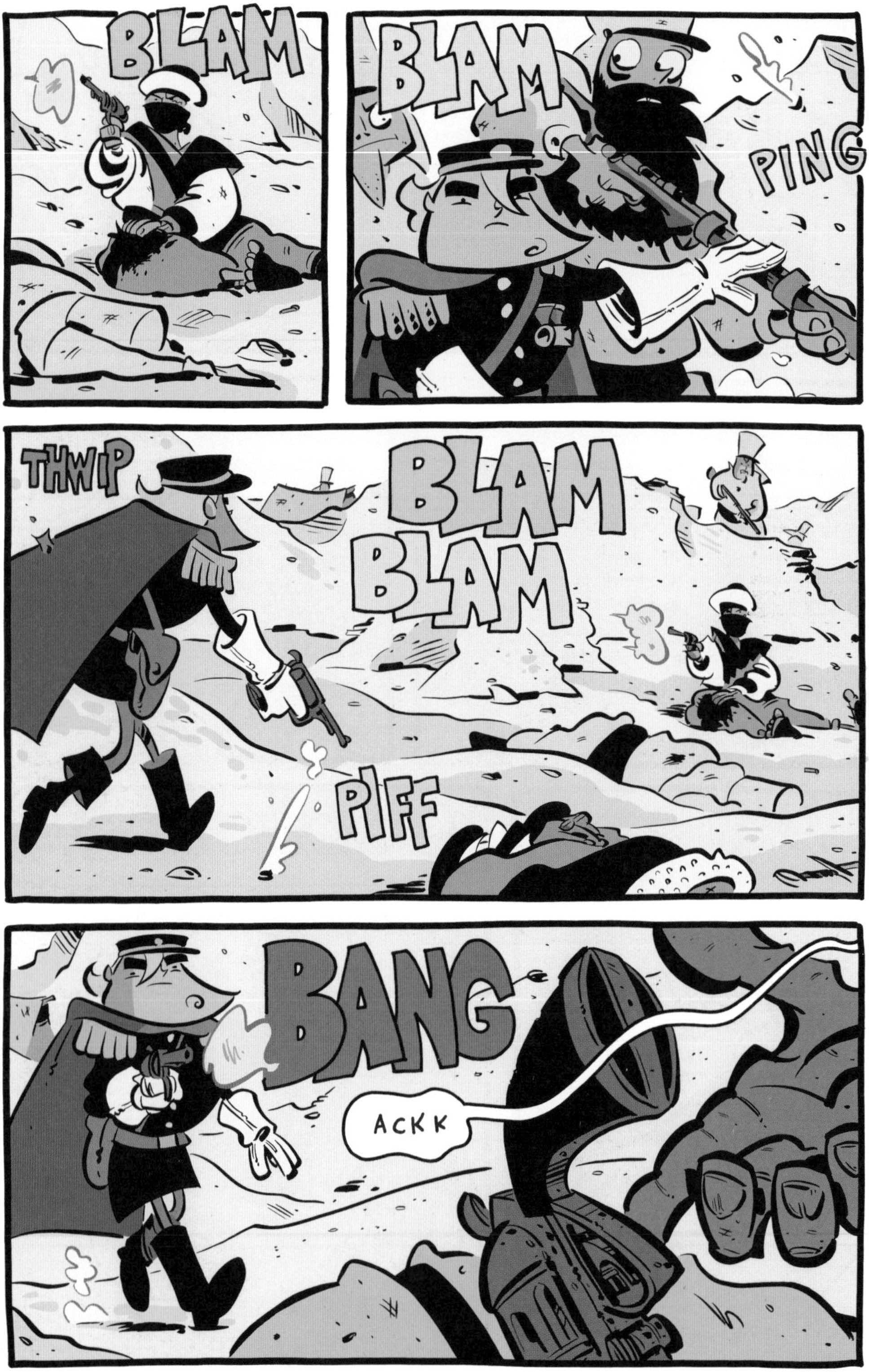
BLAM
BLAM
PING
THWIP
BLAM
BLAM
PIFF
BANG
ACKK

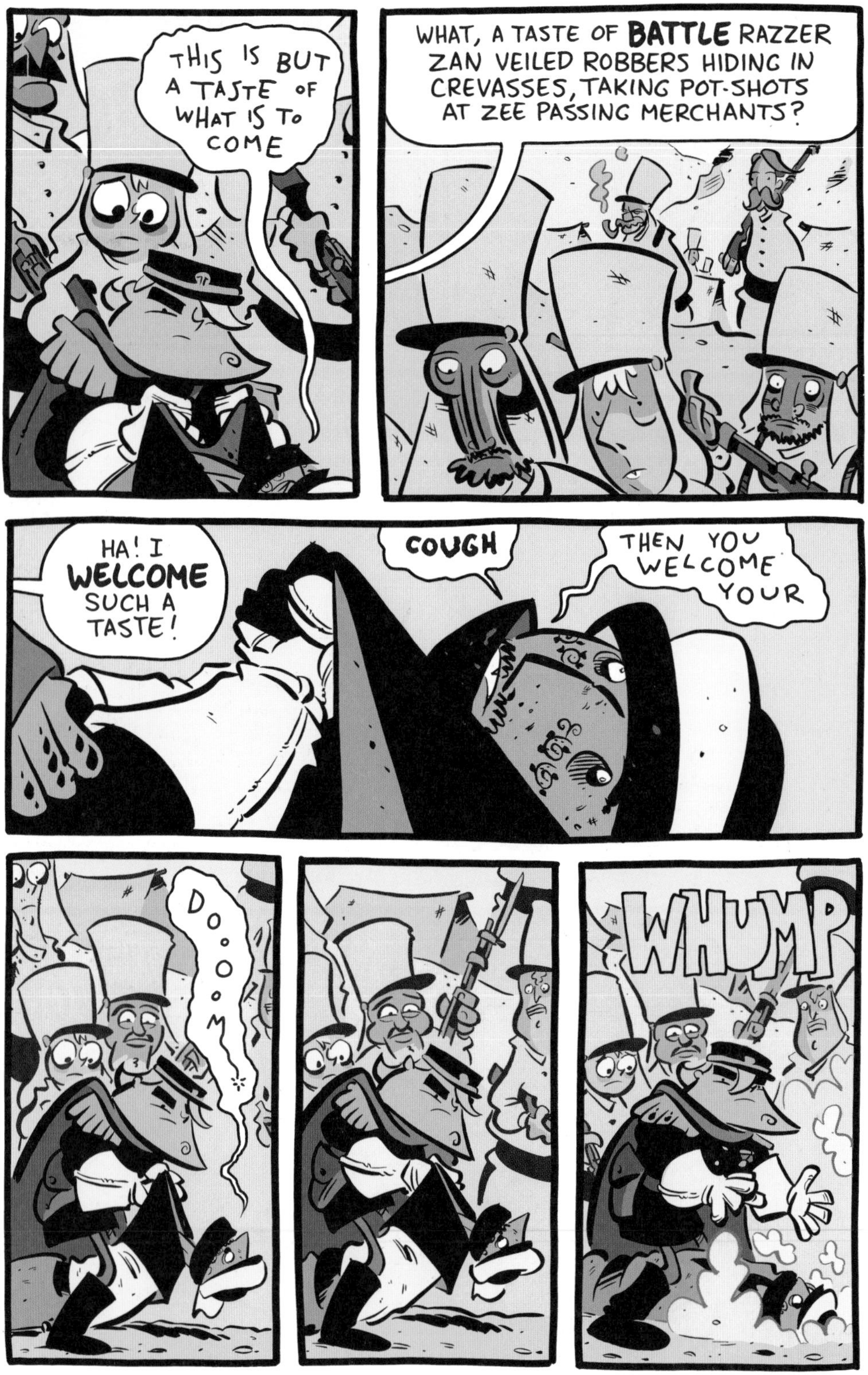
THIS IS BUT A TASTE OF WHAT IS TO COME
WHAT, A TASTE OF **BATTLE** RAZZER ZAN VEILED ROBBERS HIDING IN CREVASSES, TAKING POT-SHOTS AT ZEE PASSING MERCHANTS?
HA! I **WELCOME** SUCH A TASTE!
COUGH
THEN YOU WELCOME YOUR
DOOOOM
WHUMP

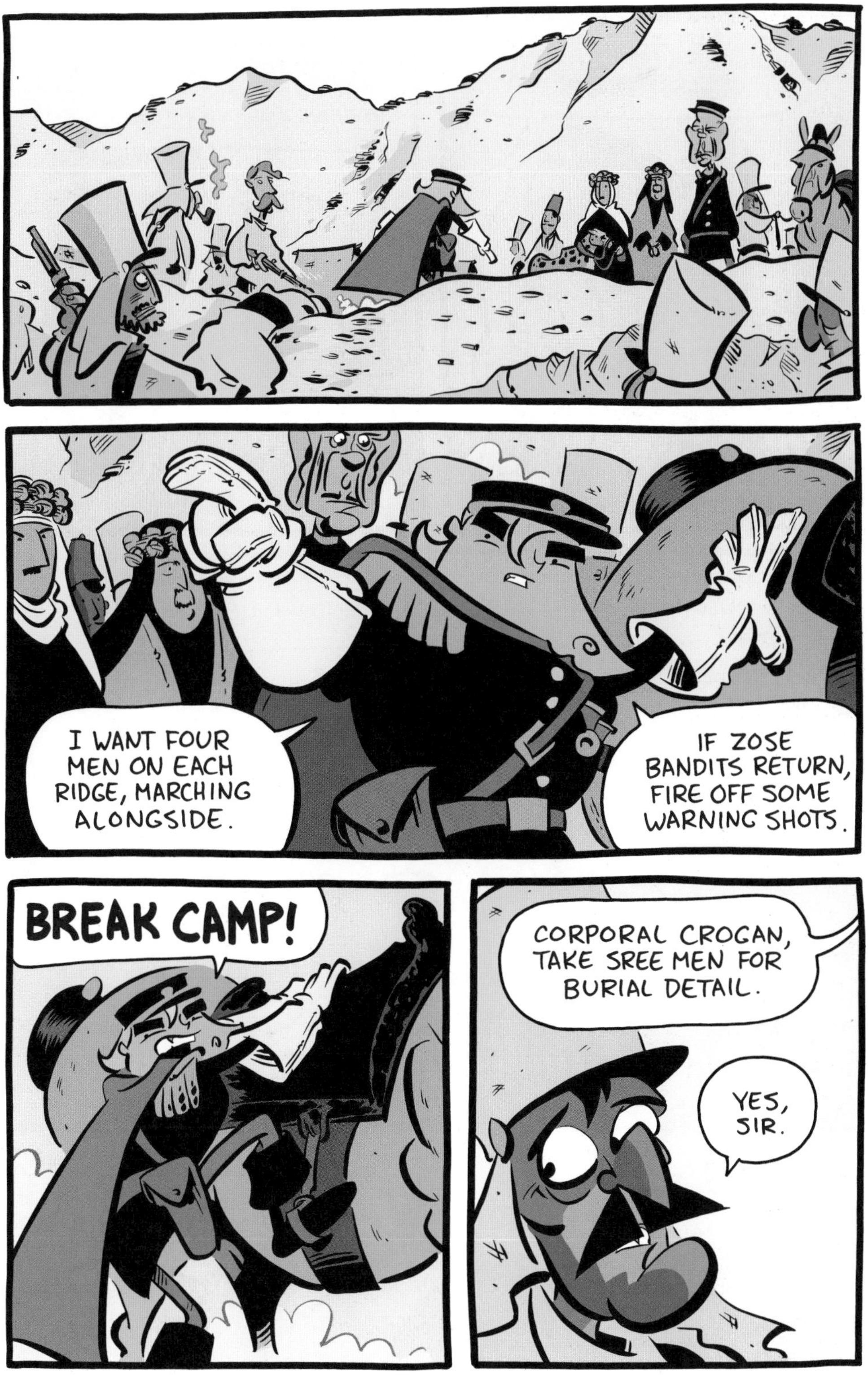
I WANT FOUR MEN ON EACH RIDGE, MARCHING ALONGSIDE.
IF ZOSE BANDITS RETURN, FIRE OFF SOME WARNING SHOTS.
BREAK CAMP!
CORPORAL CROGAN, TAKE SREE MEN FOR BURIAL DETAIL.
YES, SIR.

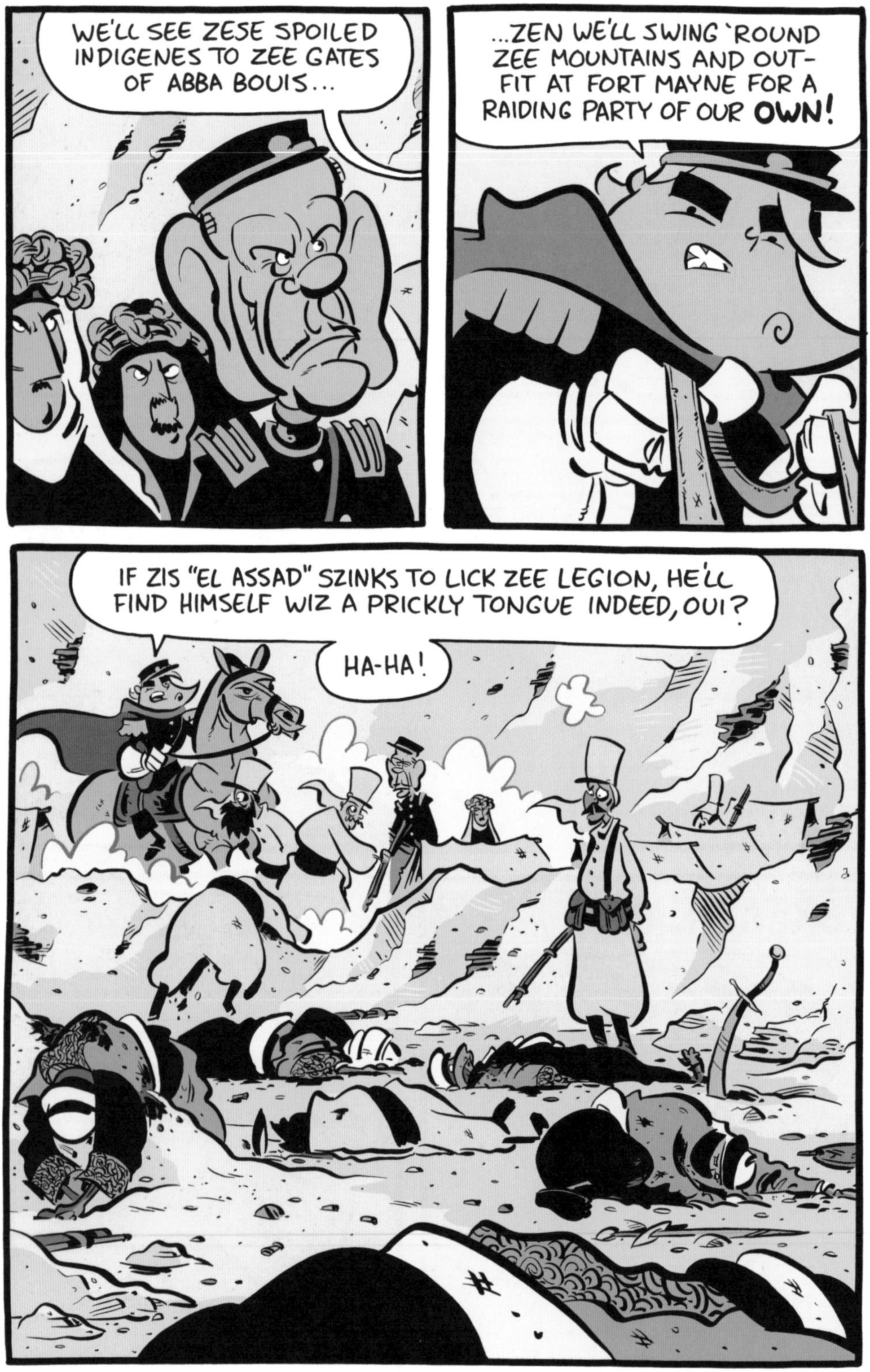
WE'LL SEE ZESE SPOILED INDIGENES TO ZEE GATES OF ABBA BOUIS...
...ZEN WE'LL SWING 'ROUND ZEE MOUNTAINS AND OUT-FIT AT FORT MAYNE FOR A RAIDING PARTY OF OUR **OWN**!
IF ZIS "EL ASSAD" SZINKS TO LICK ZEE LEGION, HE'LL FIND HIMSELF WIZ A PRICKLY TONGUE INDEED, OUI?
HA-HA!

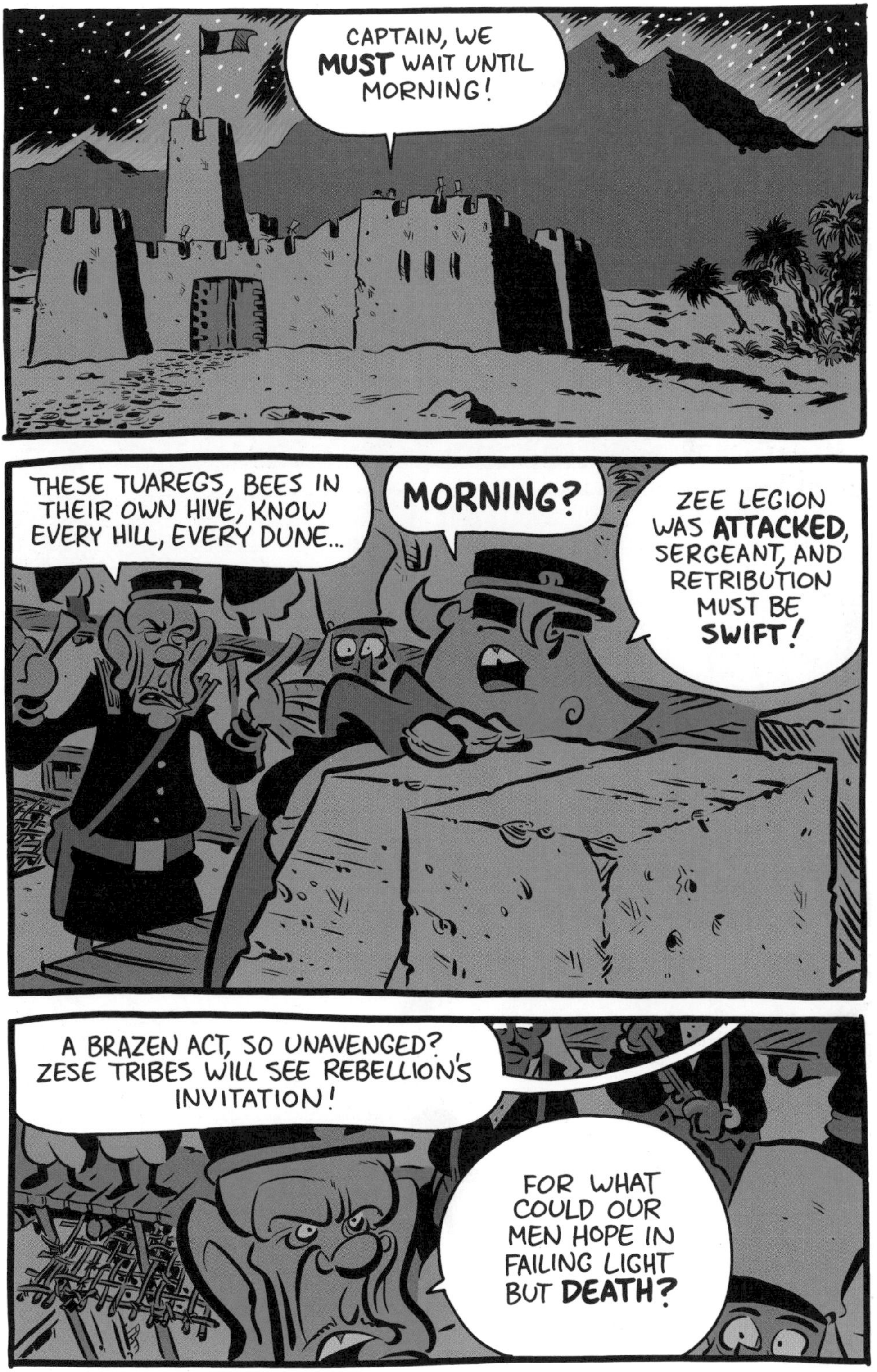
CAPTAIN, WE **MUST** WAIT UNTIL MORNING!
THESE TUAREGS, BEES IN THEIR OWN HIVE, KNOW EVERY HILL, EVERY DUNE...
MORNING?
ZEE LEGION WAS **ATTACKED**, SERGEANT, AND RETRIBUTION MUST BE **SWIFT**!
A BRAZEN ACT, SO UNAVENGED? ZESE TRIBES WILL SEE REBELLION'S INVITATION!
FOR WHAT COULD OUR MEN HOPE IN FAILING LIGHT BUT **DEATH?**

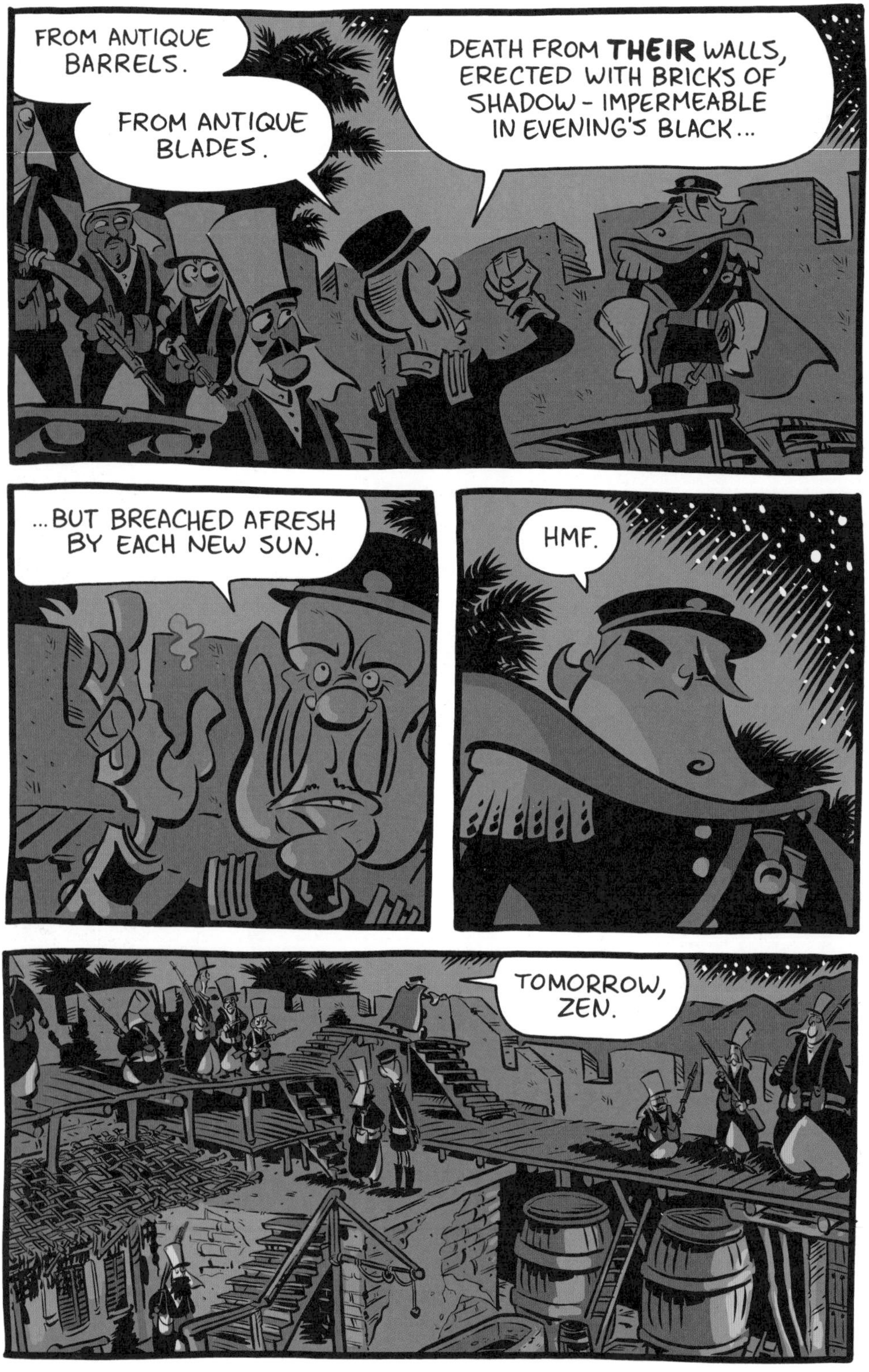
FROM ANTIQUE BARRELS.
FROM ANTIQUE BLADES.
DEATH FROM THEIR WALLS, ERECTED WITH BRICKS OF SHADOW - IMPERMEABLE IN EVENING'S BLACK...
...BUT BREACHED AFRESH BY EACH NEW SUN.
HMF.
TOMORROW, ZEN.

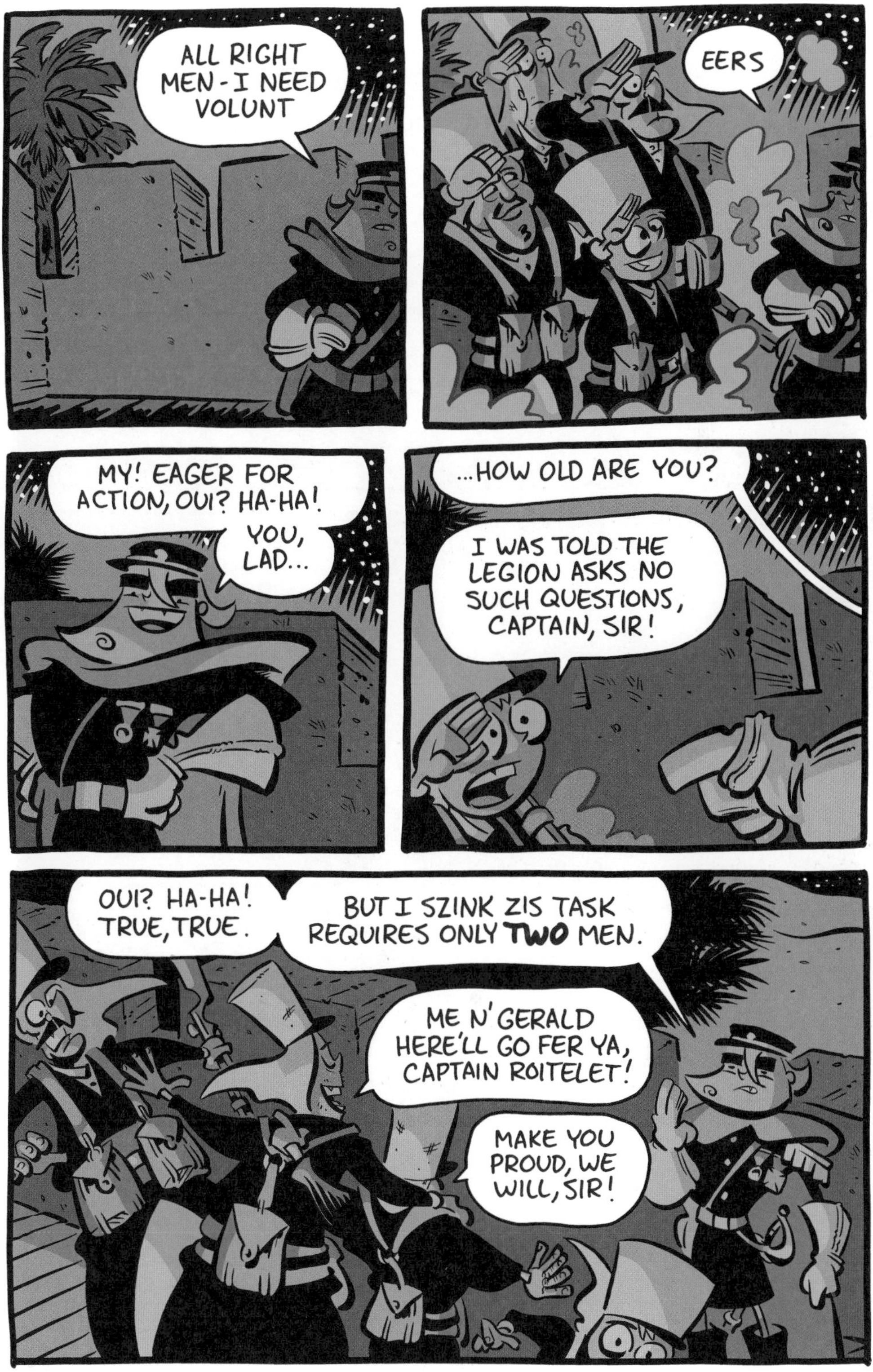
ALL RIGHT MEN - I NEED VOLUNT
EERS
MY! EAGER FOR ACTION, OUI? HA-HA!
YOU, LAD...
...HOW OLD ARE YOU?
I WAS TOLD THE LEGION ASKS NO SUCH QUESTIONS, CAPTAIN, SIR!
OUI? HA-HA! TRUE, TRUE.
BUT I SZINK ZIS TASK REQUIRES ONLY **TWO** MEN.
ME N' GERALD HERE'LL GO FER YA, CAPTAIN ROITELET!
MAKE YOU PROUD, WE WILL, SIR!

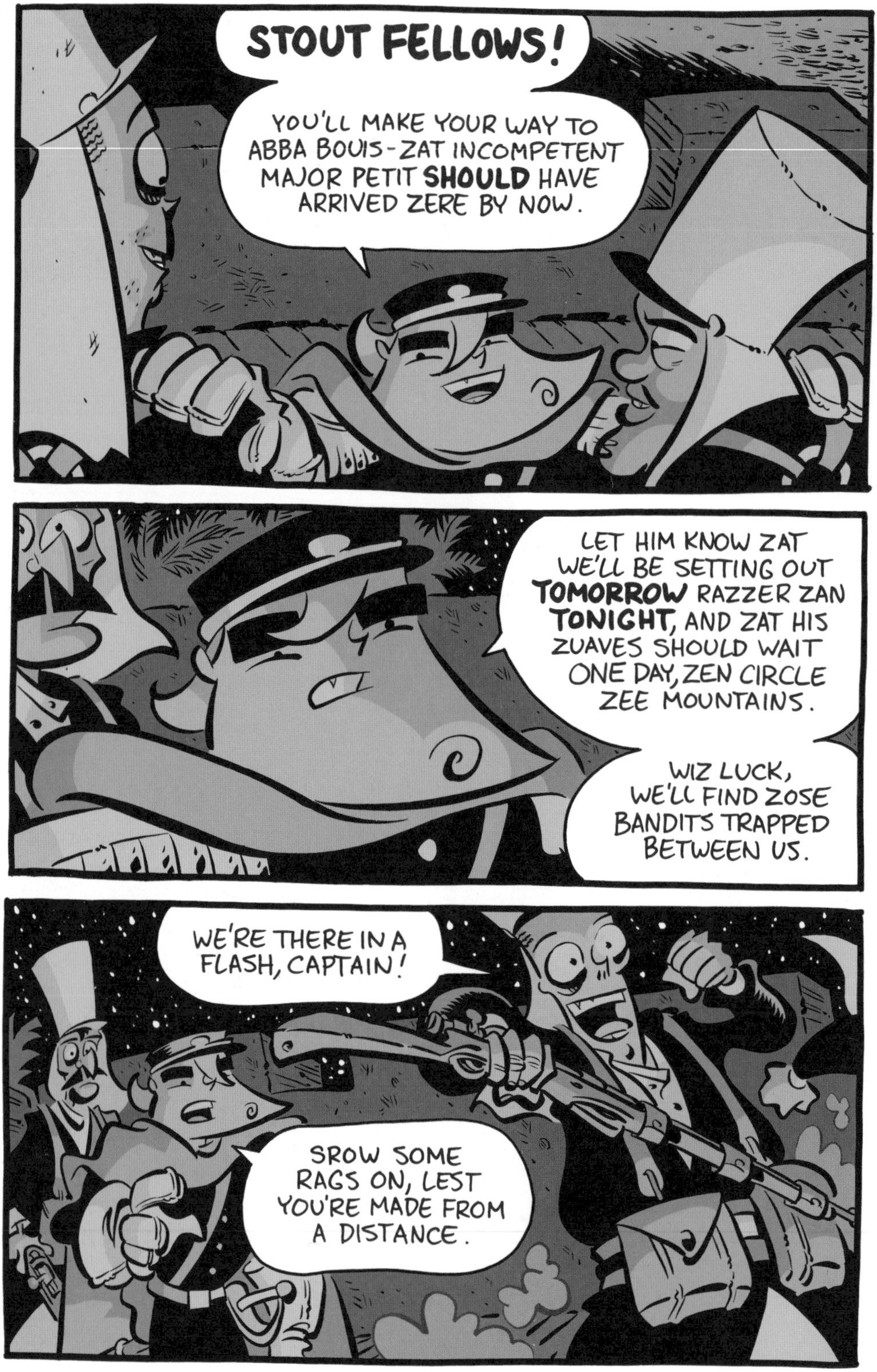
STOUT FELLOWS!
YOU'LL MAKE YOUR WAY TO ABBA BOUIS-ZAT INCOMPETENT MAJOR PETIT **SHOULD** HAVE ARRIVED ZERE BY NOW.
LET HIM KNOW ZAT WE'LL BE SETTING OUT **TOMORROW** RAZZER ZAN **TONIGHT**, AND ZAT HIS ZUAVES SHOULD WAIT ONE DAY, ZEN CIRCLE ZEE MOUNTAINS.
WIZ LUCK, WE'LL FIND ZOSE BANDITS TRAPPED BETWEEN US.
WE'RE THERE IN A FLASH, CAPTAIN!
SROW SOME RAGS ON, LEST YOU'RE MADE FROM A DISTANCE.

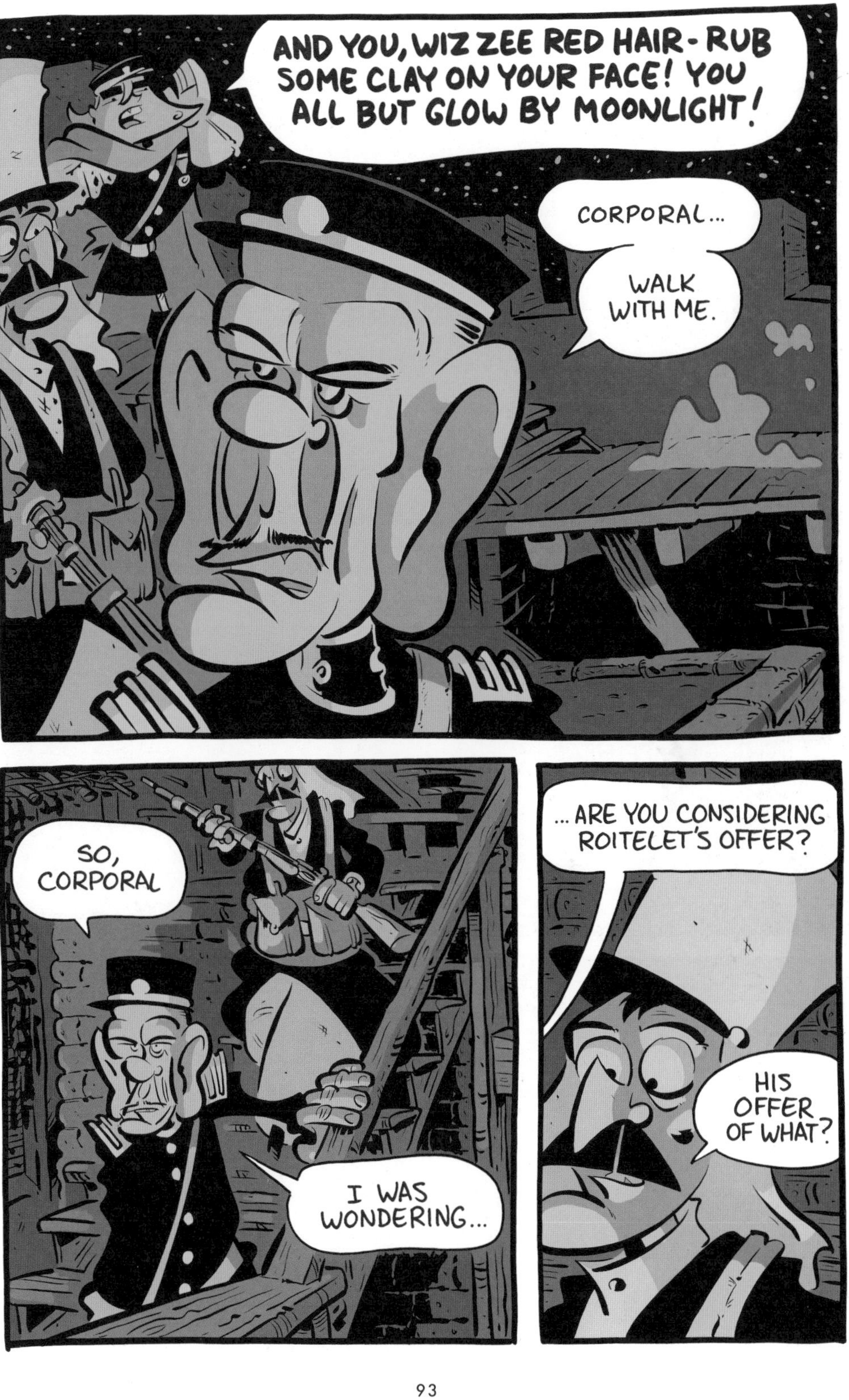
AND YOU, WIZ ZEE RED HAIR- RUB SOME CLAY ON YOUR FACE! YOU ALL BUT GLOW BY MOONLIGHT!
CORPORAL...
WALK WITH ME.
SO, CORPORAL
I WAS WONDERING...
... ARE YOU CONSIDERING ROITELET'S OFFER?
HIS OFFER OF WHAT?

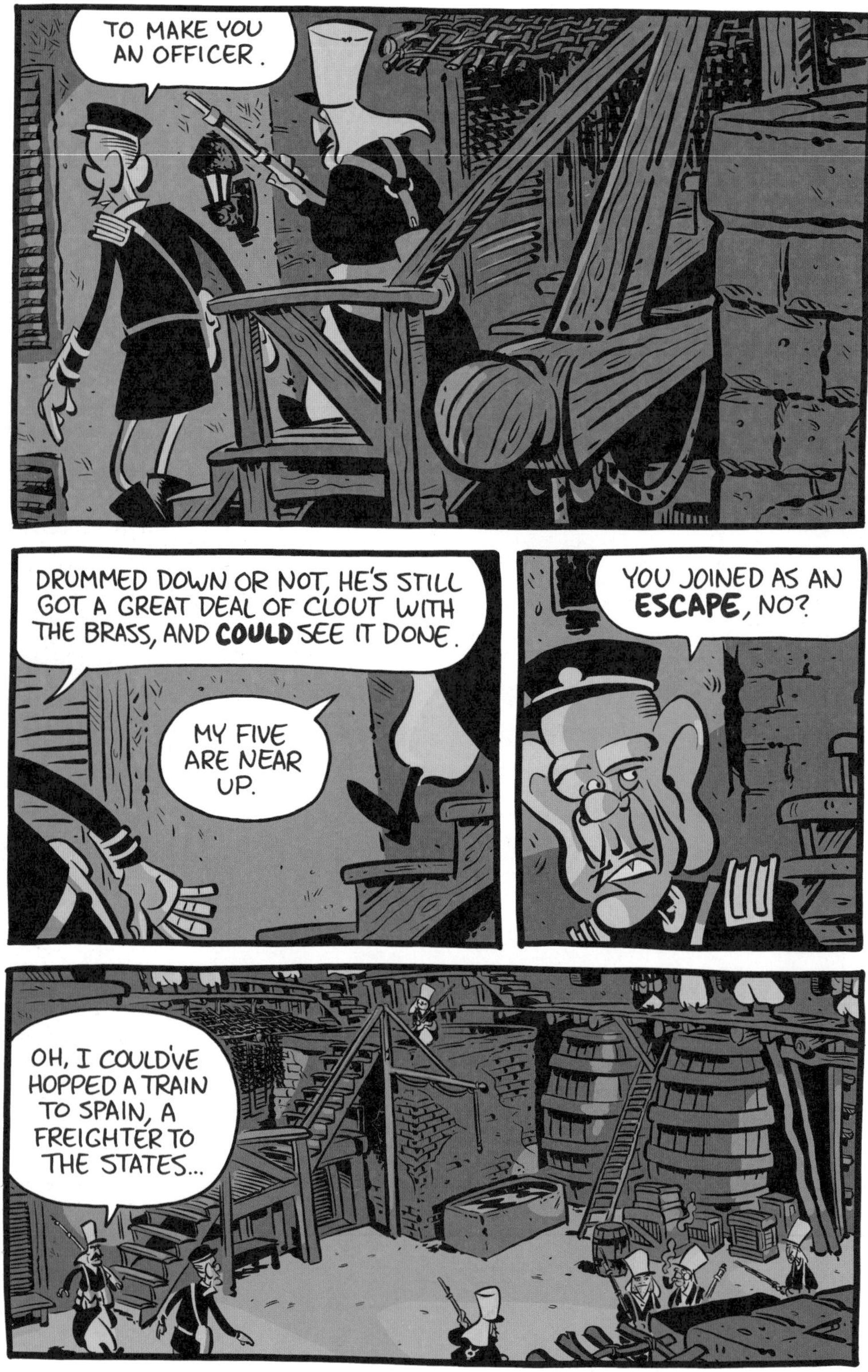
TO MAKE YOU AN OFFICER.
DRUMMED DOWN OR NOT, HE'S STILL GOT A GREAT DEAL OF CLOUT WITH THE BRASS, AND COULD SEE IT DONE.
MY FIVE ARE NEAR UP.
YOU JOINED AS AN ESCAPE, NO?
OH, I COULD'VE HOPPED A TRAIN TO SPAIN, A FREIGHTER TO THE STATES...

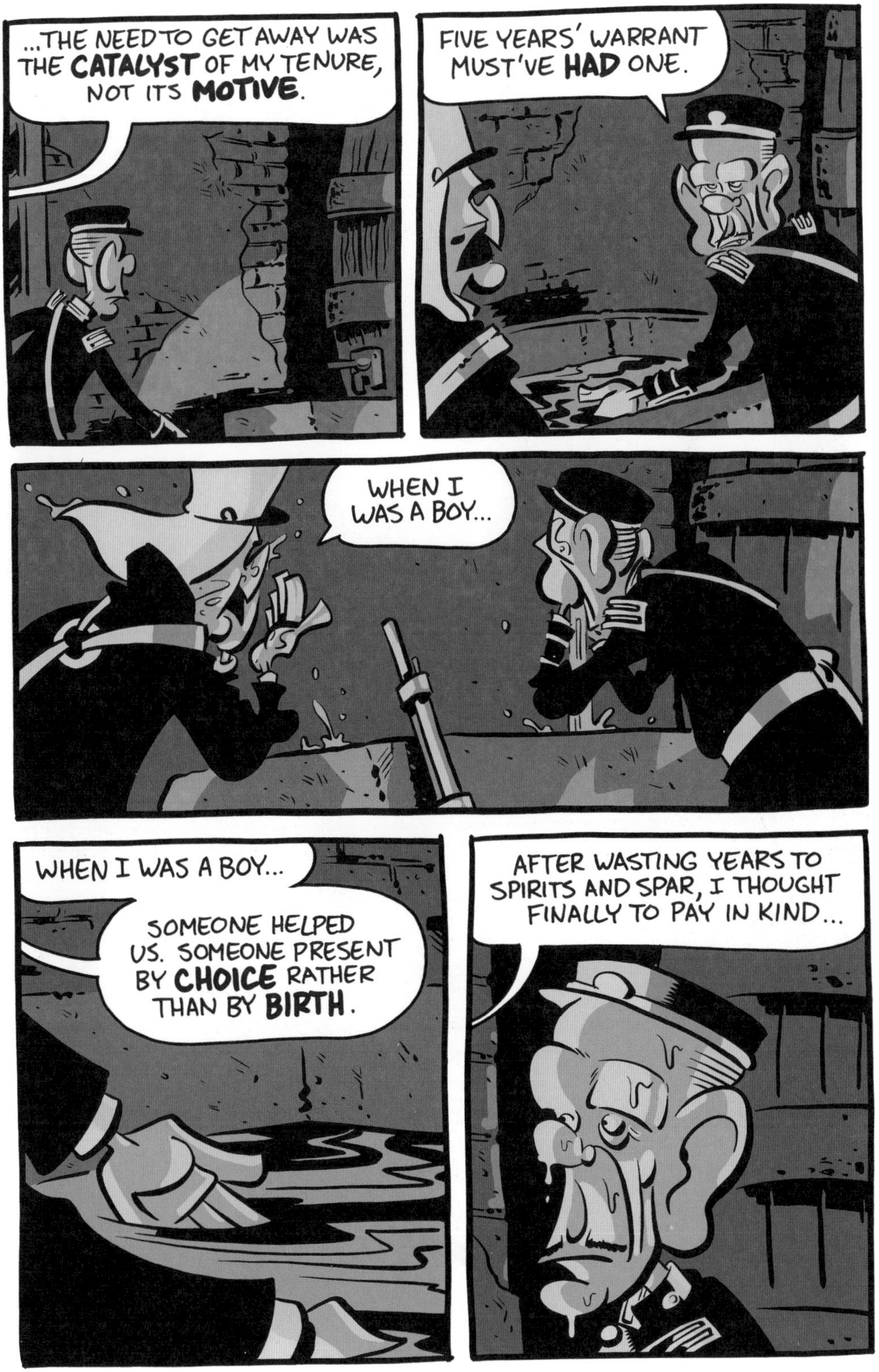
...THE NEED TO GET AWAY WAS THE **CATALYST** OF MY TENURE, NOT ITS **MOTIVE**.
FIVE YEARS' WARRANT MUST'VE **HAD** ONE.
WHEN I WAS A BOY...
WHEN I WAS A BOY...
SOMEONE HELPED US. SOMEONE PRESENT BY **CHOICE** RATHER THAN BY **BIRTH**.
AFTER WASTING YEARS TO SPIRITS AND SPAR, I THOUGHT FINALLY TO PAY IN KIND...

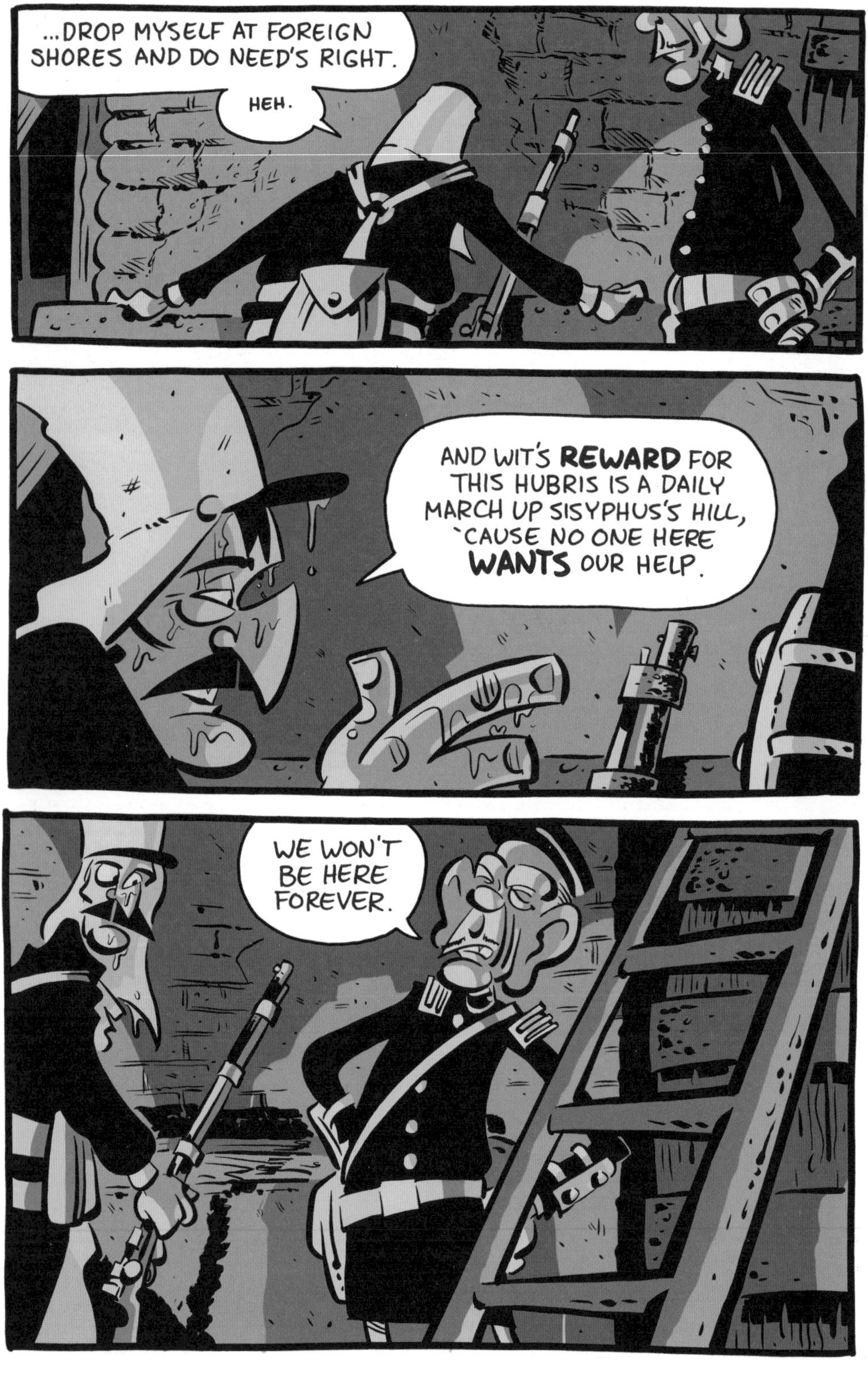
...DROP MYSELF AT FOREIGN SHORES AND DO NEED'S RIGHT.
HEH.
AND WIT'S **REWARD** FOR THIS HUBRIS IS A DAILY MARCH UP SISYPHUS'S HILL, 'CAUSE NO ONE HERE **WANTS** OUR HELP.
WE WON'T BE HERE FOREVER.

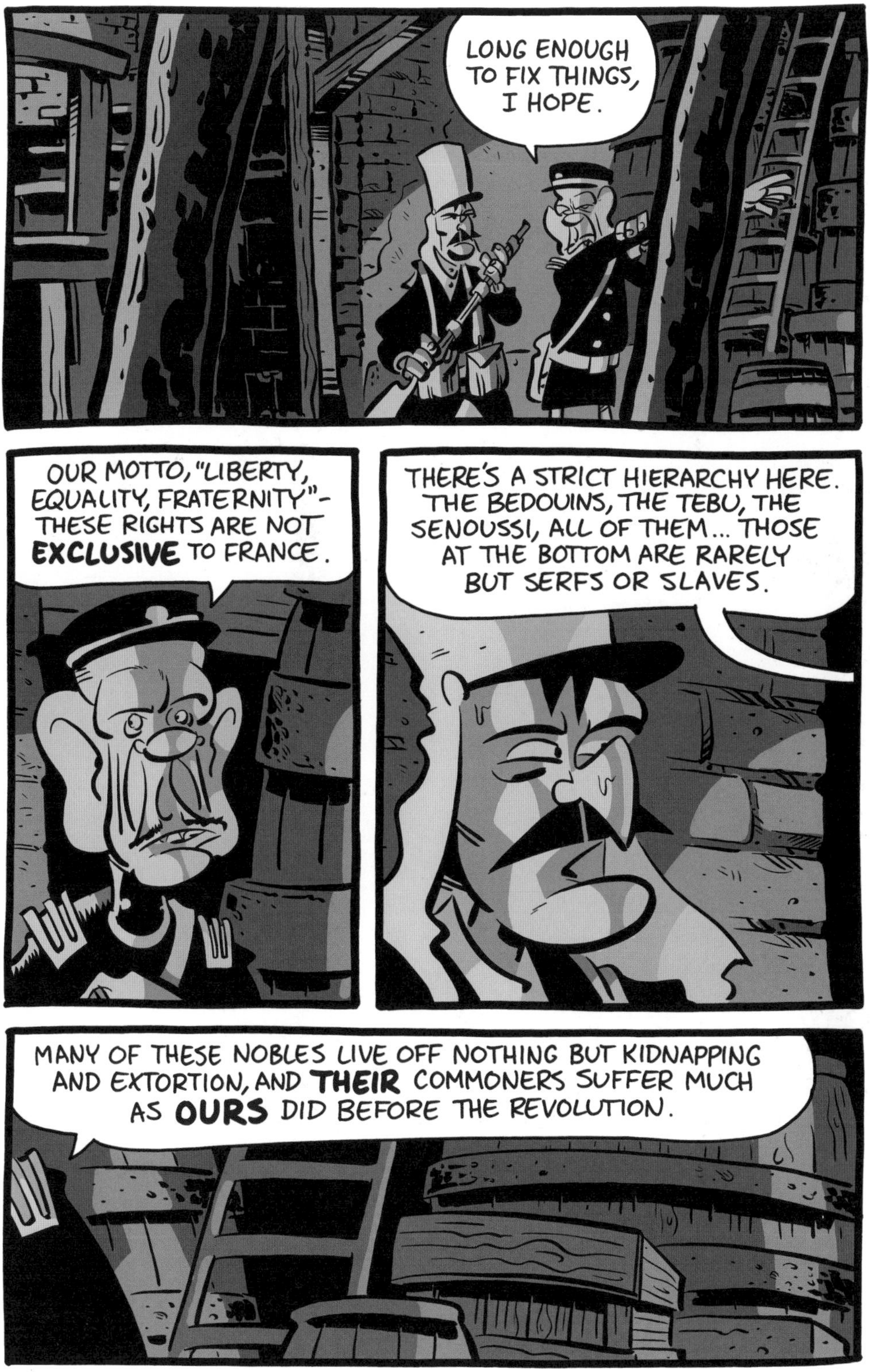
LONG ENOUGH TO FIX THINGS, I HOPE.
OUR MOTTO, "LIBERTY, EQUALITY, FRATERNITY"- THESE RIGHTS ARE NOT **EXCLUSIVE** TO FRANCE.
THERE'S A STRICT HIERARCHY HERE. THE BEDOUINS, THE TEBU, THE SENOUSSI, ALL OF THEM... THOSE AT THE BOTTOM ARE RARELY BUT SERFS OR SLAVES.
MANY OF THESE NOBLES LIVE OFF NOTHING BUT KIDNAPPING AND EXTORTION, AND **THEIR** COMMONERS SUFFER MUCH AS **OURS** DID BEFORE THE REVOLUTION.

98

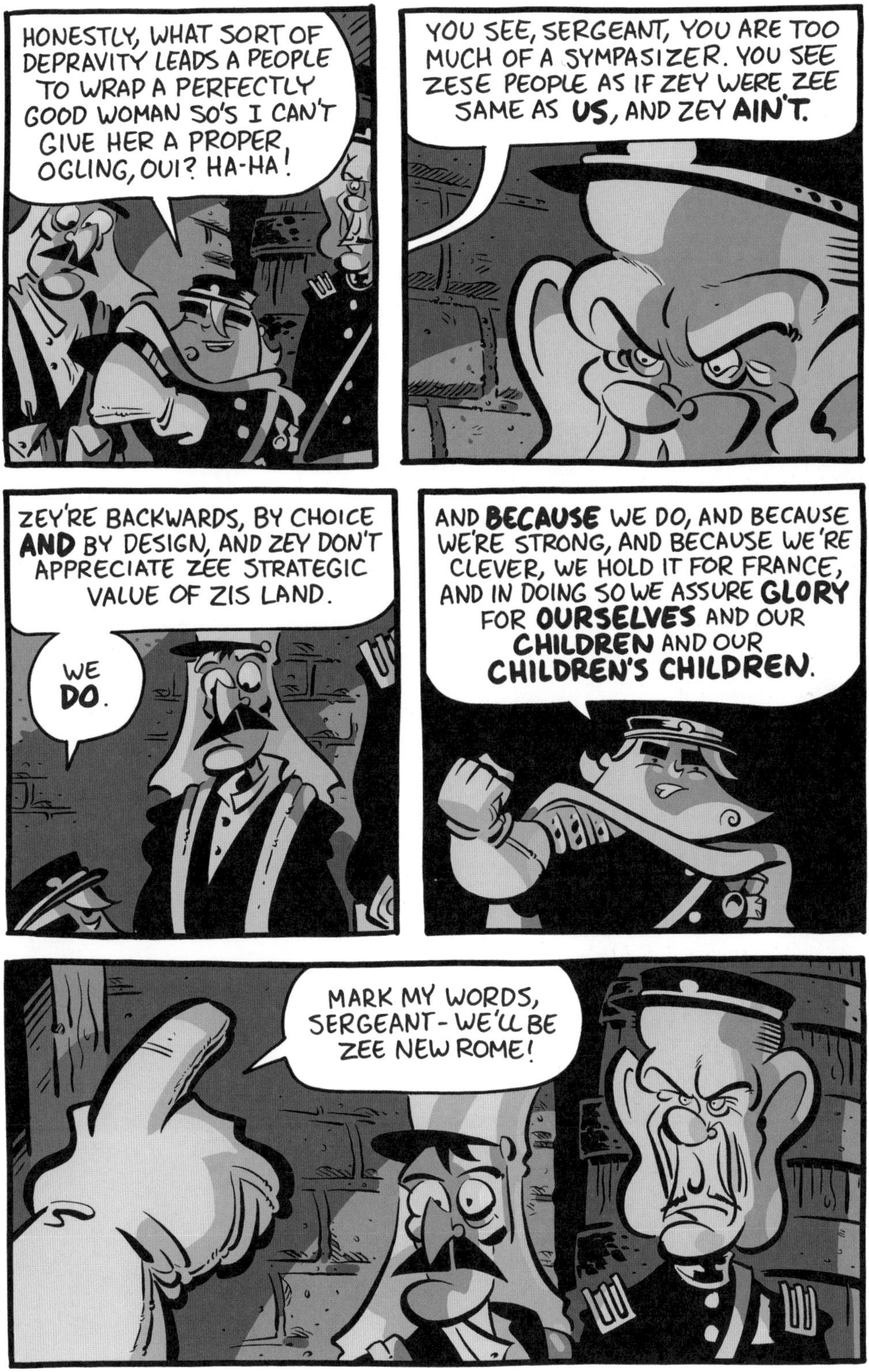
HONESTLY, WHAT SORT OF DEPRAVITY LEADS A PEOPLE TO WRAP A PERFECTLY GOOD WOMAN SO'S I CAN'T GIVE HER A PROPER OGLING, OUI? HA-HA!
YOU SEE, SERGEANT, YOU ARE TOO MUCH OF A SYMPASIZER. YOU SEE ZESE PEOPLE AS IF ZEY WERE ZEE SAME AS **US**, AND ZEY **AIN'T.**
ZEY'RE BACKWARDS, BY CHOICE **AND** BY DESIGN, AND ZEY DON'T APPRECIATE ZEE STRATEGIC VALUE OF ZIS LAND.
WE **DO**.
AND **BECAUSE** WE DO, AND BECAUSE WE'RE STRONG, AND BECAUSE WE'RE CLEVER, WE HOLD IT FOR FRANCE, AND IN DOING SO WE ASSURE **GLORY** FOR **OURSELVES** AND OUR **CHILDREN** AND OUR **CHILDREN'S CHILDREN**.
MARK MY WORDS, SERGEANT- WE'LL BE ZEE NEW ROME!

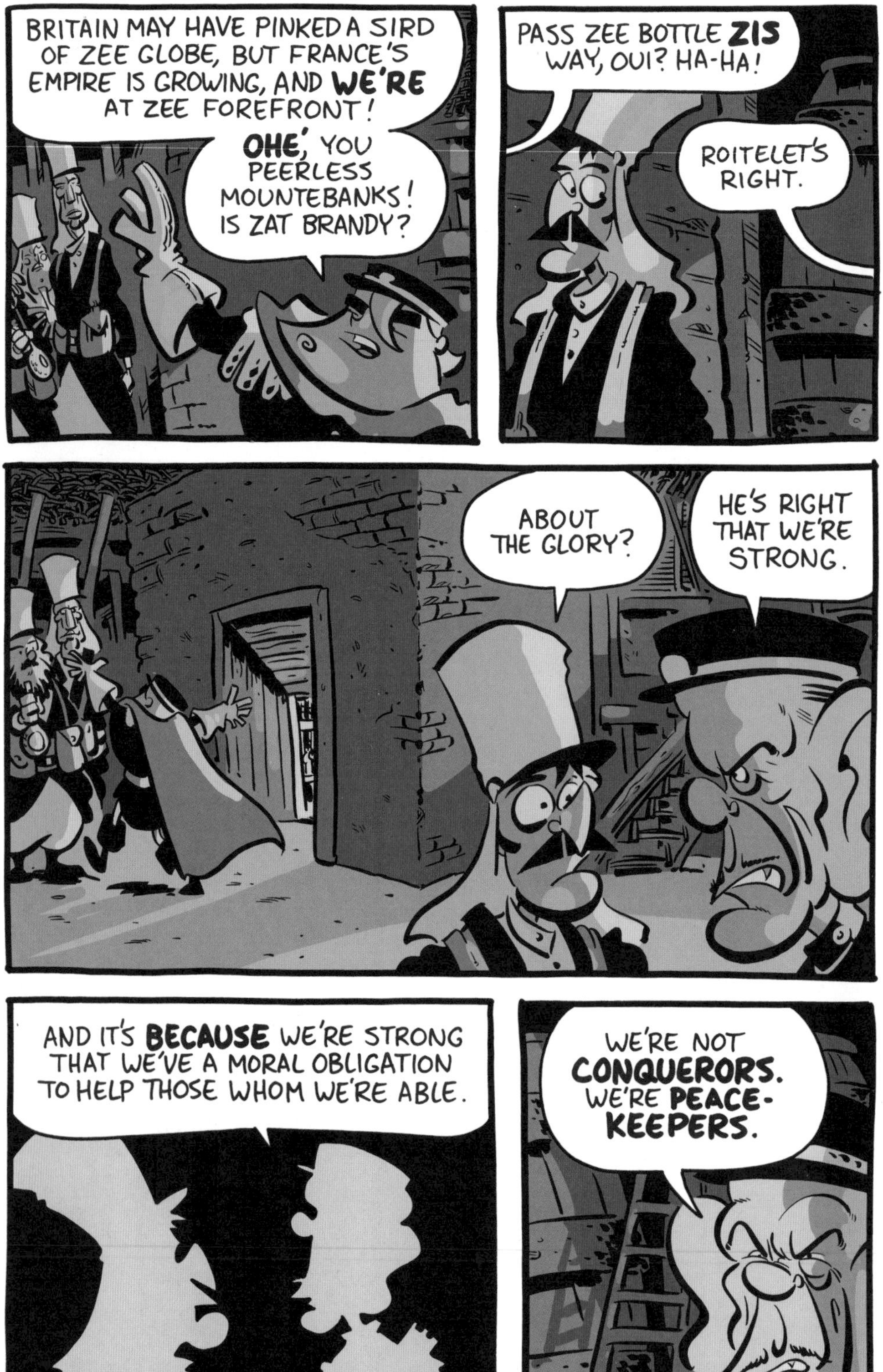
BRITAIN MAY HAVE PINKED A SIRD OF ZEE GLOBE, BUT FRANCE'S EMPIRE IS GROWING, AND **WE'RE** AT ZEE FOREFRONT!
OHÉ, YOU PEERLESS MOUNTEBANKS! IS ZAT BRANDY?
PASS ZEE BOTTLE **ZIS** WAY, OUI? HA-HA!
ROITELET'S RIGHT.
ABOUT THE GLORY?
HE'S RIGHT THAT WE'RE STRONG.
AND IT'S **BECAUSE** WE'RE STRONG THAT WE'VE A MORAL OBLIGATION TO HELP THOSE WHOM WE'RE ABLE.
WE'RE NOT **CONQUERORS**. WE'RE **PEACE-KEEPERS**.

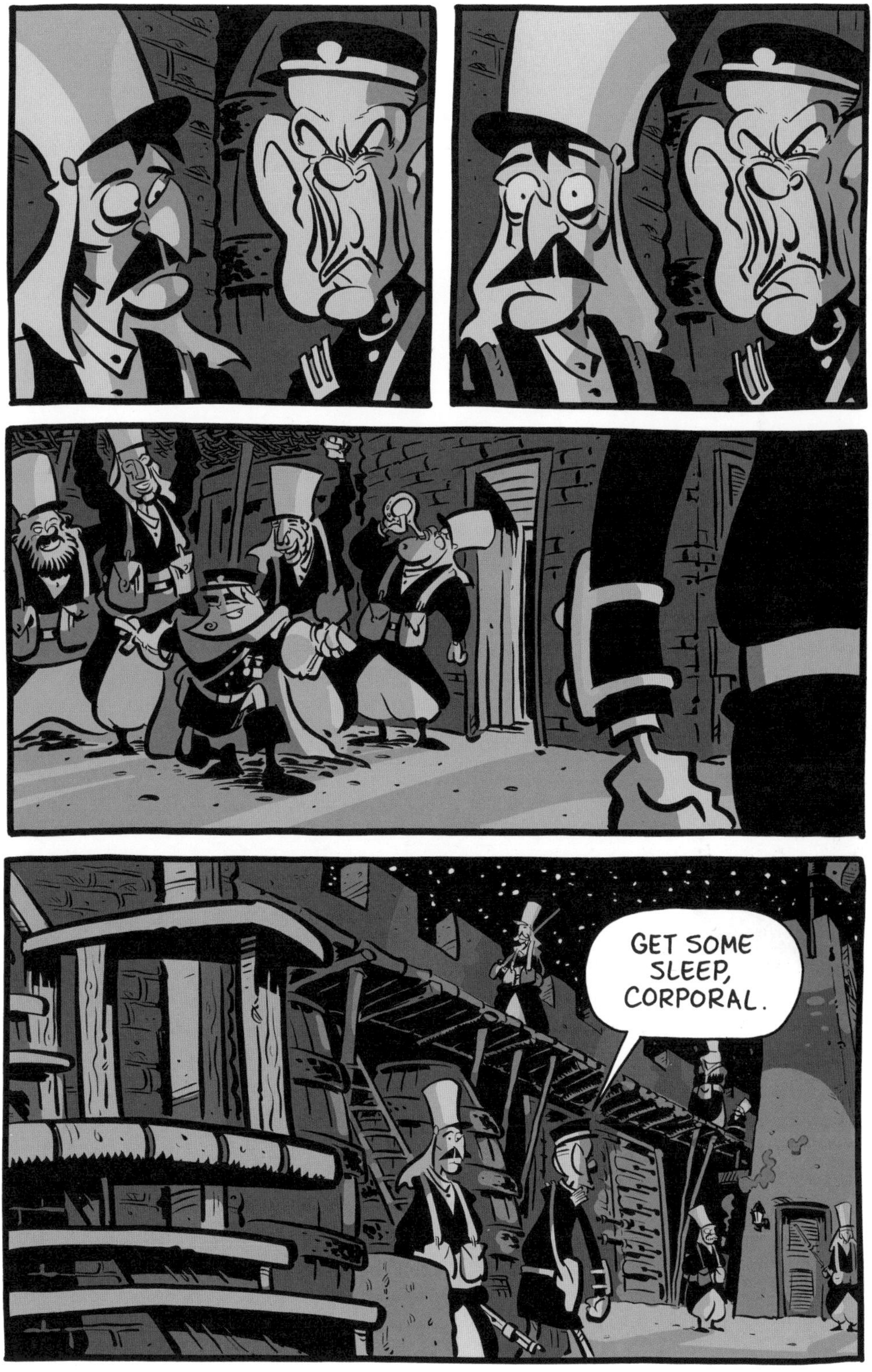
GET SOME SLEEP, CORPORAL.

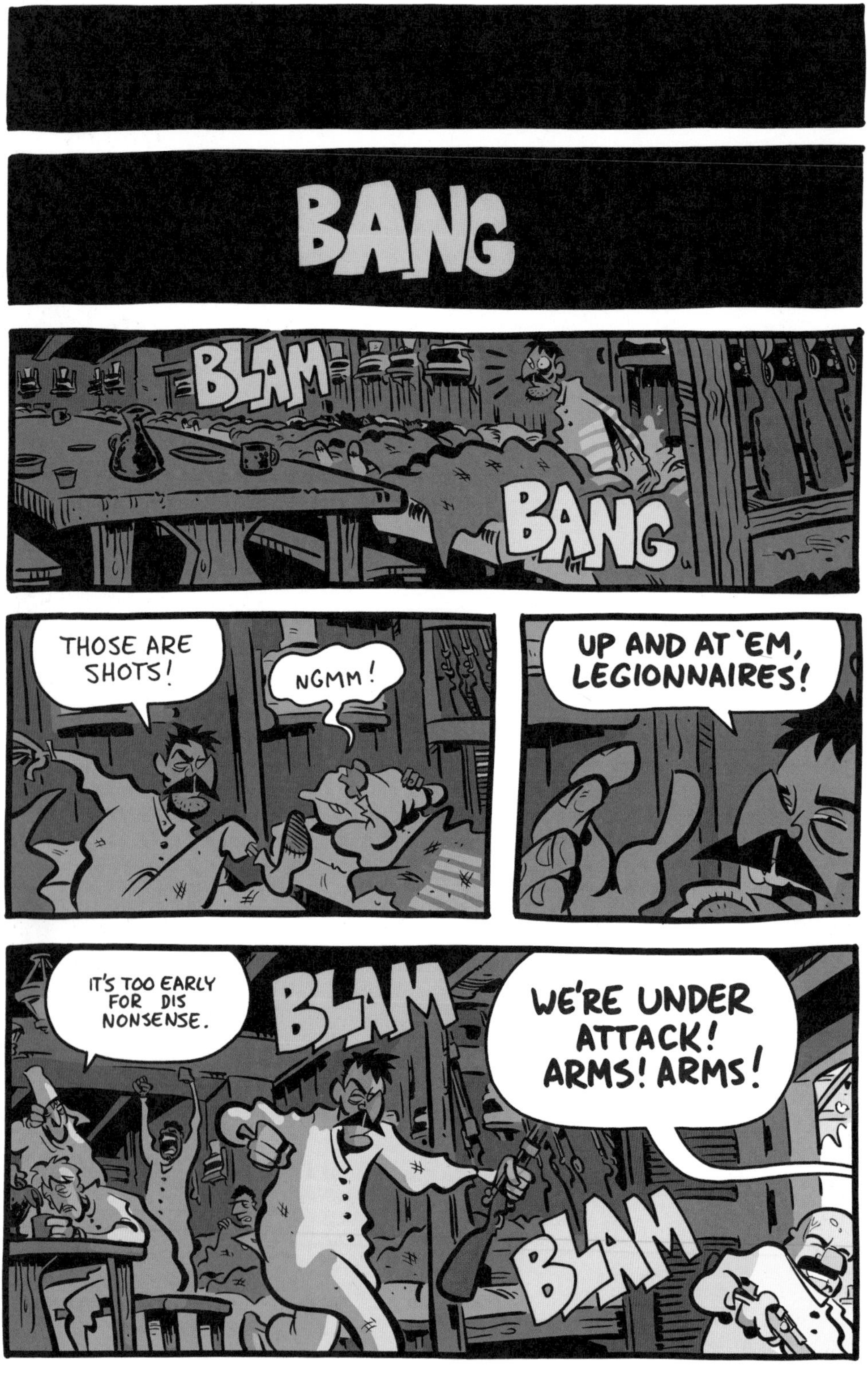
BANG
BLAM
BANG
THOSE ARE SHOTS!
NGMM!
UP AND AT 'EM, LEGIONNAIRES!
IT'S TOO EARLY FOR DIS NONSENSE.
BLAM
WE'RE UNDER ATTACK! ARMS! ARMS!
BLAM

DON'T BE DAUNTED BY THEIR NUMBERS — PROPERLY DEFENDED, THESE WALLS ARE NIGH IMPREGNABLE.

THE **GATE** IS THE CLOSEST THING WE HAVE TO A WEAK POINT, SO AS LONG AS WE KEEP THEM BACK, THEY'VE NO CHANCE OF REACHING US.

NOW **ZIS** IS WHAT YOU MEN HAVE BEEN MISSING!

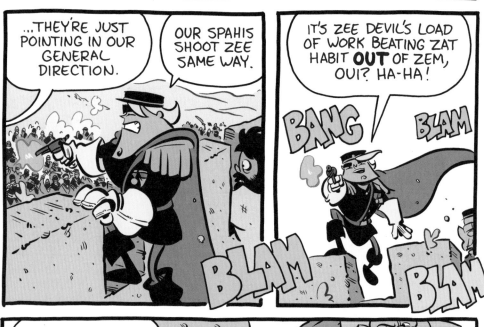

111

...I'LL NOT STAND FOR THIS ANYMORE!

STAND FOR **WHAT**, CORPORAL?

THESE INSULTS TO OUR COMMANDER, BOTH **IMPLIED** AND SPOKEN **OUTRIGHT!**

I, WITH EVERY MAN IN THIS UNIT, AM **PROUD** TO FIGHT UNDER ROITELET'S COMMAND! HAVE YOU NEVER HEARD HIS REPUTATION? HAVE YOU EVER SEEN A MAN SO BRAVE?

I'VE NEVER SEEN A MAN SO **RECKLESS.** AND HIS JEWELED REPUTATION?

"THE ONLY SURVIVOR OF **THIS** BATTLE, THE ONLY SURVIVOR OF **THAT** BATTLE"...

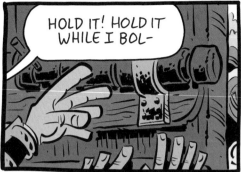

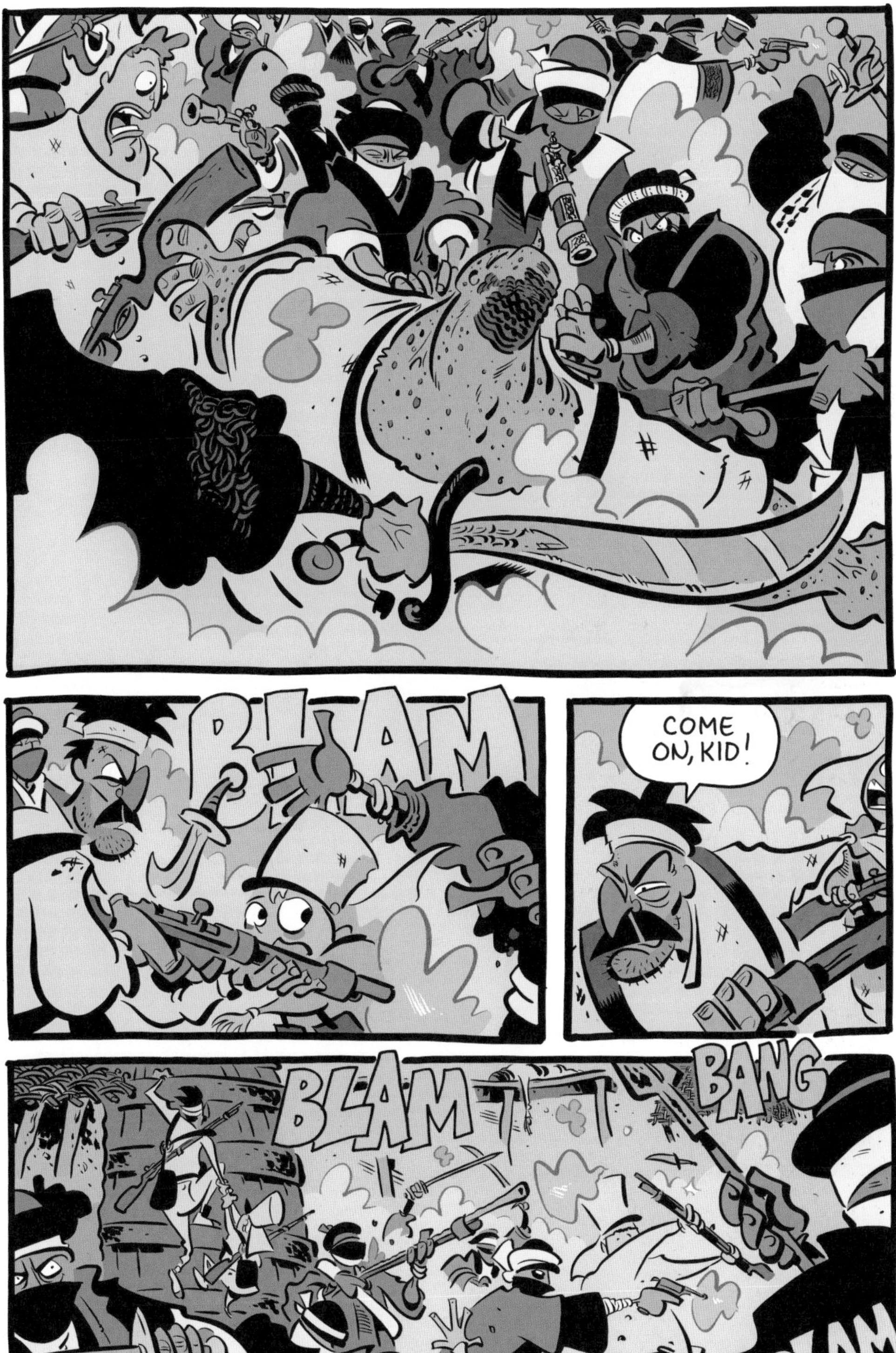
BLAM
COME ON, KID!
BLAM
BANG
BLAM

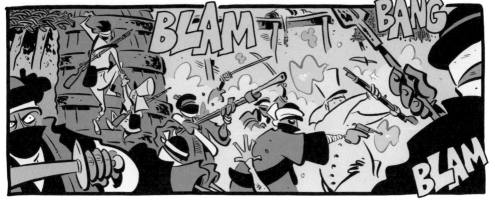

120

122

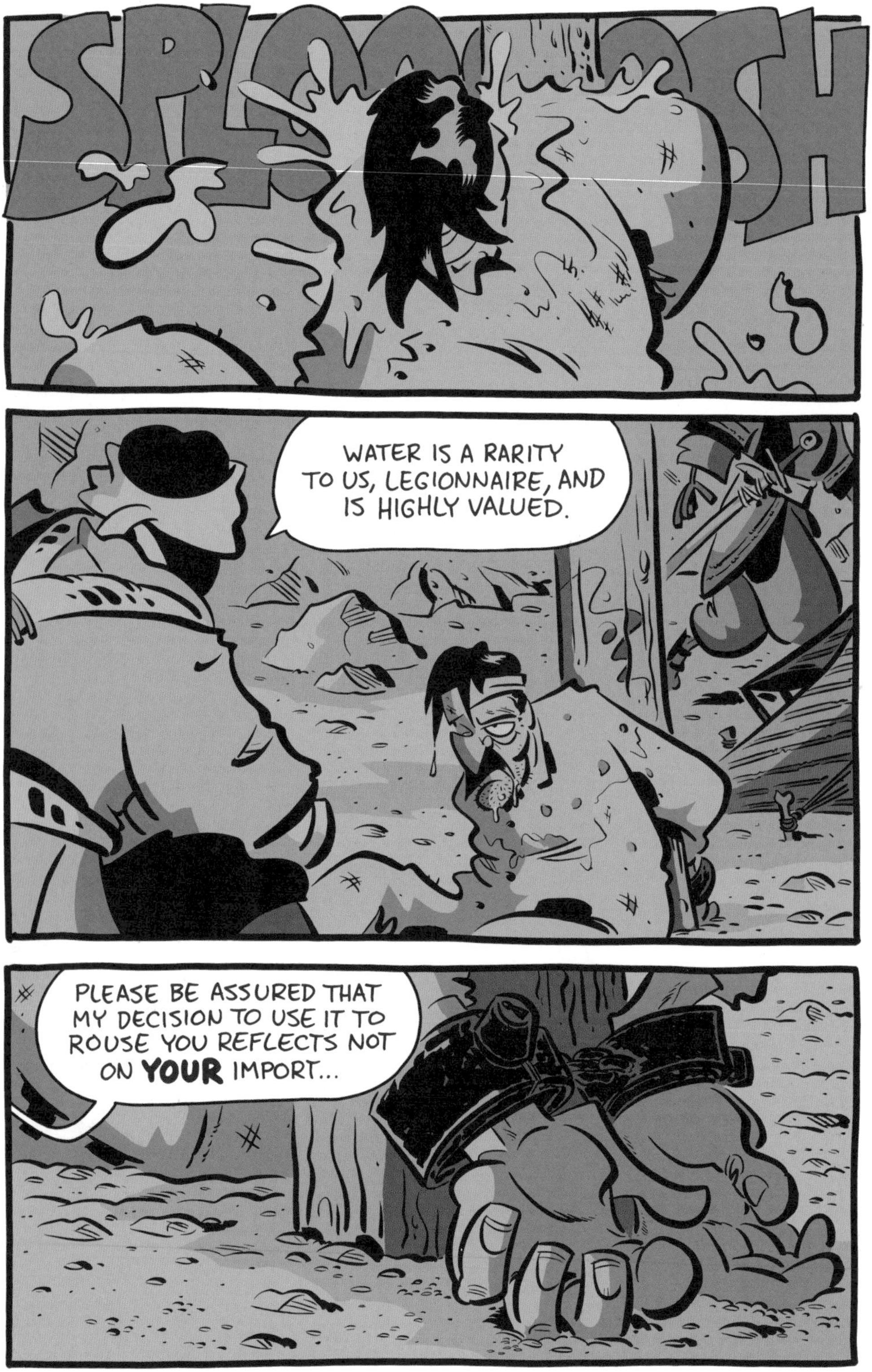
SPLOOOOOSH
WATER IS A RARITY TO US, LEGIONNAIRE, AND IS HIGHLY VALUED.
PLEASE BE ASSURED THAT MY DECISION TO USE IT TO ROUSE YOU REFLECTS NOT ON **YOUR** IMPORT...

129

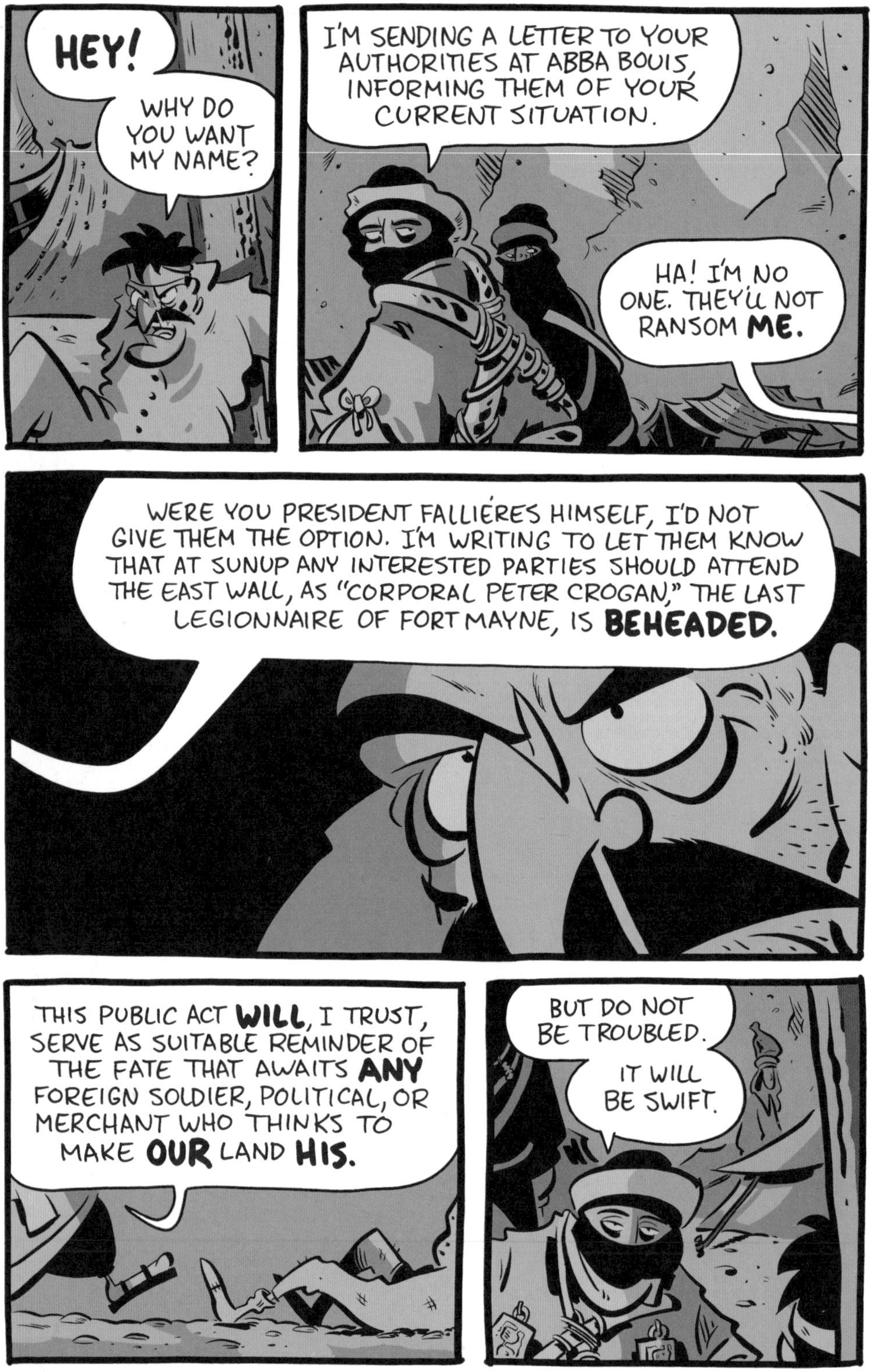
HEY!
WHY DO YOU WANT MY NAME?
I'M SENDING A LETTER TO YOUR AUTHORITIES AT ABBA BOUIS, INFORMING THEM OF YOUR CURRENT SITUATION.
HA! I'M NO ONE. THEY'LL NOT RANSOM ME.
WERE YOU PRESIDENT FALLIÉRES HIMSELF, I'D NOT GIVE THEM THE OPTION. I'M WRITING TO LET THEM KNOW THAT AT SUNUP ANY INTERESTED PARTIES SHOULD ATTEND THE EAST WALL, AS "CORPORAL PETER CROGAN," THE LAST LEGIONNAIRE OF FORT MAYNE, IS BEHEADED.
THIS PUBLIC ACT WILL, I TRUST, SERVE AS SUITABLE REMINDER OF THE FATE THAT AWAITS ANY FOREIGN SOLDIER, POLITICAL, OR MERCHANT WHO THINKS TO MAKE OUR LAND HIS.
BUT DO NOT BE TROUBLED.
IT WILL BE SWIFT.

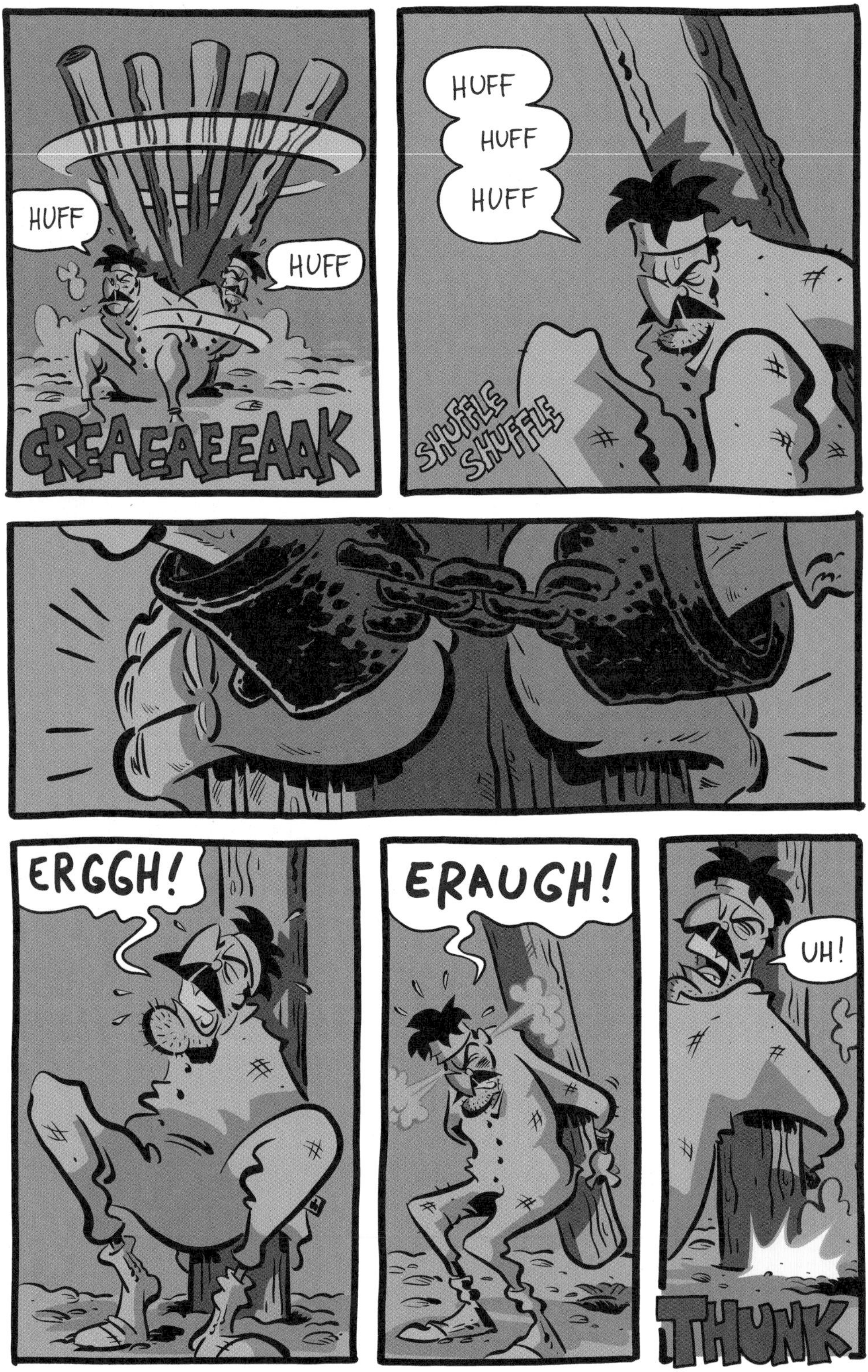
HUFF
HUFF
CREAEAEEAAK
HUFF
HUFF
HUFF
SHUFFLE SHUFFLE
ERGGH!
ERAUGH!
UH!
THUNK

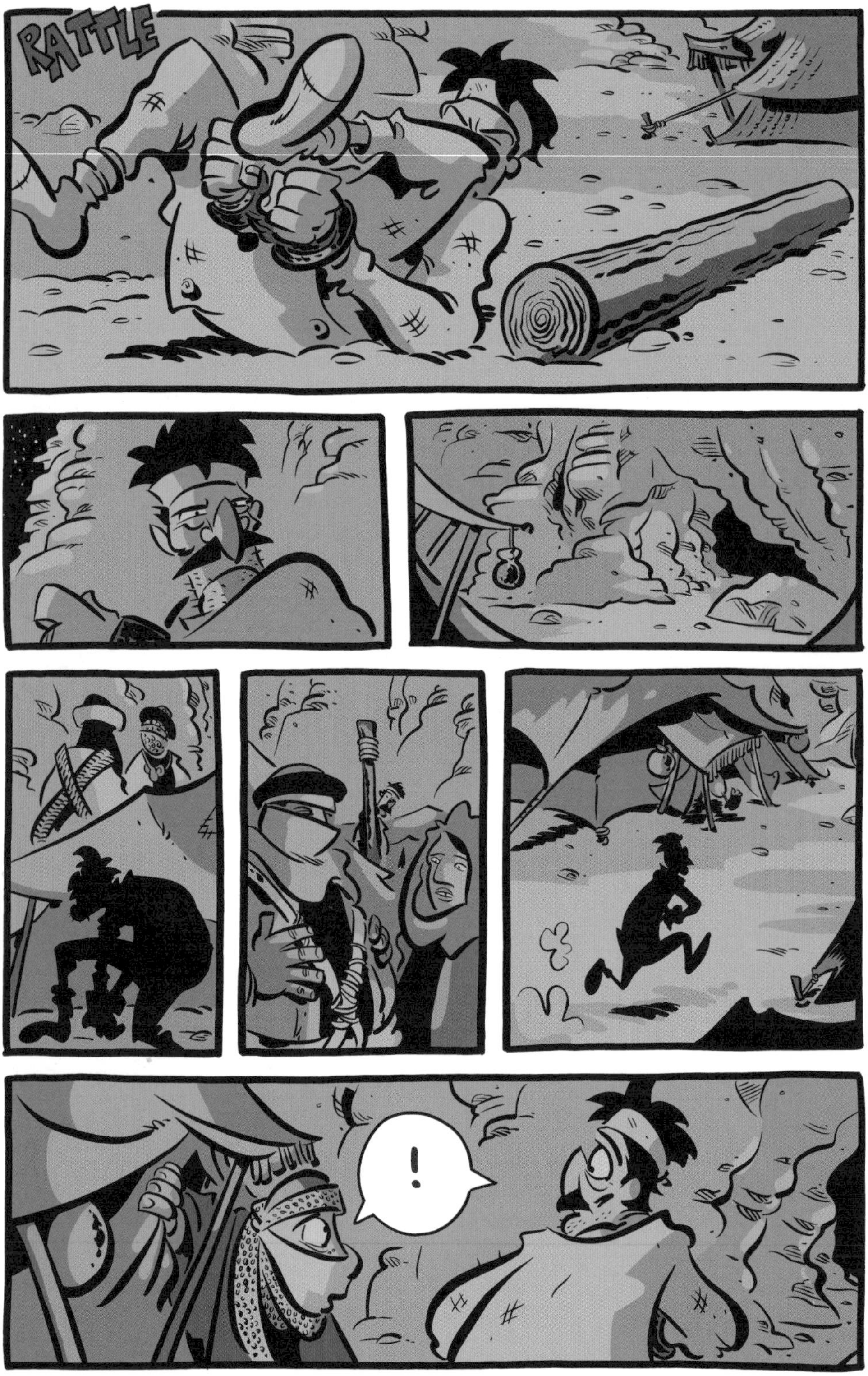
RATTLE
!

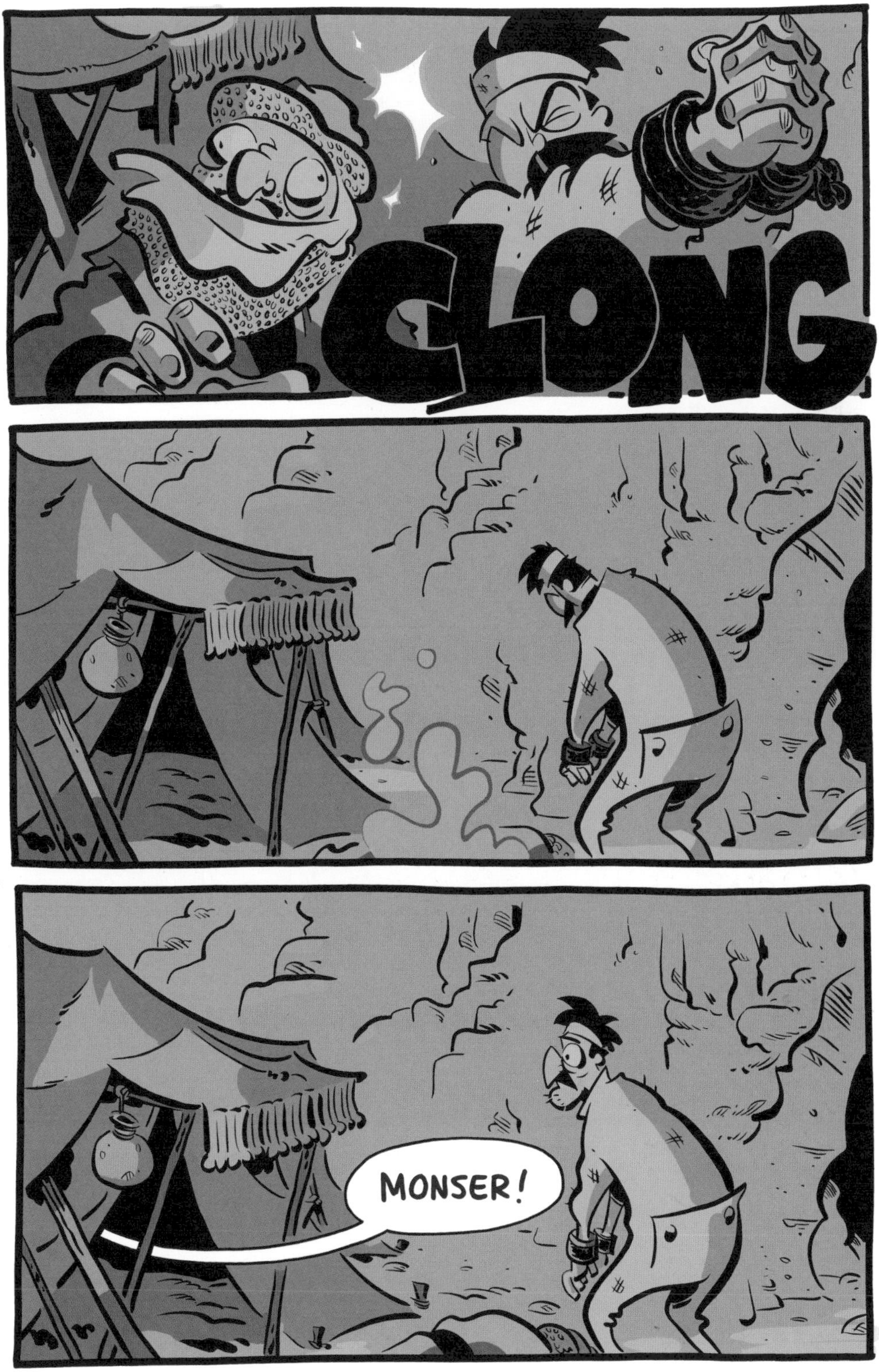
CLONG
MONSER!

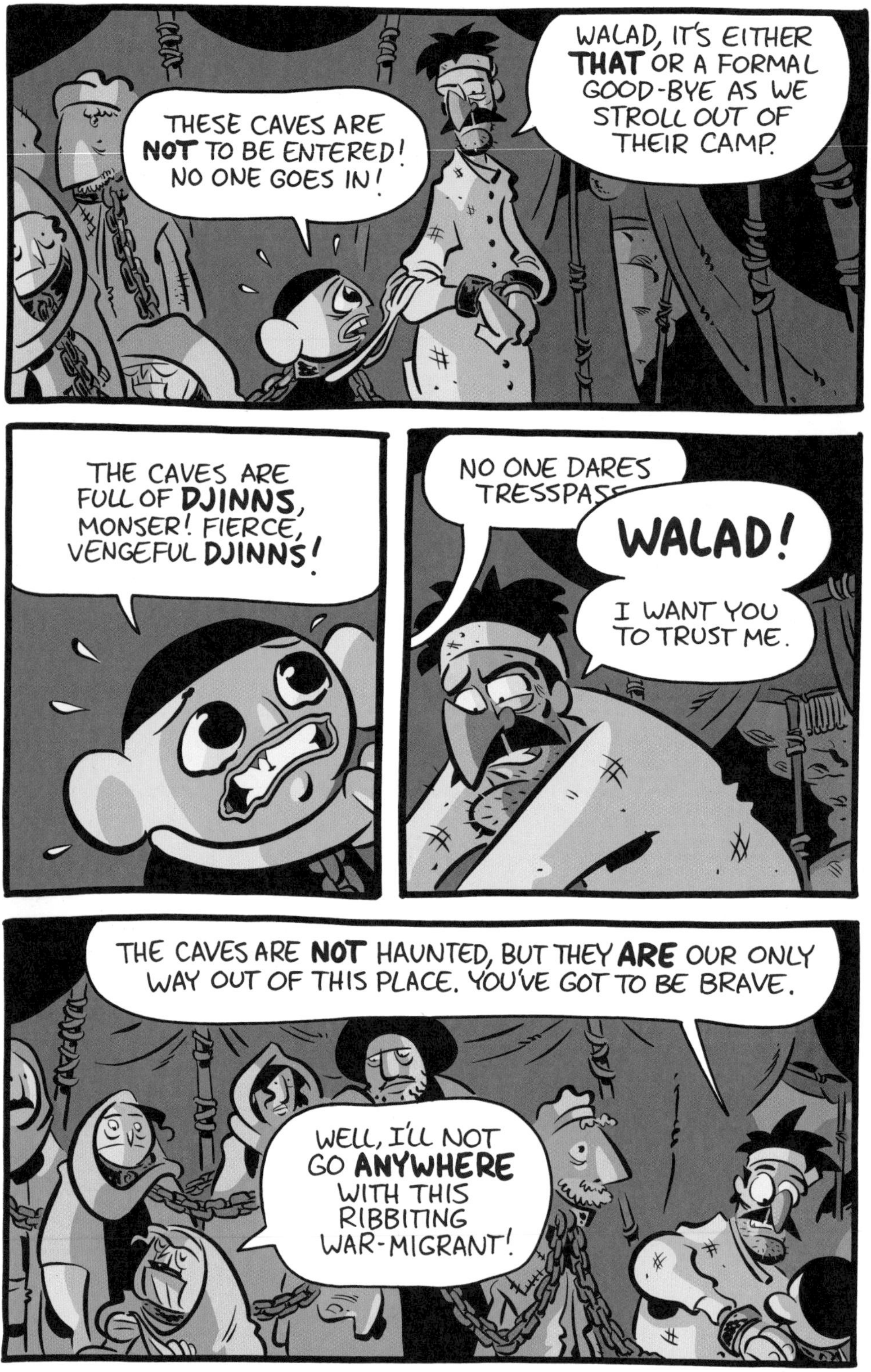
THESE CAVES ARE NOT TO BE ENTERED! NO ONE GOES IN!
WALAD, IT'S EITHER THAT OR A FORMAL GOOD-BYE AS WE STROLL OUT OF THEIR CAMP.
THE CAVES ARE FULL OF DJINNS, MONSER! FIERCE, VENGEFUL DJINNS!
NO ONE DARES TRESSPASS
WALAD!
I WANT YOU TO TRUST ME.
THE CAVES ARE NOT HAUNTED, BUT THEY ARE OUR ONLY WAY OUT OF THIS PLACE. YOU'VE GOT TO BE BRAVE.
WELL, I'LL NOT GO ANYWHERE WITH THIS RIBBITING WAR-MIGRANT!

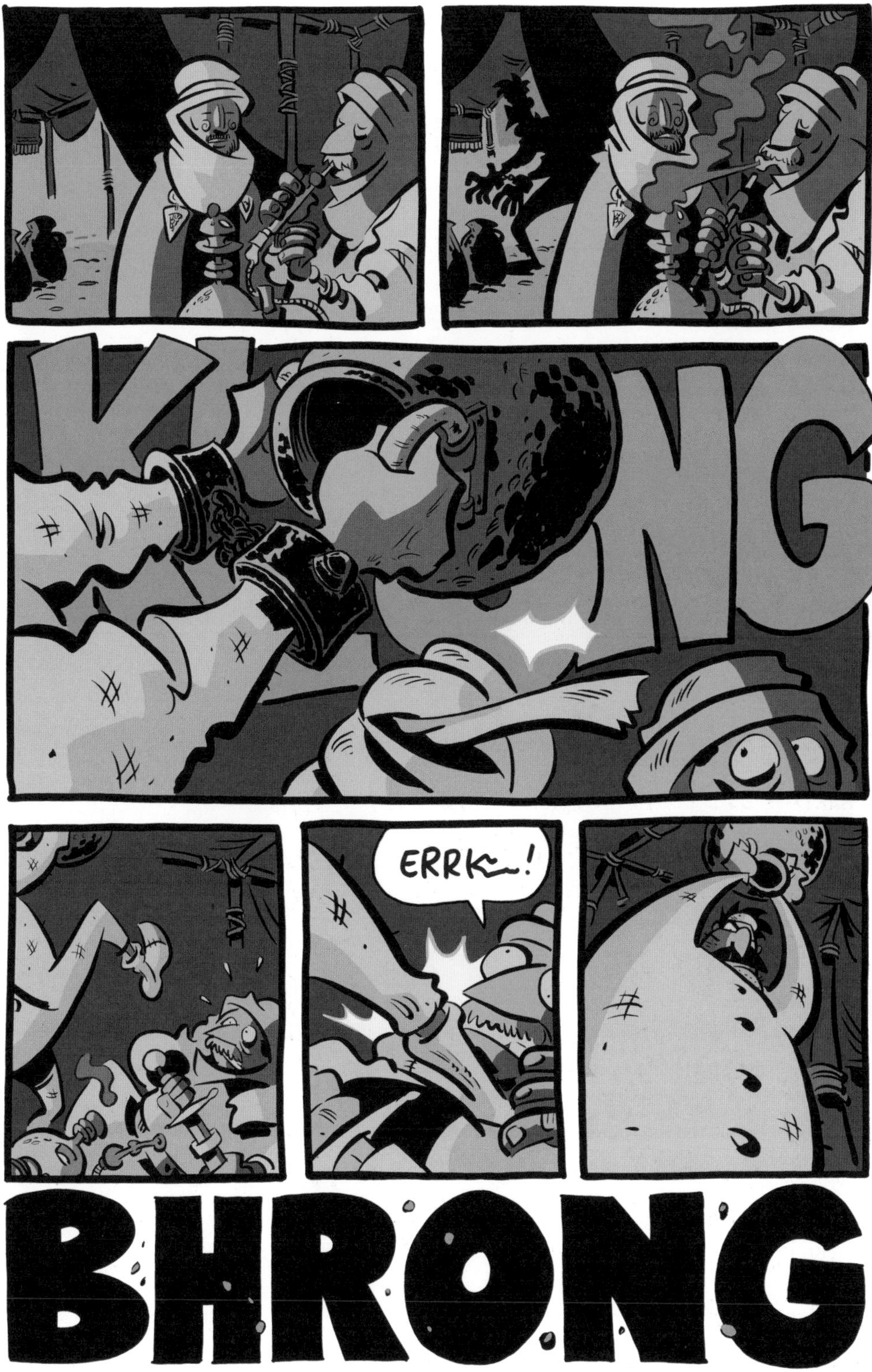
ERRK—!
BHRONG

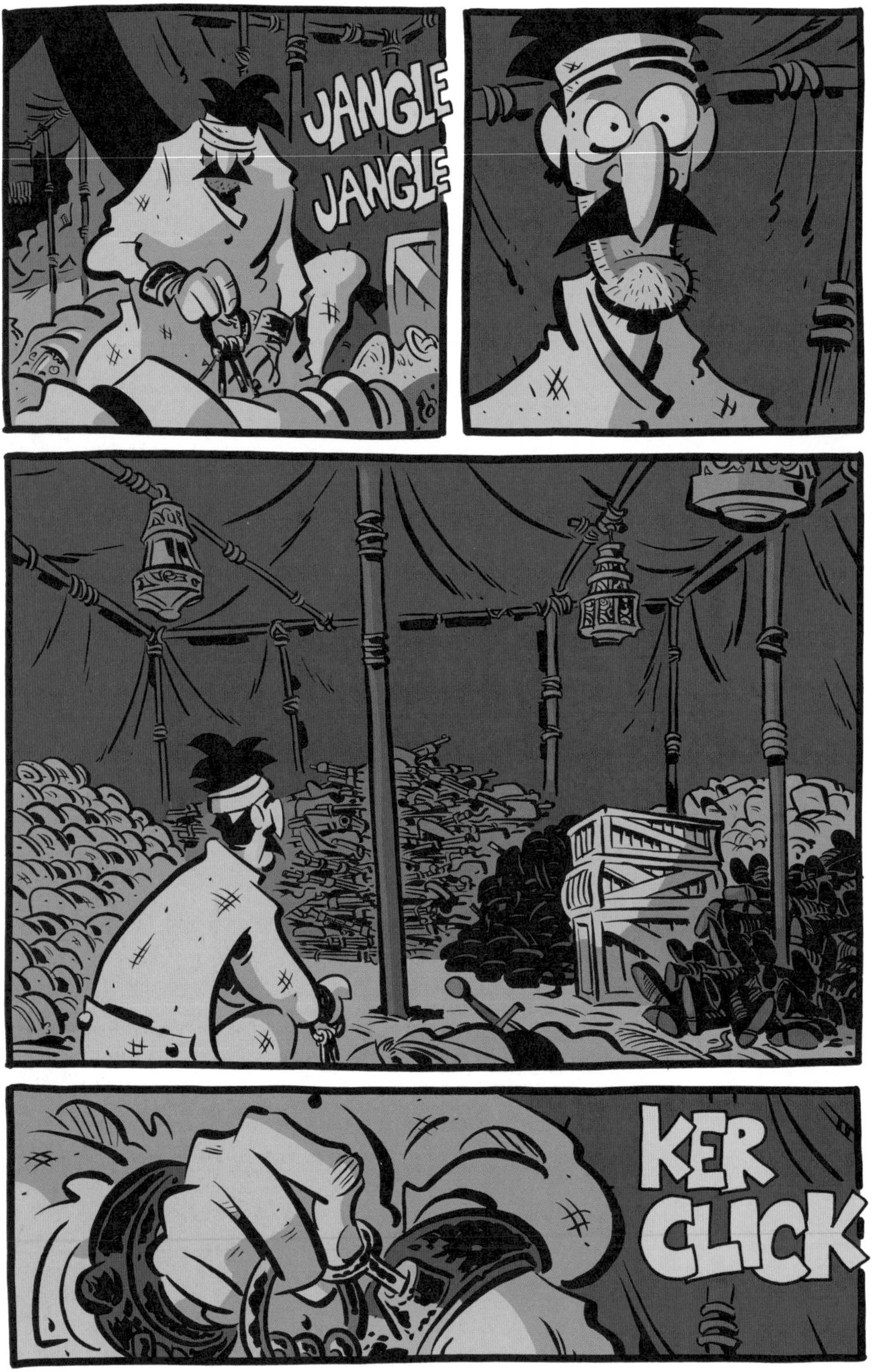
JANGLE
JANGLE
KER
CLICK

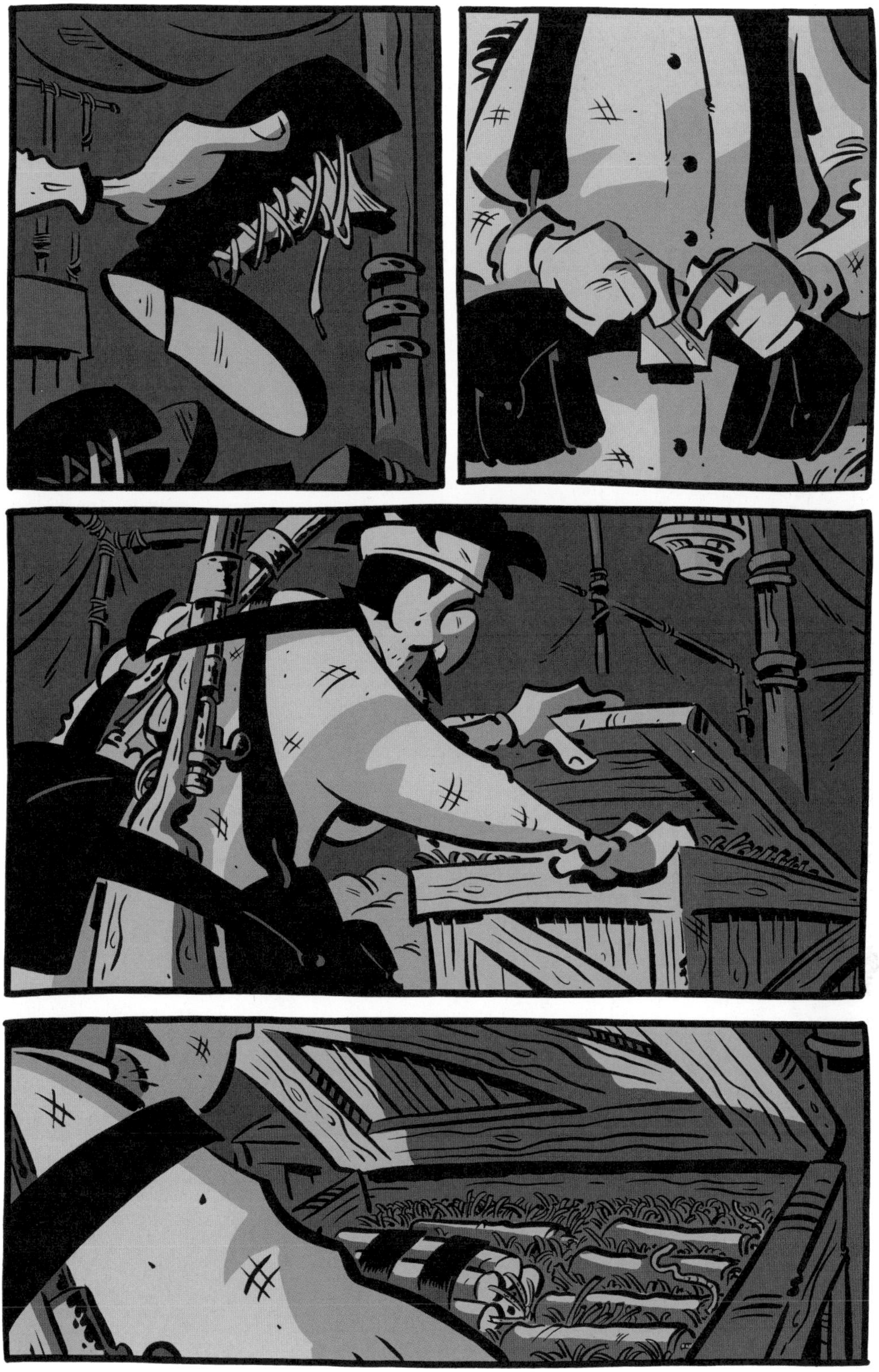

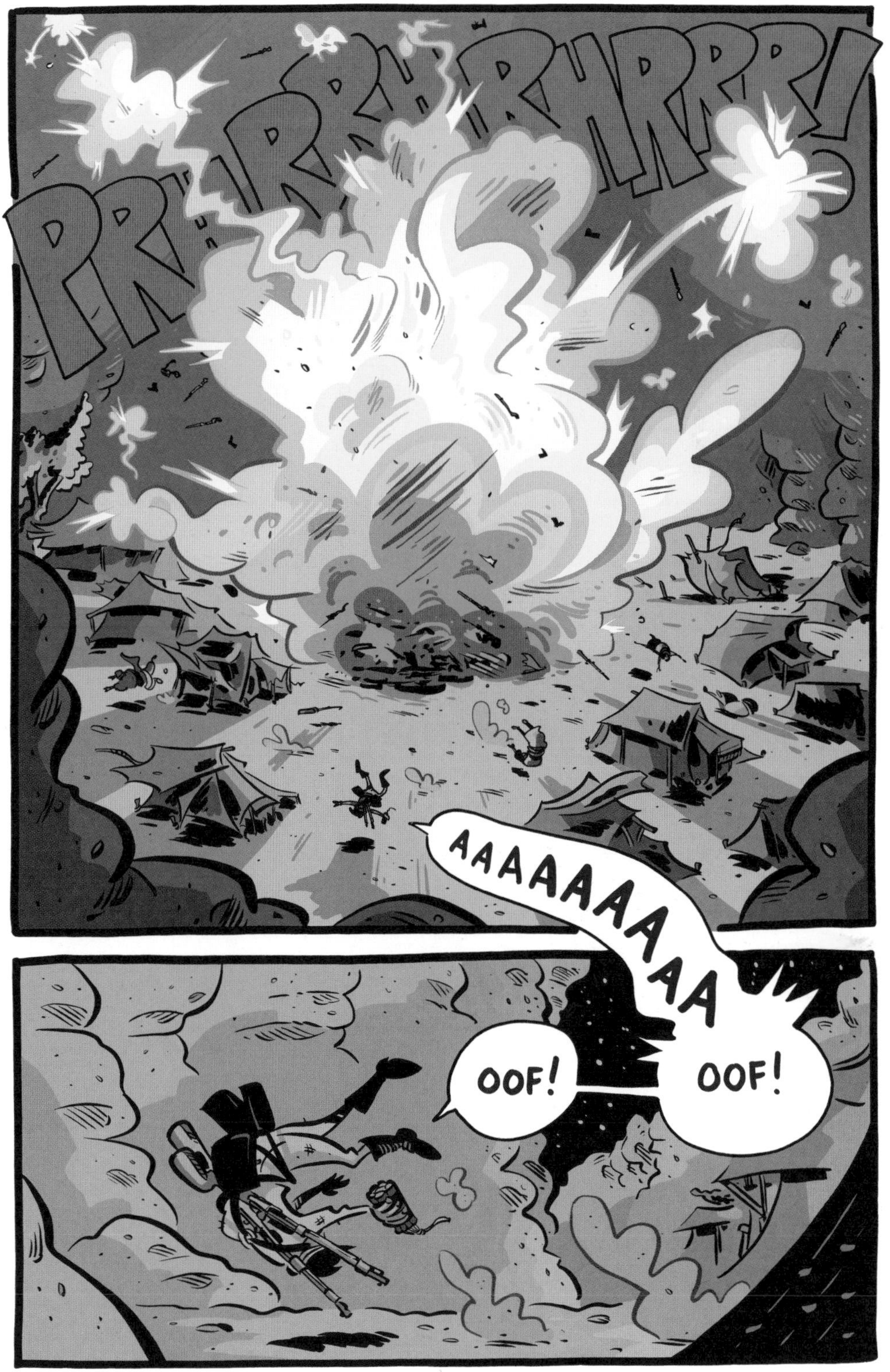
AAAAAAAAAAA
OOF!
OOF!

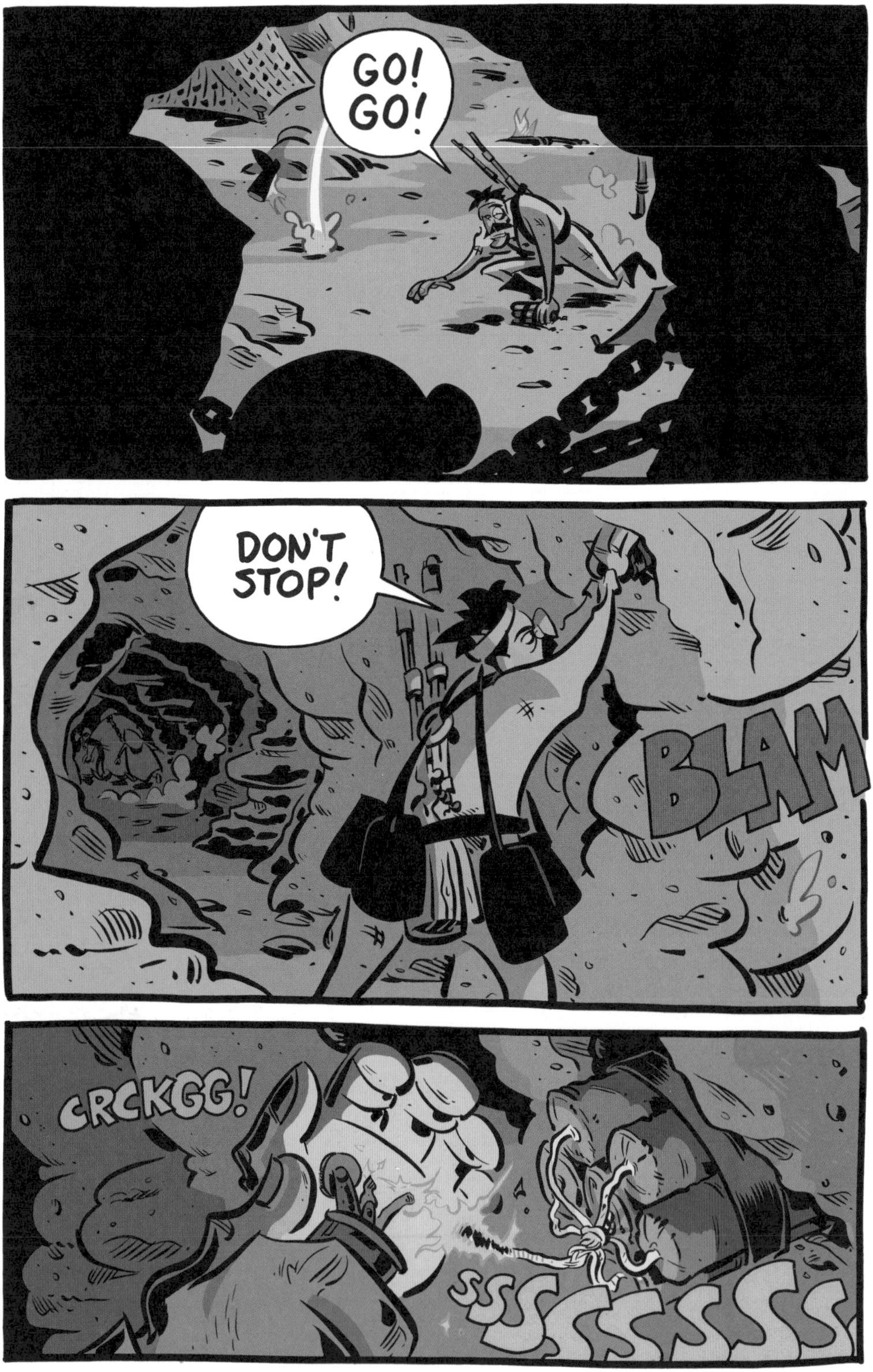
GO! GO!
DON'T STOP!
BLAM
CRCKGG!
SSSSSSSSS

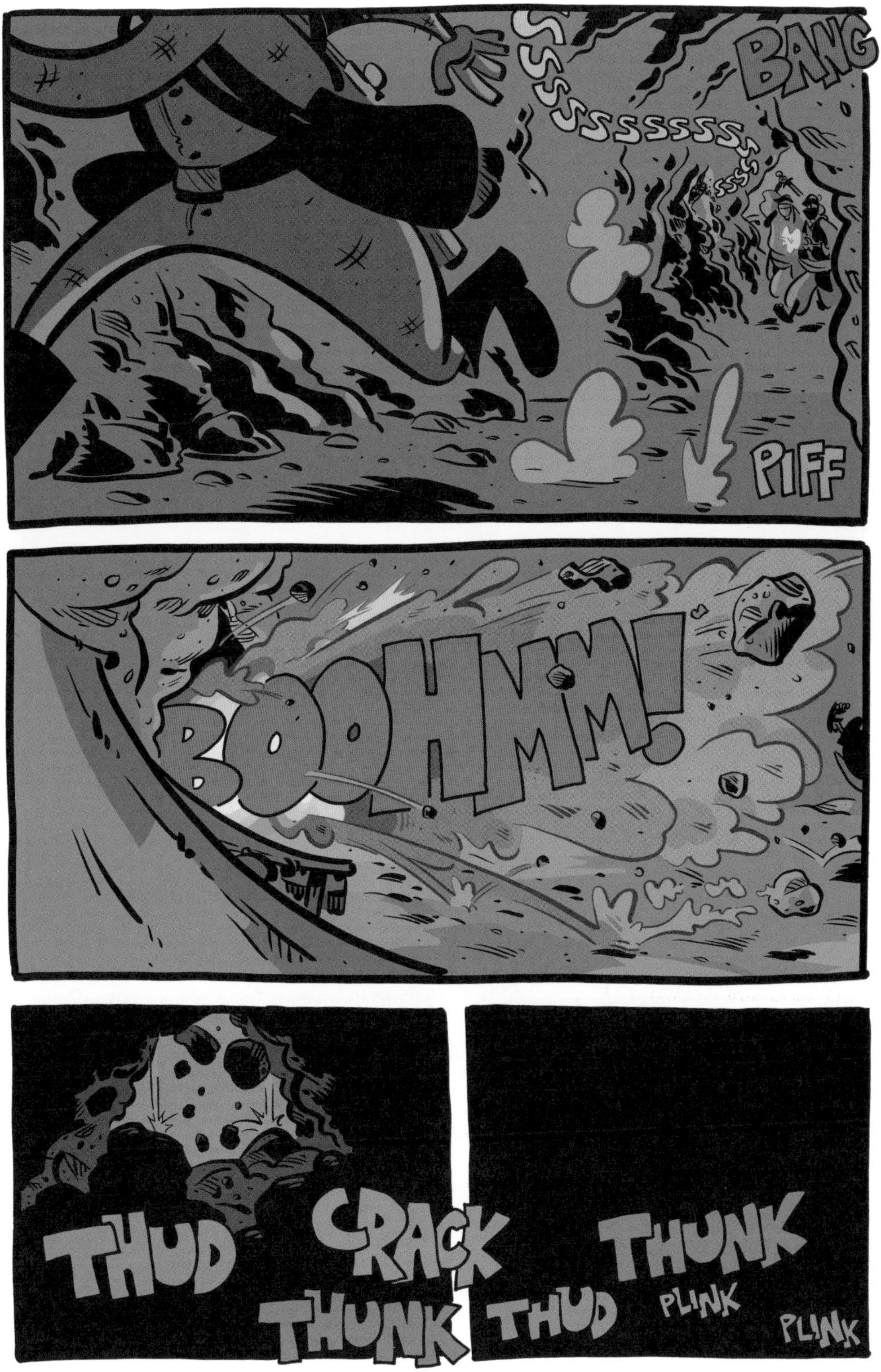
SSSSSSSSSSSSSS
BANG
PIFF
BOOHMM!
THUD
CRACK
THUNK
THUNK
THUD
PLINK
PLINK

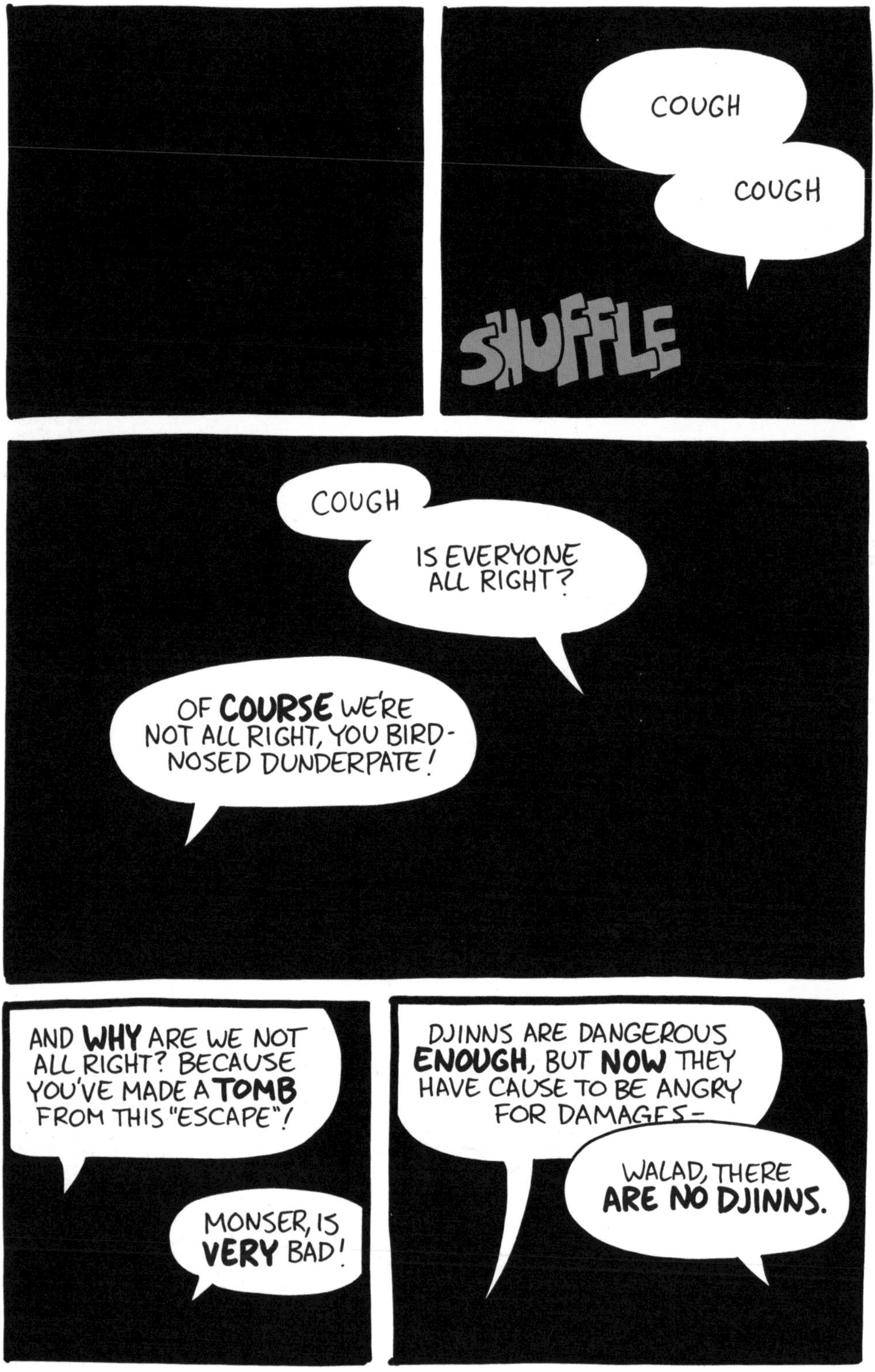
COUGH
COUGH
SHUFFLE
COUGH
IS EVERYONE ALL RIGHT?
OF COURSE WE'RE NOT ALL RIGHT, YOU BIRD-NOSED DUNDERPATE!
AND WHY ARE WE NOT ALL RIGHT? BECAUSE YOU'VE MADE A TOMB FROM THIS "ESCAPE"!
MONSER, IS VERY BAD!
DJINNS ARE DANGEROUS ENOUGH, BUT NOW THEY HAVE CAUSE TO BE ANGRY FOR DAMAGES–
WALAD, THERE ARE NO DJINNS.

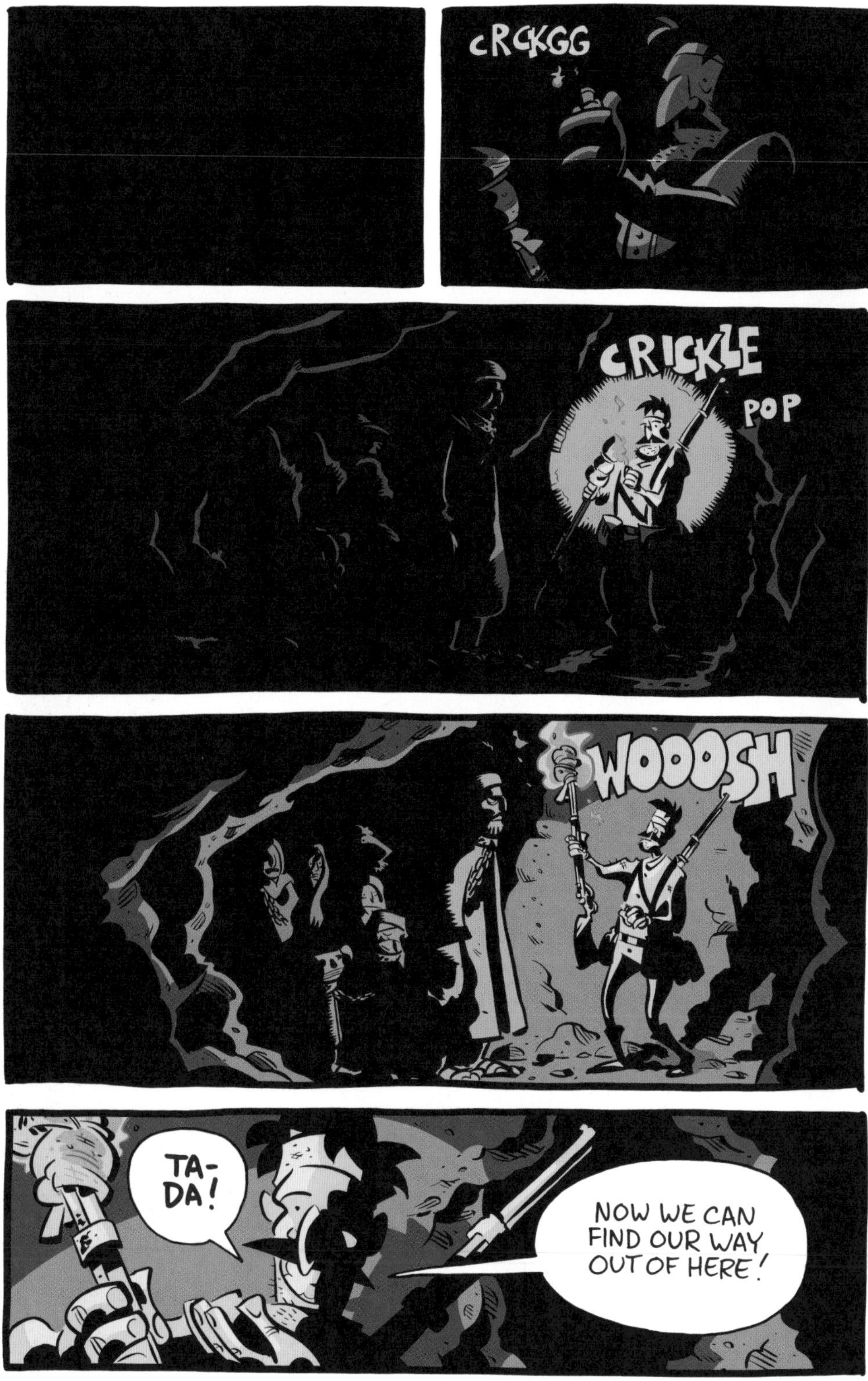
CRCKGG
CRICKLE
POP
WOOOSH
TA-DA!
NOW WE CAN FIND OUR WAY OUT OF HERE!

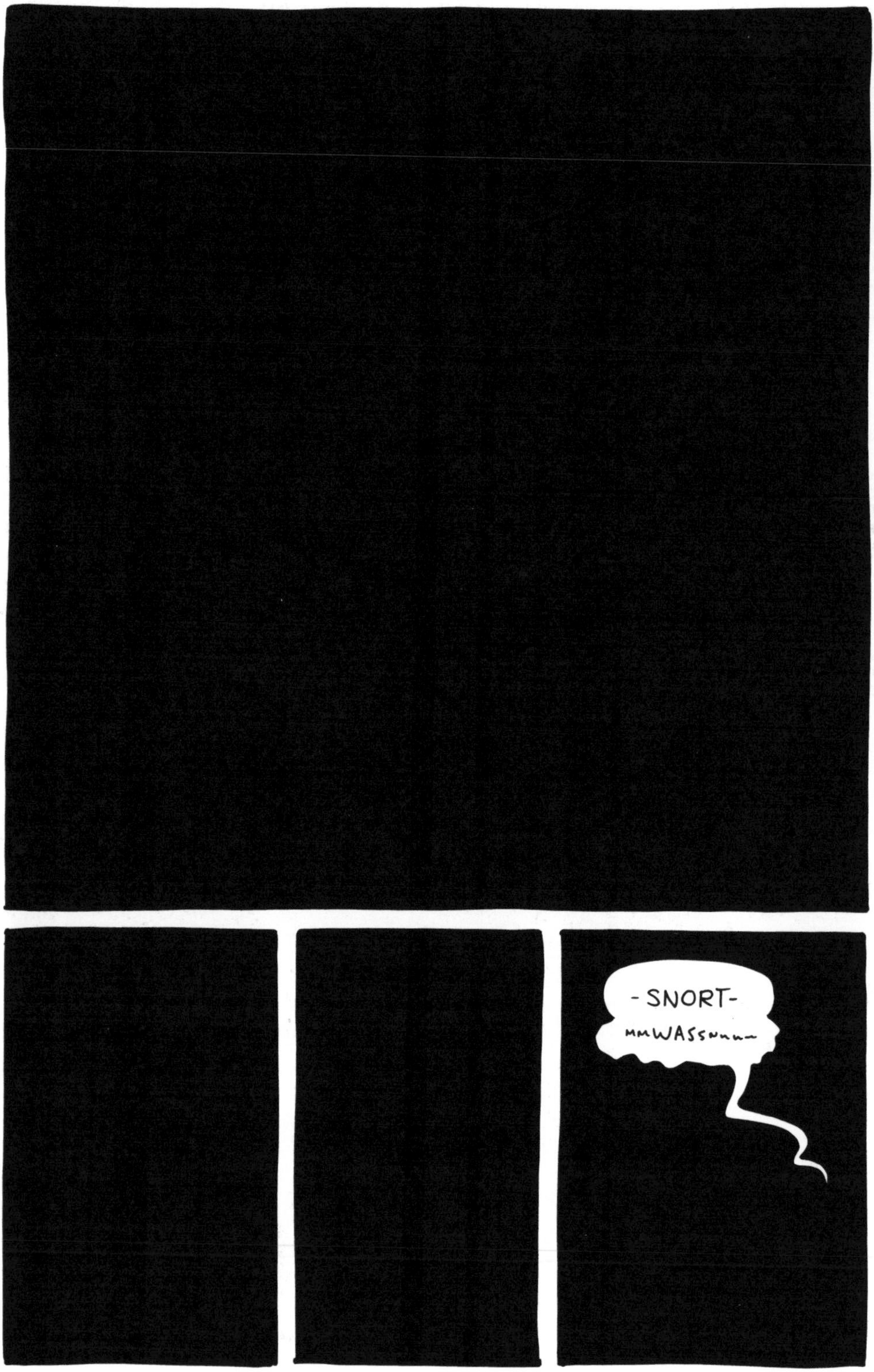
- SNORT-
MMWASSnnnn

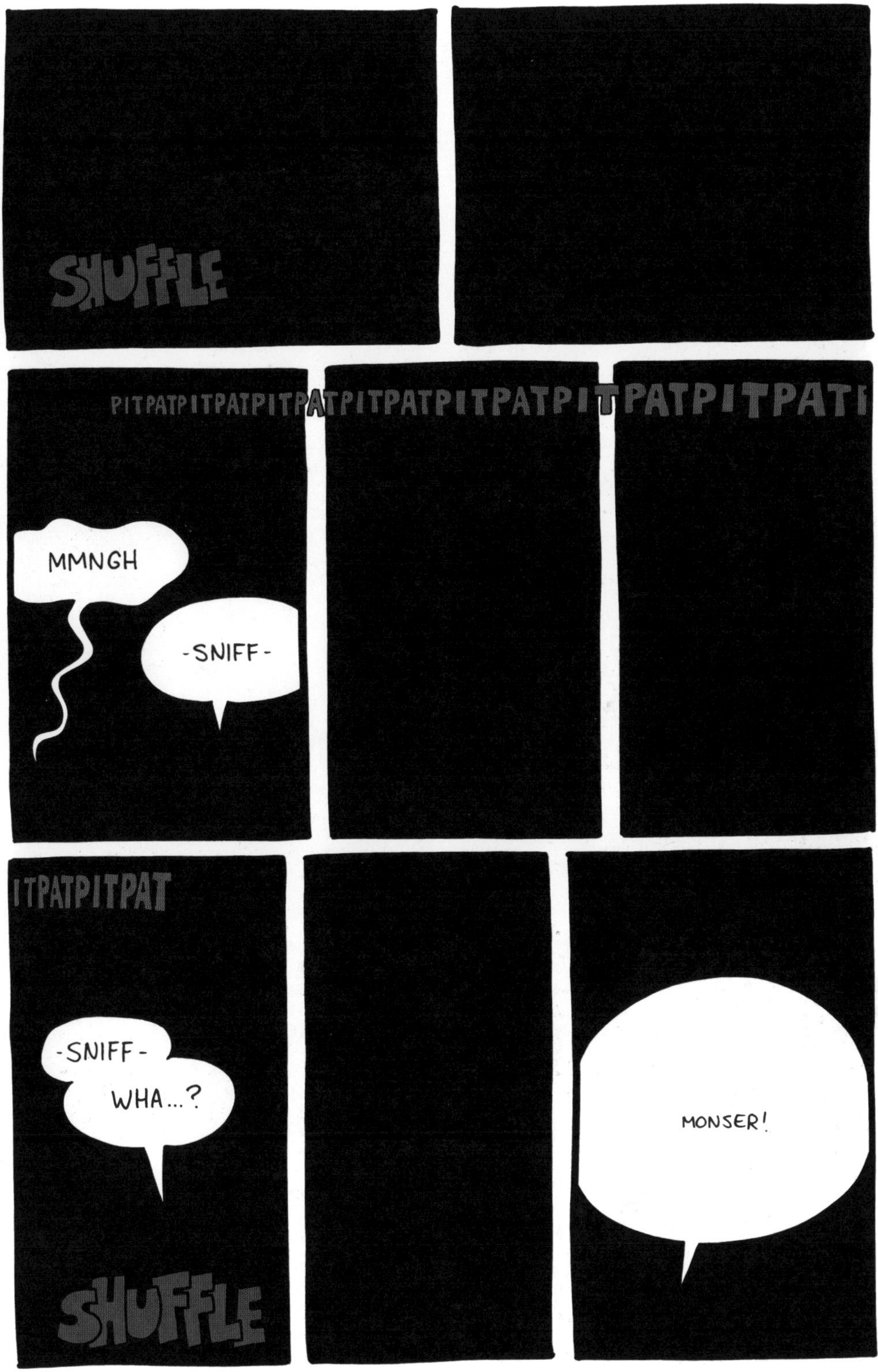
SHUFFLE
PITPATPITPATPITPATPITPATPITPATPITPATPITPATPITPAT
MMNGH
-SNIFF-
ITPATPITPAT
-SNIFF-
WHA...?
SHUFFLE
MONSER!

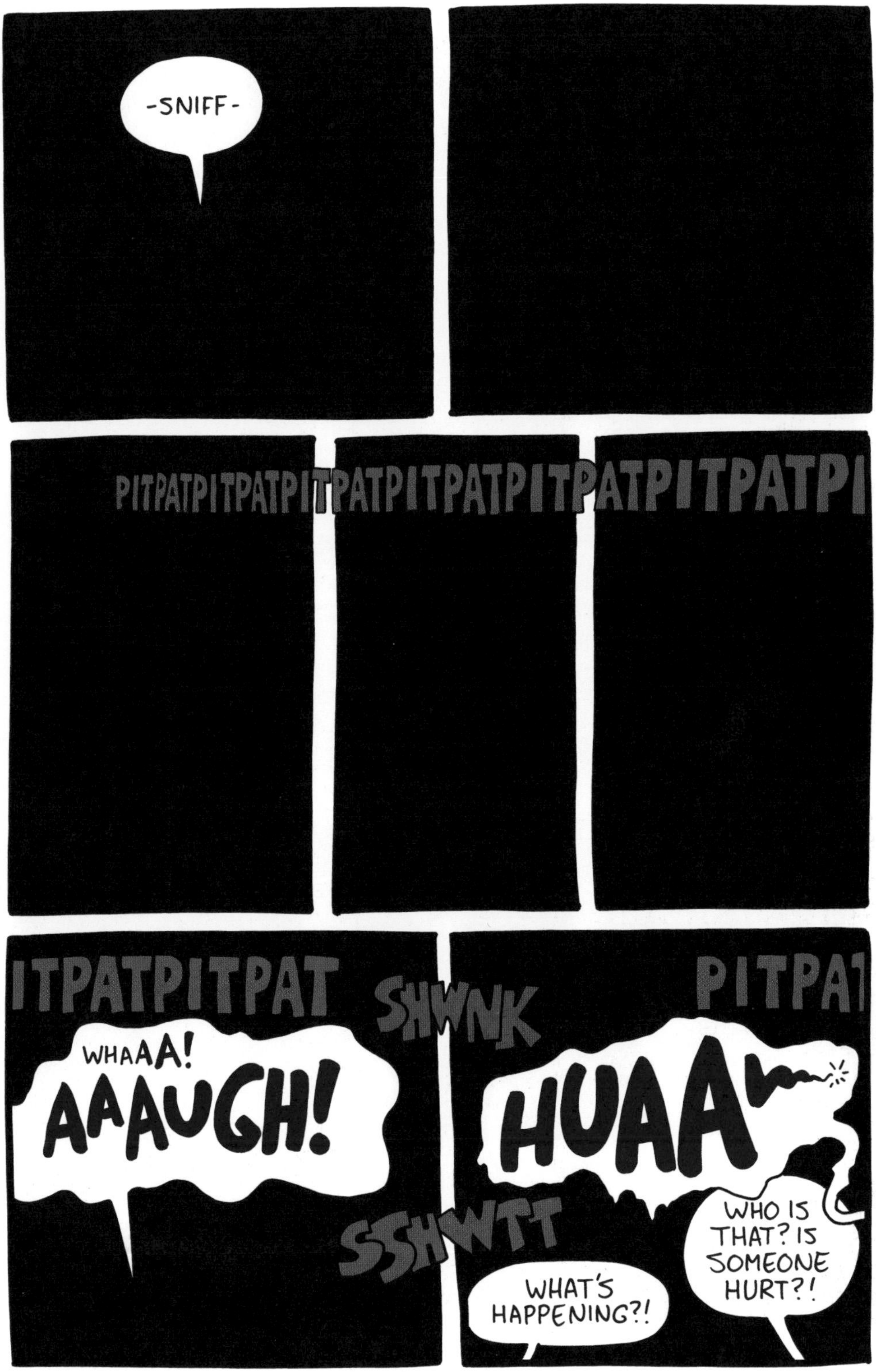

159

160

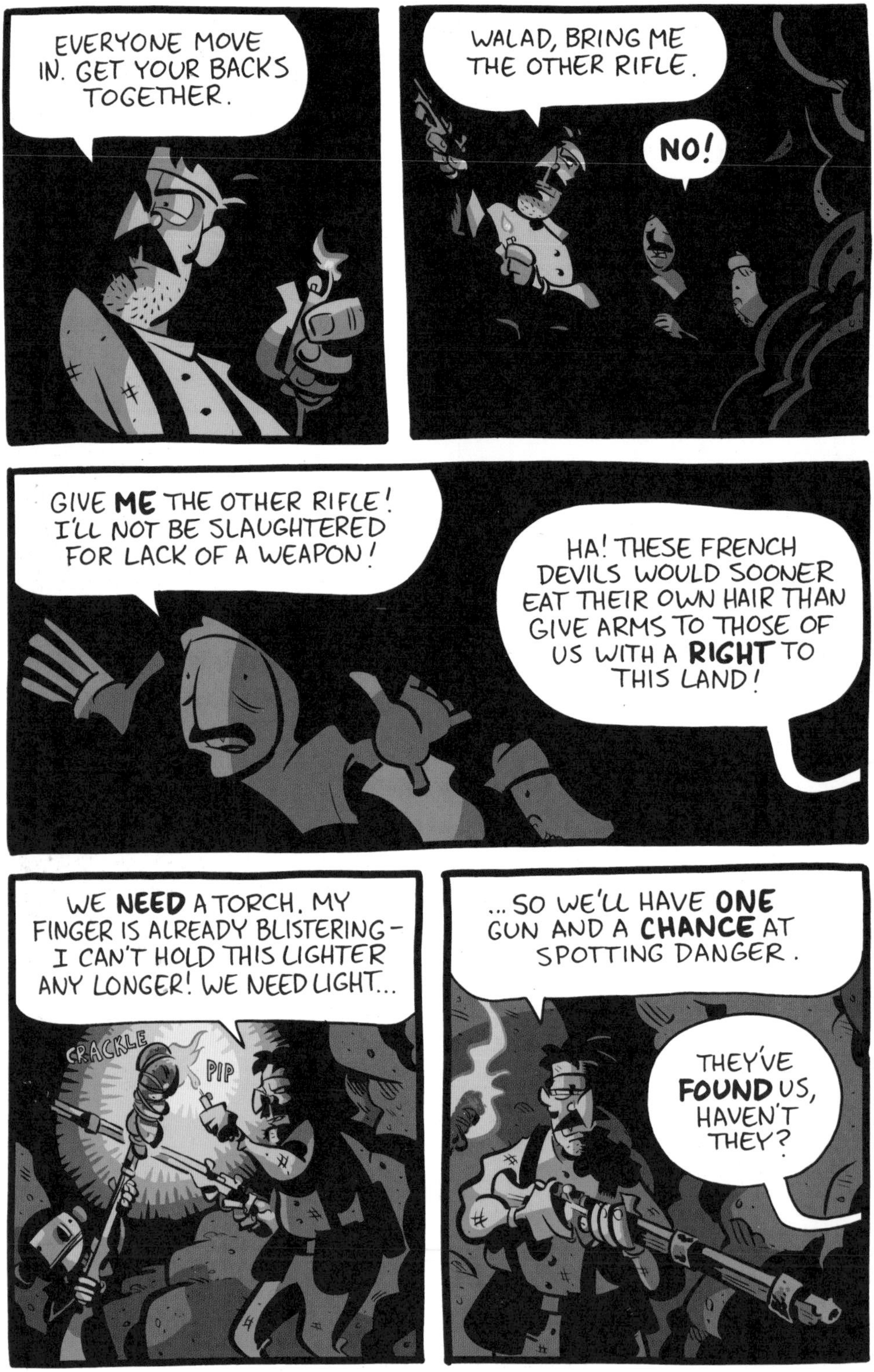
EVERYONE MOVE IN. GET YOUR BACKS TOGETHER.
WALAD, BRING ME THE OTHER RIFLE.
NO!
GIVE **ME** THE OTHER RIFLE! I'LL NOT BE SLAUGHTERED FOR LACK OF A WEAPON!
HA! THESE FRENCH DEVILS WOULD SOONER EAT THEIR OWN HAIR THAN GIVE ARMS TO THOSE OF US WITH A **RIGHT** TO THIS LAND!
WE **NEED** A TORCH. MY FINGER IS ALREADY BLISTERING— I CAN'T HOLD THIS LIGHTER ANY LONGER! WE NEED LIGHT...
CRACKLE
PIP
...SO WE'LL HAVE **ONE** GUN AND A **CHANCE** AT SPOTTING DANGER.
THEY'VE **FOUND** US, HAVEN'T THEY?

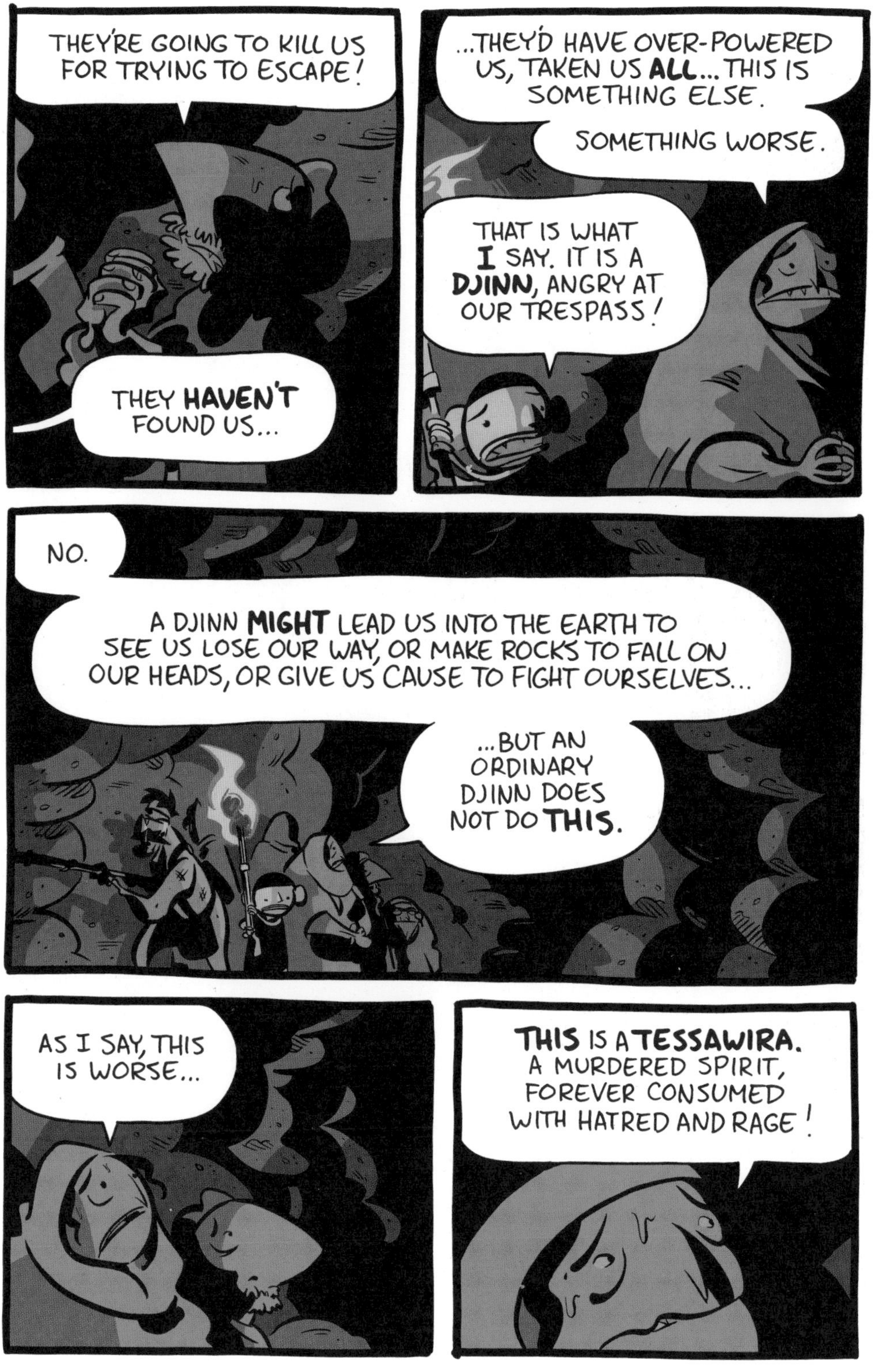

THEY'RE GOING TO KILL US FOR TRYING TO ESCAPE!
THEY HAVEN'T FOUND US...
...THEY'D HAVE OVER-POWERED US, TAKEN US ALL... THIS IS SOMETHING ELSE.
SOMETHING WORSE.
THAT IS WHAT I SAY. IT IS A DJINN, ANGRY AT OUR TRESPASS!
NO.
A DJINN MIGHT LEAD US INTO THE EARTH TO SEE US LOSE OUR WAY, OR MAKE ROCKS TO FALL ON OUR HEADS, OR GIVE US CAUSE TO FIGHT OURSELVES...
...BUT AN ORDINARY DJINN DOES NOT DO THIS.
AS I SAY, THIS IS WORSE...
THIS IS A TESSAWIRA. A MURDERED SPIRIT, FOREVER CONSUMED WITH HATRED AND RAGE!

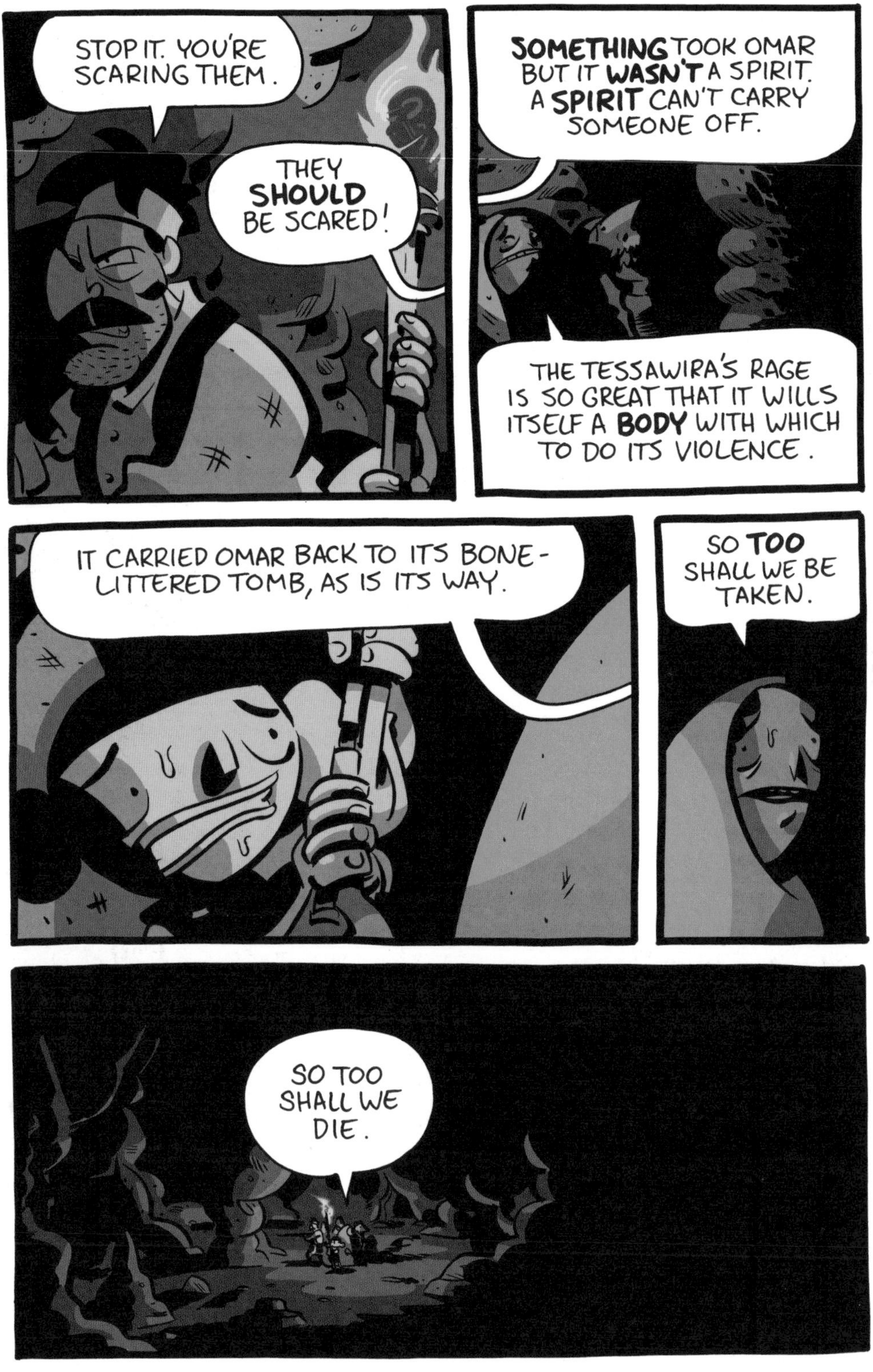
STOP IT. YOU'RE SCARING THEM.
THEY **SHOULD** BE SCARED!
SOMETHING TOOK OMAR BUT IT **WASN'T** A SPIRIT. A **SPIRIT** CAN'T CARRY SOMEONE OFF.
THE TESSAWIRA'S RAGE IS SO GREAT THAT IT WILLS ITSELF A **BODY** WITH WHICH TO DO ITS VIOLENCE.
IT CARRIED OMAR BACK TO ITS BONE-LITTERED TOMB, AS IS ITS WAY.
SO **TOO** SHALL WE BE TAKEN.
SO TOO SHALL WE DIE.

[redacted]

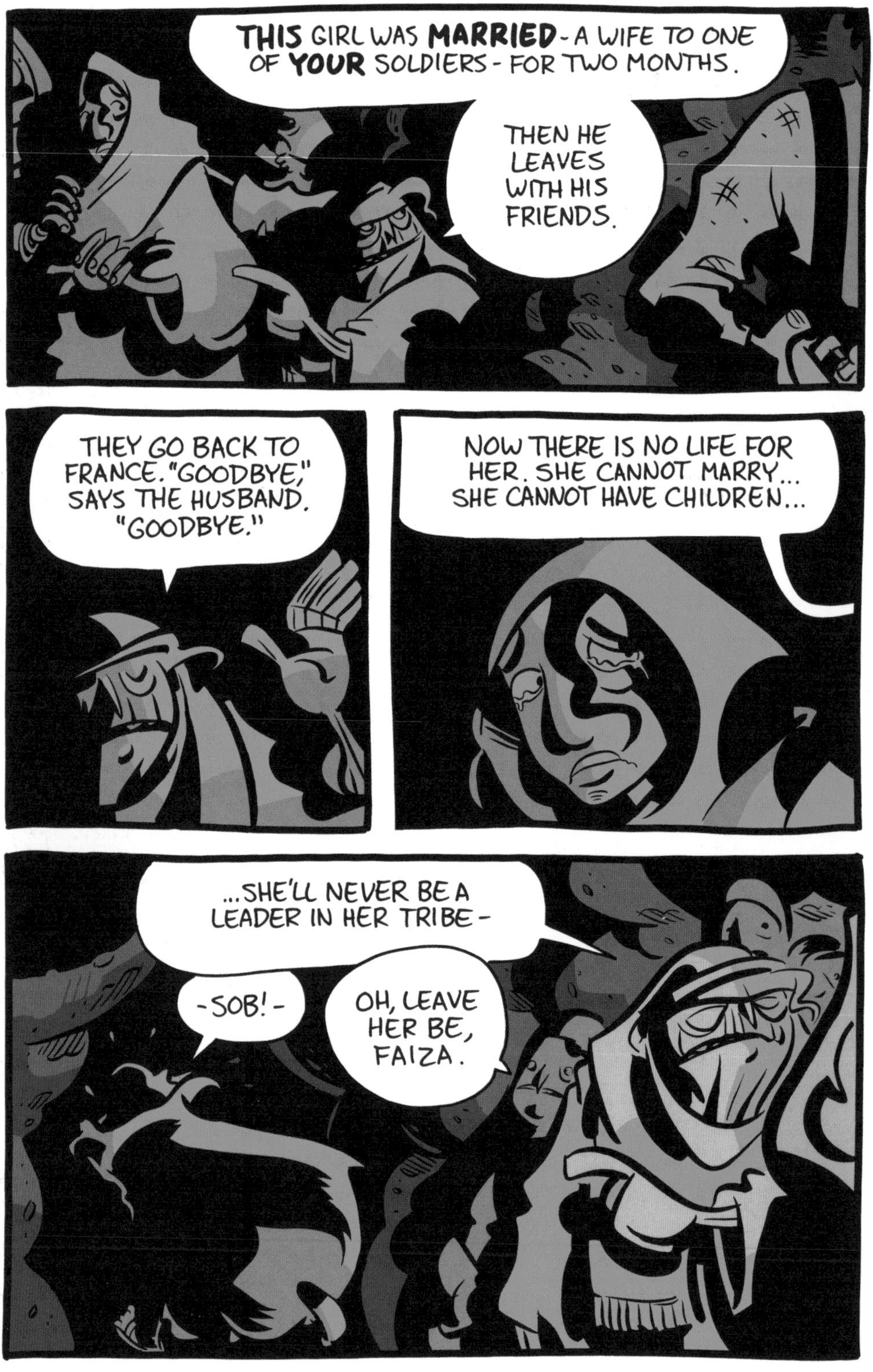
THIS GIRL WAS MARRIED - A WIFE TO ONE OF YOUR SOLDIERS - FOR TWO MONTHS.
THEN HE LEAVES WITH HIS FRIENDS.
THEY GO BACK TO FRANCE. "GOODBYE," SAYS THE HUSBAND. "GOODBYE."
NOW THERE IS NO LIFE FOR HER. SHE CANNOT MARRY... SHE CANNOT HAVE CHILDREN...
...SHE'LL NEVER BE A LEADER IN HER TRIBE -
-SOB! -
OH, LEAVE HER BE, FAIZA.

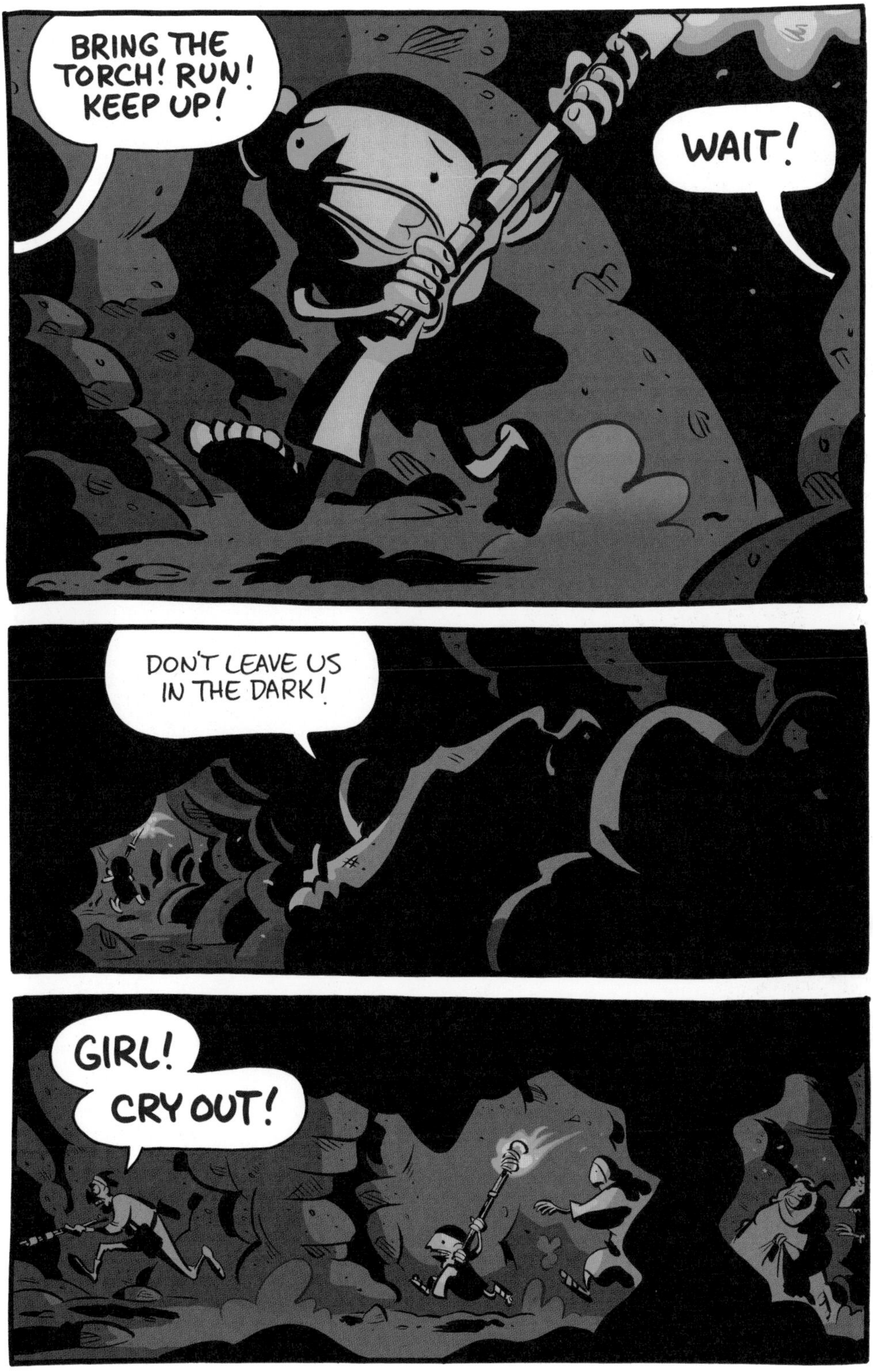
BRING THE TORCH! RUN! KEEP UP!
WAIT!
DON'T LEAVE US IN THE DARK!
GIRL! CRY OUT!

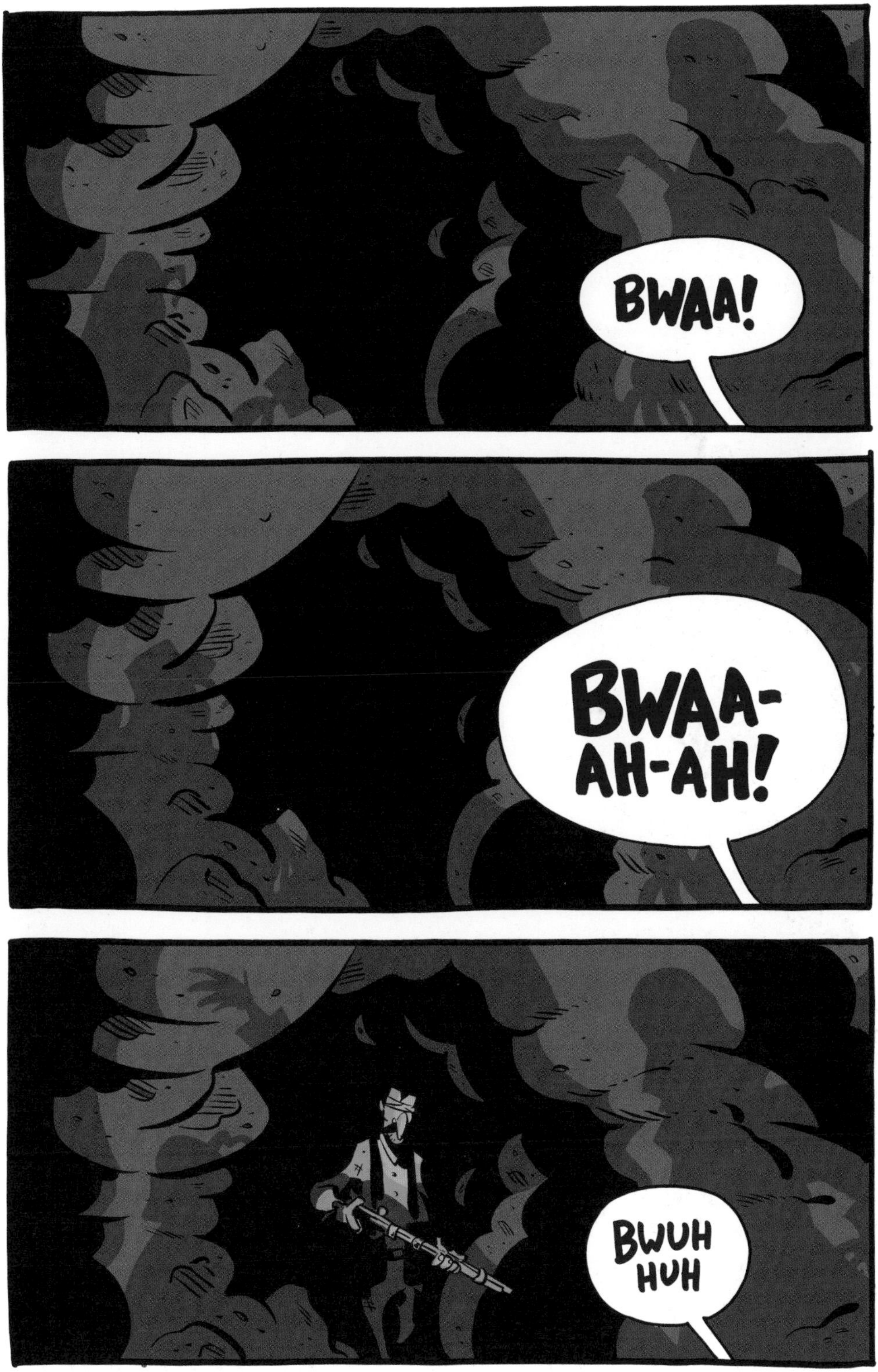
BWAA!
BWAA-
AH-AH!
BWUH
HUH

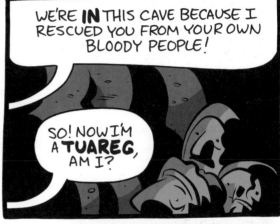

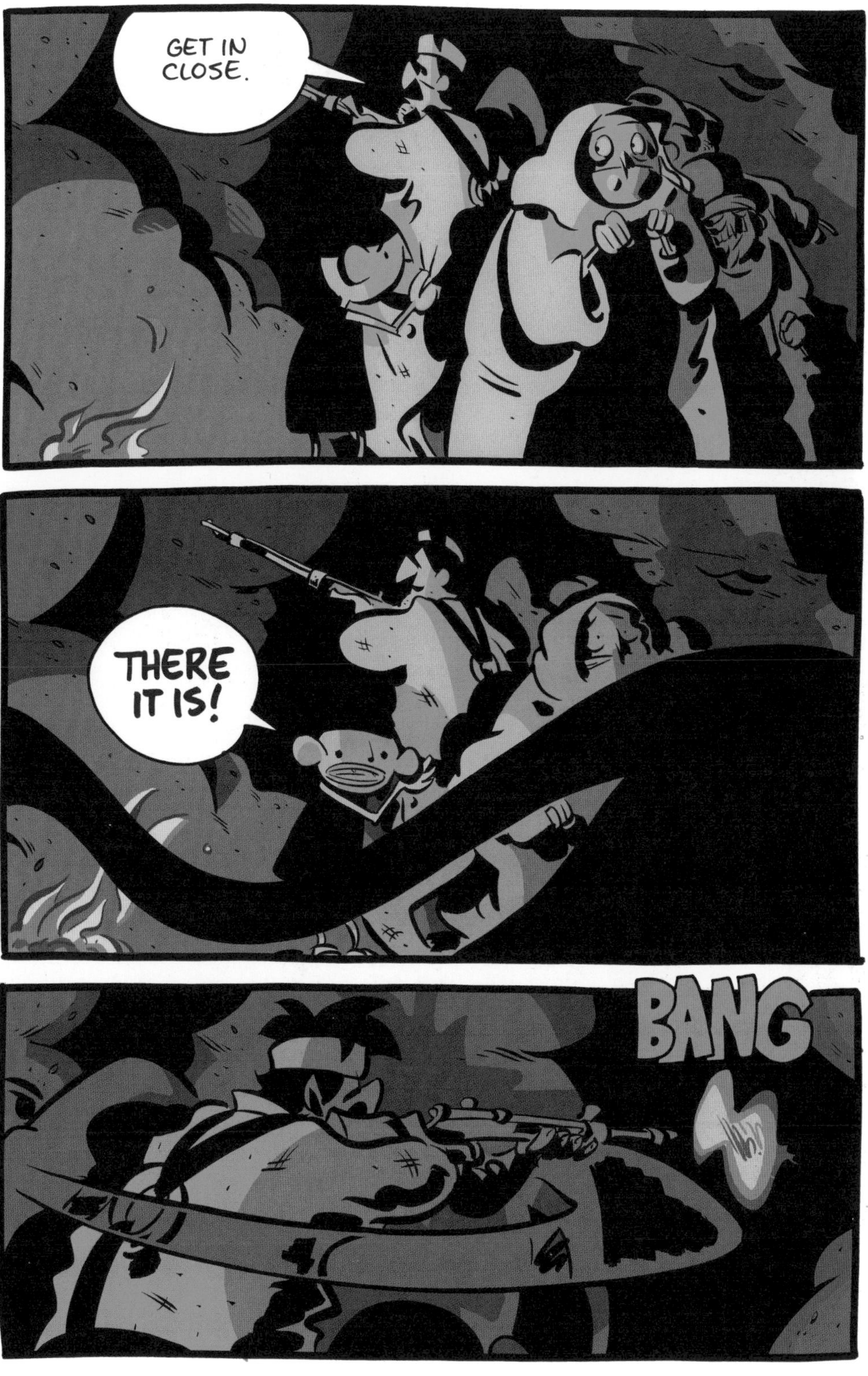
GET IN CLOSE.
THERE IT IS!
BANG

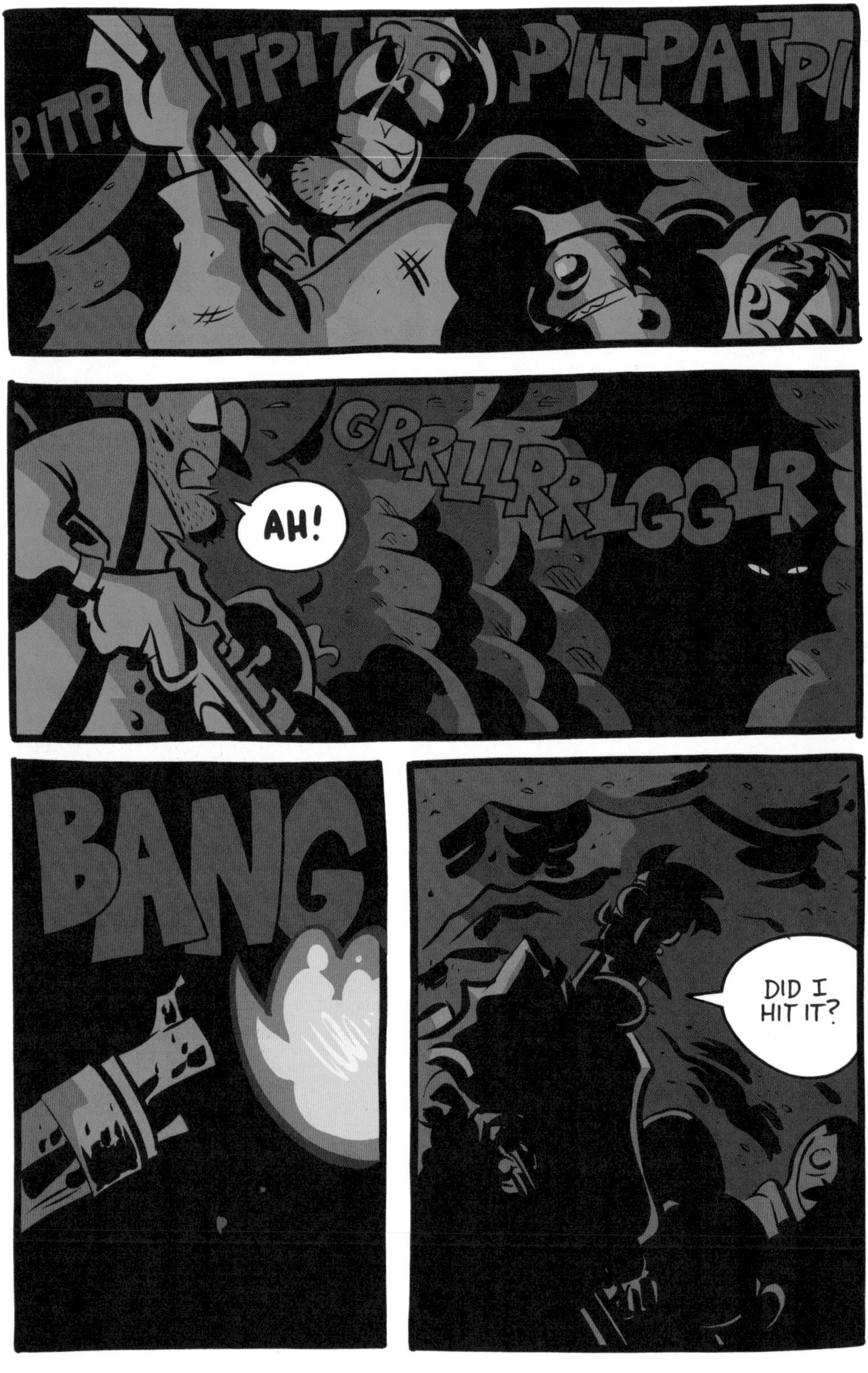
PITP
TPIT
PITPATPI
GRRLLRRRLGGLR
AH!
BANG
DID I HIT IT?

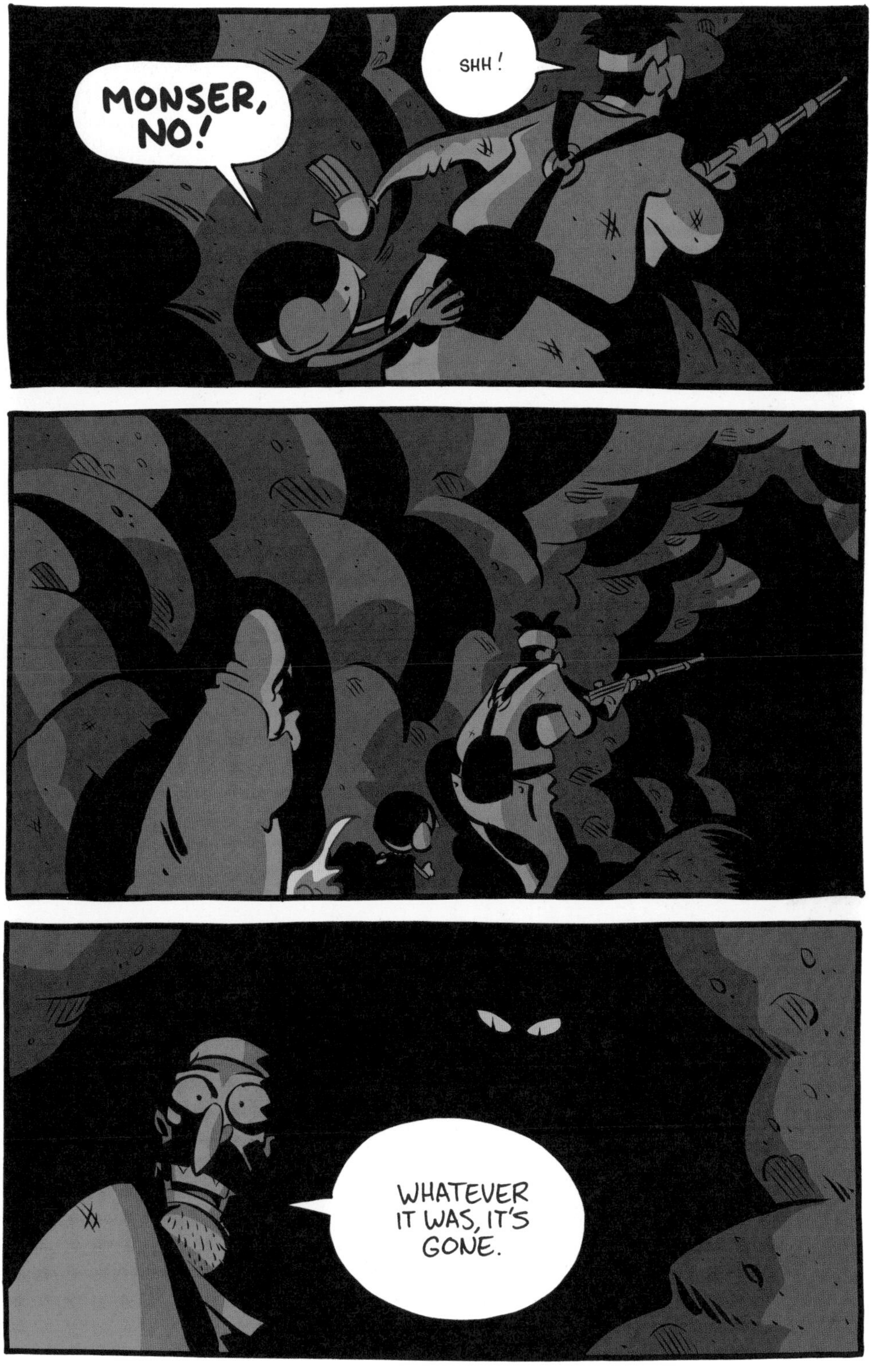
MONSER, NO!
SHH!
WHATEVER IT WAS, IT'S GONE.

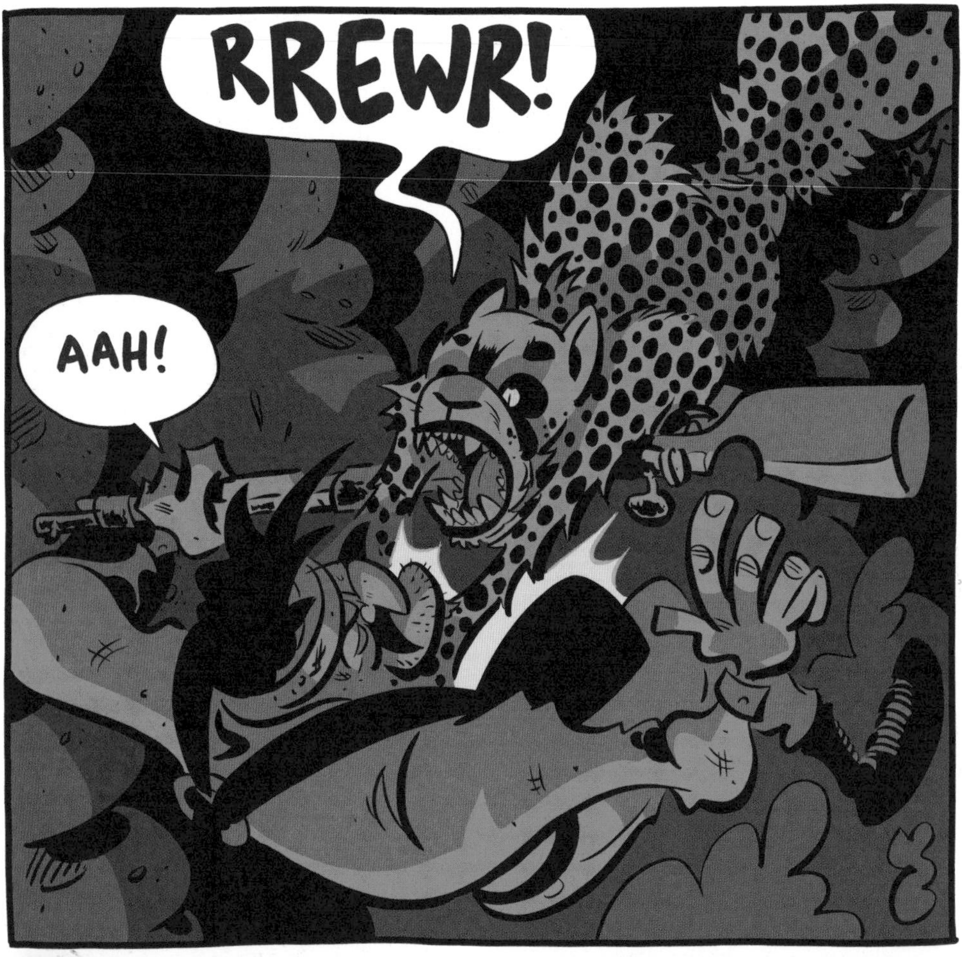
RREWR!
AAH!

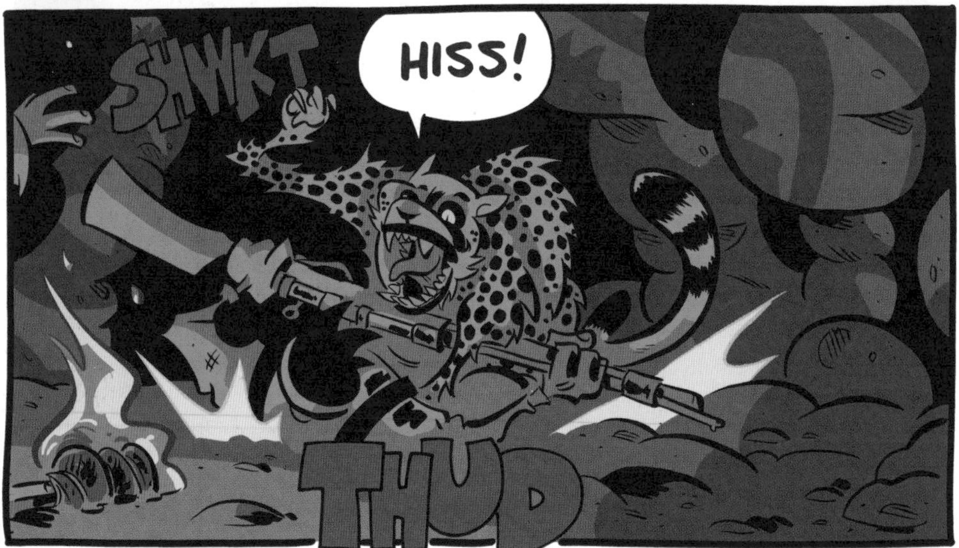
SHNKT
HISS!
THUD

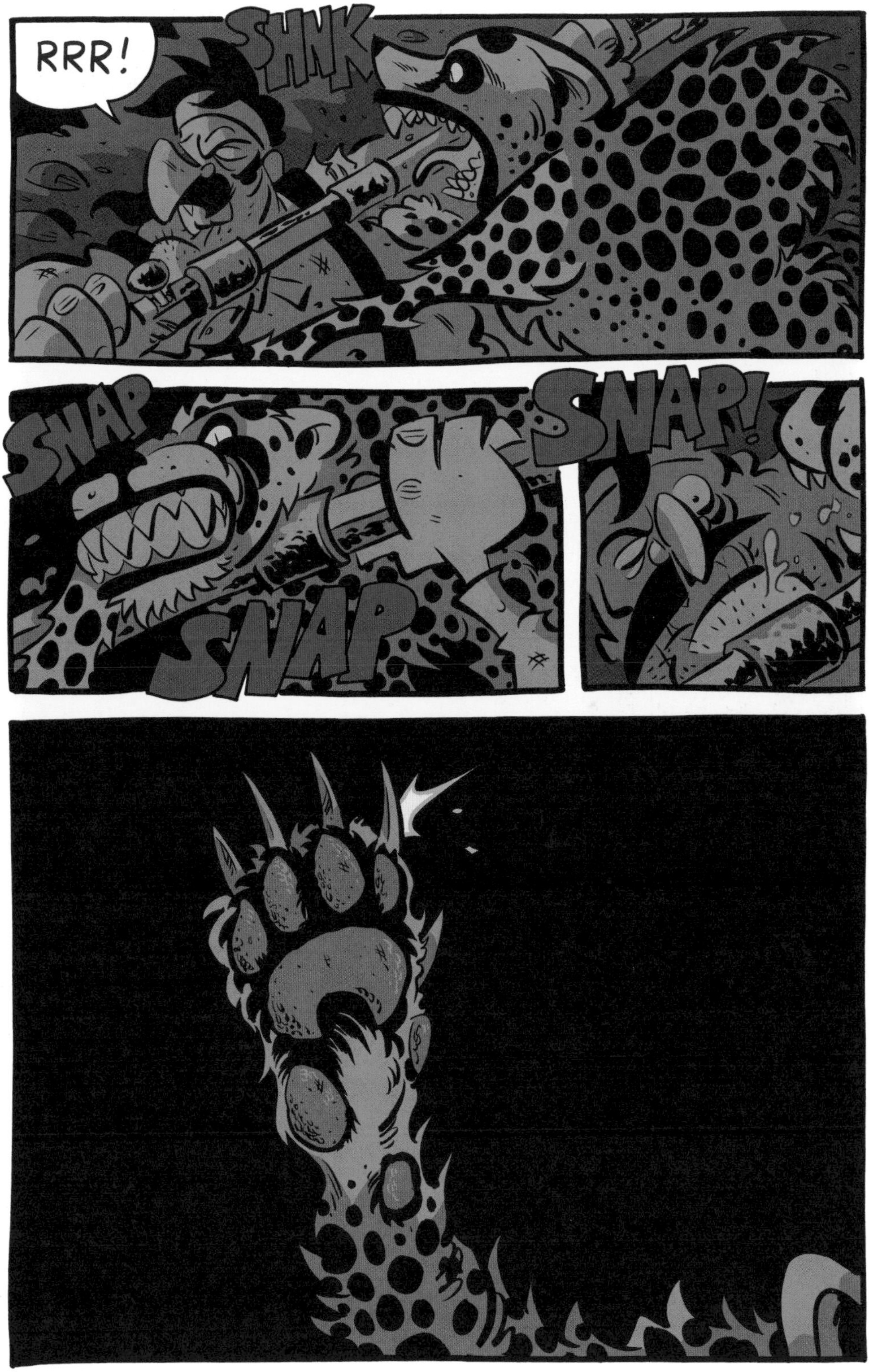
RRR!
SHNK
SNAP
SNAP
SNAP!

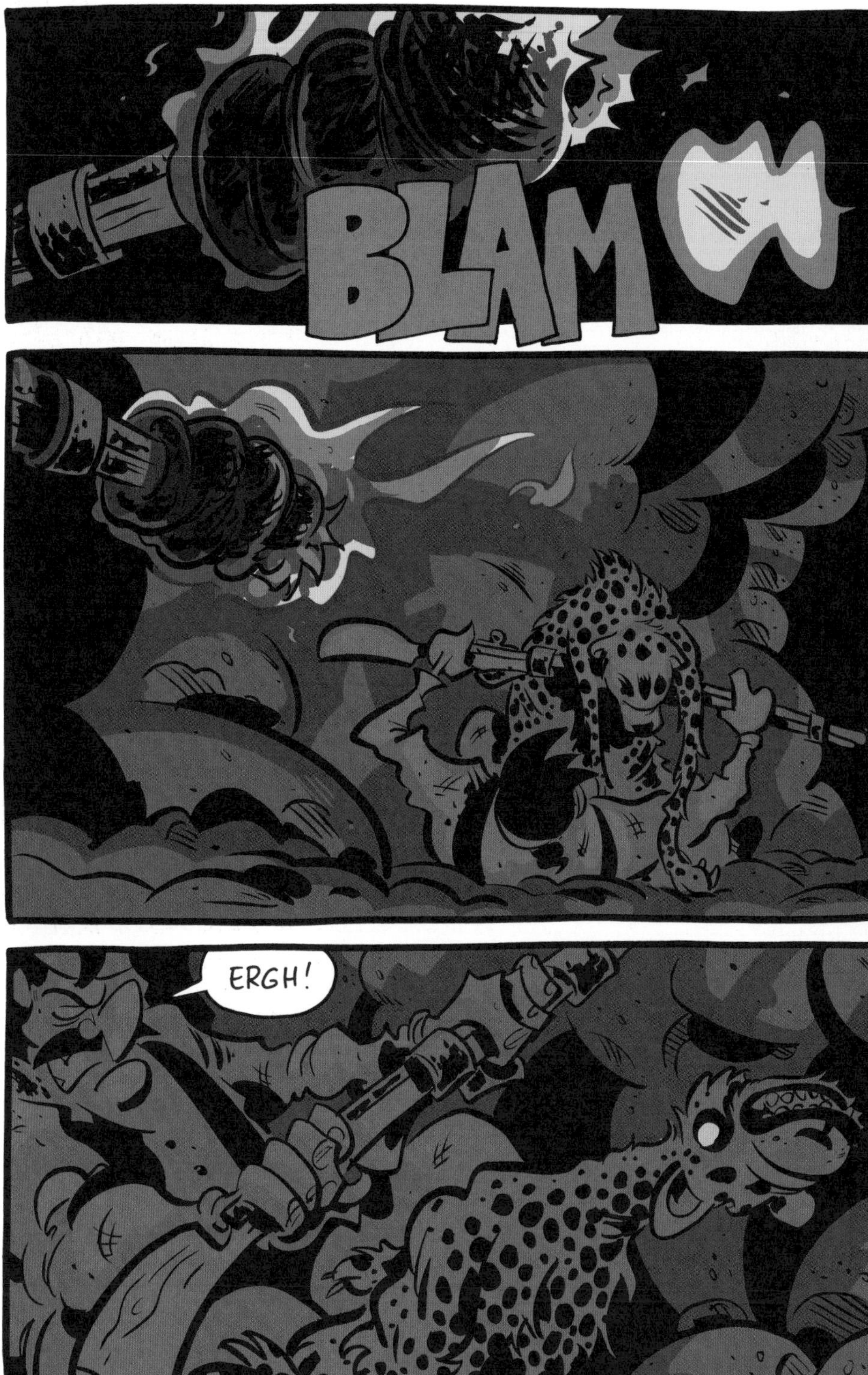
BLAM
ERGH!

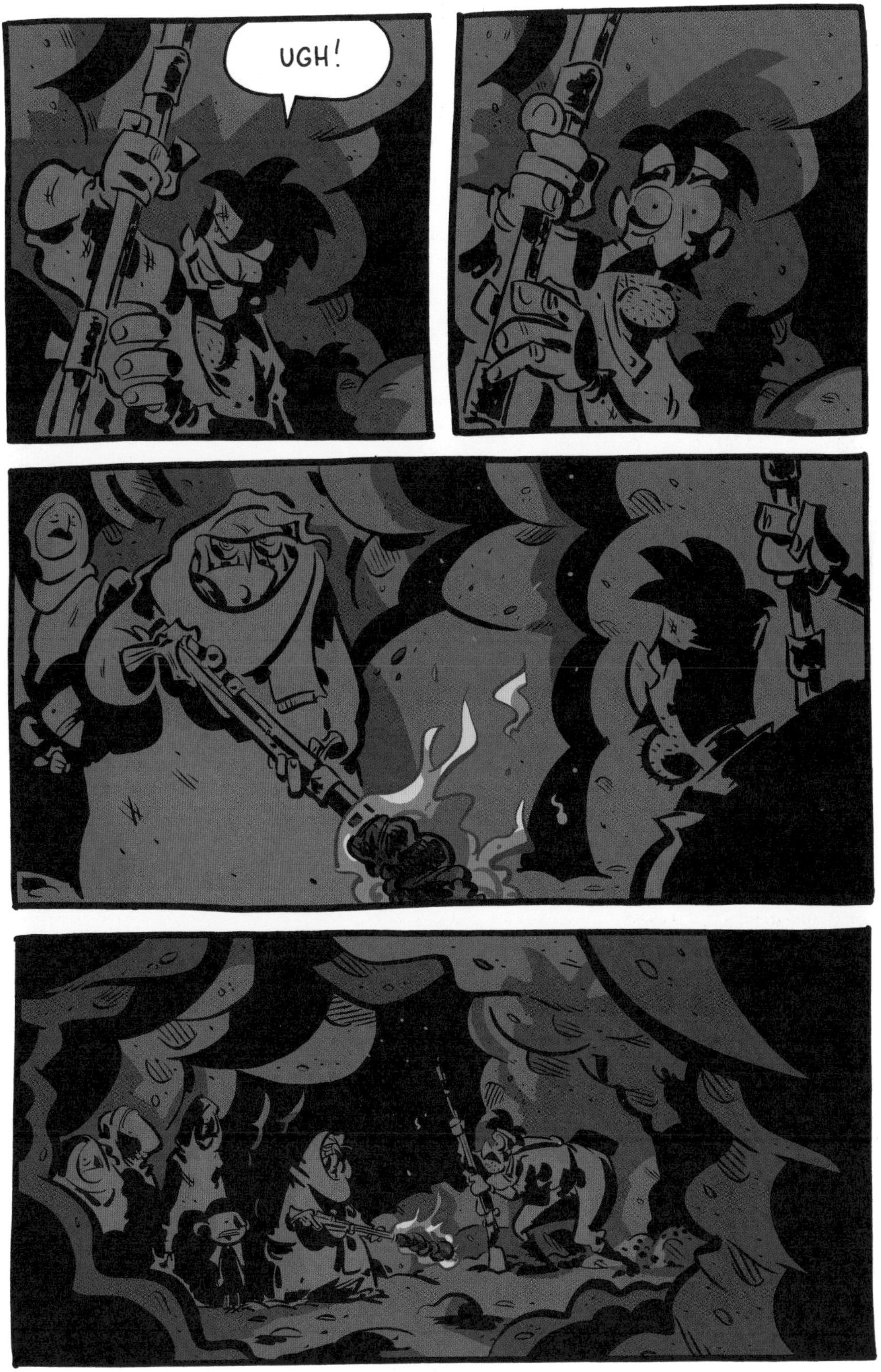
UGH!

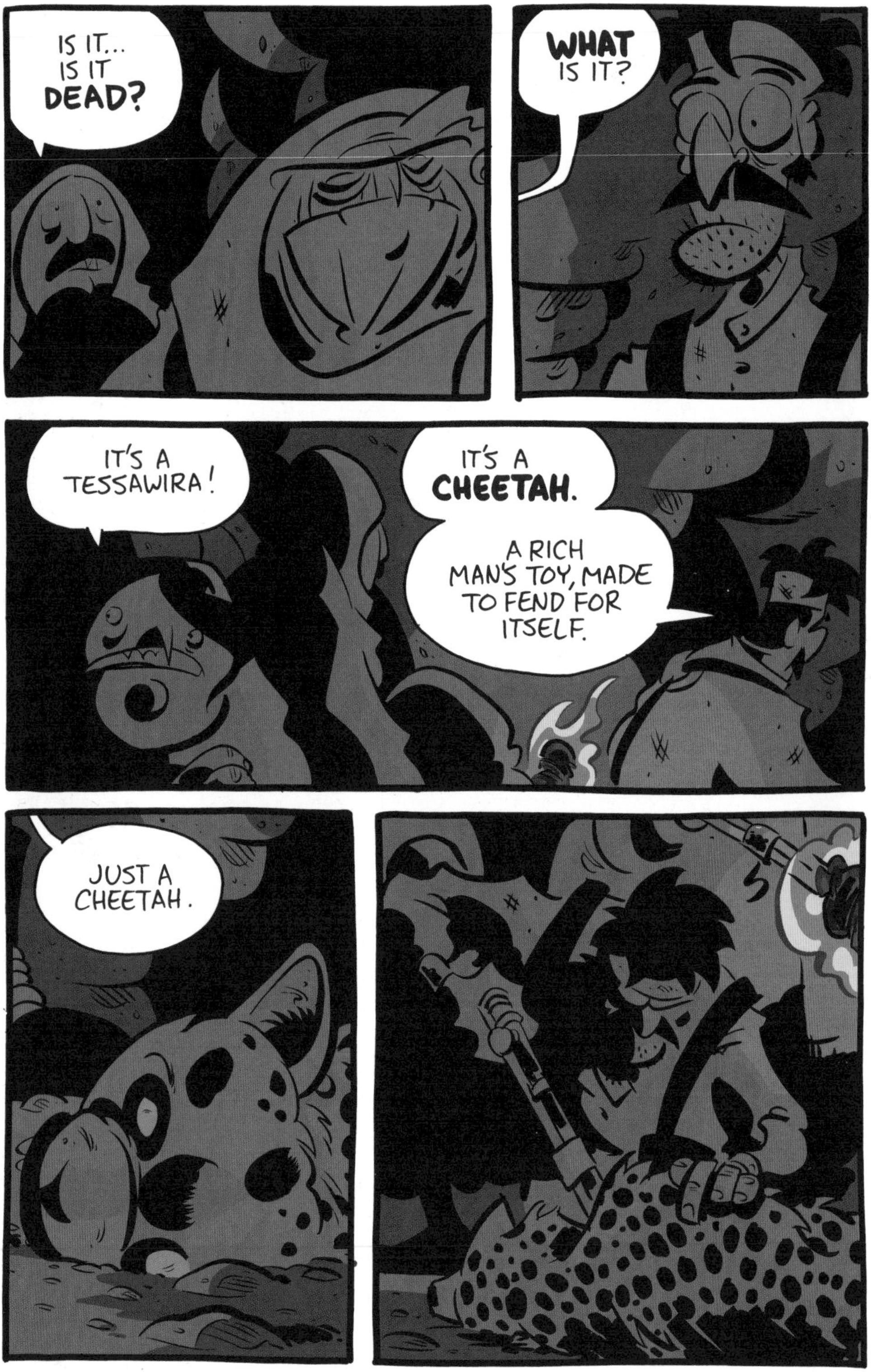
IS IT... IS IT DEAD?
WHAT IS IT?
IT'S A TESSAWIRA!
IT'S A CHEETAH.
A RICH MAN'S TOY, MADE TO FEND FOR ITSELF.
JUST A CHEETAH.

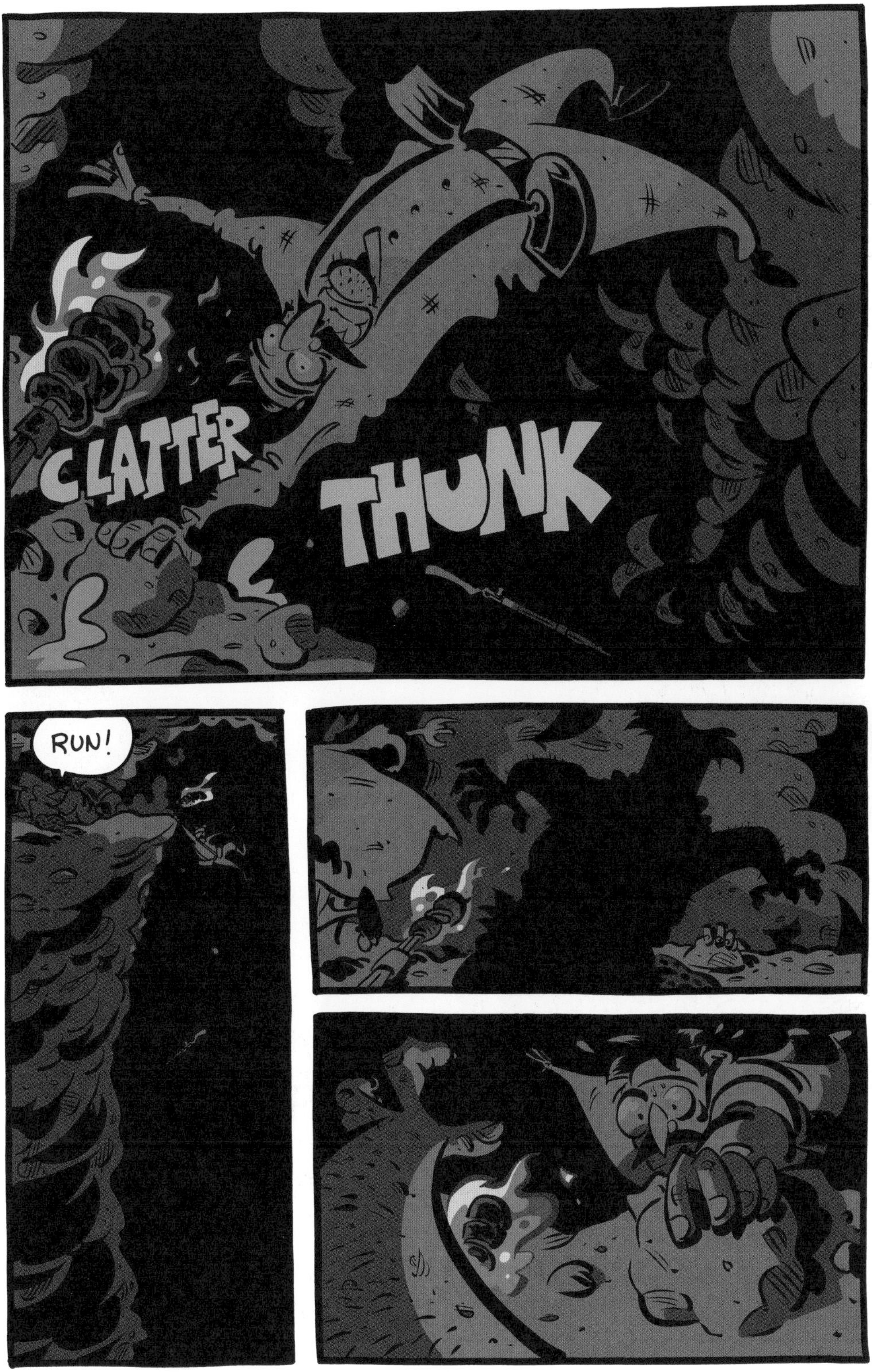
CLATTER
THUNK
RUN!

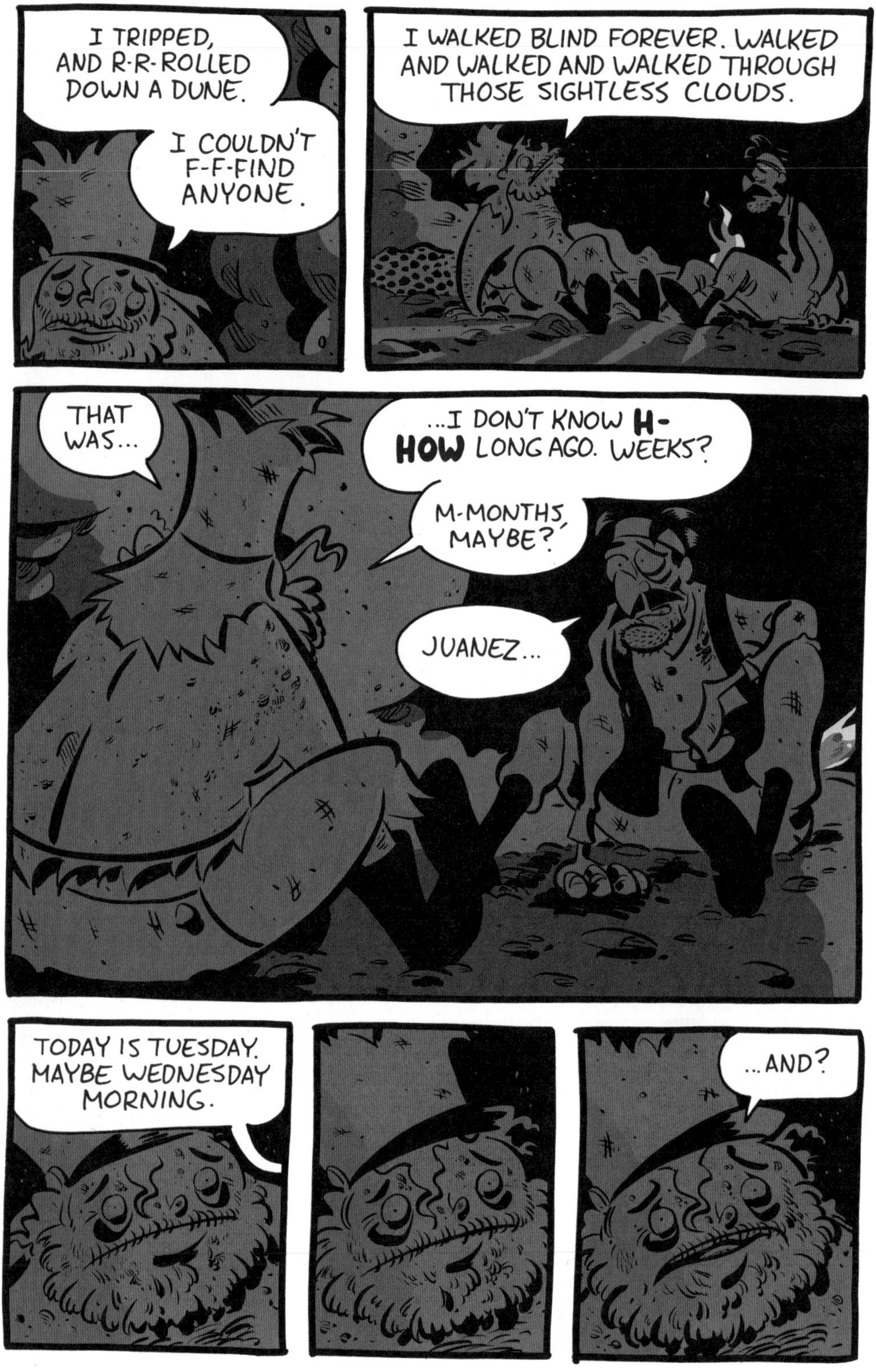
I TRIPPED, AND R-R-ROLLED DOWN A DUNE.
I COULDN'T F-F-FIND ANYONE.
I WALKED BLIND FOREVER. WALKED AND WALKED AND WALKED THROUGH THOSE SIGHTLESS CLOUDS.
THAT WAS...
...I DON'T KNOW H-HOW LONG AGO. WEEKS?
M-MONTHS MAYBE?
JUANEZ...
TODAY IS TUESDAY. MAYBE WEDNESDAY MORNING.
...AND?

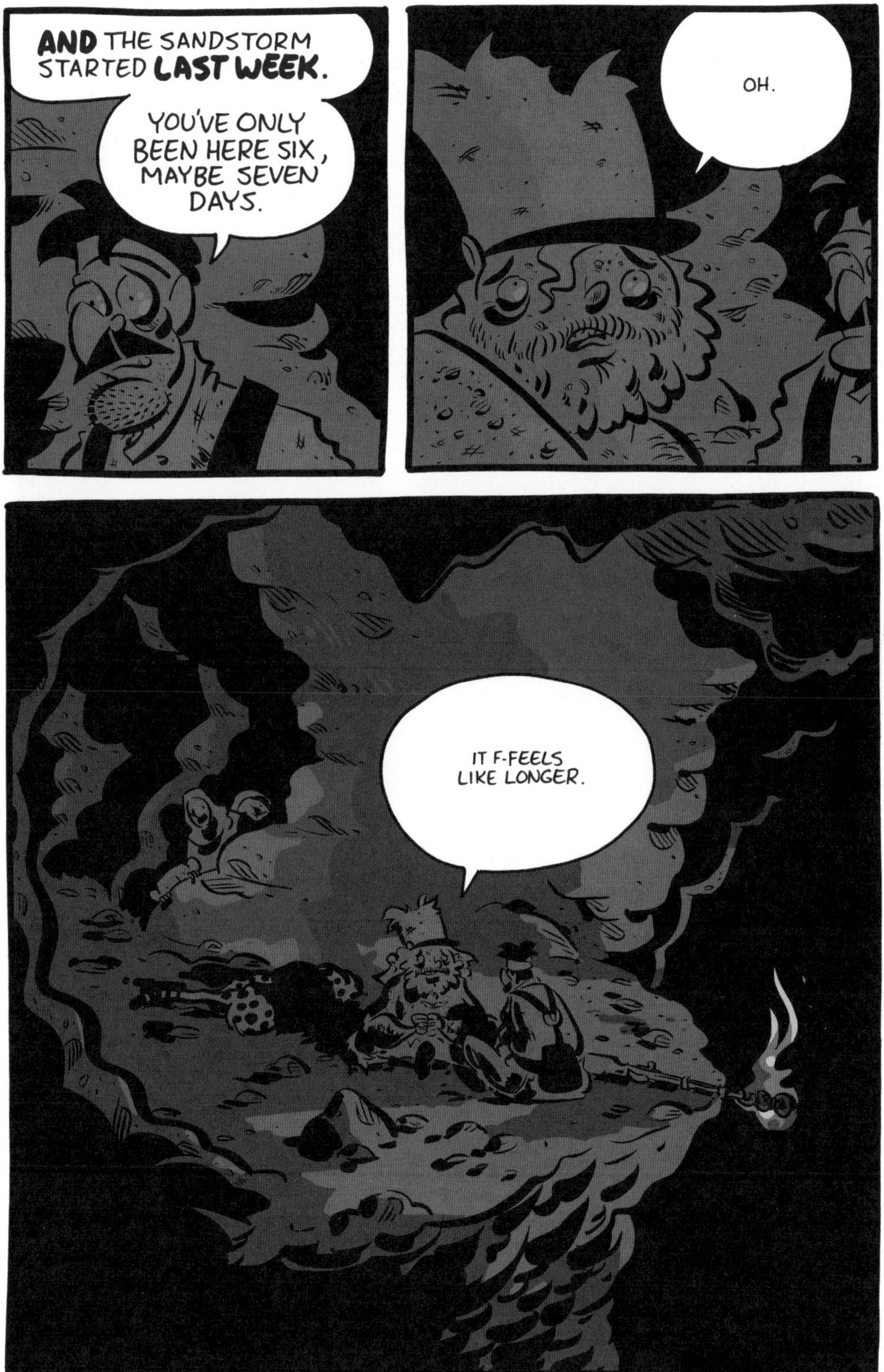
AND THE SANDSTORM STARTED LAST WEEK.
YOU'VE ONLY BEEN HERE SIX, MAYBE SEVEN DAYS.
OH.
IT F-FEELS LIKE LONGER.

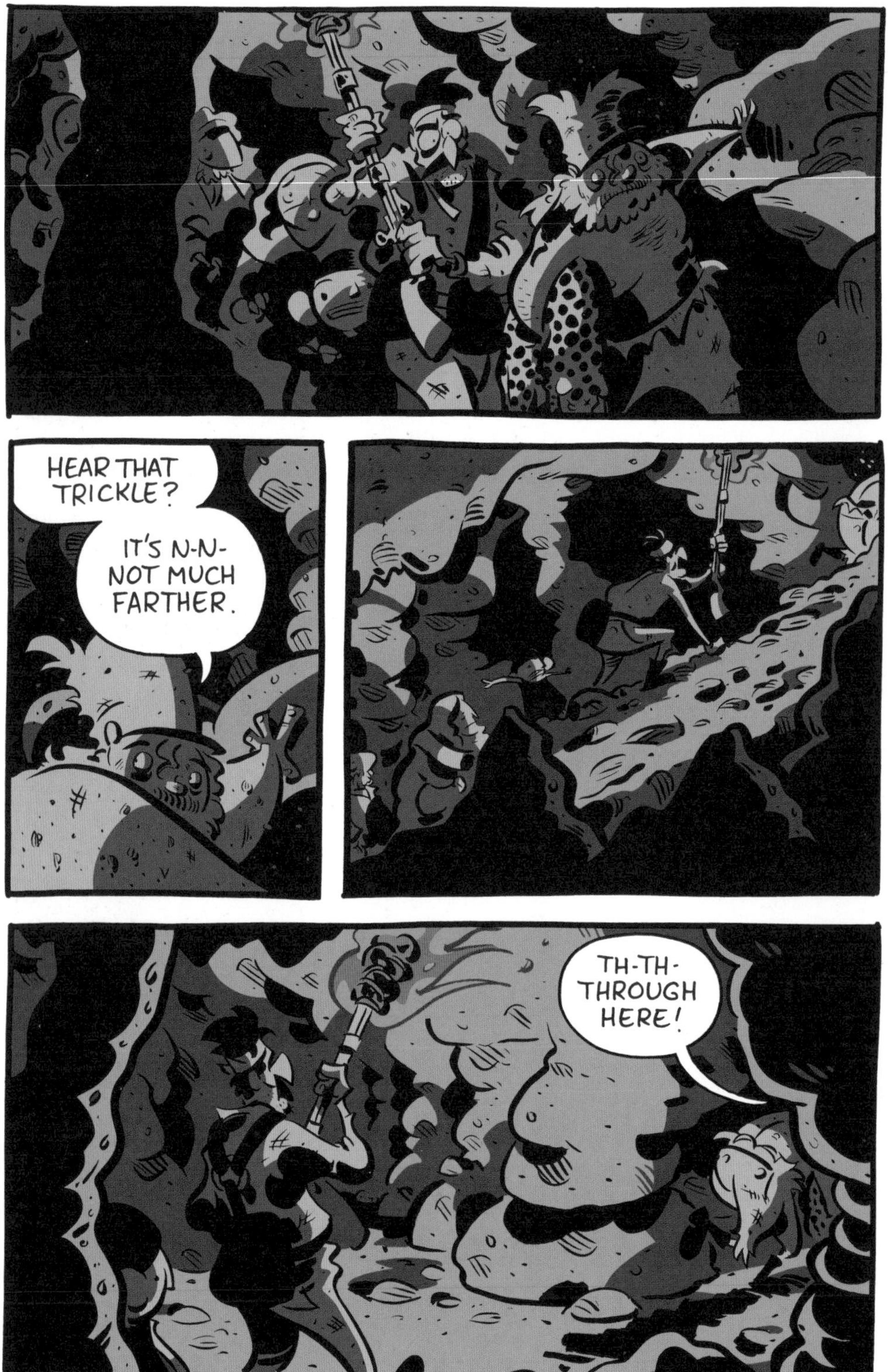
HEAR THAT TRICKLE?
IT'S N-N-NOT MUCH FARTHER.
TH-TH-THROUGH HERE!

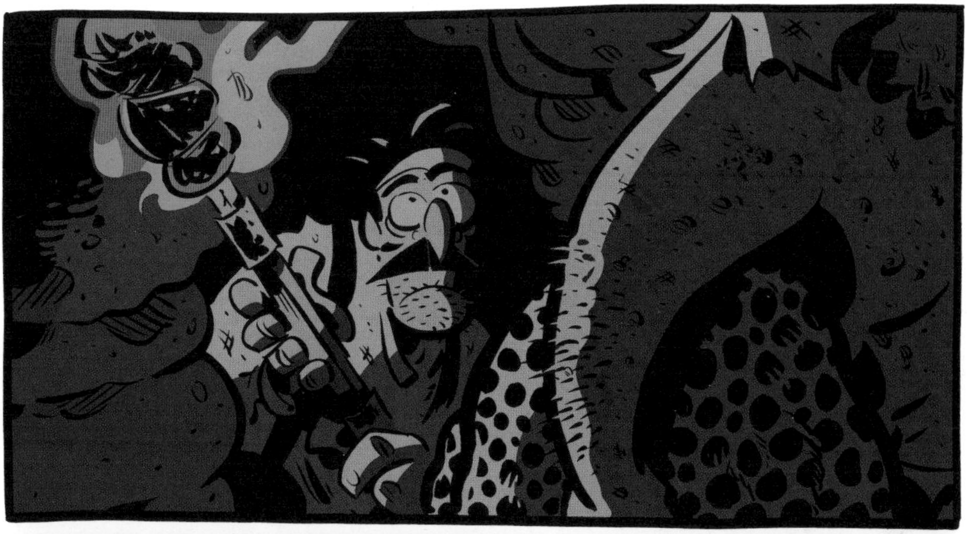

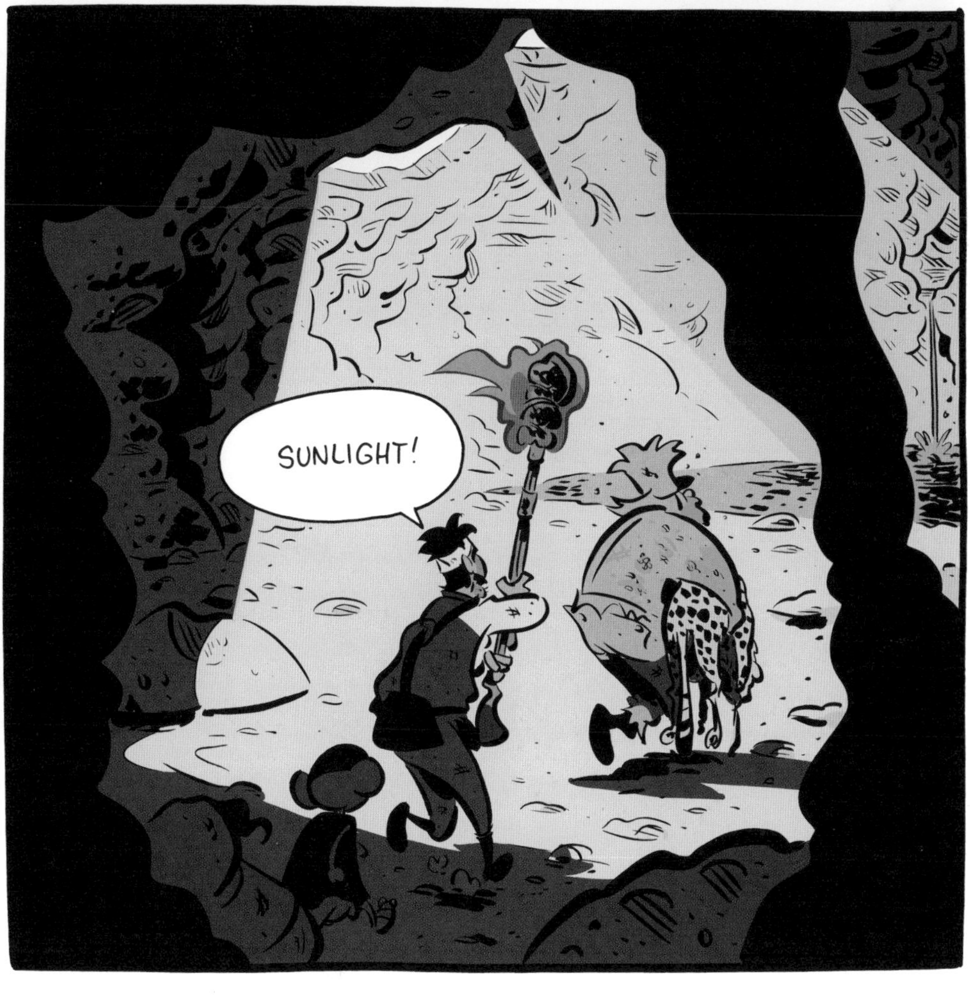
SUNLIGHT!

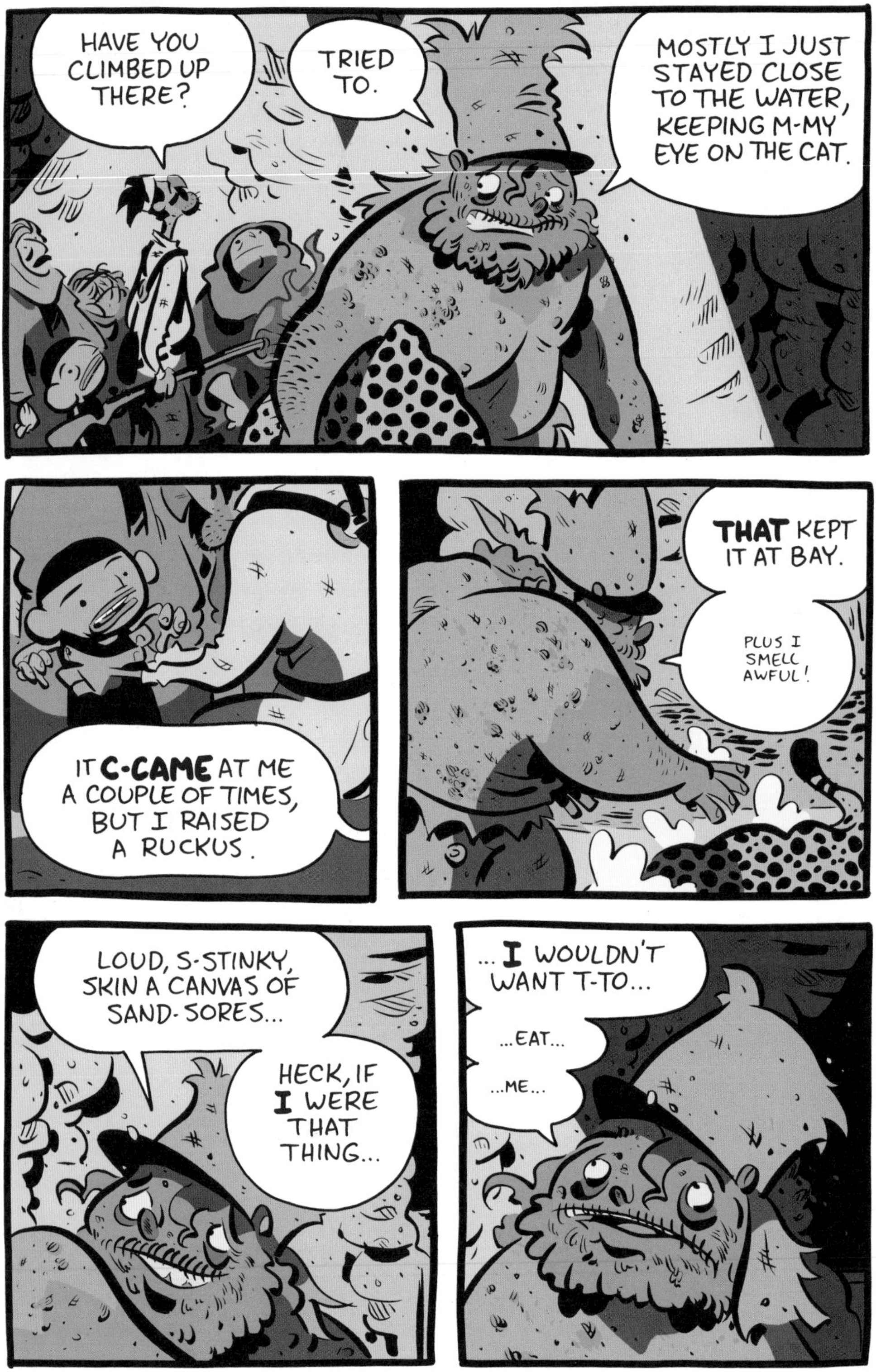
HAVE YOU CLIMBED UP THERE?
TRIED TO.
MOSTLY I JUST STAYED CLOSE TO THE WATER, KEEPING M-MY EYE ON THE CAT.
IT C-CAME AT ME A COUPLE OF TIMES, BUT I RAISED A RUCKUS.
THAT KEPT IT AT BAY.
PLUS I SMELL AWFUL!
LOUD, S-STINKY, SKIN A CANVAS OF SAND-SORES...
HECK, IF I WERE THAT THING...
...I WOULDN'T WANT T-TO...
...EAT...
...ME...

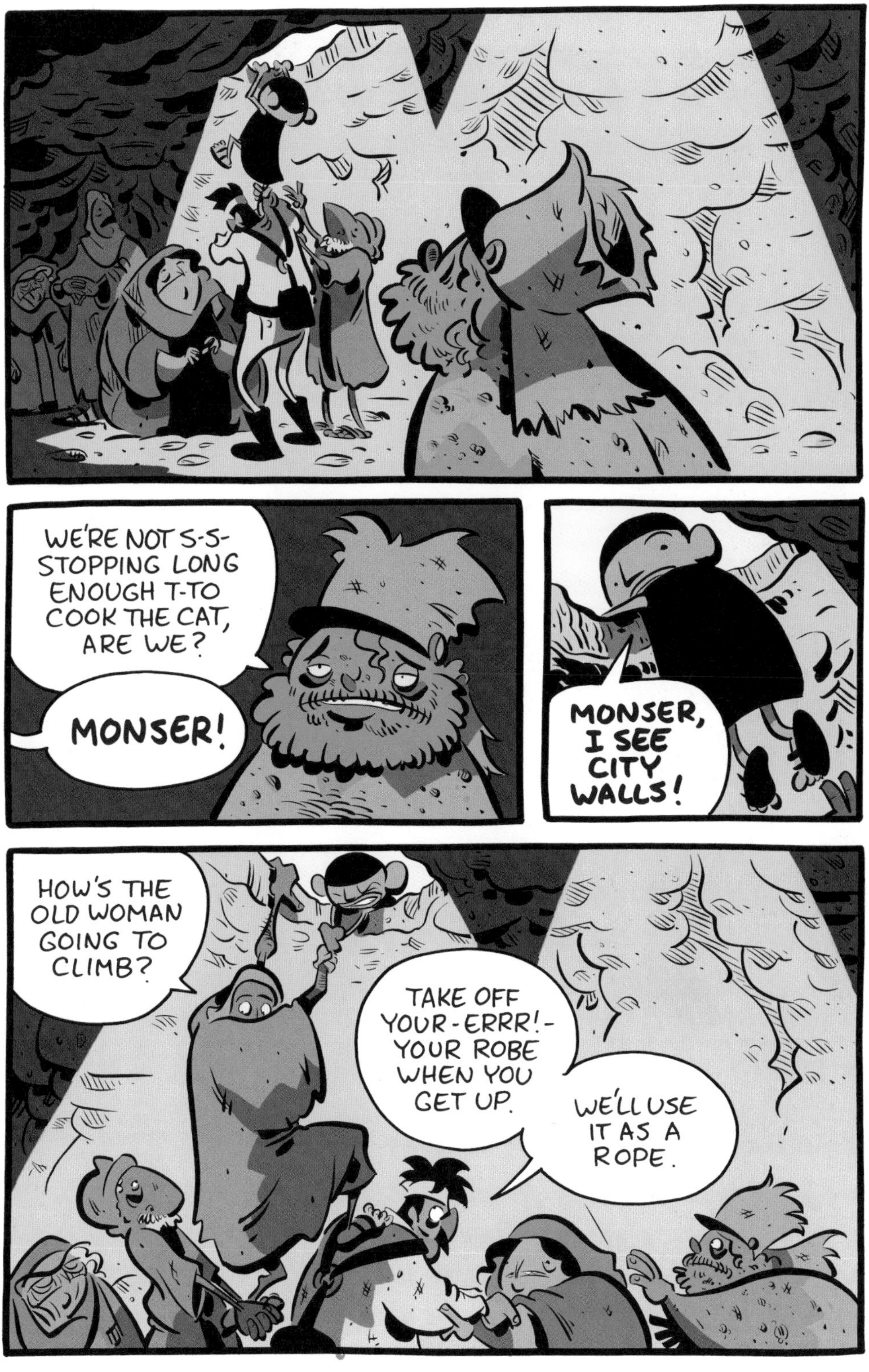
WE'RE NOT S-S-STOPPING LONG ENOUGH T-TO COOK THE CAT, ARE WE?
MONSER!
MONSER, I SEE CITY WALLS!
HOW'S THE OLD WOMAN GOING TO CLIMB?
TAKE OFF YOUR-ERRR!-YOUR ROBE WHEN YOU GET UP.
WE'LL USE IT AS A ROPE.

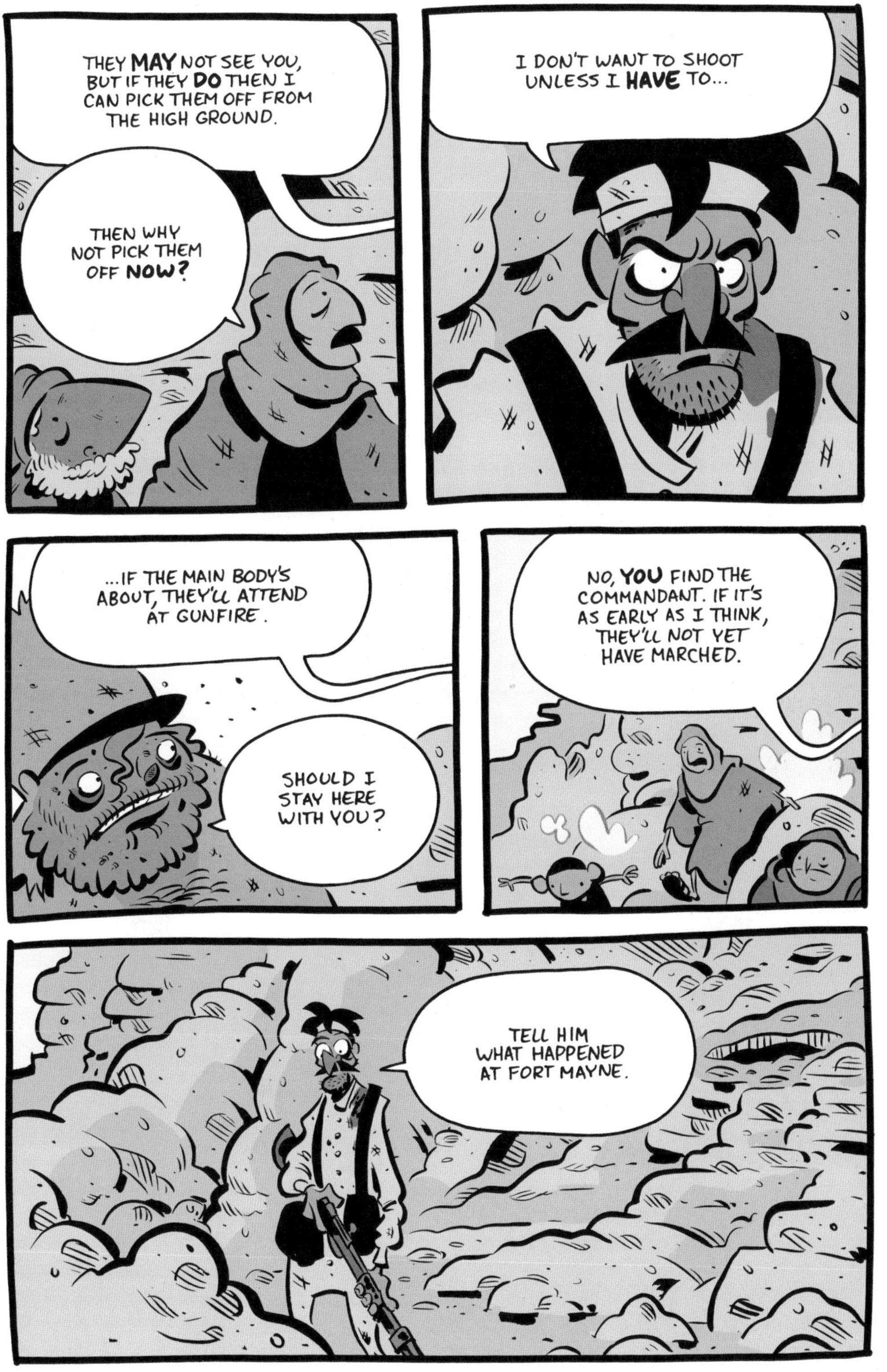
THEY MAY NOT SEE YOU, BUT IF THEY DO THEN I CAN PICK THEM OFF FROM THE HIGH GROUND.
THEN WHY NOT PICK THEM OFF NOW?
I DON'T WANT TO SHOOT UNLESS I HAVE TO...
...IF THE MAIN BODY'S ABOUT, THEY'LL ATTEND AT GUNFIRE.
SHOULD I STAY HERE WITH YOU?
NO, YOU FIND THE COMMANDANT. IF IT'S AS EARLY AS I THINK, THEY'LL NOT YET HAVE MARCHED.
TELL HIM WHAT HAPPENED AT FORT MAYNE.

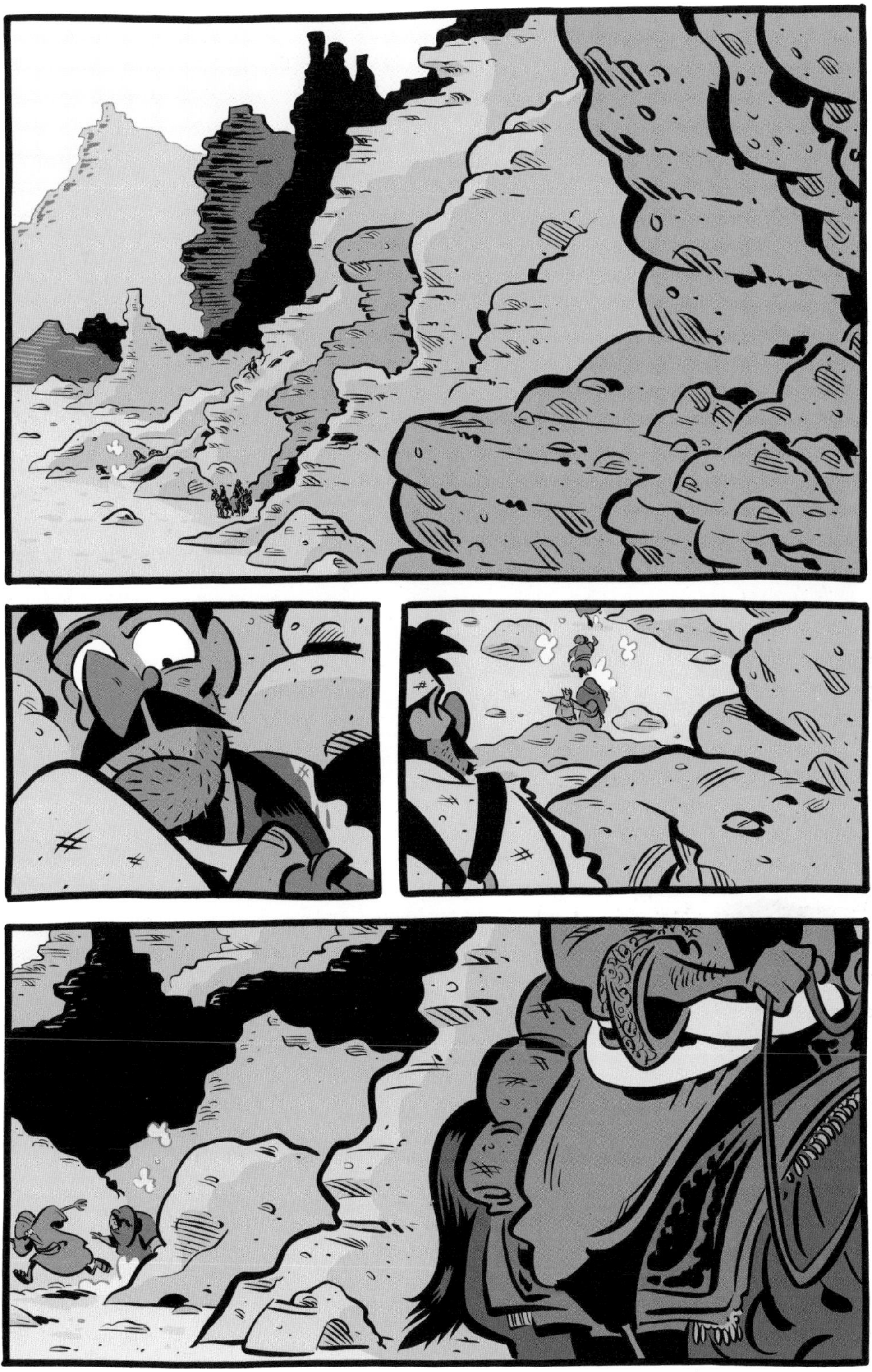

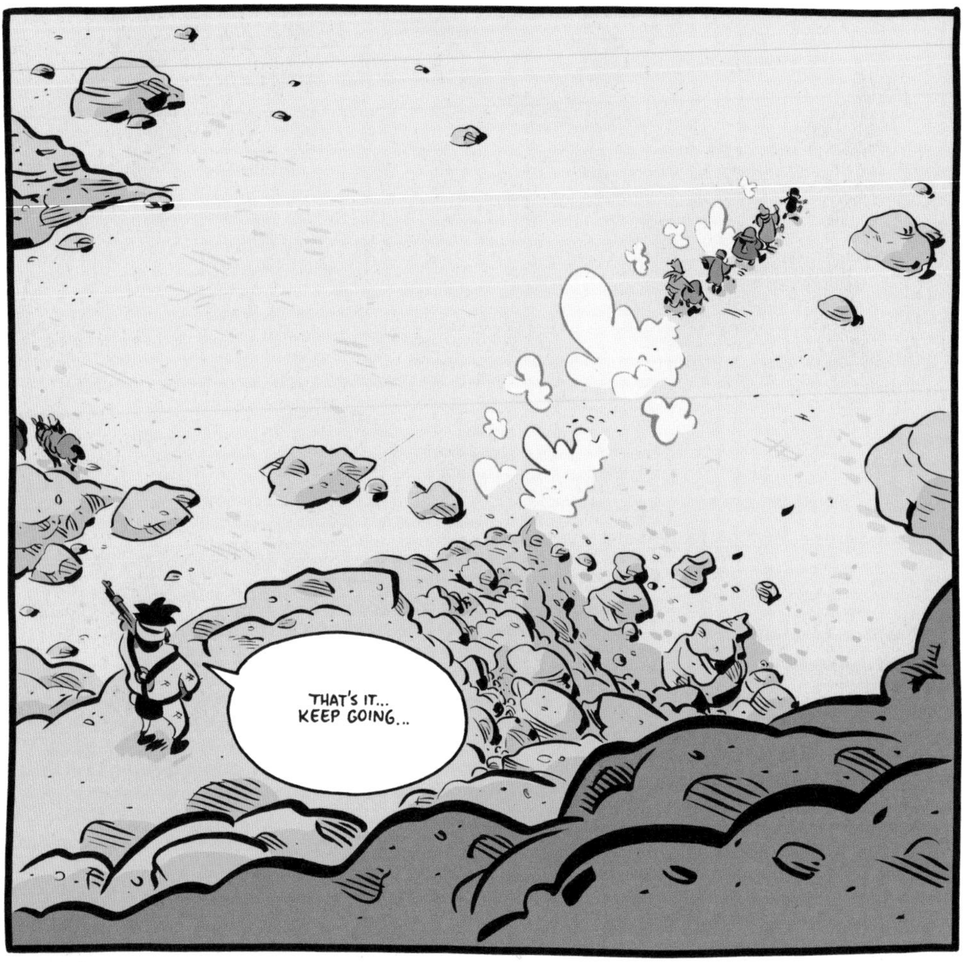
THAT'S IT...
KEEP GOING...

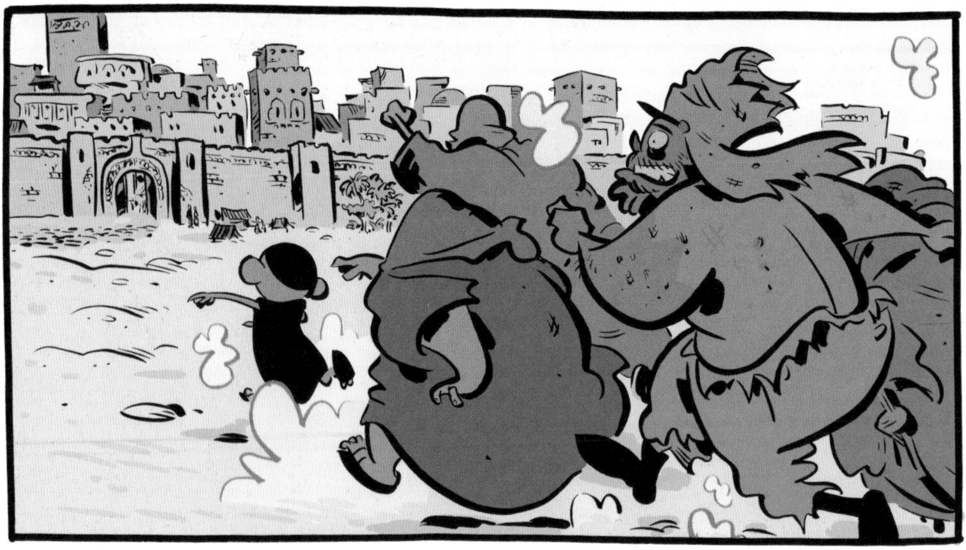

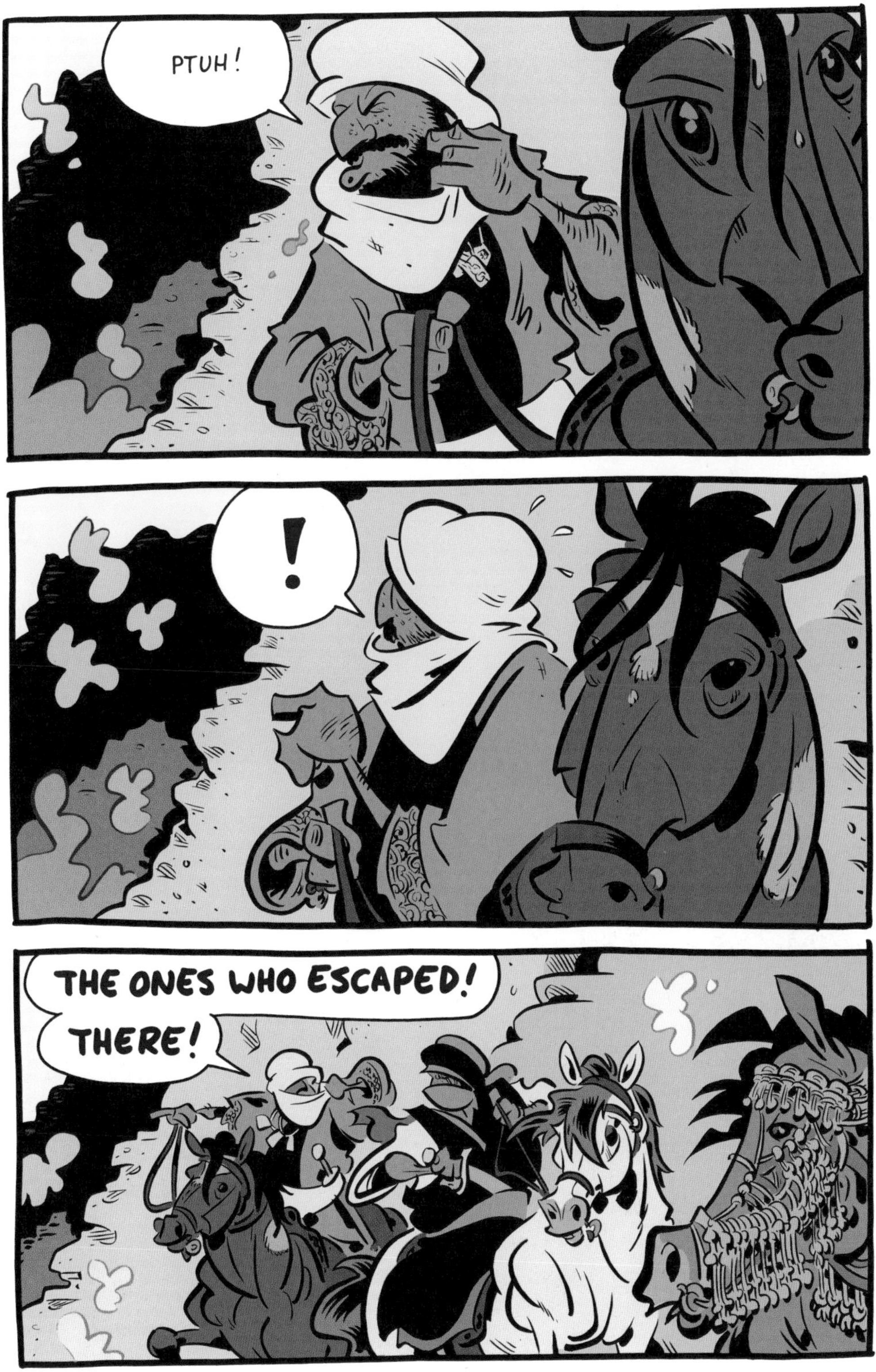
PTUH!
!
THE ONES WHO ESCAPED!
THERE!

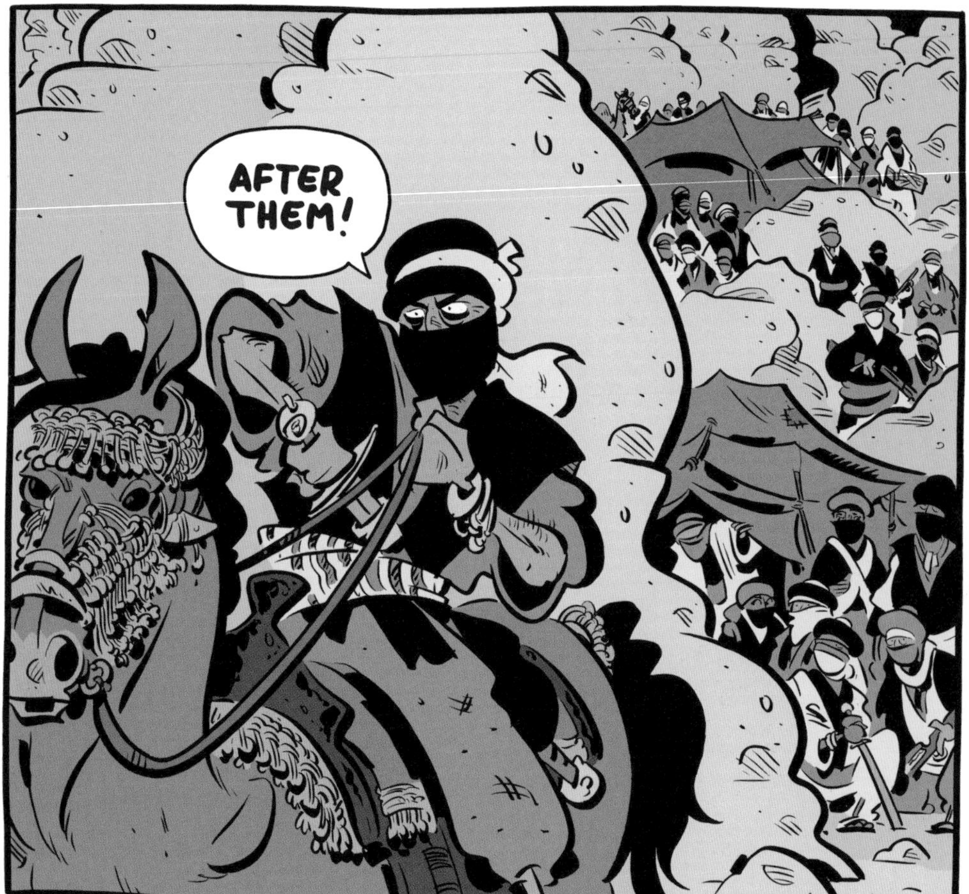
AFTER THEM!

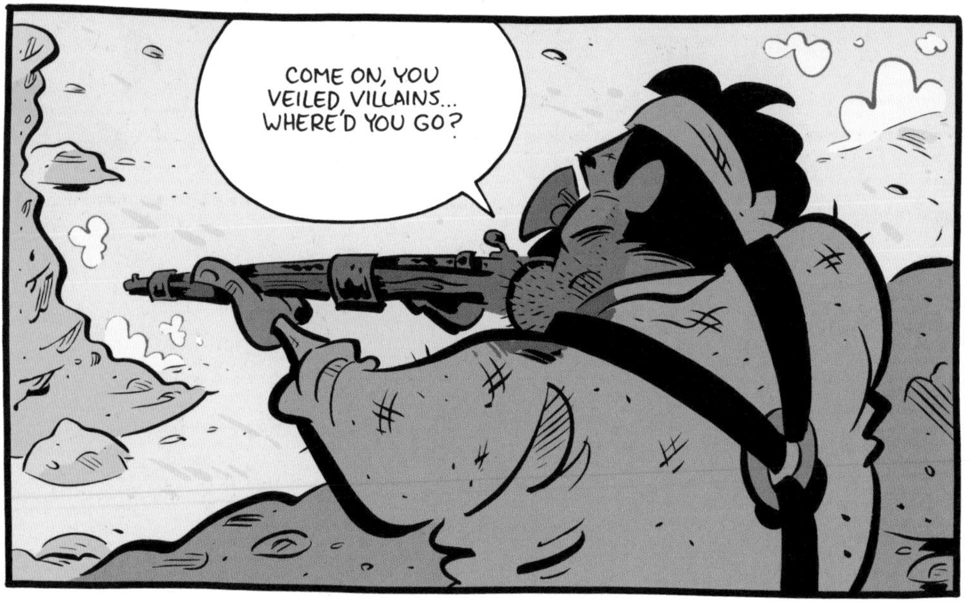
COME ON, YOU VEILED VILLAINS... WHERE'D YOU GO?

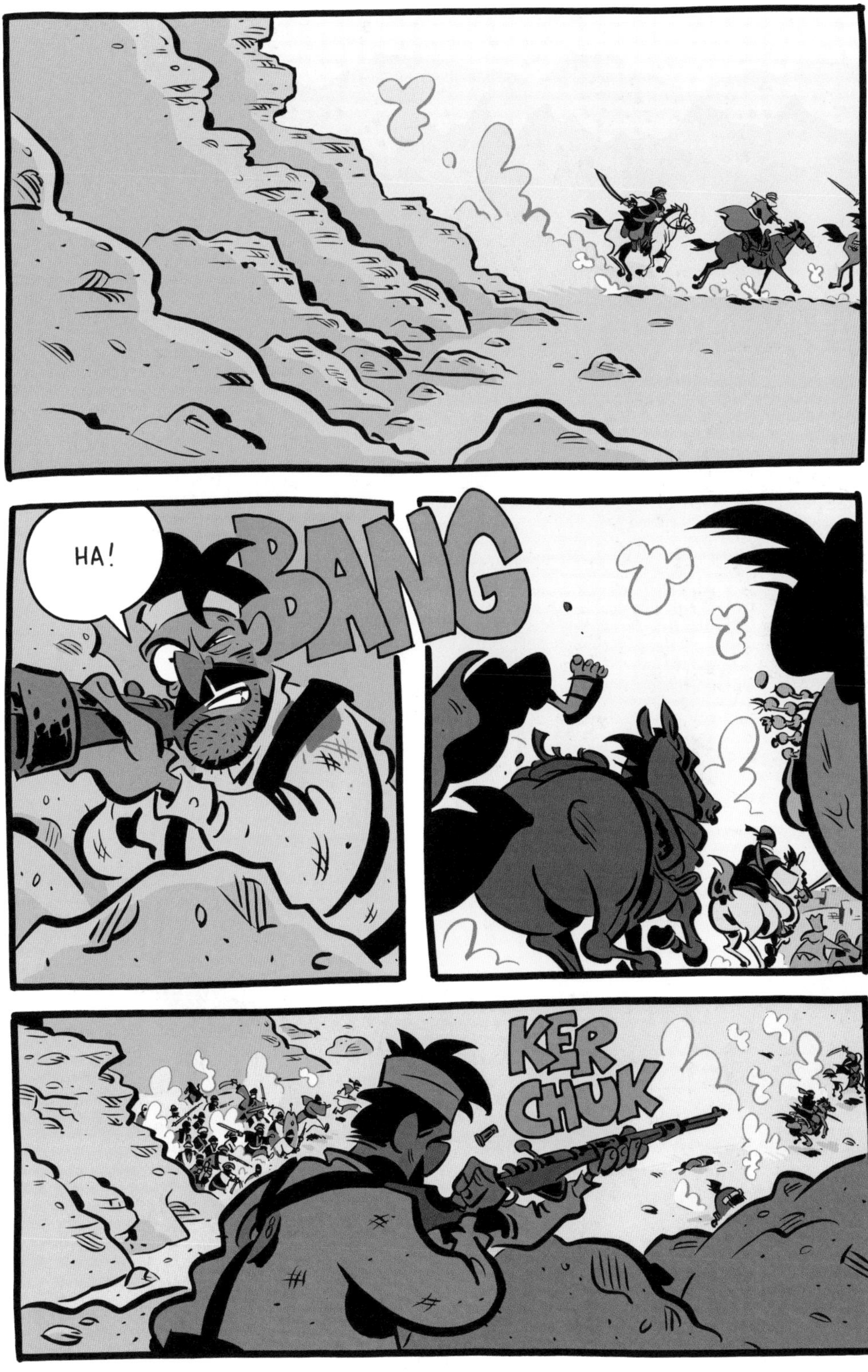
HA!
BANG
KER CHUK

TWO DOWN ...
ONE TO G-

AAH!

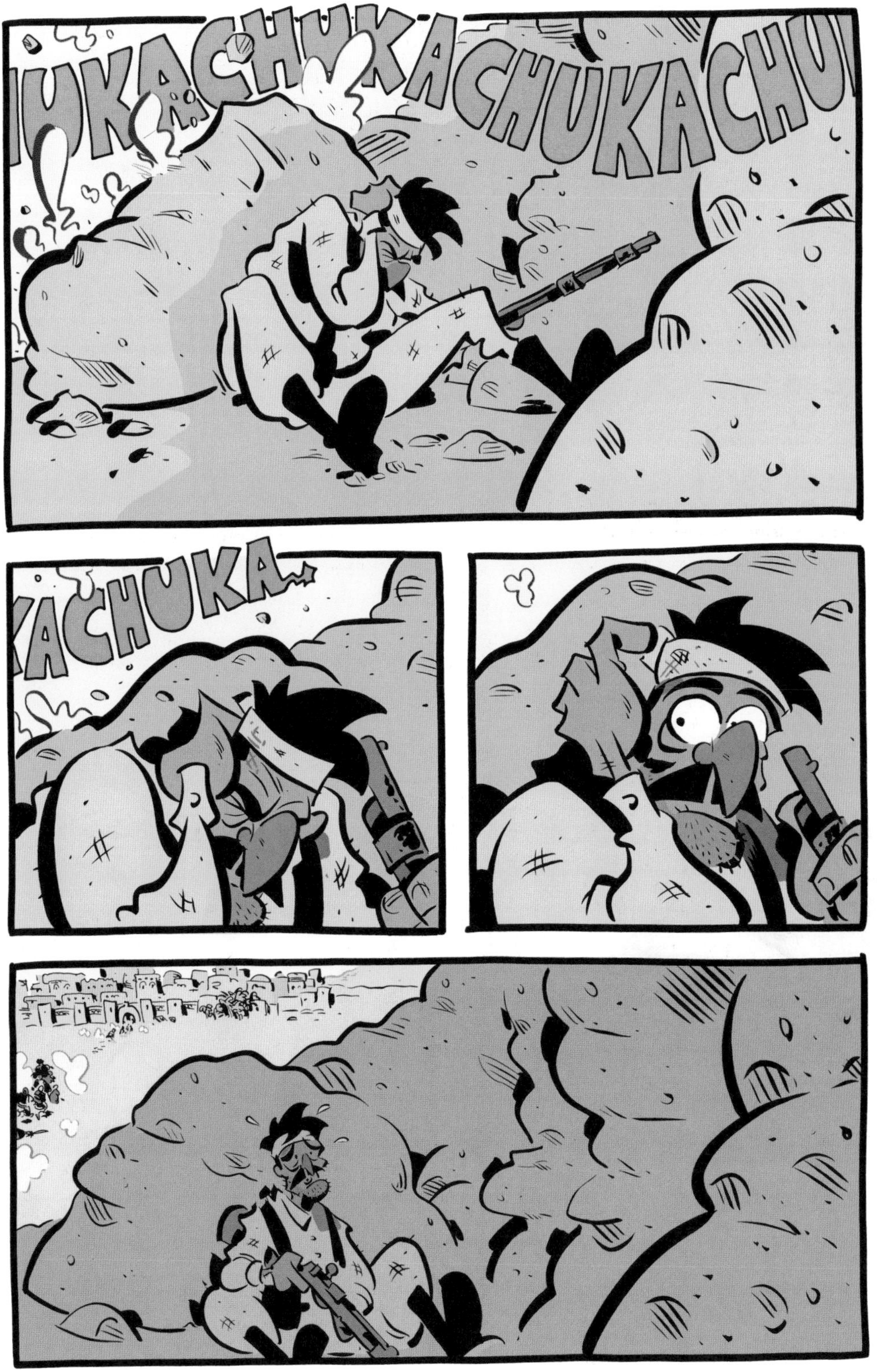
UKACHUKACHUKACHU
KACHUKA

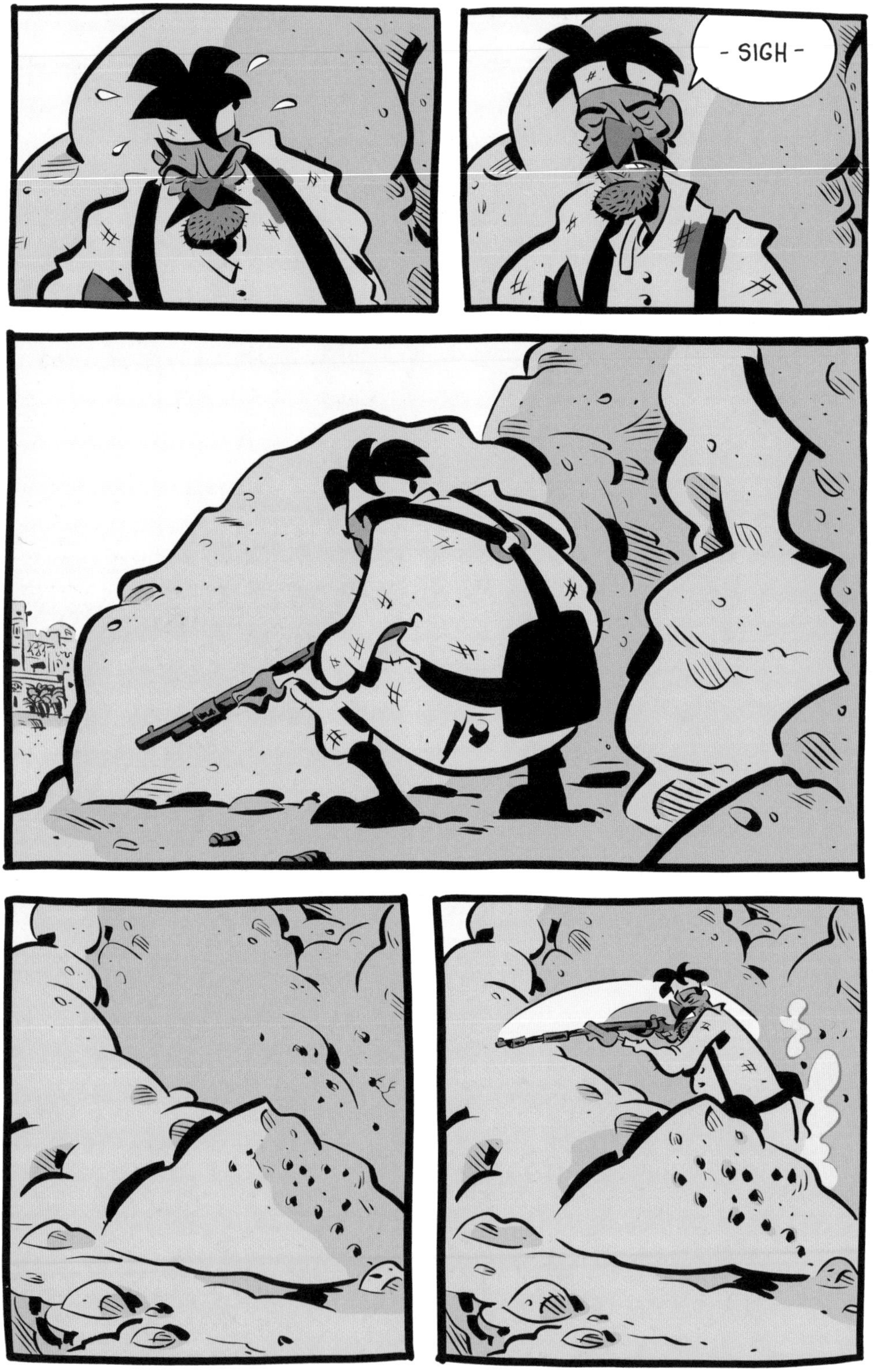
- SIGH -

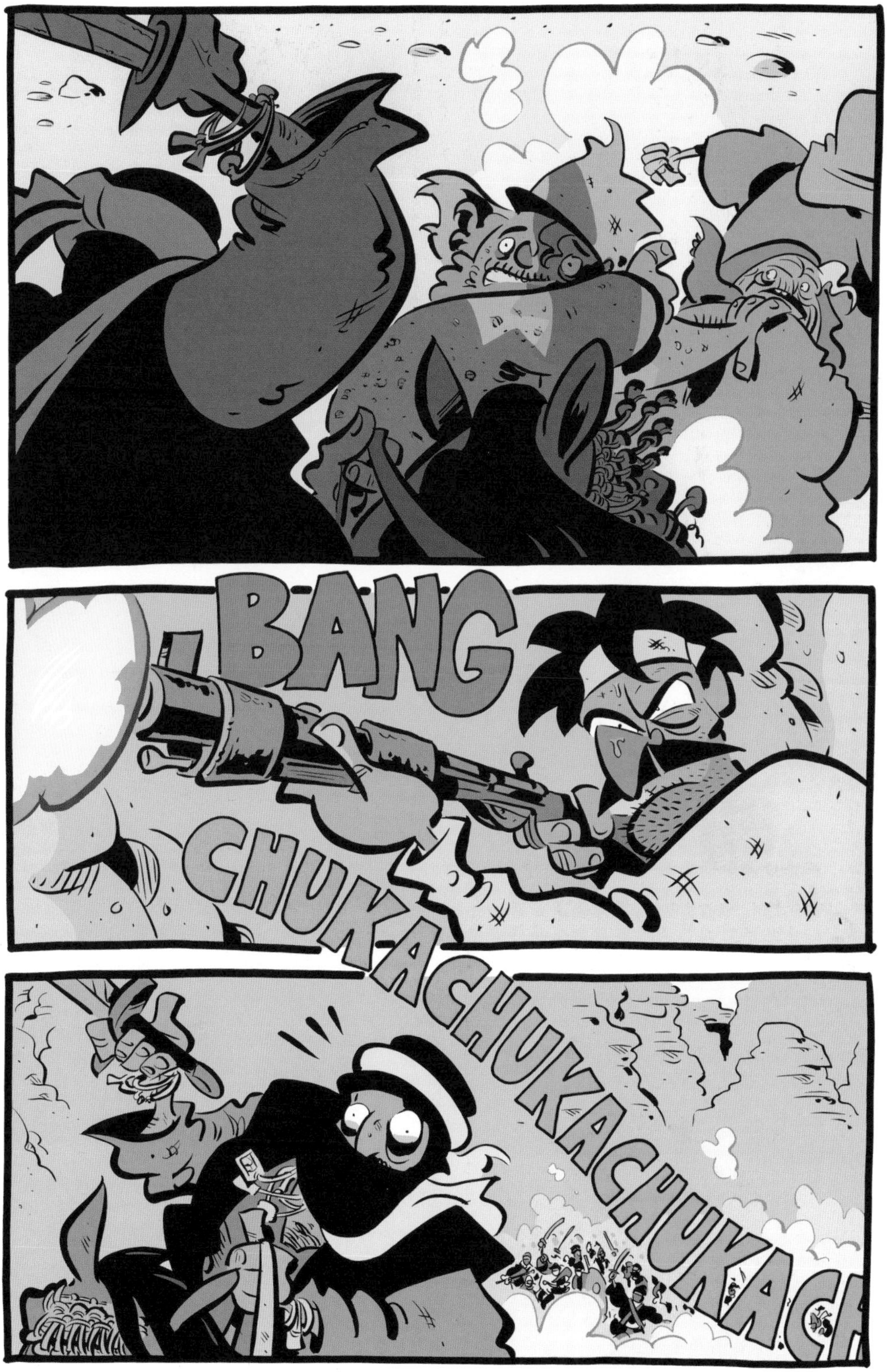
BANG
CHUKACHUKACHUKACHUKACH

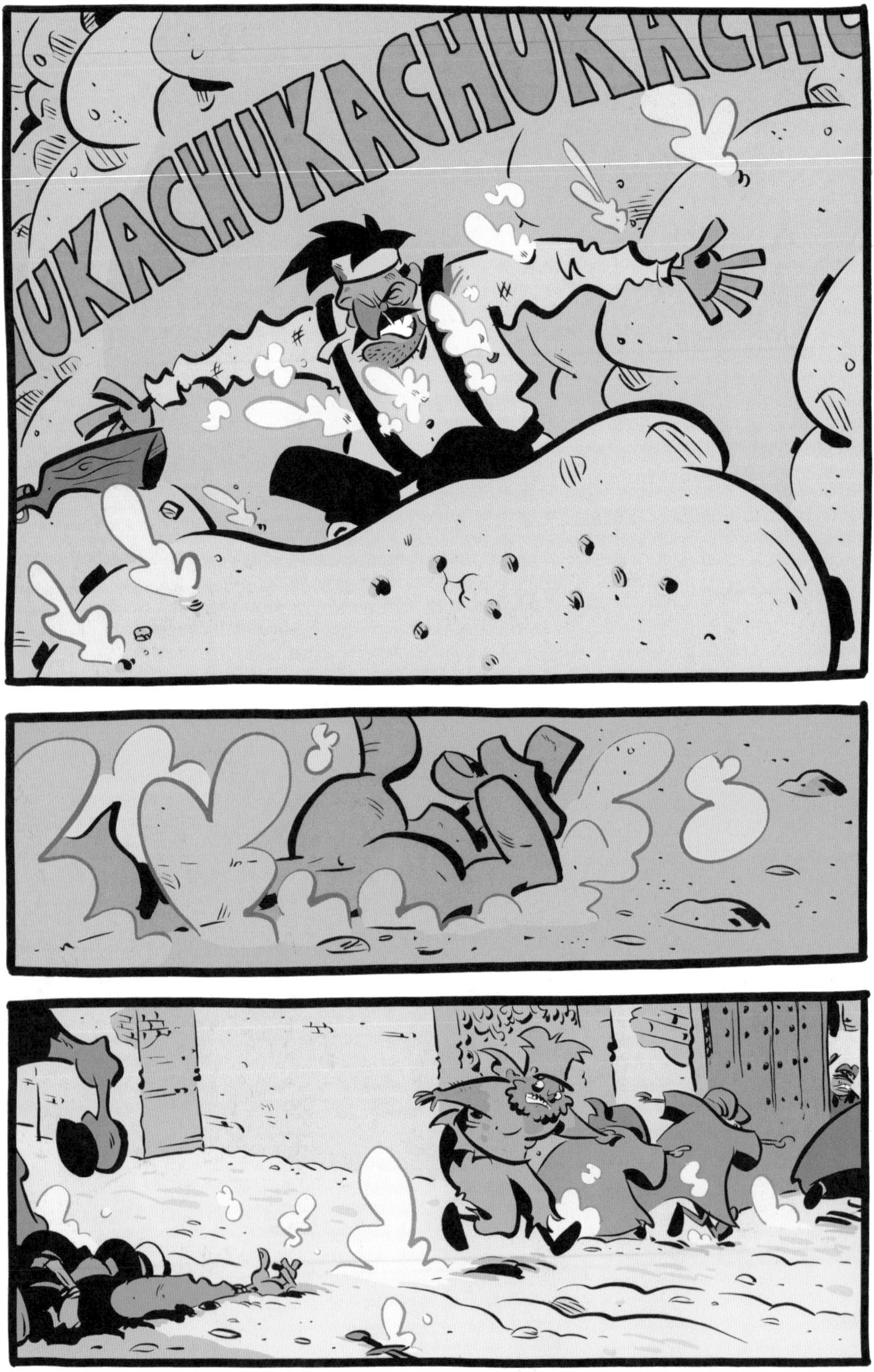
UKACHUKACHUKACHUKACHU

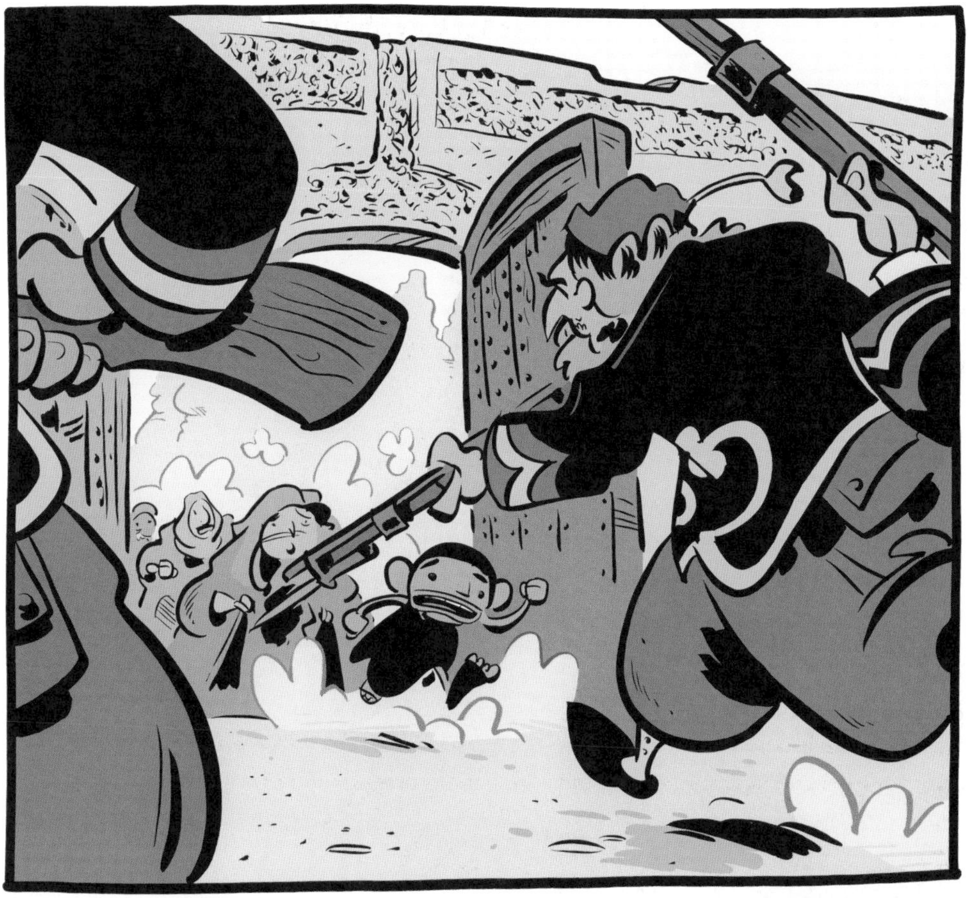

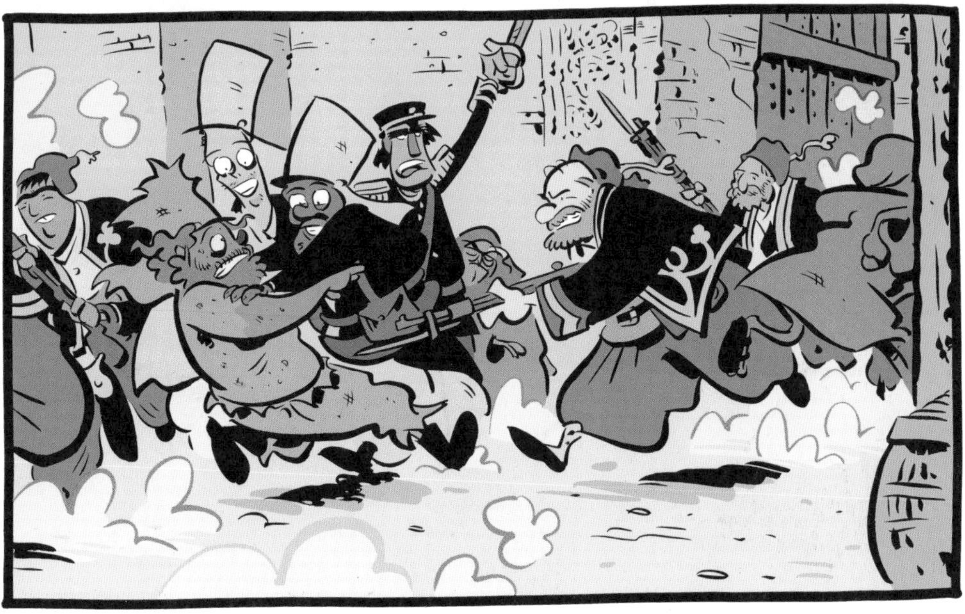

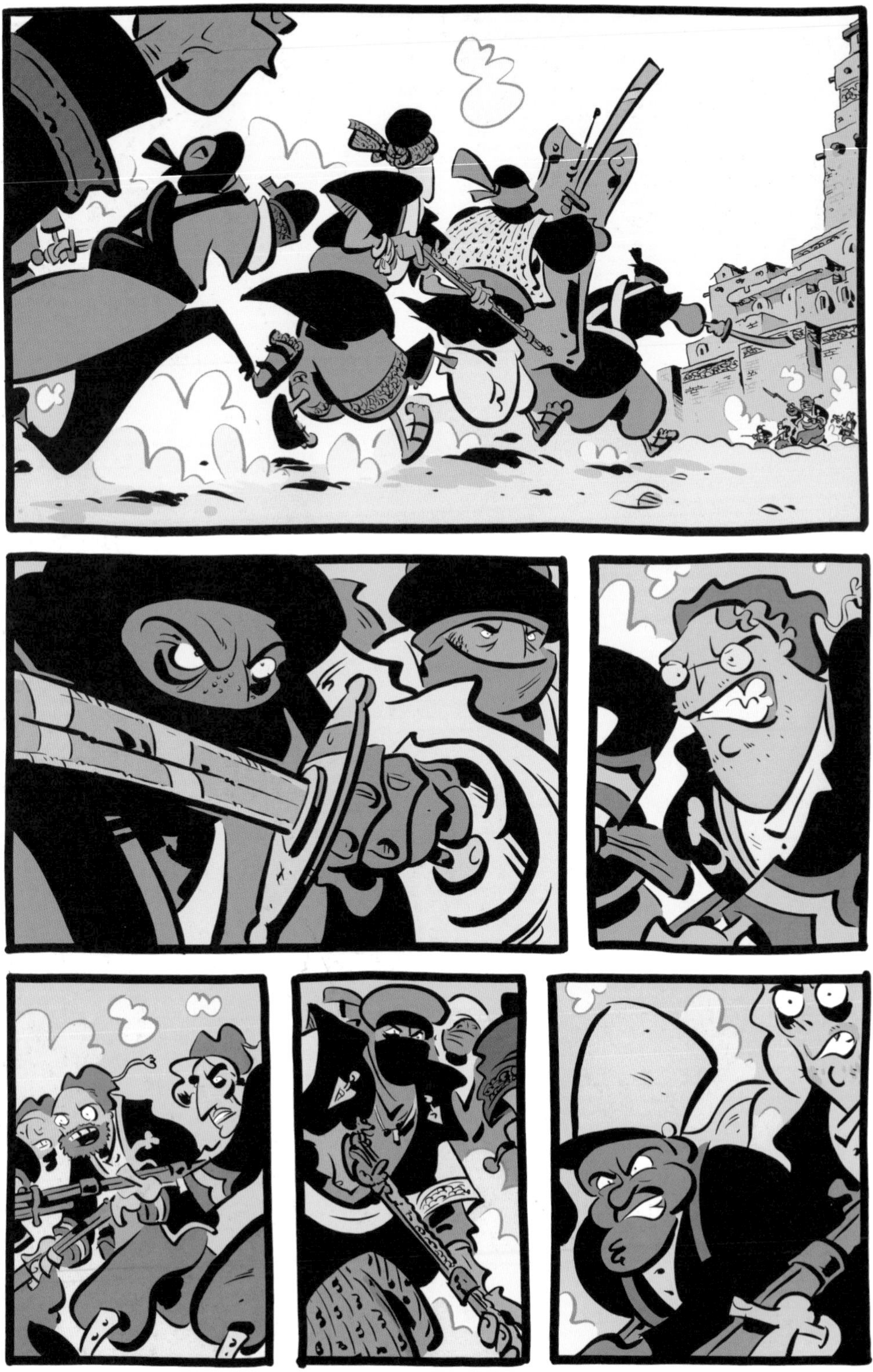

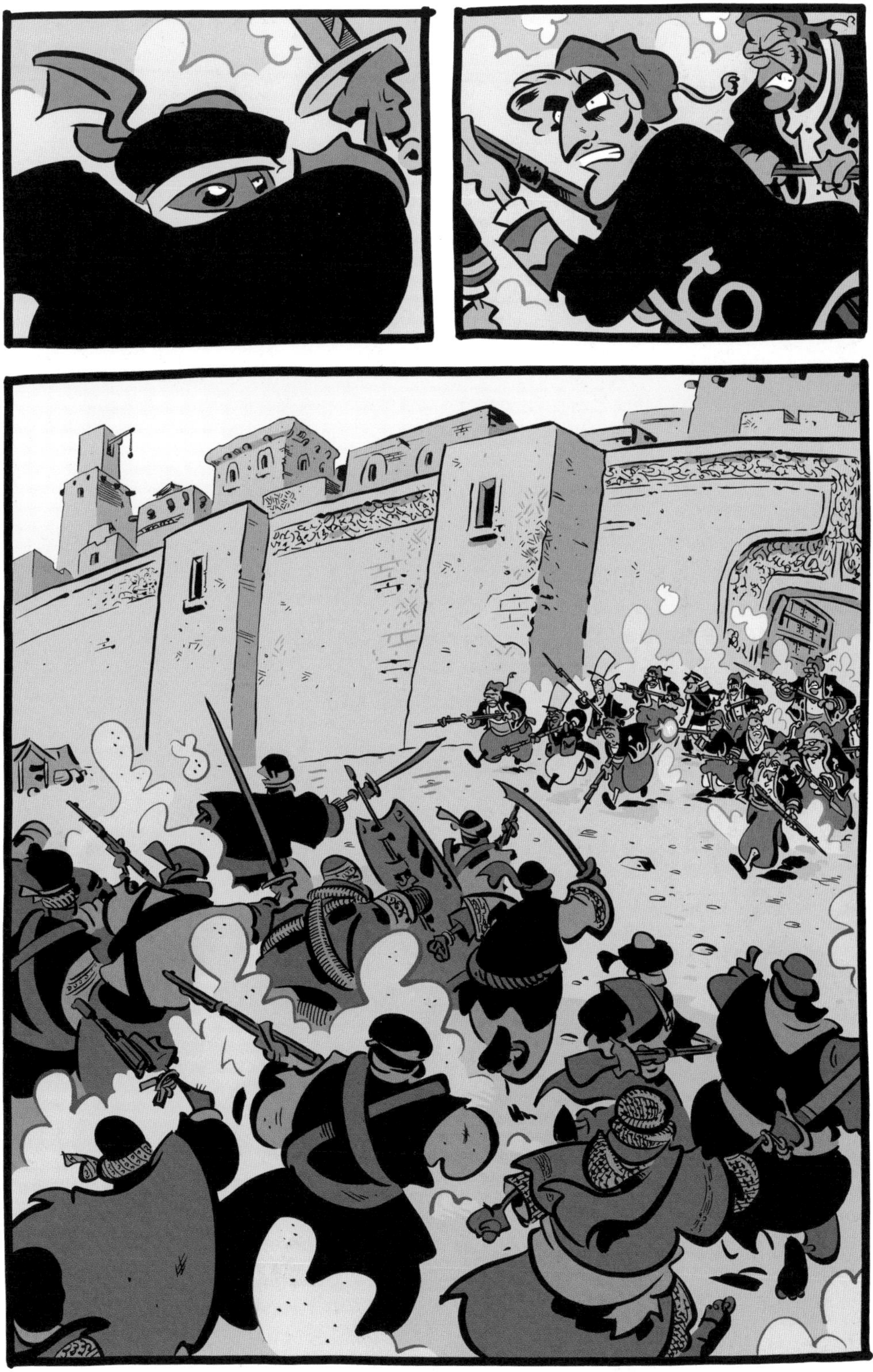

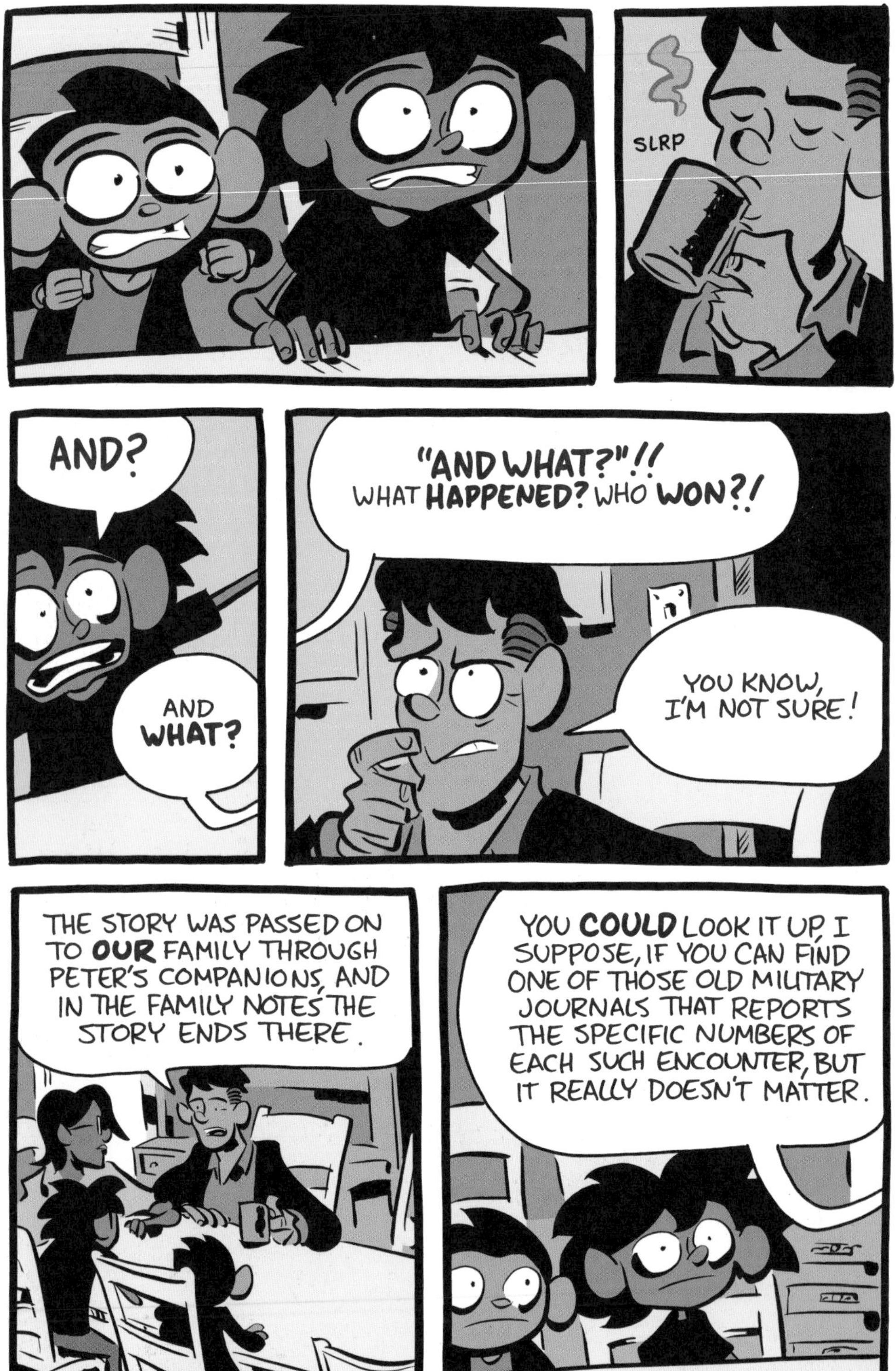
SLRP
AND?
AND WHAT?
"AND WHAT?"!! WHAT HAPPENED? WHO WON?!
YOU KNOW, I'M NOT SURE!
THE STORY WAS PASSED ON TO OUR FAMILY THROUGH PETER'S COMPANIONS, AND IN THE FAMILY NOTES THE STORY ENDS THERE.
YOU COULD LOOK IT UP, I SUPPOSE, IF YOU CAN FIND ONE OF THOSE OLD MILITARY JOURNALS THAT REPORTS THE SPECIFIC NUMBERS OF EACH SUCH ENCOUNTER, BUT IT REALLY DOESN'T MATTER.

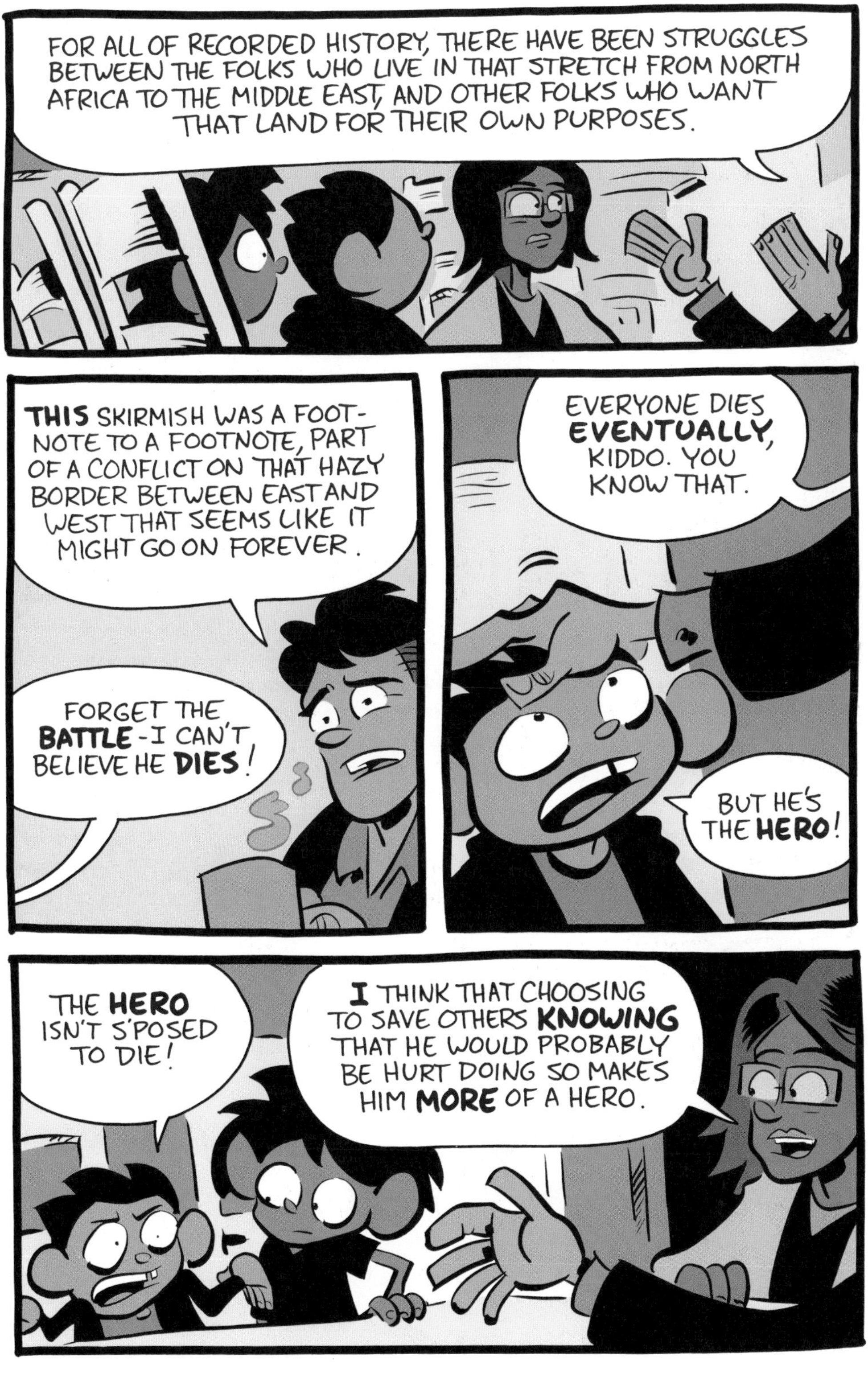
FOR ALL OF RECORDED HISTORY, THERE HAVE BEEN STRUGGLES BETWEEN THE FOLKS WHO LIVE IN THAT STRETCH FROM NORTH AFRICA TO THE MIDDLE EAST, AND OTHER FOLKS WHO WANT THAT LAND FOR THEIR OWN PURPOSES.
THIS SKIRMISH WAS A FOOTNOTE TO A FOOTNOTE, PART OF A CONFLICT ON THAT HAZY BORDER BETWEEN EAST AND WEST THAT SEEMS LIKE IT MIGHT GO ON FOREVER.
FORGET THE BATTLE - I CAN'T BELIEVE HE DIES!
EVERYONE DIES EVENTUALLY, KIDDO. YOU KNOW THAT.
BUT HE'S THE HERO!
THE HERO ISN'T S'POSED TO DIE!
I THINK THAT CHOOSING TO SAVE OTHERS KNOWING THAT HE WOULD PROBABLY BE HURT DOING SO MAKES HIM MORE OF A HERO.

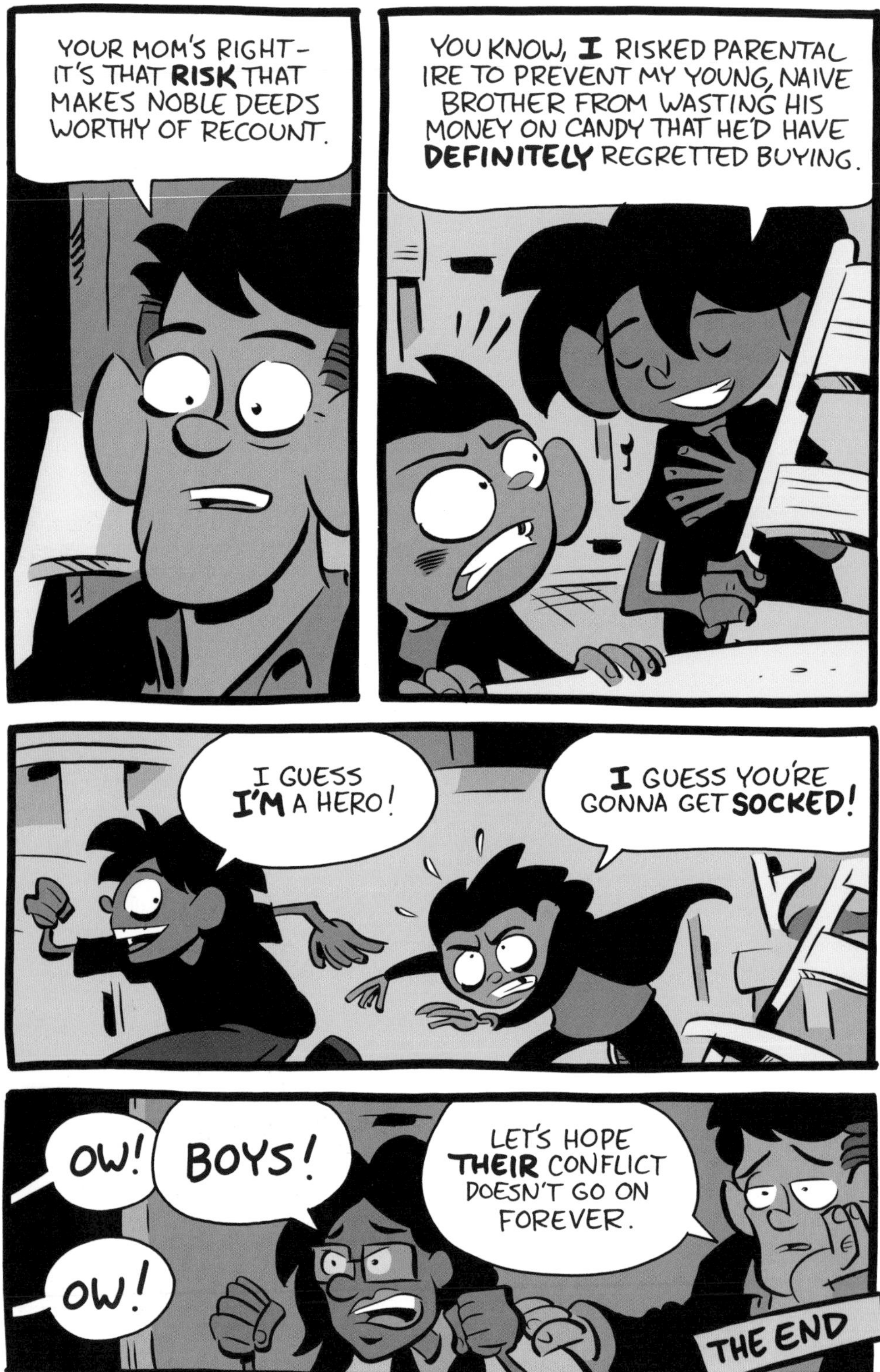

YOUR MOM'S RIGHT- IT'S THAT **RISK** THAT MAKES NOBLE DEEDS WORTHY OF RECOUNT.
YOU KNOW, **I** RISKED PARENTAL IRE TO PREVENT MY YOUNG, NAIVE BROTHER FROM WASTING HIS MONEY ON CANDY THAT HE'D HAVE **DEFINITELY** REGRETTED BUYING.
I GUESS **I'M** A HERO!
I GUESS YOU'RE GONNA GET **SOCKED**!
OW!
BOYS!
LET'S HOPE **THEIR** CONFLICT DOESN'T GO ON FOREVER.
OW!
THE END

THANKS TO:

First and Foremost, my wife Liz for her infinite patience with my sixteen-hour workdays and the occasional mercurial outbursts in which those stretches result. Her support, enthusiasm, and understanding allow me to wrap myself up in these little worlds, and the work contained herein is a direct result of her selflessness. She also filled in a lot of the black contained in the cave sequence, which helped me finish the book quicker than I otherwise might've, and for that my editor is grateful to her, too.

My mother, Donis Schweizer, for always pointing out the other side of any theoretical argument, and for creating stories to illustrate the human component of that stance. Her gift for off-the-cuff fiction is second only to the empathy she instills in it.

My father, Mark Schweizer, my editor, James Lucas Jones, and my good friend Hunter Wook-Jin Clark, for all serving as sounding boards for the plot, helping me to work out its intricacies as I went along. Hunter was especially accommodating, sometimes meeting me at the Majestic Diner in the wee hours of the morning to help me work out the details. If the story resonates, it is due in no small part to their help.

Pat Bollin, who graciously forgoes the usual congratulatory niceties we cartoonists tend to heap on each other, instead pointing out every artistic flaw he can spot whenever I show him my new pages. There have, over the course of the book's execution, been tiny but numerous artistic revisions, and most swing back to the meticulous input offered by Bollin.

Matt Kindt, who, despite his incredibly busy publishing schedule, took the time to comb for clarity. With luck, the book will be more accessible thanks to his keen eye.

Patrick Quinn, Matthew Thomas Maloney, Brett Osbourne, and Dr. Teresa Griffiths, my bosses at SCAD-Atlanta, both for giving me the opportunity to teach what I love and for creating an environment in which excellence is expected from both faculty and students. I could not imagine a program whose affiliation I am prouder to claim.

The Sequential Art faculty at SCAD-Atlanta for being a constant source of inspiration, debate, and artistic one-upmanship, and for never slacking in their desire to improve their own storytelling ability and mine; and David Duncan at the Savannah campus for being so generous with sharing his excellent class and lecture notes.

The good folks at Oni Press, for putting out this series and working hard to ensure that it finds its way into people's hands.

Lastly, the students of the Sequential Art program. Their dedication to their craft is staggering, and I feel I learn as much from them as I hope they learn from me. To see so many of them getting published before graduation is likely more a testimony to their tenacity and talent than to any lessons I impart, but it doesn't stop me from welling with pride at their accomplishments.

Chris Schweizer
Decatur, GA
November 2009

ACKNOWLEDGEMENTS:

I am indebted to the research and scholarship of many writers, but most notably to Douglas Porch, Dugald Campbell, and Lloyd Cabot Briggs, without whom I'd have been woefully ill-prepared to undertake this volume. And, of course, to Percival Christopher Wren, whose *Geste* books set a standard for Foreign Legion adventure to which I can aspire, but never match.

Photo by Liz Schweizer, circa this book's execution in 2009

CHRIS SCHWEIZER was born at the tail end of 1980. He received his BFA in graphic design from Murray State University in 2004, and in 2008 earned his MFA in Sequential Art from the Savannah College of Art & Design in Atlanta, where he went on to teach for five years. He now spends all of his time making comics, and lives in Kentucky with his wife Liz and daughter Penny.

Chris has been a hotel manager, a movie theater projectionist, a guard at a mental institution, a martial arts instructor, a set builder, a church music leader, a process server, a life-drawing model, a bartender, a car wash attendant, a bagboy, a delivery boy, a choirboy, a lawn boy, a sixth-grade social studies teacher, a janitor, a speakeasy proprietor, a video store clerk, a field hand, a deckhand, a puppeteer for a children's TV show, a muralist, a kickboxer, and a line worker at a pancake mix factory. He likes being a cartoonist best.

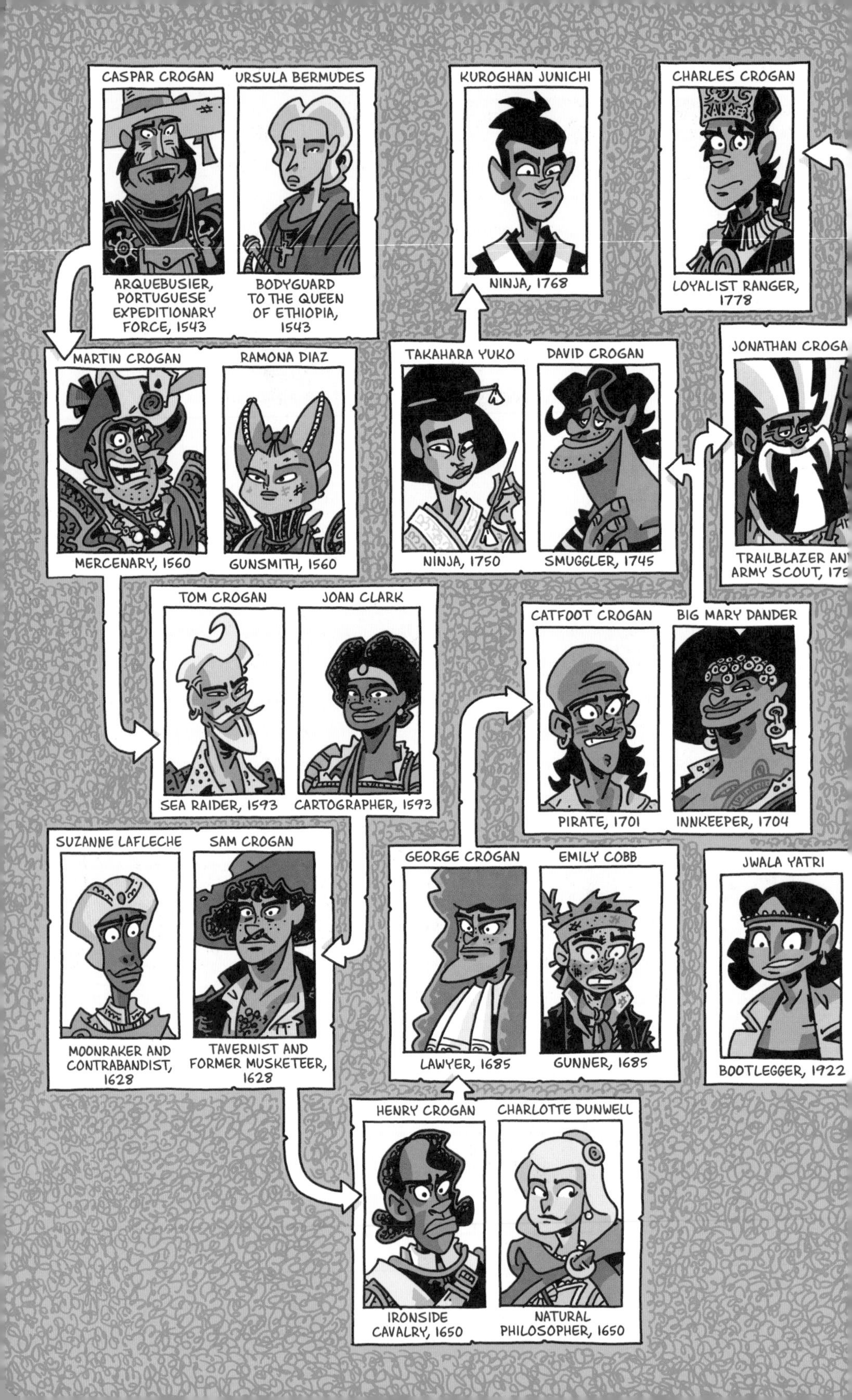

CASPAR CROGAN
ARQUEBUSIER, PORTUGUESE EXPEDITIONARY FORCE, 1543
URSULA BERMUDES
BODYGUARD TO THE QUEEN OF ETHIOPIA, 1543
KUROGHAN JUNICHI
NINJA, 1768
CHARLES CROGAN
LOYALIST RANGER, 1778
MARTIN CROGAN
MERCENARY, 1560
RAMONA DIAZ
GUNSMITH, 1560
TAKAHARA YUKO
NINJA, 1750
DAVID CROGAN
SMUGGLER, 1745
JONATHAN CROGA
TRAILBLAZER AN
ARMY SCOUT, 17
TOM CROGAN
SEA RAIDER, 1593
JOAN CLARK
CARTOGRAPHER, 1593
CATFOOT CROGAN
PIRATE, 1701
BIG MARY DANDER
INNKEEPER, 1704
SUZANNE LAFLECHE
MOONRAKER AND CONTRABANDIST, 1628
SAM CROGAN
TAVERNIST AND FORMER MUSKETEER, 1628
GEORGE CROGAN
LAWYER, 1685
EMILY COBB
GUNNER, 1685
JWALA YATRI
BOOTLEGGER, 1922
HENRY CROGAN
IRONSIDE CAVALRY, 1650
CHARLOTTE DUNWELL
NATURAL PHILOSOPHER, 1650

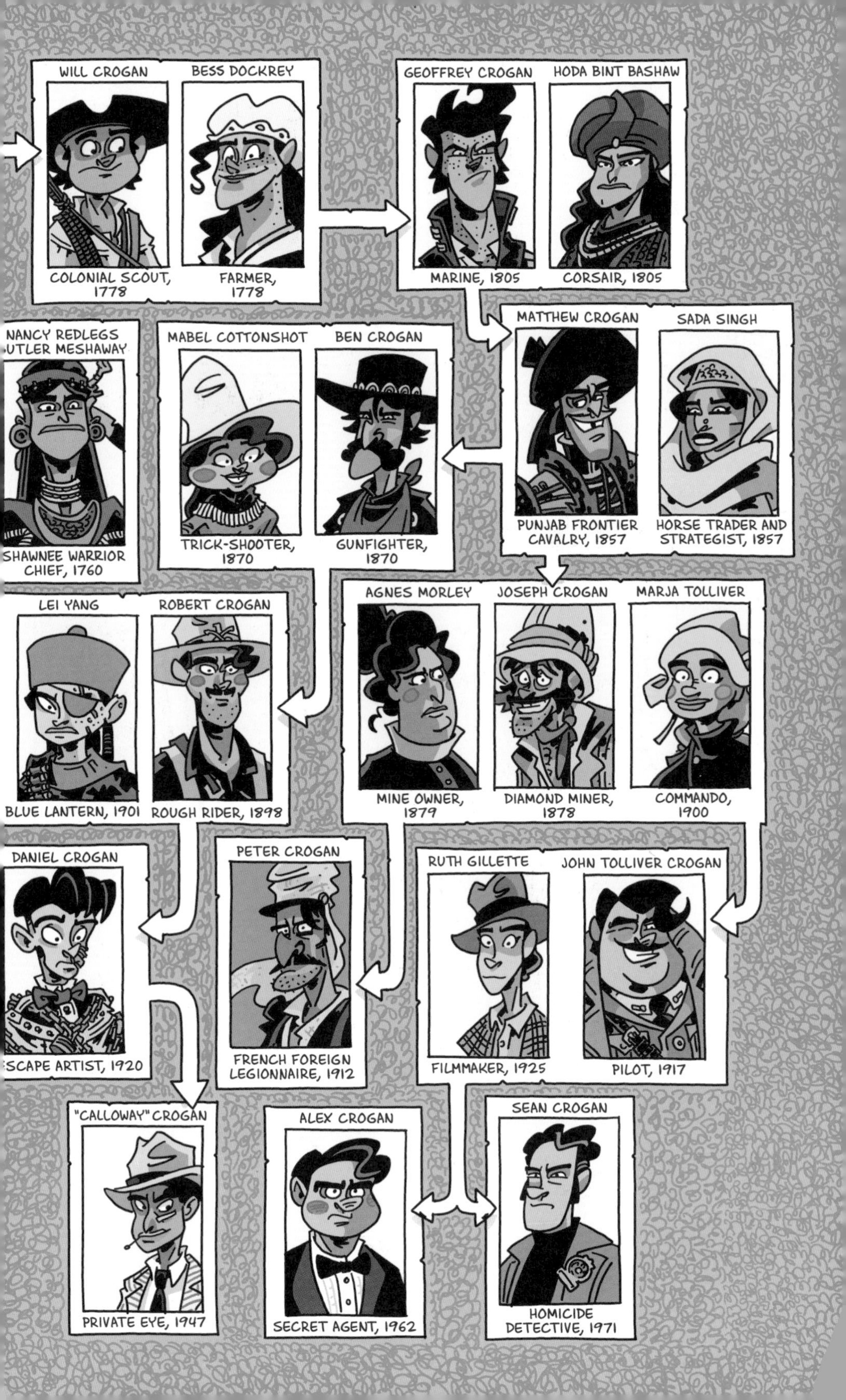
WILL CROGAN
COLONIAL SCOUT, 1778
BESS DOCKREY
FARMER, 1778
GEOFFREY CROGAN
MARINE, 1805
HODA BINT BASHAW
CORSAIR, 1805
NANCY REDLEGS
UTLER MESHAWAY
SHAWNEE WARRIOR CHIEF, 1760
MABEL COTTONSHOT
TRICK-SHOOTER, 1870
BEN CROGAN
GUNFIGHTER, 1870
MATTHEW CROGAN
PUNJAB FRONTIER CAVALRY, 1857
SADA SINGH
HORSE TRADER AND STRATEGIST, 1857
LEI YANG
BLUE LANTERN, 1901
ROBERT CROGAN
ROUGH RIDER, 1898
AGNES MORLEY
MINE OWNER, 1879
JOSEPH CROGAN
DIAMOND MINER, 1878
MARJA TOLLIVER
COMMANDO, 1900
DANIEL CROGAN
SCAPE ARTIST, 1920
PETER CROGAN
FRENCH FOREIGN LEGIONNAIRE, 1912
RUTH GILLETTE
FILMMAKER, 1925
JOHN TOLLIVER CROGAN
PILOT, 1917
"CALLOWAY" CROGAN
PRIVATE EYE, 1947
ALEX CROGAN
SECRET AGENT, 1962
SEAN CROGAN
HOMICIDE DETECTIVE, 1971

OTHER BOOKS BY CHRIS SCHWEIZER AND ONI PRESS

CATFOOT'S VENGEANCE

Sailor "Catfoot" Crogan doesn't try to make waves, but the tyrannous captain of his ship is convinced he's on the verge of leading a mutiny. Salvation comes when pirates board the ship and take control, but Catfoot finds he's stepped into even murkier waters with a villainous new first mate.

Previously published as *Crogan's Vengeance*.

LOYALTY

Charles and William Crogan are both fiercely loyal to their country, and they've taken up arms to defend it… from each other. When these brothers, each on his own mission, find themselves together for the first time since the start of the American Revolution, they must determine which comes first: loyalty to their cause, or to each other.

Previously published as *Crogan's Loyalty*.

www.onipress.com